AWAY WITH THE FISHES

Also by Stephanie Siciarz

Left at the Mango Tree

AWAY WITH THE FISHES

STEPHANIE SICIARZ

PINK MOON PRESS
Away with the Fishes
Stephanie Siciarz

Cover Art: Patti Schermerhorn
Cover Design: Andrew C Bly

Published in the United States by Pink Moon Press
ISBN: 0989686329
ISBN-13: 9780989686327
Library of Congress Control Number: 2014909553

Again,
for Barry

Honest man, early 40s, athletic, with fishing boat seeks honest woman, early 30s, with bicycle, cooking skills, and dainty hands. For immediate marriage.

On Oh I was known as a sea captain, though I wasn't one at all. Captain Dagmore, they called me. Captain Dagmore Bowles. I've never commanded on ship or shore, and I prefer a grand piano to a grand sailing vessel. But I have *traveled* the seas, plumbed their very depths, if you must know, and I consider myself a not-so-accidental expert on the islands that dot the water's surface.

An island worth its salt, I've always said, is like a well-composed sonata. I ought to know, for I've navigated the tricky terrain of more than one of each. Wind is meter, I say, to which the palms and pawpaws have to bend; tides and toads, flats and sharps that should never stray too far out of key; and the sea and sand, the staff upon which all the notes are splashed. I assure you that if ever an island was worth its salt—a bit *too* salty even—that is the island of Oh.

In fact, this is as much Oh's story as it is my own, for my life didn't simply unravel against the island's backdrop. It didn't dance methodically across the stage of Oh's sands or recite its poetry to an audience of coco palms. No, indeed. Rather, it was the island theater that dictated the actors' steps and mine. Its sun and its moon who at whim—as always—entangle the cords of the poor islander marionettes.

I lived on Oh not once but twice. And not anymore. I don't live anywhere anymore. I, the once Captain Dagmore Bowles, don't *live* at all, not in the manner of a moving, breathing man who plays piano or stretches his toes in the soft, gritty sand. I'm no longer a son, or a father. Not in the way I once was. I simply *am*. I float on

Oh's shores. I walk on its winds. I watch the goings-on, the view so much better from where I am now.

When the island sits quiet, the odd (very odd) uneventful day on Oh, I return to the beach that made me the man I once was, haunt the house that broke my heart, or sit atop the rocky peak that stole so many blissful hours from me. I could go somewhere new, I suppose, but why bother? Oh decided long ago that I (and mine) belong to her, to her mangoes and manchineels, her pineapples and prickly pear, and, above all, to her inconstant moon and her chilly sun.

Oh, the devilish undoings of *that* heavenly twosome! If ever you should come here, beware. Not just of your friends and your enemies (assuming you can tell which is which); be wary, too, of the sun and the moon, who spin around your head.

1

Stories on Oh are not of the kind that can simply be told from start to finish, like gliding through the alphabet, each letter cozily tucked between the ones before and after. The island's tales, they shift with the wind, and destinies turn on a teacup. My story is a case in point. It starts not with me, but with Bruce Kandele—editor-in-chief, copyeditor, reporter, and special correspondent of Oh's only newspaper, the *Morning Crier.*

Bruce was vexed that, of late, the best he could do in the line of front-page news was an unusually sumptuous sunset or a plum pair of rainbows. Though he enjoyed a good sunset as much as you or I—a good rainbow, too—sunsets and rainbows were not the *Morning Crier*'s usual fare, and putting them on the front page had Bruce's dander up. Oh's trim daily typically fed on lean and meaty truth, not on natural wonders, too sweet to nourish and far too everyday to stir the palate. Now if, in the bronze and salmon hues of the setting sun, a crime had been committed, some infraction infracted or conspiracy conspired; if, under the colorful arcs that graced the sky in twos and threes like ripples in a pool, a theft took place, or a ruse; then perhaps. But pretty pictures for pretty pictures' sake were not going to sell a paper, and Bruce knew this very well.

Trouble was that for the first time in the history of the *Morning Crier* (which goes back three generations, maybe four), nothing was going on. Not a mystery, a calamity, a family feud. Usually given to melodrama, Oh had grown tedious. The island simply endured, its chorus of trees and scheming moon, its fickle tides and shifty winds, all as if asleep. Worse than that, their dull and sleepy communion shunned the islanders. Shut them out, it did, like goats on the wrong side of a fence.

The hummingbirds minded their business. The mosquitoes didn't bite. Even the leaves kept to themselves, singing their rustling hymns in the most hushed of voices. Anywhere else, this would be the order of the day. But not on Oh. On Oh, the clouds cook up trouble. The stars spice up our stew. Sun and moon, as I told you, take turns playing roles in our islander tragicomedies. Bruce couldn't remember anything like it, and neither could I.

Bruce feared the island's silence to be the calm before an especially vicious (if front-page-worthy) proverbial storm. At night he studied the heavens. When would the dratted storm break? he asked them. And with what force? He checked the positions of the planets and the stars, examined the different hues that made up the nighttime sky, but he couldn't spot a single sign to ease his apprehensions, couldn't glimpse the slightest hint that whatever was stewing would be served up before long.

Part of Bruce's interest in the island's brooding mood was economic. If the best he could put on the paper's front page was a pair of galloping rainbows, the paper was sure to go broke. Equal part of his interest ran much, much deeper than that. Like the rest of the islanders, he was bored, bored and a little bit worried. How long would they tolerate an island so aloof? he wondered. What might happen if they tired, finally, of Oh's taunts and its moping about? What might the bored and a-little-bit-worried islanders be capable of if their fancies weren't tickled—and soon?

———

Bruce Kandele was not the only one who felt the way he did, though few others on Oh would have elaborated their position as eloquently (he was a journalist, after all). They would only have said that lately things seemed a bit "feeble," as if the island were dozing, or a little bit drunk on rum and juice. Take, for example, Trevor Rouge, owner and operator of the island's most popular bakery, and generally acknowledged good and jolly guy.

Trevor, after entering the world plump and promising, had grown into a man some six inches shorter than he would have liked to be. He made up for his stature (or lack thereof) with a tall-ish crocheted cap that housed his hair, with a razor-sharp wit, and a strong and admirable heart. Together they garnered him the immediate friendship and unwavering respect of everyone he encountered, and made of his bakery a sort of meeting place, a town hall dusted in flour where one was assured of warm company and warm buns, "old talk" (island gossip), and cheap cold drinks from a fridge that rocked and hummed.

Presiding as he did over the bakery court, Trevor often found himself in the midst of the islanders' muddles, a position about which Trevor's wife, Patience Rouge, had mixed feelings. Though she enjoyed the money and custom that his advice and company lured into the bakery, and liked very much to hear the island gossip he brought home, she thought it unwise of Trevor to get mixed up in the islanders' troubles. Trouble on Oh was infectious and Patience feared equally for her own health and his.

Ever-present at Trevor's Bakery, besides Trevor himself, was Branson Bowles. *Doctor* Branson Bowles, to be precise. (Branson was once my son.) He taught history at the Boys' School of Oh, the same school where Trevor and he had studied history and mathematics and literature. Rather, *he* had studied those things, while Trevor played cricket and rendezvoused with the girls and somehow in the end knew just as much as Branson did (though Branson is taller and bulkier, with no need to stuff big hair inside a big hat).

Trevor and Branson had been as close as brothers in their boy days. They still were, though Branson's time abroad, eight long years for his teacher's training, left him feeling more an outsider than an islander. Time off an island will do that to you, take it from me. Without Trevor's conspiring and enthusiastic ear, Branson's experiences far from Oh were mostly insipid, and it was with great joy that he had returned—over fifteen years ago now—to take up his post at the Boys' School, and his place at the edge of Trevor's bakery counter at the end of every day.

Like most of the islanders, Officer Raoul Orlean, Head of Customs and Excise, made the occasional stop at Trevor's Bakery, too, though his reasons for doing so were strictly professional. Raoul didn't go in search of fritters or friends, but to sniff out facts and clues. He had a soft spot for what he called truths of the plain-as-noses-on-faces variety (as opposed to island magic), and more than once he had caught whiff of one at Trevor's. His nose and his forty-odd years in the service of the island's imports and exports had propelled him to the Office's top rank (he started out a mere stamper of passports at the airport), and pushed him to the verge of retirement dozens of times. Though he threatened to leave his job on a weekly basis, the case had yet to come up that would send him packing. He cursed every time a tough one arose, then didn't sleep until he had solved it, each recovered tariff and levied fine a matter of personal and patriotic pride.

Bruce, on the other hand, checked in at the bakery at least once a day. He knew, as Raoul did, that the bakery was a hot-bed of information and buns both, and unlike Raoul, whose wife Ms. Lila cooked up all a man could ask for, Bruce had an equal need for newsworthy gossip and pineapple cake.

Around the time that Bruce feared for what Oh had (or worse, maybe *didn't* have) in store, he was not, as I said, the only one to sense the island's troubles. Trevor and his customers did, too—with the exception of Raoul, who found it rather refreshing that the mosquitoes had stopped stinging and that the islanders had stopped discerning impossible whispers in the shimmy of the trees. While Bruce fretted and pleaded with the lazy stars, and while all the bakery's patrons but Raoul talked of little else, Trevor, on the other hand, knew that nothing any of them said or did (or didn't say or do) could hasten the island's pace. He had spent his whole life on Oh, every single second of it minus those he spent swimming in the sea; he knew that the island would come around when it wanted—and not a minute before.

Trevor knew the island so well, in fact, that he perceived the exact moment when Oh's tantrum was about to end. He announced it at the bakery one late, cloudy night, over hot bread, ginger beer, and a pair of lonely hearts. *Front-page* lonely hearts.

2

"Oho!" Trevor snorted as he banged his hand on the bakery counter. "Now who do you suppose wrote that?!" He had just finished reading aloud, for the tenth time that day, the unusual (and already infamous) ad of the lovelorn man in the *Morning Crier*, the one with the fishing boat and seeking a bicycled bride who could cook.

"He put it in an envelope with money and slipped it under the door," Bruce announced. "I don't have any idea who it was."

"But the front page, Bruce? Couldn't you bury it somewhere inside the paper?" Branson asked.

"It's better than a sunset," he rebutted. "I thought it might give us all something to do. You know, we figure out who this fellow is and then we help him find a dainty-handed mate on two wheels. Preferably with a basket of macaroni pie dangling off the handlebars."

Branson didn't insist, for Bruce was loath ever to admit any error in journalistic judgment. Imagine his conviction when it appeared he had solved both of his problems in one fell swoop: the islanders were buying up the paper faster than Bruce could print it and they could talk of nothing else. The lonely fisherman had become an instant local hero. As the customers filed through the bakery for their daily bread, they elevated him to near-saint status. A hard worker! A strong and decent young man! One of Oh's finest, who sought nothing more than a dainty and capable woman with whom to go fish, to go forth and to multiply! (They never did figure where the bicycle fit in.) That such a man should be reduced to advertising his basic needs was a tragedy! A travesty! A testimony to the malevolence of every woman on Oh who would let such a catch bob sad, ignored, and unhitched in the gentle sea!

Raoul, who, generally speaking, didn't give a flying fish about lonely hearts ads, quietly took in the scene, paying particular attention to what Bruce had to say. Though Bruce and Raoul weren't the closest of friends, they went back a long way, and Raoul consulted with Bruce on cases once in a while. When he heard Bruce mention the envelope surreptitiously slipped under the door, Raoul pricked up his ears. He, too, had found a strange, unsigned message that day, and it was precisely because of it that he had stopped in the bakery to sniff for clues. Was some anonymous island trouble-maker on the loose? And what did he mean dragging Raoul into whatever he was up to?

But by the time the evening drew to a close, Raoul had convinced himself that Bruce's anonymous ad had nothing to do with Raoul's own mysterious communication, for which there simply must be some perfectly reasonable—and plain—explanation. He wouldn't give it another thought.

And yet.

Like a gnat, the strange message flitted inside Raoul's head, and he could focus on little else. He nodded distractedly to Bruce as Bruce left. He listened to, but didn't hear, the wave of talk that swelled and engulfed the bakery, finally splashing Trevor's customers out into the empty street. Through the glass of the storefront, it looked to Raoul as if they floated off into the dark, clinging eerily to their plump and plastic-wrapped loaves like castaways to buoys.

He had a very bad feeling that the gnat in his brain was about to become a fat and proper fly.

3

A gnat on the brain was nothing new for Raoul Orlean. His problems always whizzed about his head like so many winged insects, the severity of each tribulation directly proportional to the size of the fly that denoted it. At any given time, Raoul was plagued by a flurry of critters representing his daily obligations: a fruitfly for the phone bill he had to pay at Oh-Tel, a midge for the letter of reprimand to a subordinate found drunk at his post, a whole dozen of gnats for the eggs his wife asked him to pick up at the market. There were houseflies (the kitchen windowframe in need of repair) and gardenflies (a rat that had his way with Ms. Lila's melons). There were craneflies, blowflies, and bottleflies in blue and green. This day's fly, though—this Tuesday fly that turned up at the bakery—was unusual even for Raoul. It was a shocking, mocking shade of hot pink.

To start, Tuesday was supposed to be Raoul's day off. He spent every one of them at the Pritchard T. Lullo Public Library, under the watchful eye of his librarian wife, relishing the plain-as-noses-on-faces truths the library shelves housed. Only the most demanding of Customs cases or the most imperative of personal chores could force

Raoul to skip his weekly visit. What kept him from his books on *this* Tuesday was a diplomatic affair, one of utmost importance. His wife, for weeks, had been pestering him to re-paint their chipped and flaking cottage, and marital tensions had risen to the point of stand-off. Ms. Lila had flat out refused to prepare Raoul's breakfast until he started the task at hand. To emphasize her point, she had laid his place at the table that morning with brushes and scrapers and paint thinner, in lieu of his typical Tuesday coffee and oatmeal and milk. She instructed her husband to settle for a quick cup of tea and to get to work. The cottage, though expansive, was short and single-storied, and if he put his mind to it, she said as she dashed off to the library, he might get a first coat on all the way round.

Ms. Lila had decided the house could do with some brightening up while they were at it, and so she had chosen, to replace the pale yellow of its exterior, a vibrant, cheerful pink. From among the rainbow of offerings at Higgins Hardware, Home, and Garden, she had purchased what the salesman called "Playful Rose," and had had big tins of it delivered. For the shutters and sills, she bought "Coconut Cloud."

Because Ms. Lila generally demanded little, and because Raoul had learned early on what unhappy wives were capable of, he heaved a nostalgic sigh for the pages that would remain unread that day, put the kettle on, and fetched some tattered trousers and a worn-out shirt. In a corner of the yard, under an almond tree, he laid out his implements and paint tins, then he ducked back inside to sip his tea. His stomach would require more sustenance than that, but he would work for two or three hours first, then break for an early lunch.

As the sun climbed, Raoul scraped and sanded and stirred and got one whole wall completely covered in the bright, playful hue.

He stood back to admire his work, guessing by the sun's position that noon had come and gone, and rubbing his grumbling tummy, told himself he had earned some bread and cheese. He was delighted to discover that Ms. Lila, who really was a good sport, had instead left him breaded fish for lunch, which he put between two slices of her homemade bread, chasing it with warm mango and cold beer.

His belly full, Raoul went back outside just before two o'clock. The first pink wall dried in the sun as he made his way past it and on to the next one. When he rounded the corner of the cottage, so engrossed was he in evaluating the morning's work that he failed to see a paintbrush lying in his path and trod on it. It sent him stumbling off balance, and he fell.

"How the devil did that get there?" he wondered, certain he had not left any brushes lying about, especially not ones still dripping with paint.

"What in the...?" His train of thought, and the words it dragged behind it, stalled as Raoul caught sight of the yellow wall he was about to attend to. It appeared to be marred by some sort of bright pink graffiti. He looked around, but could see no mischievous youths running off, could hear no taunts and giggles from the bush behind his house. He leaned back and took in the marking on the wall. It was hastily painted and running and drippy. It seemed to say FIND A BAKER. Why would someone tell him to do *that*? Raoul had plenty of home-baked bread. And why with Playful Rose on a faded yellow wall?

He got up off the ground and backed away to take in the whole of the words. The spacing between the letters was uneven and sloppy, as were some of the letters themselves, but none of the readings he imposed on them made any more sense than FIND A BAKER.

"Stupid kids," Raoul spat, sure that the words must be a reference to some silly teenage joke or some carnival song that eluded him. He would go on with his work and not give it another thought. Then he wondered, Should he paint over it? Might he be destroying evidence? Although he couldn't answer when he asked himself "Evidence of what?" Raoul decided to skip the second of the cottage's four sides and to go straight on to the third. Perhaps later his wife would see some sense in the writing on the wall.

Raoul hummed as he worked, scraping and smoothing the wood before him, but he couldn't resist the urge to peer around the corner every so often, to see if the strange graffito was still there, and whether viewing it anew might yield any insight. He finally grew so preoccupied that he abandoned his work to search the immediate vicinity for clues.

He examined more closely the paint tins that stood under the almond tree and discovered behind one of them a small spill, into which someone—the vandal, presumably—had stepped. Not fully, not enough to leave behind proper footprints, but enough to leave a series of pink smears leading away from the yard. Raoul ran inside for his magnifying glass, but it was of no help in determining what sort of shoe or what sort of foot was attached to the guilty party. He followed the smears for as long as he could, but they gradually faded into nothing, the culprit's heel wiped clean by the woodsy brush surrounding the cottage.

"Hmm," Raoul said. He had come to the end of his property and found himself on the edge of the road parallel to his. He looked left, and he looked right, and he looked through his magnifying glass, which he held up to eye level, expecting to see heaven-knew-what sort of clue in thin air, but to no avail. He turned and made his retreat. It was nearly evening, and Ms. Lila would soon be home.

While Raoul walked, he wondered who could have painted such a silly message on his house. He turned the strange rosy words over and over in his head, dismissing them in one instant, and theorizing about them in the next. Despite his wonderings and theories, when he got back to the cottage, the pink fly that would knock against Raoul's brain later that night was still nothing more than a niggling gnat. It niggled sufficiently, however, to drive Raoul just a little bit mad. Mad enough that, without waiting to hear what Ms. Lila might make of the day's events, he had put away his paint and brushes, spruced himself up, and gone to the bakery to look for the baker.

Alone there with Trevor and Branson (at the end of the night that had witnessed the debate about the love-starved fisherman), Raoul looked on from a few feet away as the two friends, under a bulb that hung bright and naked over the smudged glass counter, snacked on fresh, steamy bread with butter, and ice-cold ginger beer. (Raoul had declined a portion.)

"This is it, you know, Bran," Trevor said, flatly tapping the folded newspaper with the lonely hearts ad against the counter's edge.

"What is?" Raoul asked anxiously.

But before Trevor could answer that Oh was waking up, before he could explain to Raoul that the island was stretching and twisting and about to jump out of its bed, the wind, which had for months sat quietly in the yard and listened to their chatter, forced its way through the window with such violence that the lightbulb swung and crashed into the ceiling. In the new and sudden darkness, Raoul heard Trevor move and chuckle, crushing with his trainers the bits of bulb that littered the floor. Raoul couldn't see him but knew that Trevor was shaking his head, in relief and resignation.

"This is it," Trevor's bodiless voice pronounced again in the darkness. "At last."

4

Perhaps I wasn't perfectly accurate before when I said that Trevor announced the end of Oh's tantrum over bread, beer, and a pair of lonely hearts. A pair of lonely hearts was to be involved soon enough, that's true. On that night, however, the second heart, which would presumably pedal its way into their lives, had yet to come forward and identify itself. Even the first remained a mystery, but at least they were certain of its existence. It wrote messages, and stuffed them with money into envelopes to slip under newspaper-office doors.

The identity of this mysterious and questing heart was cause for such speculation, it may well be that the frenzy of the islanders' conjecture is what finally awoke the wind, which in turn stirred the clouds into rain.

"I'll bet you this package of plantains in my hand it was Neal from the valley who placed that ad!"

This pronouncement came from Officer Arnold Tullsey, who, together with Officer Joshua Smart, represented the cream of the island police force and of the law-enforcement football club (striker and goalkeeper, respectively). The pair of them were headed home on Dodger Bent's bus, which careened around the corners and up the hill to the village of Thyme, where both of them lived.

"You know Neal from the valley," Arnold continued, "always alone down there with his chickens and his dogs. How else could he find himself a nice lady?"

"Neal? Nah," Dodger disagreed as he drove, glancing at Arnold in the rearview mirror. "It couldn't be Neal. The man said he had a boat. It has to be a fisherman. Someone who lives by the beach."

"What, you never heard of anyone from the valley going fishing?" objected Jarvis Coutrelle, conductor and change-maker on Dodger's bus. "Could be someone from the country, too. Lots of men move of a morning to fish, and keep a boat anchored at the shore."

"I don't think Neal owns a fishing boat," Joshua Smart said matter-of-factly.

"Whoever he is, why would he want a woman with a bike?" Dodger asked no one in particular.

"Could be that waiter from Val-de-Trop," suggested Joshua. "You know the one. With the green and white boat he's always repainting?"

"He does more painting than fishing with that boat," Jarvis remarked as he counted up the coins he and Dodger had collected over the course of the day.

"In truth, I've only ever seen that boat up on the beach. Not once in the water!" Arnold confirmed, and all four of them laughed at the waiter's expense.

"I still think it's Neal from the valley," Arnold insisted.

"Nah. No way it's Neal," Dodger repeated.

"I say it's the waiter," Joshua said. "What's his name?"

Before anyone could advance an answer, without warning, Dodger jerked the minibus to a stop in the middle of the road.

"Why are you stopping?" Arnold asked.

"Is it Alain Gilbert?" Joshua wondered aloud.

"In the road?" Arnold asked.

"No, his *name*," Joshua said, so stuck in their discussion that he hadn't noticed Dodger stopped-dead. "The name of the waiter from Val-de-Trop, is it Alain Gilbert?"

"That's a tree!" Dodger cried.

"They named a tree Alain Gilbert?" Arnold asked, confused.

"No! There's a *tree* across the road," Jarvis explained, standing up and peering through the windscreen.

"Oh." (Arnold.)

"Ah." (Joshua.)

"Mm." (Dodger.)

Dodger and Jarvis found themselves still two miles away from Thyme, with their two police passengers and a good part of the road blocked by a downed breadfruit tree. The battered breadfruit was apparently the work of the violent wind and rain, which had begun to knock against the windows of the bus somewhere between Neal's chickens and the waiter's painted boat.

Dodger put the bus in reverse, intent on winding his way down the hillside until he found an alternate route to climb back up. His first backward maneuvers were met with such frightful squeals from the policemen on board, however, that Jarvis forced him to stop. Officers Arnold and Joshua, in an effort to reclaim some authority, jumped out of the bus then with official urgency, examined the road, and determined that Dodger had just the space he needed to inch the vehicle forward between the tip of the heavy, fallen tree and the two-foot ditch on the road's edge.

"Are you mad?" Dodger said to them. "I can't fit through there."

"You can, I tell you!" Joshua insisted.

"We'll direct you," Arnold said.

They did, and he couldn't. About thirty seconds later the bus was stuck, its front wheel sunken into the sewage ditch.

"Well, that's that," Arnold announced. Resigned to a rainy walk home, and unable to do anything more for Dodger or Jarvis, he reached inside the bus, collected his package of plantains and covered his head with it. While Joshua did the same, his own improvised raingear a discarded plastic bag that had fluttered through the bus the whole trip, a pair of headlights pulled up on the other side of the fallen tree and shined into the face of Dodger's vehicle. As luck or the awakening island magic would have it, Randolph Rouge was just then coming down the mountain in his bread truck, having finished his deliveries to the tiny shops scattered atop the hill. Randolph, Trevor's son, was as small-statured and as big-natured as his father; he offered to carry the officers up to Thyme, and Jarvis into town. Dodger could stay with the minibus until Jarvis returned with a tow truck, which Randolph would help him fetch after the policemen had been sorted out.

Randolph's truck was smaller than the minivan-bus, and he moved it agilely, so it took but a few seconds before he was facing in the right direction, Dodger's minibus at his back. Jarvis got in next to Randolph, and Arnold and Joshua made do inside the truck's empty and seatless back half. When the flour-dusted officers had been safely deposited in Thyme, Jarvis and Randolph went back down the mountain's other side, a loud calypso marathon blaring from the radio.

"Who you think we can find to pull out Dodger's bus at this hour?" Jarvis asked. It was close to ten o'clock by then.

"My uncle will do it," Randolph said, bouncing his shoulders up and down in time to the music. "We'll go back to the bakery and call him from there."

So apart from the mystery of the lonely hearts ad, the night's problems had worked themselves out. Dodger's passengers were home and mostly dry. The night's deliveries were made. The rain was slowing down. Randolph's uncle would rescue Dodger's minibus before too much longer.

Randolph liked it when things fell into place, and if they did so to calypso rhythm, why, then all the better. These were his thoughts as he happily tapped the steering wheel and followed the curves down and into Port-St. Luke.

But Oh was just waking up, remember. Just stretching and twisting and about to jump out of its bed. The wind had stirred, and stirred up the rain in turn. I'm sure that calypso beat only inspired the island's antics. Suddenly everything stilled and the moon shone bright on Randolph's and Jarvis's path. It shone on the asphalt, where there was any, and on the puddles where the road was rough and torn. On the unmoving leaves, the shiny wet trunks of the trees that had withstood the just-finished storm—and on the bent and mangled remains of a bicycle that Randolph slammed on the brakes to avoid.

The two men looked at each other, then both jumped out of the bread truck and rushed to survey what they assumed to be the remnants of some terrible accident. The bicycle was nearly crushed, but they found no blood or clothing or shoes or any other piece of evidence to indicate that the rider had been thrown or harmed. They checked the ditches and the woods in the general vicinity, even going so far as to knock on doors and to ask if anyone had seen or heard what happened. No one saw or heard anything, no one seemed to be missing, and no one had ever seen a bicycle like the one that lay in the middle of the road.

This last part is what's most unusual, for on Oh it's impossible to own something without your neighbors knowing. Equally impossible is it to avoid loaning out that very same thing to any neighbor who should ask. A bicycle was a commodity that would not have gone overlooked. Randolph decided to put the bike in the truck and to take it back to the bakery, where his father would surely know what to do about it.

"Looks like a lady's bike, doesn't it?" Jarvis observed, as they picked it up from the road. Randolph didn't answer, and on the way home he kept the radio off.

And there, at home, at Trevor's Bakery in Port-St. Luke, the second bit of the story joins the first. Branson and Trevor were still sipping ginger beer (Trevor had replaced the bulb by then) and Raoul was trying not to think about what he had decided not to think about, when the boys arrived and told their tale in all its particulars: Neal and the waiter from Val-de-Trop, the toppled breadfruit, and the bicycle abandoned in the road. Had Randolph and Jarvis happened upon evidence of the second, bicycle-owning lonely heart? Trevor shook his head again and smiled wide and bright.

"Ho ho," he said. "This is it. This is really it."

Raoul didn't answer, but under his breath he cursed the madding gnat that had sent him to find the baker.

5

Some little bit of madness is intrinsic to life on Oh. To life on *any* island—and I've visited many—but on Oh especially. For one thing, you can most easily and literally find yourself running in circles on an island. Worse, your circular jog will carry you endlessly past every monument to your troubles: past the ravine where you twisted your ankle, up the hill where you were butted by a goat, down the lane where your wife cheated on you with a man half your size. Of course the monuments to your success will always be there, too, the cricket pitch where you scored a half-century and the mango tree where you tasted true love. While it's good, even wise, to illumine your course with the flashlight of the past, you may find its beam falls too easily on familiar pitfalls, too readily on roads best traveled. You might ignore an unexpected gulley and stumble, or overlook a lush but untried path.

On Oh, this running in circles and in the subjective rays of your own history, maddening enough on its own, is exacerbated by the island's capricious terrain. A wink from the moon, and clouds unleash terrific storms, turning ditches into rivers overnight. A sneeze from the sun, and the frangipani's blooms triple, blocking your view and choking you with their powerful perfume. A loud and angry wind will blow the leaves off of every last tree, and there won't be a patch of shade for miles. The assaults to your sanity and your senses are quite thorough.

Which is why, to cope, most of the islanders on Oh choose to see, hear, smell, taste, and feel things not as they are, but as they wish them to be. Flooded river banks? Just a generous Oh throwing its plentiful fish right up on the grassy shores. Vicious sunlight? Why, the better for the islanders' deep mocha complexion. Believe you me, spend enough time on Oh, and you will convince yourself that the weeds are the sweetest of roses, and a traitor your very best friend. Here denial and delusion are as soothing as tea and fresh scones.

6

An abandoned and mangled bicycle was as newsworthy as it got, all the more so in light of the anonymous lonely heart who sought a bicycled mate. Trevor couldn't possibly have known what complications the island was cooking up just then, nor could he guess that Bruce would be the finishing touch, the cherry on the waking island's cake.

Randolph and Jarvis had just finished their stormy tale when Trevor picked up the phone. First he called his brother-in-law, Ernest, who had a truck with a hitch on it and was happy to rescue Dodger's bus. He called Patience to tell her he wouldn't be home for a while. And he called Bruce, because Bruce was a newsman in search of news, and so a friend in need. Also, Bruce was the only one of them who owned a camera. Trevor thought they ought to shoot the scene, and Raoul, who had experience in such matters, agreed.

"The scene of what?" Branson asked.

"If we knew that we wouldn't be here puzzling over a mashed-up bike in flour dust at midnight, would we?" Trevor told him.

As a matter of fact, it was hardly eleven-thirty, but they were indeed standing in front of Trevor's Bakery, gazing perplexed into the back of the bakery truck at the bicycle the boys had carried home. Randolph wanted to get it out, but Raoul thought it best to photograph the bike as it was, just once-removed from the scene of the crime, not twice.

"What crime?" Branson asked. "The boys said they looked for clues and there weren't any."

"Since when does no clue mean no crime?" Raoul asked, though it was more an observation than a question.

"Don't the police have cameras? Maybe we should just call the police," Branson suggested. In response, Trevor looked knowingly at Raoul and did something of a cough and a snort combined. It was the sound he made whenever he wished to remind Branson that his years off Oh had rubbed away a few layers of islander varnish.

"The police? They'll fill out a dozen forms, cite me for covering the evidence in flour, and call in experts from Killig who'll file a report." (Killig is Oh's island neighbor, known for its rum and for robbing Oh of a lucrative pineapple trade.) Though Raoul counted himself among Oh's government ranks and almost took offense at Trevor's characterization, over the years he had witnessed more than one pickle at the hands of the Island Police, and so he held his tongue.

Trevor cough-snorted again and went on. "Then *our* police will file a report about *their* report and before you know it, the trail's gone cold."

"What trail?" Branson asked.

"The trail from the bike to its rider," Trevor said with a bit too much glee.

Though Branson listened to his best friend sort out the islanders' troubles every evening at the bakery, he forgot how much

Trevor fancied a really good riddle. Which is what the mystery of the mangled bicycle was becoming.

"Have it your way," Branson said and let his hands fall to his legs with a loud slap. It was the sound *he* made whenever he wished to *acknowledge* his thin islander veneer (a Bowles hallmark, alas, this thinness). Which was not so thin, mind you, that he didn't guess Trevor's ulterior motive for involving the *Morning Crier.*

Trevor wanted to stir up talk, a foolproof island remedy for any island problem. In this, too, Raoul agreed with him. Though Raoul himself was a man of few words, and much preferred the permanency of those printed in his library books, he had long since discovered the power of some old-fashioned island gossip.

———

Bruce arrived shortly after (he only lived a few minutes away on foot) and began to assemble his reportage of dog-eared notepad pages on which he scribbled Randolph's and Jarvis's account, and snapshots of the bike from every angle. Raoul and Trevor finally allowed the removal of the bike remains from the truck, and Bruce photographed them upright, too, or as close to upright as the boys could hold them.

"If you don't mind, Trevor, I'll get a start on the story here, while it's all fresh." Bruce tapped his temple with his index finger and cleared some space on the counter. "I might need to ask the boys for more details as I go along."

"Suit yourself," Trevor said. "We have to wait for Ernest anyway."

Wait they did, Trevor, his son Randolph, Jarvis the bus conductor, Branson, and Raoul, in silence, seated on the low concrete step outside the bakery. Randolph and Jarvis, still shaken by their discovery, drank beer from sweaty brown bottles with slippery labels. Trevor drew with his fingers in the dirt between his feet, and Branson stared at the moon, fuller-faced than any he could remember for quite some time. He half-noticed that the tree-frogs and crickets, too, chirped louder than they had in weeks.

Only Raoul's mind was racing. He was troubled, he was. By the hot-pink message that had sent him scrambling to the bakery, by the news of Bruce's anonymous ad, by the bent and twisted bicycle the baker's son had found in the road. It seemed a terrific coincidence that bikes were turning up in newspapers and on shortcuts alike, or that Bruce and Raoul should both receive unsigned letters in the space of two days. As much as Raoul hated to admit it, it seemed that Trevor had got it right. Oh was wide awake, and the rainy moon was just the beginning. Unless—and Raoul thought this the better guess by far—the rain was the only *real* coincidence and he could find some connection between the BAKER, the bicycle, and the bashful bachelor hungry for a wife.

While Raoul wondered how to go about such a strange and formidable undertaking, his head a-buzz with more questions than answers, Ernest Peachtree pulled up to the bakery. His noisy exhaust pipe battled the reggae tune that poured from his truck's radio, the cacophony accentuated by hoots of his horn.

"Good night, all. Good night!" he shouted from the open window as he wildly swung the vehicle into the small lot in front of the bakery. He cut the motor and hopped out. Jarvis stood to greet him. "Thanks, man. Good of you to help," he said.

"Doesn't sound like Dodger, getting himself stuck in a ditch," Ernest answered. "What happened?"

"He listened to the police, that's what."

"Police?" Ernest was confused.

"I'll explain it on the way," Jarvis said as he patted him on the back. "Let's go rescue the bus."

"Hold up!" Ernest said. "Trevor, you got a bun or something? I'm hungry."

They all went inside and Trevor gave Ernest warm bread with some sausages from a tin.

"Bruce! What are you doing here?" Ernest asked cheerfully, when he saw Bruce at work over his notepad. It struck him, then, that the presence of Raoul Orlean there, at that hour, was unusual as well. "What's going on?" Ernest asked, filled suddenly with more worry than cheer.

"Randolph and Jarvis found a bike in the road and Bruce is writing a story about it for the paper," Trevor explained.

"You mean a lost and found kind of thing?" asked Ernest.

"Something like that," Bruce said, with a strange smile on his lips. Strange enough that Trevor and Branson exchanged a puzzled look, and Raoul's fly pitched in his head.

"Jarvis will tell you the whole story on the way. Go ahead and get Dodger now. I'll wait up for you here," Trevor said.

"Wait!" Bruce shouted, waving his tattered notepad in the air and following after Ernest. "Can you drop me at the *Crier* first? I want to get this in tomorrow's edition."

"Sure. Let's roll."

The rest of that night went uneventfully enough (what happened in the morning was far more intriguing). Ernest and Jarvis found Dodger asleep in his bus and pulled the bus from the ditch.

The vehicle was undamaged, so once freed, Dodger was up and running. He took Jarvis home and then went home to bed himself. Raoul went home, too, where he had some explaining to do to Ms. Lila, about his whereabouts that evening and his painting that day. Back at the bakery, Randolph, Trevor, and Branson played dominoes until Ernest returned. When he did, they re-examined the evening's events all over again (the ad in the *Morning Crier*, the night's rain, Dodger's bus, the breadfruit, the bicycle, Bruce) in light of Ernest Peachtree's new and fresh perspective.

Little did they know, an even fresher one was taking shape inside the grimy-windowed newspaper offices a few doors down the road.

Hit-and-Run on Thyme Shortcut
Baker, bus driver key witnesses

Late last night on the secondary road that leads from town to Thyme, an unidentified motorist collided with a bicycle, knocking a female cyclist, also unidentified, to the ground. The bicycle, which was badly damaged, was discovered in the road by baker Randolph Rouge of Port-St. Luke and bus driver Jarvis Coutrelle of Beaureveille, who were forced to take the shortcut after last night's storm downed a tree, blocking the primary Thyme road. Though the two young men acted quickly at the scene of the crime, their efforts to apprehend the guilty party were fruitless. Equally futile were their attempts to identify the injured young woman, who fled the scene presumably in search of medical care. Rouge and Coutrelle proceeded to clear the road of all evidence, namely one lady's bike, silver with yellow handles and yellow seat, which they carried back to Port-St. Luke, careful to preserve its integrity in light of the soon-to-be-ongoing police investigation. It is unclear if road conditions played a role in the accident. When questioned as to the velocity at which the hit-and-run driver was moving, Rouge exclaimed, "I didn't see a thing!" prompting this reporter to speculate that both the driver's breakneck speed and the wet and bumpy backroad were contributing factors. The attempted vehicular homicide of a female cyclist is particularly noteworthy in view of an advertisement published in this same newspaper only yesterday, in which a female cyclist with cooking skills and dainty hands was sought. It is unknown whether the missing victim possesses these attributes. This reporter is moved to speculate that she does, and to appeal to the citizenry of Oh to disclose any information that might bring to justice the dangerous driver, and evil thwarter of romance, responsible for this shameful act.

Ah, Bruce! His journalistic integrity as in need of a dusting as was the floury bike!

If you're wondering how he could have made such a mess of the facts, you needn't. He would tell you it wasn't a mess at all, but a calculated and pointedly crafted interpretation of the events. He too was a believer in the island philosophy that talk leads to truths—and to Bruce it didn't matter if the talk was triggered by a few little black-and-white lies.

7

Though Raoul Orlean was not a big believer in luck, of the good kind or the bad, even *he* had to admit what a stroke of good fortune it was to find Ms. Lila softly snoring under the sheets as he tiptoed into the bedroom. Raoul had had an exhausting day. He had painted one whole side of the cottage, crept through the bush for clues, strained his brain on a rosy-pink riddle, and stayed at Trevor's Bakery far later than he had planned, lending his official expertise to the evening's ado. His head ached from the fly that taunted him, his hands itched from the solvent he had used to clean them, and the last thing he wanted to do was explain to his wife why he hadn't managed to "get a first coat on all the way round," or why one of the cottage walls was covered with letters. Heaving a sigh of relief, and thanking his lucky stars before he could stop himself (he was on principle against such superstitious practices), Raoul slid gently into bed alongside her and immediately fell asleep.

When he awoke, Ms. Lila's side of the bed was empty. She was already up and at her morning's ablutions and duties, and in the easy quiet of the bedroom, Raoul stretched and smiled, calm and rested. It wasn't long, however, before the events of the previous day came to mind—the graffiti, the bakery, the bike, the bachelor fisherman. When they did, Raoul was filled with a sluggish, heavy dread, his predilection for truths-plain-as-noses-on-faces prodding the fly in his head to a frenzy.

"Good morning," his wife greeted him, as he dragged himself into the kitchen and slumped into a chair. "What's the matter with you? Too much to drink last night?"

"Nah," Raoul replied. "What *I* have can't be fixed with a stiff cup of tea."

Ms. Lila rushed over to him, concerned, and touched his forehead. "You don't feel fevered," she said. "What's going on?"

"Have you seen the house?" he asked her, motioning with his chin towards the out of doors.

"Ooh, I almost forgot!" She clapped her hands together. "I went to the market after the library closed. My hands were so full when I came home, I walked straight in. By the time I thought to go back out and have a look, the rain was coming. Did you get very far?"

"Well," Raoul began, and he went on to tell her in painstaking detail about everything that had happened. He told her about the first wall he painted and about the message he found, and how after that he went to look for a baker, and how at the bakery he found Bruce, who had *also* found a message, one that happened to involve a bike, and, to conclude, he told her about the hit-and-run.

"And?" she said, when he had finished.

"And what?"

"And what does any of that have to do with anything?"

Raoul was flabbergasted. "Don't you see? Some hooligan is on the loose and sending secret messages! Now there's been a hit-and-run besides!"

Ms. Lila, dear heart, was used to the frenzies to which her husband was prone, the random variables he tried to string together into neat equations, and she sometimes heard the flies in his head buzzing even before he did. She was sure she heard one now—one that was going to interfere with the repainting of her cottage—and she meant to put her foot down and squash it.

"Not that this hooligan, assuming he exists, is any business of yours," she told him, "but let's go have a look at this nonsense you're talking about." She spun on her heel and headed outside, Raoul trailing behind.

After duly admiring the first coat of paint on the one finished wall (she was quite pleased with her choice of color), she turned and looked at the message on the second wall.

"See?" Raoul gushed, feeling vindicated by the strangeness of the writing. "FIND A BAKER. So that's what I did. I went to Trevor's Bakery for clues."

"That doesn't say FIND A BAKER," Ms. Lila objected. "This one's an R," and she touched the letter in the middle. "And see this? It's a definite dot. The message isn't FIND A BAKER, it's FIND R. BAKER."

"What's an R. Baker?" Raoul asked her.

"Not *what*," she answered impatiently. "*Who!*"

"What does that mean? Who's R. BAKER? And why should I go looking for him?"

"My point exactly. Unless he's a housepainter, I suggest you put him right out of your mind, cover up this mess as soon as you get home from work, and get on with it. The rain's good and broke now. We'll only have a few more weeks of sun before the wet season, and I'll not have the house looking like a striped Easter egg for half of the year!"

"But what if this is evidence?" Raoul pleaded.

"Evidence of what?" Ms. Lila asked him sternly.

Raoul of course had no answer to this. He simply stood, mute, looking at his wife.

"I thought so!" she said and went inside to prepare his breakfast. "Hurry now, or you'll be late to the office."

At the headquarters of Customs and Excise later that morning, Raoul struggled to focus at his desk. He read and re-read Bruce's report in the *Crier*, trying to figure out how the bicycle accident might be connected to the lonely-hearted fisherman—if, indeed, it was—and what possible reason the same anonymous fisherman might have for painting strange instructions on the side of Raoul's cottage. Try though he might, Raoul could read nothing between the printed lines of the paper to help him make sense of the nonsense of the day and night before. On the contrary, the more he reflected and mulled things over, the murkier they became. Still, these were no random events that Raoul could just ignore. They couldn't be! He would have to do some sleuthing. How else to free the plain and simple truth from the words and letters and messages in which it was so mysteriously entangled?

First, though, official duty called. Raoul folded the newspaper in half and tucked it in his drawer, then he turned back to the work on his desk. There were budget ledgers to review, import (and export) applications to process and approve, and holiday requests to sign off on from at least a dozen members of his staff. As he worked, turning pages and shuffling forms and signing and stamping and stapling, he noticed every letter in a way he never had before. It seemed that every word spoke directly to him, as sure as if it were standing in front of him wagging its finger at his nose. The entries in his ledgers hissed and twisted, like little black snakes on soft, green grass. The alphabet tabs of his accordion folders sprang to life and whispered to each other. The carbon-copy request forms mocked him, flaunting their layers of pink and yellow that displayed the same words over and over, as permanent as paint. Raoul rattled his head back and forth and repeatedly blinked his eyes, which he focused squarely on a dull and empty grey wall. "What's going on?" he asked it, irritated.

He put his hand to his ear and listened, but he could hear only the sounds that sneaked in, diluted, from beyond his office door: the muffled conversations of his coworkers, the ring of a phone, the whir of a pencil sharpener. From the window behind his head, he heard the brush of leaf against leaf and the distant tinkling of a windchime. (The breeze hadn't died down since the night before.) He did not hear a single hiss or whisper. Nor, as near as he could tell, was any slip of a form making fun of him. Reassured, he rattled his head again and returned to his business.

The minute he did, the words were at it again. The A's and R's toyed with him, morphing one into the other and back. Signatures disappeared before his eyes, rendering every request and memo an unsigned taunt. And—could it be?—Raoul swore the pale pink pages before him blushed playfully to bright rose.

"Ahh!" Raoul spat, fed up. In one violent move, he stood up and pushed the chair away from his desk with the backs of his knees. There was no getting any work done, not with this fresh pink fly buzzing in his head and his ledgers hissing and spitting. He decided to take an early lunch. Perhaps some sea air would clear his mind, he thought, and he set out on foot for the harbor in the heart of town.

But though his body worked with the aim of delivering him to the water's edge, muscle and joint in blissful, ignorant synergy, his mind's purpose was another entirely. It wandered off, indifferent to the clarity Raoul sought, twisting his nose this way and that and landing his eyes on sniggering consonants and vowels. There seemed to be no escape. Was he going mad? So seemed to indicate the billboard for Mad Mabel's rum shack. Was he under some kind of magic spell? he wondered, at the sight of the sign for Nut-Magic Nutmeg Tonic and Cure-All, available at Dimwell's pharmacies island-wide.

"Bite your tongue!" Raoul said out loud to himself. He hated that word—*magic*—and he refused to entertain the notion that it had him in its grasp, or for that matter, that it was capable of grasping so much as a flea on a mutt on a soggy beach!

Lucky for Raoul, his legs, unthinking, continued to carry him to the harbor, for his mind, which had till then played tricks on him, was wholly occupied in a head-on attack on all things magical, supernatural, supernormal, extra-ordinary, and occult.

"Rubbish all of it," he muttered under his breath. "Don't know what they see in it!" *They* were the islanders in general, the citizens of Oh, so inured to the pranks and meddlings of the stars and the streams that they tended to see magic—nay, to look for it—where there was none. Ever since Raoul, as a young man, had developed his love for facts and for truths, he had found himself at odds with friends and family members, who refused to deny the island's magical charms. Charms that, as far as Raoul was concerned, could be explained away to a mathematic certainty, if only one tried hard enough.

For years he had considered this uniquely Oh issue, and though his theories were many, he had yet to determine why exactly his neighbors remained so desperately certain of the island's sorcery. Did they hope to secure some better fate for themselves by bowing to the ocean breeze? Were they too lazy to take life in hand? Was it simply easier to blame the moon for their misjudgments, the palms for their peccadilloes? To chastise the tide when they fell short? It never crossed Raoul's mind, as he sat down finally on a bench and looked out to sea from the port in Port-St. Luke, that the islanders might just have it right. That sometimes, no matter how hard you tried to hold on, a swift island wind could blow you right off your feet and out to sea, if it really wanted.

It was precisely because of magic, or, more precisely, "magic talk," that Raoul went to the harbor to clear his head that day and not to the Belly to spend his early lunch break. The Buddha's Belly Bar and Lounge, which Raoul frequented almost daily, was tucked into the lower level of the Hotel Sincero, owned and run by one of Raoul's three best mates, the flashy but practical Cougar Zanne. At the Belly at lunch hour, Raoul was likely to meet not only Cougar, but his other two best mates as well, cab-driver Nat Gentle and the crooning, juggling, musician they all called Bang. Any of them would notice immediately that Raoul had a fly in his head, and when pressed, he would have to tell them about his pink graffiti, and how it must have something to do with the mysterious lonely hearts ad and maybe even the hit-and-run. They would no doubt, like Trevor, attribute all the goings on to the awakening island and the drama it loved to stage. They would tell Raoul to forget about investigating, to save himself the trouble and to let Oh work what magic it wanted—especially if it was working it on the side of Raoul's own house! Didn't he realize what forces he was up against?

Raoul rattled his head yet again and admired the sea that glistened in front of him. He saw boats being emptied of cargo and wondered about the places they had been. A ship's captain caught Raoul's eye and tipped his cap.

"Now that's a man who knows real life," Raoul said, raising his hand to return the captain's greeting. "The stars above him, the sea below, and his ship and cargo in between. I bet *he* doesn't fuss over magic."

A short distance away, a pair of deckhands sipping beer and eating fish-and-chips noticed Raoul talking all alone. They laughed at him and shouted something, but Raoul paid them no mind. When he was lost in thought, or in sleuthing, he didn't care what anyone had to say about him. His methods were a little unconventional, it was true, but what plain truth wasn't worth at least a spot of humiliation?

Raoul's thoughts flitted back to the Belly, and he grew agitated again. "Magic talk! It's all they do there!" he complained to the ships in front of him. "Ever since the damned place opened up." Raoul recalled one of his very first visits to the Belly. In those days, forty years before, it wasn't yet a full-fledged Bar and Lounge, but an overhang Cougar had stuck to the outside of a then-tumble-down Hotel Sincero. Some silly fool had sat and asked Raoul for advice, sure that island magic was keeping him from his one true love. Raoul couldn't remember who it was, but he remembered keeping their discussion short and sharp.

Resigned to the islanders' magical obsession, Raoul calmed his mind now and took in the beauty of the silent, simple sea and the massive man-made boats that rested on top of it, like the sugary flowers Ms. Lila put on cakes for special occasions. He saw huge wooden crates unloaded and knew they were headed for Customs, where his colleagues would clear them and tax them. He watched as the deckhands finished their food and drink and took themselves back on board. The ship's captain gestured and gave orders and walked the length of the pier, and suddenly Raoul's memory jerked.

"What do you know about that!" he said, moved to a sorry smile and shaking his head in disbelief. He remembered now. He remembered the man who had asked him about magic all those years ago at the Belly, the man who couldn't win over his one true love. Dagmore Bowles was his name. *Captain* Dagmore Bowles. (Who, I might add, won over his one true love in the end!)

Well, well. Even amidst the waves, Raoul marveled, Oh's magic lay in wait. If a wandering and worldly old sea-captain like Dagmore had fallen for its humbuggery, then the still and islandy islanders didn't stand a ghost of a chance.

8

The Captain Dagmore Bowles that I once was, the one Raoul once met at the Belly, was not born a captain, or even a Dagmore. Nor was he born on Oh. He was the fruit of an island neighbor, but from exactly which tree he fell, I couldn't tell you. Although he was orphaned from a very young age and got off to an unhappy start, the stars had aligned a grand future for him. A future as brilliant as the stars themselves, I always thought. At least for a little while.

Growing up on that same island that gave him life, the boy that would one day be Dagmore knew himself simply as Quick. The islanders had so dubbed him for his quick legs and his quick wit, and, while none had the space or means to take Quick under wing, they all pitched in and saw that he was dressed and fed, with hand-me-downs and leftovers, respectively. In exchange he used his legs and his wit to run the islanders' errands and to trap their rats. He slept on the beach, which suited him fine, and bathed in the salty sea. Thus cared-for by all and by none, he confronted and conquered the ages of four, five, and six.

When he was seven, he was struck by a terrible case of wanderlust. His feet itched so badly that he ran around the island quicker than ever, which made his small island seem that much smaller. He knew every inch of it by heart and longed to explore the other islands he spotted off shore, adrift and beckoning and promising of adventure.

Though not every island boasts a dose of magic equal to that found on Oh, where it gushes about like so many raging rivers, each island has a trickle, a stream, a brook that springs to life now and again after an especially hearty rain. Quick's island was no different. Right about the time that his feet were too itchy to bear, a droplet of magic with Quick's name on it burst like silver fireworks in a still, dark sky, leaving Quick gaping wide-eyed in awe.

A ship had laid anchor off the island's shore!

Quick had never seen anything like it. The biggest craft on *his* island were simple fishing boats. Once in a while some slightly bigger fishing boat arrived from he-knew-not-where with supplies and mail for the islanders, but those boats were mere toys compared to the one he stood staring at (a pirate ship, for sure!) on the day of the magic droplet. It wasn't long before the monstrous craft lowered a smaller vessel into the water, filled with six white faces all capped with blond hair. So that's what a pirate looks like! he said to himself.

A nearby clump of manchineel trees hid Quick from view as the pirates dragged their boat ashore and readied themselves to explore. They had sacks and spyglasses, compasses and charts, maps and blades. They spoke something close to Quick's language, which didn't startle or surprise him, for he was seven and words were words. That there might be other varieties of them never crossed his mind.

The so-called pirates were in fact nothing of the sort. They were sea-faring merchants and a scientist or two, who sought profit and specimens of leaf and bug to take back home—"home" a great white bear of a faraway land that had once briefly hugged Quick's black and tiny island in its colonial paws. So the men Quick spied on (or rather their troublesome grandfathers) were not entirely unknown to the sand on which they tread. And because the sins of the fathers are the missteps of the sons, the landing party had hardly covered fifty meters, when one of its men put his foot into a hole.

"Ow!" the unlucky devil cried out.

"What is it?" This question, as near as Quick could tell, came from the pirate leader.

"My ankle! I think it's broken."

"Take off your shoe. Let's have a look," said the man with the biggest sack of all.

Curious as he was to see the white, naked ankle, Quick's wit and his legs conspired to other ends, forcing him from his hiding place while the men were distracted. What's more, they sent him headlong into the men's temporarily abandoned boat. While just a few yards away the man with the big sack poked and palpated his companion's swelling foot, Quick rolled up his lithe little body and squeezed himself under the boat's stern-most plank of bench.

His wits had told him in a flash that this ankle might mean trouble. It might send the landing party rushing back to the ship instead of reconnoitering on land, and Quick would lose his chance to stow away.

As usual, Quick's wits were dead on, and outwitting a pack of pirates proved no more difficult than trapping a pair of rats. He had just tucked his knees up under his chin when he heard the men's voices growing louder and closer.

"Leave me here. I'll wait in the boat while you go have a look around," said the injured man, presumably.

"It looks like rain anyway. What's say we move on, Captain? These tiny islands are all the same. We've seen a dozen already and not one any different from the next. Can't we cross this one off the list?"

The man's words set off a flurry of questions in Quick's speedy brain. To which of the remaining faces did this new voice belong? Was the captain the man that Quick had identified as the leader of the other pirates? What did the strange voice mean, all islands were the same? Why, even small and insignificant Quick knew this wasn't true. He could see from the shores of his own island that the others around were different. One was tall and green, one flat. Another, a little bit of both.

Quick listened to the men debate and argue, back and forth. One of the group was especially vehement in his conviction that the island must be explored. His research would lose all credibility if incomplete, he said. But between the impending rain, the swelling (and now purplish) ankle, and the captain's short temper (he hadn't slept the night before on account of losing the last hand of cards), the man's conviction was trampled on, as convictions often are, and the party left the island straightaway. Quick melted into the dark of his hiding place and left the island with them, the six men none the wiser.

You can imagine what brave, young Quick must have been thinking as his body lurched across the waves toward an unknown and exciting destiny. What would he eat? Would he fit in? Would there be people to talk to? Would they want to talk to him? He worried about these things, mind, because the real worries, the particulars of life off an island, like urgency and noise and too many people, were too foreign even to imagine. Could Quick have ever dreamed what he was in for?

He wondered, too, if when he returned to his island home, assuming he survived and made it back, the islanders would remember who he was. Poor Quick! He couldn't know that they would mostly miss him when they smelled a rat.

And what of the island? As he sailed unknowing into the future, did he sense a faint breath of remorse on the breeze, a cool hint of lust from the isle that gave him life? Little matter, because another island entirely had set its sights on young Quick, and *that* island's shifty winds would blow him rough-and-tumble onto her sunny, sandy shore.

9

Trevor's Bakery buzzed like a beehive in the full of activity that next day when Bruce's article on the hit-and-run appeared in the paper. The customers that hovered busy and curious around the counter and the open front door sought answers and explanations to go with their cakes and their honey croissants. In exchange they offered rumor and theory with their coins and rainbow bills. (Oh's legal tender made up in color what it lacked in economic worth.)

"I couldn't believe my eyes when I read that headline!" Angela Ratte, elementary school teacher, exclaimed to Trevor, who was busy brushing butter on tops of bread loaves. "Just think of poor Randolph coming upon a lady in the middle of the road like that."

"It didn't happen so! It says that right here in the article," chimed Buster Torrent, carpenter and especially fond of Trevor's guava tarts. (He ate one every morning, sometimes two.) "'Equally futile were their attempts to identify the injured young woman,' it says."

"Identifying the young woman and seeing her are two different things," Angela rebutted. "Did Randolph see her or didn't he?" she interrogated the baker.

"You can ask him yourself." Trevor motioned with his head in the direction of the door, through which Randolph was entering, his arms piled high with large, empty bread baskets.

"Ask me what?" Randolph deposited his load on the floor behind the counter and slapped away the flour from his trousers.

The island, it seems, had no time for Angela's queries, for it allowed her not to utter so much as a syllable in response, before police officer Arnold Tullsey busted, bellowing, through the bakery doorway, followed by fellow police officer Joshua Smart.

"Where's that scoundrel, Bruce Kandele?! The door's locked down at the *Crier*. Is he here?"

"Haven't seen him yet today. Why's he a scoundrel?" Trevor asked, arranging his loaves into lines on a long aluminum tray, while Angela, angry at having been supplanted in the conversation, picked up her pies and shuttled them home.

"Why, for half a dozen reasons!" Officer Smart said. "Undermining the law, disrupting an investigation, unauthorized tampering and photographing of evidence—"

"Just a minute," Trevor stopped him. "Disrupting *which* investigation, would that be?"

"Trevor, you know very well which investigation," Officer Tullsey continued. "This bike business. Bruce should have called in the police. All of you should have. How can we investigate a crime if no one tells us about it?"

"Alleged crime, Arnold," Officer Smart corrected.

"Well, that's exactly what Bruce did, isn't it?" Trevor asked. "He told everyone about the crime at once. Easier that way, you don't find?"

"You know that's not what I mean," Officer Tullsey replied. "He made us look like fools, 'soon-to-be-ongoing investigation'! What are we supposed to say to that?"

"Can I get another guava tart?" Buster intervened. (Listening intently he had devoured the first one in record time.) He laid two large coins on the counter.

"Where's the bike?" Officer Smart asked. "We should take that down to the station. We'll need your statements, too."

"Help yourselves. It's out back in the shed," Trevor said, and off the two officers went.

It must have been about the time that Officers Joshua Smart and Arnold Tullsey were puttering around in the shed—and Raoul was ruminating about magic at the port—that Branson ran into Bruce buying swordfish at the fish market. Branson, who had seen the early edition of the paper first thing that morning, chided Bruce for the inaccuracies in his hit-and-run article, but Bruce defended every last one.

"You didn't even get Jarvis's job right," Branson told him. "He doesn't drive the bus, Dodger does."

"I know that," Bruce said, as if Branson had made the most idiotic of all possible observations. "I'm not a simpleton, am I? But every little bit counts in these cases."

"These cases?"

"Getting people talking! The 'inaccuracies,' as you call them, are icebreakers. Someone says, 'Hey, isn't Jarvis a conductor, not a driver?' and someone else agrees, and before you know it, they've examined the whole case and maybe come up with some idea or with a clue. How else are we gonna solve this mystery?"

"How can you be so sure you'll hear every idea and clue they come up with?"

"That's the easy part," Bruce said. "I just hang around the bakery. Every piece of gossip worth chewing on comes out between a bun and a banana cake at Trevor's. Same holds for clues and theories, good ones and bad ones alike."

Flawless logic, Bruce's, and so impossible to debate any further.

Fresh swordfish in hand, Branson and Bruce set off together for the bakery, where the police had already loaded the bike onto their truck and were taking statements from Trevor and Randolph. Buster had finished his second guava tart but lingered, relishing the spicy police conversation. While Officer Tullsey asked the questions, Officer Smart took notes.

"Please tell me exactly what happened." Officer Tullsey directed the first question to Trevor.

"I was here at the bakery, chatting with Branson and with Raoul Orlean, when Randolph and Jarvis showed up. In the back of the bakery truck they had a mangled bike they found on the road to Thyme. I heard what the boys had to say, and then I called Bruce to take some pictures of it. After that we sat outside and drank some beer."

"Did your son drink, too?" Officer Tullsey asked.

"He did."

"Hmm." Officer Tullsey rubbed his chin. "Okay. We'll take his statement next. I hope he wasn't so drunk that he's forgotten what happened." Officer Tullsey nudged Officer Smart. "You get all that?" he asked. "I'm going to question Randolph now."

"Got it," Officer Smart confirmed, scribbling on his notepad. "Drank beer. Drunk."

Randolph opened his mouth to object, then shrugged his shoulders and put his hands in his pockets.

"Randolph, tell me what happened on the road up there," Officer Tullsey began.

"Not much to tell," Randolph said. "I was in the truck with Jarvis, coming back to town on the shortcut, to get help for Dodger. That's when we found the bike in the road."

"What happened next?" Officer Tullsey asked slowly, studying Randolph.

"Nothing. We picked up the bike and brought it home."

"Did you search the scene for clues?"

"We had a look around. I don't know for clues."

"You find anything? See anyone nearby?" Officer Tullsey asked.

"Nah."

"No young woman fleeing the scene, like the paper says?"

"Nope."

"You sure?"

"Yep."

Officer Tullsey ran his fingers through his hair, frustrated, then dismissed Randolph with a wave of his hand.

Their civic duties seen to, Trevor and Randolph began to fill the empty bread baskets still resting on the floor. It was then that Branson and Bruce walked into the bakery.

"Well, well," Officer Tullsey remarked as he looked at Bruce. "We just took Randolph's and Trevor's statements. I don't know what's worse, Bruce, the fact that you looked into the case without calling us, or the fact that you did such a shoddy job of it."

"C'mon, Arnold, no hard feelings. I can't sell papers full of rainbows forever, can I?"

"That article's all wrong!" Officer Tullsey complained.

"It isn't!" Bruce insisted, a staunch defender of his particular brand of journalism. "It's one-hundred percent true to my intentions."

"What about the facts of the case?" Officer Smart demanded. "That article was irresponsible, you know."

But the island, it seems, had as much time for Joshua Smart's demands as it had for Angela Ratte's earlier queries. Before Bruce could utter a syllable in response, the widow Corinna arrived.

"Halloo, halloo! Good Morning! One pineapple cobbler, please." The widow Corinna, nearly ninety years old and nearly deaf, pushed her way through the crowd of Officers Tullsey and Smart, the spectating Buster, a silenced Bruce, and ever-present Branson. She stood leaning on her walking stick in front of Trevor's counter.

"Good morning, Corinna," Trevor said. "I got one for you just now coming out of the oven."

"Seven? I paid six last time!"

"No. I say it's coming from the oven," Trevor repeated, a bit louder.

"Well, where else would it come from? You're not getting in cobblers from Killig, are you? I want a fresh one!"

"No, no, don't worry. This is one of ours and it's fresh."

"That's still no reason to charge me more this week than last week." (Corinna bought a cobbler every week for her grandkids.)

"I'm not charging you anything more," Trevor nearly shouted.

"I should hope not," Corinna said. "My word!"

After Corinna left, the police tried to pick up the thread of the conversation she had cut off, but to no effect: Bruce saw no reason for their reprimands, Buster now wanted cobbler for his mother, and Randolph began to carry his newly full baskets to the bakery truck outside. Branson suddenly remembered the swordfish in his hand, which had already begun to sweat, and asked if he and Bruce could put their packages in the fridge.

The thread was too thin for such yanking about and broke.

Their investigation stymied for the moment, Officers Tullsey and Smart unbuttoned their jackets and slipped off their official demeanors. Now simply longtime pals Arnold and Joshua, they helped themselves to cold drinks, while Trevor made sandwiches.

"So what do you make of this bicycle business?" Trevor asked them as he worked. "You think someone got hurt?"

"Well, after hearing what Randolph had to say, I can't figure who it might be," Arnold said.

"It's surely strange, no one in the area knowing about a lady with a bike, nobody seeing what happened. You can't make a move on this island without somebody somewhere seeing something," Joshua (correctly) pointed out.

"We'll go ask more questions tomorrow, up by where it happened," Arnold said. "See if we find out more than the boys did. Get a statement from Jarvis, too. And from Mr. Orlean."

"What about that lonely hearts ad? It couldn't really be connected, could it?" Branson asked, his islander veneer not so thinned that he had lost all interest in Oh's affairs. (But thin enough that the officers had seen no point in questioning him.)

"Don't see how," Arnold said.

"Awful coincidence, though, isn't it," Joshua mused.

"Yes, indeed," Bruce agreed, with the same strange smile from the night before.

"What? You're not cooking up another half-invented story, are you?" Branson asked.

Bruce sighed. "I'm getting a little tired of explaining the finer points of journalism to the likes of all of you. If you don't mind, I have a newspaper to run." He left, feigning injury and indignation.

Branson rushed out after him. As he stepped outside, the sun angrily emerged from behind a cloud and, catching him unawares, nearly blinded him! All of its brilliance was concentrated into two pinpoints of light aimed straight at Branson's eyes, and *his* eyes alone, or so it felt in that split second. He stopped dead on the bakery step and shaded his face with his hands. By the time his stinging, watery vision re-adjusted itself, Bruce was an already small silhouette, getting smaller with every step.

Branson looked up, squinting and cautious, to where the sun burned a hole in the sky. It dazzled bright and innocent. And completely ordinary. He could detect no sign whatsoever of the malice he had sensed only a second before, could discern no hint of ill will. Not that he should have, for what had he ever done to incur the sun's wrath?

He remained on Trevor's step, however, unable to shake the foolish and self-aggrandizing sensation that the sun had indeed driven two purposeful spears of light into his pupils. Certainly not to impede his pestering Bruce?

Despite the heat, Branson shivered. He recalled suddenly the stories his captain father used to tell about go-rounds with the island elements. Branson had always thought the tales as tall as papayas. Huh. Maybe not!

Maybe Dagmore Bowles really *did* fight with the moon and the stars, and clash with the capricious tide.

"What are you doing out here alone?" Trevor poked his head through the doorway. His words undid Branson's daydream, dragging him from his father's affairs back to the step in front of the bakery. "Did you catch him?"

"Who?"

"Bruce."

"Nah, that's okay. It doesn't matter."

"What about the fish?"

"What fish?"

"You didn't go after him to tell him he left his swordfish in the fridge?"

"Oh. Right. He'll come back for it. You know Bruce. There's no stopping him when he hits his stride."

Back inside, cold with sweat and prickly with foreboding, Branson leaned against the wall and let the others talk. The police team had a football match coming up, and Arnold and Joshua proceeded to analyze the holes in the opposing team's line-up.

"We can beat 'em with our eyes closed," Joshua said. "Their team's been fighting like cats and dogs."

"Fighting over what?" Arnold asked.

Joshua took a deep breath. "After they won a game last month, Shoop, the goalkeeper, got some fish and cooked up by his place. His grandma gave him the potatoes and the breadfruit and the dasheen, but he didn't have any flour. So he couldn't make the dumplings. The first man comes and takes his bowl and says, 'The soup is nice, but you didn't make any dumplings?' So Shoop says, 'Nah man. No flour.' Then the next man comes and takes his bowl and says, 'Shoop, you ain't put no dumplings in the broth?' And Shoop again says, 'Nah man. No flour.' Each time a new man reaches the pot, the man says the same thing. It got to be a bigger and bigger joke, and Shoop got more and more vexed. You know Shoop. By the time the tenth man got his bowl and said, 'Shoop, man...,' there was no reasoning with him."

Buster and Arnold started to laugh, and Joshua continued. "Shoop threw 'em all out. He snatched the bowls right from their fingers. 'I'll eat the whole pot for myself!' he cried. They call him 'Dumpling' now."

Even Trevor, more sensitive than the others, was chuckling. "Poor Shoop."

"Every time he lets a goal slip by, the rest of the team harasses him. They yell at him on the field, 'Why you do that, Dumpling?' and 'Open your eyes, Dumpling.'"

By this time the men were all laughing so hard, they had tears running down their faces. Their cheerful talk went from Dumpling to Dumpling's girl to someone else's girl and, before they knew it, they were debating the Prime Minister's latest tax hike and the new pizza shop opened in town.

Together they ranted and reasoned, joked and gibed. Their chatter was loud and jovial and filled the air like balmy fog after a tropical rain. It rubbed against the humid walls, caressed the glass of the bakery counter where Arnold and Trevor leaned, even melted the chill that shadowed Branson's thoughts and his skin. It wrapped itself around them all, warm and benevolent, like a rainbow around a cool and stormy sun.

10

While one half of Oh discussed the lonely heart who got thrown from her bike in the night, and the other half debated whether the lonely-heart fisherman who placed the ad to find her was even a fisherman at all, a real lonely heart on Oh suffered something fierce. It belonged to Madison Fuller (a fisherman himself, though this was incidental to his pain). Madison's heart ached for his lost girlfriend, Rena Baker. Not the metaphorical sort of "lost," one heart tiring of another and thumping off to new adventures; no, Madison had truly and literally lost Rena. She was nowhere to be found.

Every afternoon Madison met Rena at the roundabout, the one that spun out roads to Beaureveille, Fort Tuesday, and Glutton Hill (where Rena lived), and every afternoon she gave him a steamy homemade lunch (sometimes an even steamier dessert). But now two days had passed without so much as a heel of bread and cheese. Madison was sick. Sick with worry (had Rena fallen into the river and drowned?), sick with hunger (who could eat at a time like that?), sick with sorrow (how would he survive without her?). Rena had left no message or note. Could she have gotten lost? he wondered. Or simply run away? (This happened on Oh from time to time.)

Madison borrowed a vehicle from a friend and drove all over the island looking for her. Rena loved to walk. She never ever took a bus or accepted a ride in a car. Perhaps she had taken a long, long walk and was late in getting back, which had happened once or twice before. Madison drove and drove, but found not a trace of Rena or his lunch. He returned home exhausted and confused and too upset to think straight. He collapsed on his bed without removing his shoes, and sought refuge in the long, thick sleep of the sad and hopeless. Not even when Madison's sister, May, pounded on the door of his room to offer him dinner could she rouse him.

Poor Madison! Sound asleep with no inkling of the nightmare about to come knocking! When Oh's whims and rains whisk away your one true love, they rarely stop at a tap on the front door. They drag you out of bed, rummage through your cupboards, and so ravage the walls of your house, that it feels like any place but home.

———————

Officers Tullsey and Smart (or, Arnold and Joshua), after conducting their initial investigation at Trevor's Bakery, spent the next day in full-on policing. The scene of the crime had to be examined for clues and bus-conductor Jarvis Coutrelle needed questioning, as did Raoul Orlean.

They started off with Jarvis in his village of Beaureveille, just up the road from Thyme. They traveled in a marked police pick-up truck, Arnold driving and Joshua thinking aloud.

"From Beaureveille we can take the shortcut back down to town, pass by where the bike was found, maybe get out and ask a few questions."

"Good," Arnold said.

"If Jarvis can't tell us anything, we'll need to sniff around the crime scene and see what we can dig up ourselves."

"I got some shovels in the back."

"Good," Joshua said. "We'll get to the bottom of this before you can say '*Morning Crier.*' Teach that Bruce a thing or two," he snorted. "He forgets we're trained professionals."

"Exactly," Arnold agreed. "I bet we get back to the station tonight with the name and full description of the lady who got knocked off that bike. For surety she's from one of the villages near where the accident happened."

"Exactly."

Such was the rhythm and gist of their talk as they bounced up the rough and rocky road to Beaureveille. They speculated and extrapolated, spouted theories and invented clues, sang reggae with the radio when they got bored. Then after about twenty minutes, they pulled off the main road and into the gap where Jarvis lived in a small wooden house. They parked their truck as far off the narrow road as they could and headed for Jarvis's front door, calling out his name as they approached.

"Mr. Coutrelle? Are you there? We need to ask you a few questions."

Jarvis, who lay dozing on the verandah, opened his eyes and focused on the two approaching figures.

"Arnold? Is that you? What's this 'Mr. Coutrelle' business?"

"We're conducting an official investigation, that's what," Joshua said. "We need you to tell us about the bike."

"Nothing to tell. Randolph and me, we found it in the road. On the shortcut. Don't you guys read the paper?"

"We're not interested in Bruce's version, we want to hear yours."

"I told you. Nothing to tell. We looked all around. Not sure for what, but there was nothing to find. No body, no clothes, no packages rolled in the ditch. Whoever she was, she just...I don't know, man. Disappeared. There was a full moon that night, you know."

"Well, won't that look good on our official report?" Arnold said. "'Woman done in by full moon.'"

"Can't you tell us anything else?" Jarvis asked. "What happened after you searched the ditches?"

"We knocked on a few doors, but nobody had heard or seen a thing. Nobody was missing. Nobody was missing a bike. Nobody even knew anyone who owned a bike."

"What then?" Arnold asked.

"That's it. We had to move the bike out of the road so we could pass. Randolph thought his dad might know what to do about it. We loaded it up and took it with us to the bakery. Then Bruce showed up. Then Randolph's uncle, Ernest. Then Ernest and me, we went to get Dodger and the bus. End of story."

End of story, indeed. Jarvis's statement, which in their zeal the officers had forgotten to write down, proved to be of no help whatsoever. A complete waste of time. Arnold and Joshua said hurried goodbyes to Jarvis and jumped back into their truck. A sniff around the crime scene was most definitely in order now. Wheels spinning in the dirt, they sped off toward the secondary road that went from Thyme to town.

When they reached the spot where the bike had been found (or what they believed to be the spot where the bike had been found, for not the faintest trace of the accident remained), Arnold and Joshua went over it with a fine-toothed comb, so to speak. They bent down and touched the dirt, sifted fistfuls of sandy pebbles that they let fall back to the ground like noisy rain. They circled the spot, kicked at suspicious nicks and holes in the road with the toes of their shoes. They measured the spot's circumference and diameter and its distance from every nearby ditch. They even dusted the dusty spot for fingerprints. Nothing.

"Huh," was all that Arnold could say. He stood with his hands on his hips wondering what to do next, while Joshua crouched in the road, still gazing intently at every tiny stone.

"Seems clear to me," Joshua said. "Someone has carried off every last clue. Someone doesn't *want* us to find out who got knocked off that bike the other night."

"Yes!" Arnold agreed. "Now why would anyone do that?" He started circling the spot again, tapping his chin and thinking.

Joshua stood up and did the same. "I think someone tried to get rid of someone else."

"Yes!" Arnold agreed again. "There's just one problem."

"What's that?" Joshua asked.

"No one's missing. Jarvis said so." Arnold and Joshua continued to circle the alleged scene of the alleged crime, stopping intermittently to glance across it at one another. At a shop not too far away, a shopkeeper and his customers marveled at their investigative dance. In turn the officers stopped, held up their index fingers and opened their mouths to share some grand idea, then closed their mouths again on second thought, before a sound slipped out.

Finally, Joshua got an idea worth setting free. "Maybe," he said, index finger pointing straight up to the sky, "maybe no one was missing when Jarvis asked. But what if someone's missing *now?*"

Arnold sensed a flaw in this new theory. He tasted it on the tip of his tongue for the briefest of moments, but was unable to spit it out, and by then the moment had passed. "Yes!" he agreed once more. "Let's go see."

Close to the shortcut that had witnessed the officers' investigation and their conclusion was a string of half a dozen houses and a shop. Not a village proper, just a small hamlet on the side of a hill. Arnold and Joshua knocked at every front door, but their questions evoked answers identical to those relayed by Jarvis an hour earlier. No one knew anything, no one had seen or heard anything, nobody was missing a bike or knew anyone who was. Everything was in order.

"Check in the village," the shopkeeper suggested. "Maybe someone there can help."

For want of a better strategy, the officers obeyed. They left the string of houses behind them, walked back to their truck at the scene of the crime, and set off for the village closest by.

Glutton Hill.

They arrived after only a minute or two, leaving their vehicle at one end of the main road, which they planned to canvass on foot. Their first stop was the pharmacy, owned and run by a Nathan Broom. "Good morning," he greeted them as they walked through the door. "Can I help?"

"Hope so," Joshua said. "You know anything about the bike accident that happened near here?"

"Only what I read in the paper. Quite a mystery."

"So you didn't see or hear anything unusual?" Arnold asked.
"No."

"You know anyone around here owns a bike?" Joshua asked.
"No."

"How about missing ladies? You know of any of those?" Arnold asked.

"Now you mention it, I did hear someone say something about Rena Baker missing. Didn't think much of it, though. Rena's like that. Probably just went off to clear her head and couldn't be bothered to tell anyone."

Arnold and Joshua looked at each other anxiously. "Did Rena ride a bike?" Joshua asked.

"No. Never saw her ride one in my life. Rena's a walker."

Arnold and Joshua thanked the pharmacist and continued their stroll down Glutton Hill's main road. They visited a supermarket, a bar, a mechanic's garage, and a seamstress's shop before reaching the road's other end. At every stop en route the conversation ensued much as it had at the pharmacy. No one knew anything, except that headstrong Rena Baker hadn't been seen for a while. No one was especially concerned or in the least bit convinced that Rena had been riding the bike in question.

Before turning back down the road again, Arnold and Joshua stopped to collect their thoughts. "What do you think of all that?" Arnold asked Joshua.

"I think it's obvious. We just found our missing lady."

"What about the bike? They all said she never rode a bike."

"You find that significant?" Joshua asked Arnold.

"I don't know. I guess not."

"Rena Baker is the only lady who's missing. It *had* to be her who got knocked off that lady's bike," Joshua said.

"So now what?" Arnold asked.

"Now, we find out who it was who knocked her off."

They set off in reverse, stopping once more at the seamstress's, the mechanic's, the bar, the supermarket, the pharmacy. They asked everyone they encountered for more information about Rena Baker. What did she look like? What did she do? Who did she frequent? They found out that Rena was as stubborn as she was slender and dainty, with a teeny tiny waist and a great big heart. They discovered that she liked to take long walks around the island all alone. They learned that her boyfriend was a fisherman from town (that meant Port-St. Luke), whose name was Madison Fuller. And they learned that every day, rain or shine, Rena prepared her boyfriend Madison Fuller a picnic lunch, which she delivered to him at the Glutton Hill roundabout.

They left Glutton Hill and returned to town, the next step in the investigation clear: Madison Fuller must be questioned, for he might very well know when Rena was last seen.

"He might even have been the last one to see her," Joshua suggested.

"You mean before the accident?" asked Arnold, who was driving their truck.

"I mean *at* the accident," Joshua replied ominously.

They rode in silence until the truck rolled up to the house where Madison lay sleeping. Arnold switched off the motor and looked over at Joshua. "You think he knocked her off that bike?"

Joshua jumped out of the truck and slammed the door, then leaned in toward Arnold through the truck's open window. "More than that," he said. "I'd bet his fishing boat on it."

II

Getting to Oh is tricky. There is one flight a day from neighboring Killig, and this, usually booked up by wealthy tourists—who fall in love with the island then fly out again, never to return. So getting *away* from Oh is tricky, too. The odd yacht lays anchor long enough to take on supplies, but is hardly likely to offer you passage. A fisherman might be more generous, but his fishing boat won't get you very far. Still, if leaving Oh is a chore, then staying is even worse. Few outsiders boast the requisite patience or the gumption to endure Oh's hardiness. The islanders are tough coconuts to crack.

Which is not to say that once in a while someone doesn't do it, find the right hammer, I mean, and enjoy the islanders' softer insides. This someone might, say, buy a little piece of land, build a lovely house, and settle in for a perfectly lovely little life, confident that he's dented the unyielding islander shells. And perhaps he will have done. At least for a little while.

But what of the island itself? Will his hammer be steady enough to master that, too? Sometimes even a local admits defeat in the face of Oh's trials—the nosey birds and the pungent, eavesdropping sugar cane—and hops a barge that will take her to freedom, wherever that may reside.

The beauty of Oh is that it knows how to balance its subjects. Sun, moon, fish, flower, all in perfect measure. No bird has a feather too many, no forest a tree too few. And for every someone who hops a barge, someone else is forever bound.

12

Quick and his pirates reached the island of Oh after a sea journey of three days, during which Quick managed to live undetected on the ship. By day, he slept hidden under bunks or lay eavesdropping on the boat where he had first stowed away. At night, he crept about below deck, by light of a stolen candle, snatching food and marveling at the strange objects of the captain and his men (their books, their drawings, their scribbles and symbols). When the moon was full and the night crew drunk and dozy, Quick climbed amid the ropes the men maneuvered to control the ship. They enchanted him, those cords as big as his fist, wrapped around wood so smooth and polished he could see his warped reflection in its sheen.

Quick relished every aspect of this lonely stowaway's existence. He enjoyed being privy to the men's private talks, enjoyed eating what tickled his tummy on any given night, enjoyed sleeping tucked up against wood that smelled of the sea. By day the men's voices were his company, and by night, the stars and moon, who watched over and guided his travels without his ever knowing.

When the ship got to Oh, the first stop it was to make since leaving Quick's island on that cloudy day, Quick was eager and filled with glee. So eager that he could barely keep his body still under the stern-most plank of bench in the boat where he once again hid. So filled with glee that he almost giggled as the boat was lowered from the ship to the sea and began its short journey to the island. Once the boat was pulled ashore, he waited for the men in the party to disembark and collect their things and set out on their way. It seemed to him that one pirate took an eternity to find his leather notebook, and the pirate captain another ten years to decide if they should turn right or left at the mango tree that stood a stone's throw from the sea's edge.

Decide he finally did, and as the men's voices were lost to bird-song and windsong and the buzzing of bees, Quick crept out of the boat. His eyes didn't know where to look first. There were mangoes and palms and papayas, bougainvilleas and buttercups, crabs in the sand and dogs in the shade. Everything he recognized from home. Yet Oh wasn't his home at all. When he looked to the east he saw great rolling hills instead of the distant sea. And to the north there was no village of islanders in need of a trapper of rats. Here, the villages dotted the island's southern tip. Quick was sharp enough to know that these differences must be just the tip of the iceberg, if you will, and so off his legs carried him to explore his first foreign land.

He found waterfalls and rivers. His island had these, too, only they were different from the ones on Oh. Different in number and different in depth. He found craters and hot springs, and the lushest forest he had ever seen, with a monkey atop every tree. His island certainly did not have one of those! Quick hoped that somewhere else on Oh just then the foolish pirate was realizing how wrong he'd been: islands are most definitely *not* all alike!

Quick even talked to some of the islanders. He found a lady washing clothes in a river and greeted her, "Good morning!"

"Good morning!" she replied. "Who are you?"

"I'm a pirate, lady. I'm traveling all over the world in my ship."

"Whose boy are you, son? Where's your mother?"

"I don't have a mother and I don't have a father. I just have a ship. Good morning, lady." And off his legs took him again.

He found a boy roasting corn cobs over a fire and greeted him. "Hello!" he said. "I'm a pirate. Could I try some of your corn?"

"You don't look like a pirate to me."

"I am so a pirate! I even have a ship. The biggest ship you ever saw."

"If I give you some corn, will you show me your ship?"

Quick was reluctant. "I guess so." (He was possessive of his ship, but he was hungry, too.) The two boys ate and Quick was disappointed to note that the corn tasted just like the corn back home. When they had finished, he led the way to the shore beyond which the ship was anchored. His explorations had taken him from one end of the island to the other and it wasn't until he saw the dark silhouette of the pirate ship against the setting sun that he realized just how long he'd been away. His heart was struck with terror. Had they returned to the ship without him? Had he missed the boat? From the tall hillside where the two boys stood, it was impossible to tell.

Quick concentrated all his energies on stifling the tears that tried to spring to his eyes. A pirate couldn't cry in front of an island boy who roasted corn! He looked toward the sun and held his breath. The yellow ball burned back at him, daring him not to turn away. He was sure he could hear it whisper in his ear. Cry-baby Quick! it said over and over. Cry-baby Quick!

The sun on *his* island never did that.

"Did you hear something?" Quick asked his new friend.

"Hear what?"

The sun started to laugh.

Quick's cheeks burned with anger. He would *not* cry. He was a pirate! He stared the sun in the face, his eyes open as wide as they would go. He knew if he closed them the tears would come—a satisfaction he would never give this taunting, foreign sun.

The sun, which could have blinded him in an instant, backed down, or, rather, ducked behind a passing cloud, and as it did, Quick heard the faint voices of his pirate companions. Had he not still feared the sun's jeers, he would have cried from sheer relief. He hadn't missed the boat! The pirates hadn't left without him!

Quick turned abruptly and patted his friend on the shoulder. "Thanks for the corn," he said. "I have to go." He nearly tumbled down the hillside, so fast were his happy feet carrying him. His friend said nothing. He simply stood rooted in the dirt, in awe of the great ship that loomed in the distance and of the very first pirate he had ever met.

Quick, on the other hand, barreled through brush and branches, scraping his skin in a dozen places. As he got closer to the familiar voices, the voices he usually heard from under a bench or a thick canvas tarpaulin, he was able to see the faces out of which each one came.

"Nothing but a bunch of pineapples on this one," a tall, bony man with a map and a cap said.

"That's no surprise. Oh's known for 'em," a hairy man furiously writing in a leather book said.

"You ever taste one sweeter than what you had here?" asked the oldest pirate in the party, with a long cutlass hanging from his belt.

How funny to see the voices embodied! Fat-sounding ones coming from thin men and ones that sounded clean-shaven exhaled past fuzzy, matted beards. Just in time, Quick fought the urge to shout out to the pirates and share the joke with them. He suddenly remembered that, though *he* considered them *his* companions, they hardly considered him theirs. Terror gripped his heart again as he realized that with the pirates in view, with them all so close to the boat, he had no way to sneak back into it before they rowed off to the ship.

The mocking sun, which took its sweet time setting that night, shrugged off the cloud donned a few moments before and beamed into Quick's crestfallen face. Still Quick didn't cry. He would figure something out. He was smart and he was fast. If he just kept his eyes on the men, he would find a way to slip past them, like a furtive gust of wind. Closer and closer he positioned himself, never abandoning the cover of the woods that lined the shore. He listened and watched as they sniffed leaves, picked up shells, made notes, and collected samples placed gingerly into a sack. He watched for what seemed like hours (though in truth it was but a quarter of a one), and as he watched, his heart sank with the sun, its descent as long and as labored.

Tears were all that Quick had left. It was getting dark (not dark enough for him to sneak past the pirates) and soon they would embark and row away from him forever. The sun snickered, the first tear tried to fall, and the moon, bless her, the moon rolled up her sleeves. She beamed so brightly of a sudden that the beach turned silvery white. Every leaf of every tree glowed. The men started. In awe, they turned from the coastline toward the woods, to pick the fruits that sparkled more beautifully by night than they had by day. The moonlight so illuminated the scene that Quick feared discovery as the men approached. Like a bullet, he shot up an almond tree, more uncertain than ever of his future. If the sun wasn't laughing at him, the moon was betraying him. What a funny island, this!

Quick clung to a branch and waited. Perhaps if they dawdled long enough, the cloud that had blocked out the sun would block out the moon. Then in the dark he could trail them to the boat and slip inside it, he told himself, not ever believing he'd manage it. He knocked his fist against his head to stimulate some idea. He knocked it so hard that the branch on which he lay grappled swung and pitched and knocked a branch of the manchineel tree next to it, sending a wave of silvery green fruits cascading to the ground. The men rushed over, intrigued by the noise, and the captain, first to reach the attractive apple-like spheres, stretched out his hand, picked one up, and lifted it to his mouth.

"Noooo!" With a ferocious shout and a leap out into the air, Quick threw himself from the almond tree, limbs flailing, and aimed his body for the captain's head. "Doooooon't!"

In an instant he had landed spot on-target, his legs wrapped around the neck of the stunned and supine captain, his gangly arms entangled in the captain's hair. For a moment nobody moved or said a word. You can imagine their surprise, attacked by a wriggling, roaring projectile from out of nowhere for picking up an apple. When they finally did collect themselves (all but the captain, whose head remained pinned by Quick's midsection), the oldest pirate freed his cutlass from its sheath and held it ready; the tall, bony man bent forward, arms outstretched and hands wide open in defense; and the hairy man scribbled so fast he dropped his pencil.

Quick sat on the captain's neck, rather stunned himself, until the pencil knocked him on the head and snapped him out of it. He climbed off the captain and apologized, his voice dry and brittle with fear. "Sorry, sir. I didn't want you to eat it." He pointed to the apple that had fallen from the captain's hand.

"Why in God's name not?" the captain asked, rolling onto his side and easing his shaken body upright. "Are they yours?"

"No, not mine. They're bad. You'll be sick if you eat it."

"Bit green, they are, but not for an ache this belly can't handle." He was sitting now, the captain, his legs out in front of him, and he rubbed his head. Quick didn't make a sound. He could only think that now he would never get back on the ship. Worse than that, he was trapped on Oh, with its pineapples and its corn and perhaps not a single rat at all. He hadn't spotted one the whole day.

While Quick fretted, the hairy man (it turned out his name was Enoch) flipped through his leather book.

"Captain! I believe the boy's right, sir. Look!" He showed the captain a sketch. "The manchineel, sir. Common in these parts. The sap in that fruit would have blistered your insides and killed you."

"Fat lot of good those books of yours do us! I could have poisoned myself if the boy hadn't come along! What's your name, son?"

"Quick, sir."

"Quick? What kind of a name is that?"

"Don't know, sir. I never had a real name."

"What do you mean you never had a real name? Where are your parents?"

Quick explained that he had lost his parents even before he found them. He explained about the village and the rats, about his island and his itchy feet, about the broken ankle and his stowing away. He confessed to stealing candles, admitted to eavesdropping, and pleaded to re-join the other pirates on board the ship.

The men looked from the boy to the captain to each other as Quick told his incredible tale.

"Your name's more believable by the minute," the captain remarked. He rubbed Quick's head and explained to him that his men weren't pirates or on a pirate ship. They were merchants and scientists and they were on an expedition, he said. He explained what an expedition was and asked Quick again if he was sure he had no parents.

"I'm sure." And in the darkness that had finally fallen, he hung his head and cried.

———

I should tell you that this particular captain, one Thomson Bowles, had set out on the expedition in question to run away from a ghost. Two ghosts, as a matter of fact. Captain Thomson had lost a wife and son to childbirth and everywhere he turned on land, any land, he saw the pair of them, mother and baby, cooing and cuddling. The vast sea and a creaking vessel (sturdy, but creaking) were the only things bleak enough not to call his departed family to mind. On the dry land of Oh, however, in the moonlight, they had shown themselves to him again. They splashed in the surf and softened his lonely heart to Quick's desperate tears.

The captain adopted the boy right then and there, on the beach, and christened him Dagmore. "In a land I once visited," he said, "this name means 'long life.' For this day on Oh, this day on which you saved my life, Dagmore will be your name forevermore."

Thus, with a word—a name—one life ended and a new one began. Quick thought it was the best name he had ever heard. Dagmore. He was even beginning to like the sound of Oh, with its corn and its pineapples. Oh. Yes, it was a beautiful name when you thought about it. Almost as beautiful as his own.

But Oh was not Dagmore's immediate destiny. Other, bigger, islands awaited, and so he left her, a sailor if not a pirate. His brilliant future, which was only just beginning, would see him schooled not only in weather and navigation, but in science, philosophy, and music. It would take him far and wide and back again, like one of the capricious piano sonatas that Dagmore would learn to master—renouncing its motif and taking it up again, a gentle refrain between *sforzandos* and *appassionatos*.

13

The Fuller house lay shadowed in the newly fallen dusk, its small front yard a mosaic of heavy greys and tired purples, bordered in shaded buttercup. Overhead the sky hung confused, belonging neither to night or day, hints of both sun and moon at its edges. The air was thick with the scent of cooking callaloo and sweet potato, with the perfume of rosebush, and the smell of cooling earth. Across the verandah, two kitchen windows curtained in worn, flimsy cotton took turns revealing May's rapt and delicate figure as she tidied and hummed, willing her cheerfulness into the air that the evening breeze spread throughout the house. In her brother's nearby bedroom, Madison's soft, regular breaths soothed away his stress and strain, then joined her muffled song.

May knew that when Madison awoke, so too would his worries, and she hoped, early though it was, that he was in bed for the night. In the light of the morning, after a hearty breakfast of bacon and porridge and homemade bread with mango jam, things would look brighter indeed. May even suspected that by morning Rena would be back, begging everyone's forgiveness for having walked off so far and so foolishly.

May was dead wrong, of course, but hardly the first islander to be fooled by the prospect of the island's morning sun.

———————

Officers Arnold Tullsey and Joshua Smart made their way across the yard and onto the verandah, where they called out to May in the kitchen.

"Good evening!"

"Good evening." May opened the screen door and leaned outside, scrutinizing the officers in their uniforms. "Can I help?"

"We'd like to speak to Madison Fuller, please," Joshua said.

"He's asleep." May sensed trouble. Had something happened to Rena?

"Could you wake him for us? Please," Arnold added, following Joshua's lead.

"This isn't about Rena, is it? What's happened to her?" May asked Arnold.

"Can we come in?" Arnold asked May.

May showed the officers into the sitting room. She was as frightened to hear what they had to say as she was anxious to know the reason for their visit. Had they found Rena? Was she harmed? Had they come to deliver bad news? It broke her heart to think how Madison would suffer.

"Please, you must tell me what's going on," she begged. "Is Rena all right? Where is she?"

"That's exactly what we're here to find out," Joshua told her.

"What do you mean?" May wrung her hands. "Madison looked and looked, but he couldn't find her anywhere. You haven't found her either?"

Arnold and Joshua exchanged a look that made May shiver. She had sensed trouble, for sure, but of the wrong kind. The officers weren't here to tell her brother about Rena, they were here to accuse him!

"I think you better wake your brother up now, miss."

"You don't think he had anything to do with Rena's disappearance?" she protested. "He's out of his head with worry. He drove all over the island today."

The officers weren't interested in what May had to say. They had set the sights of their investigation on Madison and were loath to veer or detour, lest they lose track of the truth.

With difficulty, May finally woke her brother from his deep and desperate sleep, and he confronted the policemen in his home.

"What's going on?" Madison rubbed his still-tired eyes.

"You tell us, young man. We're trying to find Rena Baker," Officer Tullsey said.

At the mention of Rena, Madison suddenly awoke. "So am I! Have you got any leads?"

"As a matter of fact we do." Officer Joshua Smart proceeded to lay out the case for fisherman Madison Fuller: "We are inclined to believe that the missing female victim of the hit-and-run that took place on the Thyme shortcut, and your girlfriend, Miss Rena Baker, are one and the same."

"What? That's crazy. Rena never rode a bicycle in her life," Madison objected.

Officer Smart continued. "We are also inclined to believe that you were the last person to see Miss Baker alive."

"Alive?" Madison and May exclaimed in chorus.

"Are you suggesting that Rena is...dead?" Madison struggled to say the word aloud.

"Would you care to tell us your whereabouts on the night in question?" Officer Tullsey chimed in.

"What night would that be?" Madison asked.

"Night before last. The night of the hit-and-run."

"I...I...I don't know," Madison stammered. "Here, I guess. Sleeping." He scratched his head.

"Can you attest to this, miss?" Officer Smart looked at May.

"Yes. I was here too."

"Were you also asleep?" Officer Smart asked her.

"Yes."

"If you were asleep yourself, then you didn't actually *see* your brother asleep in his room," Officer Tullsey countered.

"No. But I know he was here."

"Just a minute!" Madison jumped up from the sitting room sofa. "What is this? Some sort of trial? What are you driving at?" He moved close up to the officers, who were seated next to each other in matching armchairs, and stared down into their faces.

Officer Smart stood up. "I'll tell you what I'm driving at. Did you happen to see an ad in the *Morning Crier* a few days ago? An ad for a lady? An ad for a lady with a bike?"

"Yeah, what of it?"

"An ad placed by a fisherman?"

"Yeah, I saw it. Everybody did. What does any of this have to do with Rena?"

"Tell me, Mr. Fuller, what is your occupation?" He sat down again, and Madison followed suit.

"I fish for a living, but if you think I placed that ad, you're out of your head. I still don't see what this has to do with Rena."

"It's perfectly clear to me what this has to do with Rena. You needed a new girl and you placed an ad to find one."

Like one of his prize catches, Madison's body twitched in disbelief, his mouth gaping and speechless.

Officer Smart continued, unrelenting: "Rena Baker. Did she or did she not prepare lunch for you every day?"

"So?"

"Would you care to tell us what she prepared for you?"

"I don't know. Fish."

"What kind of fish?"

Madison was losing his patience. "Swordfish, flying fish. I don't know."

"What else did she make to go with the fish?"

"Plantains. Cabbage. Rice and peas. Macaroni pie. Does it matter?"

Office Smart nudged Officer Tullsey. "Are you getting all this down?"

Officer Tullsey pulled a pencil and pad from his pocket and made a note. "Got it. Peas. Macaroni pie."

"Well, I never!" May puffed, aggravated, astonished, and at a general loss for words.

"This so-called fish that she prepared," Smart continued. "Where did it come from? Did Miss Baker buy it at the fish market or did she get it from you?"

"Sometimes she cooked what I caught and sometimes she bought it. Honestly I don't see *what* this has to do with—"

"Don't you?" Officer Smart interrupted. "Tell me, when Rena Baker buys you fish from the fish market, who pays?"

"What?!"

"The fish money. Who puts up the fish money?"

"Well, she does, I guess."

"You reimburse her?"

"No, but I buy her all kind of—"

"You expect me to believe that a man, a *fish*erman, who makes his girlfriend buy him fish and cook him cabbage on the side isn't capable of murder? What happened after you got rid of her? You got hungry, didn't you? You got a hankering for those nice plantains of hers and that's when you slipped your ad under the door at the *Morning Crier.*" He stood up again and looked down into Madison's face. "Didn't you?"

"Murder. *Morning Crier,*" Officer Tullsey noted. "Got it."

"But I love her!" Madison jumped up.

"This is ridiculous!" It was May's turn on her feet. She was furious. "How dare you come into our home and accuse my brother of such madness without a shred of evidence? Murder, indeed! I want you out of here now." She stuck her arm straight out and pointed to the door.

"Well, if you're refusing to cooperate, miss—"

"Now!" she shouted.

"You're just complicating the investigation. We'll be back with a warrant, you know. To search the place for evidence."

"Fine. Get all the warrants you want. But for now, get out of my house."

The officers looked at each other and quietly obeyed. Partly they feared May, a force to be reckoned with just then and of hurricane strength. Partly they were tired, having been up and down the whole of Oh's southern half that day. And, partly, they weren't sure what the law said they should do next (or if they should have done what they already did). Yes, perhaps it was best to leave quietly and consult the Chief of Police. The next step could well be an arrest, and neither officer had the nerve to assume responsibility for that.

With the officers out of her house and her hair, May set about setting the table. Her answer to just about anything was something to eat, and Madison's callaloo soup still awaited. They would sort everything out over dinner. Of that, May was determined.

Madison, on the other hand, was in shock. His beloved Rena missing and now this? Accused of doing her in? He had no appetite, but May insisted, so mechanically he raised the spoon to his lips until he had emptied the bowl. While she ranted, he didn't say a word.

"Do you believe the stupidity of it? What on earth can those two be thinking? If they expect me to stand for it one minute, they're in for a surprise. What should we do first?"

May waited, but still Madison sat unspeaking, too sad and too scared to think straight. May would have to find a solution herself, she realized. With her dainty hands in her apron pockets, she circled the kitchen table, thinking.

They could hire a lawyer, but how much would it cost? Surely more than they could afford. And why should they waste hard-earned money if Madison had nothing to explain or hide? Even so, May debated with herself, those officers seemed pretty convinced. Once an idea took root on Oh, it was damn near impossible to pull it up and chuck it out.

"I've got it!" May snapped her fingers and beamed at Madison, who tore his gaze from the empty soup bowl in front of him and looked up at his sister.

"Call your friend Randolph," she said. "His father will know exactly what to do."

———

May Fuller was not the only islander that night whose digestion would be disrupted by the alleged disappearance of Rena Baker. Before Officers Tullsey and Smart took their discoveries to the Chief of Police, they would first question Raoul Orlean about his role at the bakery the night of the accident. When they knocked at his still-yellow door, he was midway through a portion of pigeon with pineapple. Because Raoul had quite a reputation among Oh's official ranks, for his position and years of service (not to mention his eccentric investigative techniques), and because Arnold and Joshua, who had already quite possibly bent the rules a bit too far that day, could see the steam rising from his piping hot plate, they kept their questions to Raoul short and sweet. In truth, they hardly questioned him at all, but instead relayed to him the facts as they understood them to be, and waited for him to confirm they had got it right.

Wasn't it true that Mr. Orlean was present when Randolph and Jarvis showed up at the bakery with a mangled bike?

Raoul nodded. Yes, it was.

Wasn't it also true that Randolph and Jarvis had no idea to whom the bike belonged or what fate had befallen its rider that night?

That certainly appeared to be the case, Raoul agreed.

Hadn't the boys searched the site of the accident for clues?

So they said, Raoul answered, adding that the boys had no reason to lie.

The officers went on to report to Raoul that they had found no clues at the scene of the crime and were wondering if perhaps that was because Randolph and Jarvis had already removed them.

Raoul shook his head. Doubtful, he argued, that the boys had done any such thing.

Just one last question, then: Had Mr. Orlean witnessed any tampering of the evidence at the hands of Trevor or Bruce or anyone else present that night?

Certainly not!

Good to know, the officers assured him, wanting very much to ask why Raoul, seeing as how he was a government official, hadn't insisted that Trevor call the Island Police first thing. Thankfully, though, Raoul's reputation made Arnold and Joshua reluctant to insist.

As they renewed their apologies for the disruption and, hats in hand, backed toward the door to take their leave, Raoul asked the officers how their investigation was proceeding, for he seemed to gather that they knew nothing new.

Why, yes, they did, as a matter of fact! Not only had they identified the mashed-up bike's missing rider, who they presumed must be dead, but they had even come up with a prime suspect.

"Already?!" Raoul asked them, astonished by the rather uncharacteristic example of official island efficiency.

"Yes, sir," they replied in unison, barely hiding how pleased they were that their exemplary performance should be revealed to such an illustrious superior.

"You don't say! A murderer on Oh?" Raoul humored them, not believing for a minute that this was the case.

"Yes, sir," Arnold replied. "He goes by the name of Madison Fuller."

"I see," Raoul said. (He didn't. The name was vaguely familiar, but that was all.) "Well," he continued, "I trust that if this Madison Fuller really is guilty, you will find irrefutable proof to that effect." (He trusted precisely the opposite, that they would find no such thing, and was eager to get back to his pigeon.) "Carry on," he said, ushering them off the verandah and into the road.

"Yes, sir. Good night, sir," Joshua bid him as they headed toward their vehicle. "We're off to submit our report just now."

Without responding, Raoul waved a fatherly hand and turned back toward the house, not giving them much further thought. If this Madison Fuller was connected to Bruce's fisherman and to his own pink mystery writer, it would certainly not be the police who would figure out how. Raoul made a mental note to look into this young man, Fuller, the following day. It wasn't until a mosquito wheezed past his inner ear that Raoul thought to ask the officers one question more.

"Wait!" he cried out after them, as the truck started to pull away.

"Yes, sir?" Joshua asked through the window.

"You didn't tell me who it is that you've determined to be missing. I'm curious, is all."

"Certainly, sir. A lady is missing, sir. Madison Fuller's lady, to be precise. Her name is Rena Baker."

"I see," he said, turning back to the house. "Good work, men." He didn't see at all, not immediately. Not until he had a mouthful of now not-so-hot pineapple perched at his lips did he see, very clearly, what was going on.

"Good god!" he exclaimed to Ms. Lila, stopping his fork in mid-air.

"What's wrong?" she said. "Did it get too cold?"

"The missing girl," he told her. "Her name is Rena Baker."

Ms. Lila just looked at him, not sure of what point he was making, and so he re-phrased it.

"According to the police," he said, "there is at present an R. BAKER who is nowhere to be found."

14

By the time the moon had overtaken the nighttime sky, Madison Fuller, the so-called prime suspect in the murder of Rena Baker, was on his way to Trevor's Bakery. He had come out of his initial shock, much to May's relief, and he sincerely hoped that Trevor Rouge would have some answers. As Madison walked, he struggled to grasp the situation in which he found himself. He was lonely and miserable, missing Rena something terrible, and he was stunned and terrified that the police might think him responsible for her disappearance. He wished, wherever she was, that she would come home. He longed to touch her and to look into her face. That she might be dead was too painful a notion to entertain, even more painful than the policemen's accusations.

Though Madison headed toward the home of his good friend, where help (he hoped) awaited, he felt utterly alone, as if the world had abandoned him when Rena did. The island had most certainly abandoned him. The road he walked was deserted, and the stars hid behind clouds. The crickets were quiet, the frogs asleep. Only the moon kept him company, her beams derisive, exposing the desolation he felt. Even his sandals mocked him, slapping his heels to mimic each step he took.

At the bakery, meanwhile, Randolph tried to bring Trevor up to speed (no mean feat, considering Randolph wasn't quite caught up himself).

"He said they think he killed her," Randolph told his father.

"Killed who?" Trevor wanted to know.

"Rena. No, not Rena. The girl with the bike. Well, both of them, I guess."

"The police think he killed *two* girls?"

"They think Rena was the girl...*is* the girl...with the bike. I think."

"Have they found her?"

"Madison didn't say anything about bodies. But they must have something on him. He sounded pretty shook up."

"He didn't do it, did he? What's he worried about?"

Luckily Madison reached the bakery right then and Randolph was spared any further efforts to answer Trevor's questions.

"Good night," Madison said as he nodded to Randolph and extended his hand to shake Trevor's. "'Night, sir. I'm in a bit of a jam. Did Randolph tell you?"

"He told me bits and pieces, but none of them seem to fit together too well. Tell me what you know."

Madison began at the beginning. He told Trevor and Randolph about his missing lunches and his drive around the island to look for Rena. He told them of his despair, his nap, and his rude awakening when the police arrived. He relayed the officers' questions and repeated his alibi, said the last straw was when they claimed he placed the ad for a lonely heart. "They think I'm advertising for a new girl 'cause I killed my old one!" he screeched. He described May's demeanor after that and how she threw the officers out, then he ended his account with the callaloo soup and May's brainstorm. He concluded with "and so here I am."

Madison's tale told, the bakery was silent. Madison and Randolph looked expectantly at Trevor, who didn't say a word right then but was clearly thinking furiously. After a minute, or maybe two, Trevor fired a rapid round of questions at Madison.

"Do the police have any real evidence to implicate you?"

"I'm not sure."

"Do they plan to arrest you?"

"They didn't say."

"Do they know for certain that Rena and the girl on the bike are one and the same?"

"They seemed pretty sure."

"Do they know for certain that Rena or this other girl is dead?"

"I don't think so."

"Or that you killed either one?"

"They implied it."

"How so?"

"May was asleep, so they think she can't vouch for me."

"Is that it?"

"That, and the ad."

"Is there a body? Is there even *one* dead body, let alone two?"

"I don't know."

"I do," Trevor announced. He stood and delivered his assessment, punctuating his words with fists on the bakery's counter. "Of *course* there's no body or you'd be sitting in jail *right now*. They want a *quick* solution and they're stabbing in the dark. Until they find some *real evidence*, they *can't* touch you."

"What if some evidence turns up?" Randolph looked for holes in his father's theory.

"Did you do it?" Trevor asked Madison sharply.

"No, I didn't do it!"

"Even so," Randolph said.

Trevor thought for a minute. "I see what you mean," he agreed, looking at his son. "On Oh they solve the crimes first and then find the clues they need after. Heaven help you if they decide you're guilty."

Madison breathed a desperate sigh.

"Now, now." Trevor patted his shoulders. "Finding clues is one thing; finding dead bodies is another."

"What if that missing bike lady turns up dead?" Randolph asked.

Trevor counted his rebuttal on his fingers. "There's no proof that the missing bike lady is even a lady. There's no proof that she's dead or gone. There's no proof Rena is dead or gone. And there's no proof Madison placed any ad."

"True." Randolph and Madison said in unison, not sounding entirely convinced.

"'Course, it would help if that silly girlfriend of yours turned up from her mysterious walk."

Randolph and Madison looked at each other helplessly.

"Here's what we do," Trevor continued. "Madison, get yourself home now and have a good night's rest. Tomorrow, you and your sister wrack those brains of yours. Try to figure out where Rena could be, and you go get her. Randolph, you keep your eyes and ears open when you're out with the truck making deliveries. Somebody knows something. Look for clues and listen for talk."

The boys nodded their consent.

"I'll have a go at Bruce," Trevor said. "I don't believe him for a minute. He knows who placed that ad. We get him to say so and maybe that clears Madison, if the police are so sure the ad points to the killer."

As if in agreement, the bakery fridge jolted to life just then, its noisy pulse filling the room. They all turned to look at it, as if they expected it to speak, to comment on their plan or to suggest another.

"Well?" Trevor said finally, his eyes back on the two young men. "What are you waiting for? Madison, go home. Randolph, give him a lift." The boys nodded and moved toward the door.

"I'll get Bruce over straightaway," Trevor continued. "Go on, off you go."

Heading home in the bakery van, Madison felt more and more like himself. Trevor had made good sense. His advice, and Randolph's help, dissipated the loneliness of his walk earlier that evening. Madison felt hopeful. Cheerful, almost, as they rode under the stars that waved and winked at him. The night was loud now, the frogs awake, the crickets in song, the leaves rustling in chorus. The moon shone brightly still, though its light washed away the despair it had previously revealed. Perhaps May was right. Perhaps in the morning, in the light of the rested sun, Madison's future would look brighter and clear.

Back at the bakery, Trevor, too, hoped this would be the case. Reluctant, however to rely on the sun's good graces alone, he contrived to employ the island paper. He rang up Bruce, apologized for involving him at such a late hour, summoned him to the bakery, and promised him a front-page scoop. Bruce, home in his favorite chair, feet propped, watching two moths dance on the rim of a light fixture, hid his excitement poorly as he vowed to rush over right then.

Next, Trevor phoned his wife, Patience, to tell her he would be late. Then he leaned on the bakery counter, his forearms pressed to the glass, and waited for Bruce to show.

———————

On the other side of Port-St. Luke, while Bruce made his way to the bakery by light of the moon, Officers Tullsey and Smart were in conference. From Raoul's house they had gone straight to the Police Station (stopping only for flying fish sandwiches and chips on the way), where they requested a meeting with Chief of Police Lucas Davenport. Chief Davenport was a commanding and (mostly) serious man, his temperament reflected in the shine of his uniform's brass buttons, his moral fiber in the well-pressed cloth of his stark black uniform. His fingernails were as trim as his waist and filed as precisely as his case dossiers. He believed in (mostly) by-the-book law enforcement and showed no mercy once he had convinced himself of a criminal's committed crime.

For this reason, when Arnold and Joshua presented their case, they emphasized Madison's guilt and minimized their own less-than-by-the-book interrogation. It was a lucky strike indeed that May had kicked them out of her house. Heaven knows the trampled protocol, had she endured them longer than she did! Though neither officer would admit it, each was thinking just this as he sat opposite the imposing chief, whose disposition was as dark as his lapels. He looked from Joshua's eyes to Arnold's and back, speaking in a ferocious near-whisper.

"Am I to understand that you as much as accused this suspect without a shred of physical evidence? Without so much as a footprint to put him at the scene of the crime?"

"May I point out the fishing boat, Your Honor. I mean, sir," Joshua corrected.

"What of it?"

"The man who placed the ad in the *Morning Crier* owns a fishing boat," Arnold said.

"So do half the men on Oh, if I'm not mistaken."

"Yes, sir, but half the men on Oh have not just lost a girlfriend under mysterious circumstances," Joshua said.

"Mysterious circumstances?"

Joshua continued. "Yes, sir. The suspect's known girlfriend, Rena Baker, is gone. Her whereabouts are, therefore, a mystery." (He paused after "therefore" for dramatic effect.)

The police chief was confused. "I thought we were discussing the case of the missing lady cyclist and the hit-and-run. Who is Rena Baker?"

"Sir," Arnold explained, "we believe that Rena Baker is the cyclist, done away with by her boyfriend, Madison Fuller, who then placed an ad in the newspaper for Rena's replacement."

Chief Davenport rubbed his chin. "It's an intriguing theory, I admit." He thought for a moment then went on. "Have we found the girl's body?"

"No, sir."

"Any witnesses?"

"No, sir."

"A single clue?"

"No, sir."

"Then it seems to me like you gentlemen are playing a parlor game, not conducting an investigation."

Joshua opened his mouth to speak but the Chief silenced him with a raised hand and went on. "What's more, a guilty man may walk free because of your clumsiness."

"Sir?" Joshua said, offended. "Clumsiness?"

"Clumsiness," the Chief repeated. "Thanks to you, our prime suspect has been tipped off. He knows now to get rid of the evidence. And, thanks to you, he has all the time in the world to do it. While we sit here chatting, he's probably burning her clothes and tossing her body into the sea."

"What do you suggest—?"

Before Arnold could finish his thought, Chief Davenport had ordered the officers to write up a full report and to complete the forms for a search warrant. He wanted them back at the Fuller house by sunrise.

15

I did say that Raoul Orlean was known for his eccentricities. The night Officers Tullsey and Smart pleaded their case to Police Chief Davenport was a case in perfect point. Although Raoul, for years, had refused to entertain the notion of island magic, he was starting to re-think his position on island luck; it struck him, as he connected the missing Rena Baker to the R. Baker on his wall who needed finding, that had the police shown up at his house any earlier than they did, there may well have been enough daylight for them to catch sight of the incriminating message on his two-hued cottage wall. If such a thing as island luck did exist, then, Raoul didn't want to push *his*. Wasting not a minute, he abandoned his dinner plate, changed his shirt, and strapped a bright light onto his head.

Were Raoul married to anyone but Ms. Lila, this sort of behavior would have triggered no end of marital discord and culminated, no doubt, in a trip to the psychiatric hospital at the edge of Port-St. Luke. Ms. Lila knew better, and when she saw Raoul emerge from their bedroom like a miner from a hole, all she said was, "I'll feed your pigeon to Fragile."

Fragile was Ms. Lila's dog, the third one to be named so over the course of nearly two decades of married life. Like her predecessors, Number Three (as Raoul liked to call her) was small and fearful and rarely made a peep (let alone a bark) or left Ms. Lila's side. Most days Fragile accompanied Ms. Lila to work, where she (the dog) watched her (Ms. Lila) from the vantage point of a low Medieval European History shelf (which, as a rule, the islanders rarely consulted), and where Ms. Lila had placed a satin pillowcase stuffed with feather down and stitched tightly shut.

While Ms. Lila used her fingers to separate the meat from the tiny bird-bones and Fragile panted anxiously at her feet, Raoul collected his paint and brushes and went outside to cover the anonymous message painted on the house. He decided that, if it were indeed evidence, he was better off to cover it up than to let the police get the faintest wind of it. They would turn his house into People's Exhibit heaven-knew-what and make a terrible mess of his yard, all the while failing to decipher the message's true intent. Not only that, they might somehow twist things around and turn him into a suspect. He could never find Rena Baker if he landed himself behind bars.

Raoul couldn't help but wonder if just on Oh, or if everywhere, innocent men were forced to take up paintbrushes in the night to protect their innocence. Surely somewhere, on Killig maybe, they were more civilized than this! As he painted by the light of the moon and the lamp on his head, Raoul thought again about Rena and Madison and, especially, about the police. Raoul knew he wouldn't get to sleep unless he got some answers first, and there were only two places on Oh to find those: the bakery or the Belly. Tonight, though, the answers Raoul was looking for had "BAKER" written all over them.

———

As Raoul cleaned himself up to go to sniffing for clues at Trevor's, and Chief Davenport finished up with Arnold and Joshua and their witless policing, Trevor found himself in a battle of wits with Bruce. He told Bruce what he had learned from Madison about the officers' bogus investigation, based on which they had decided Rena Baker was the missing girl from the bike.

"Rena Baker? Who's she?" Bruce looked up from the notepad where he was jotting down Trevor's every word.

"She just happens to be from Glutton Hill, right near the bike accident. She also just happens to be missing, stupid girl. And she happens to be the girlfriend of Madison Fuller, who, as you know, owns a fishing boat, which is why the police have decided that he killed Rena and put an ad in *your* paper to find a new girl."

"Fancy that!" Bruce exclaimed, genuinely delighted. He chuckled to himself, sure that no rainbow would grace his front page for a good long while.

"Don't you see what this means?" Trevor tried to reason with him.

"It means I might sell a few papers is what it means."

"What about Madison?"

"What about him?" Bruce asked.

"He's the most honest man in Port-St. Luke," Trevor argued. "I don't believe for a minute that he killed Rena Baker or anyone else."

"You're probably right," Bruce said, not sounding as though he cared either way.

"Will you say that in your story?"

"It wouldn't be much in the way of journalism if I did, would it? Im-par-ti-al-i-ty," he said. "That's the key." He wagged his pencil smartly at Trevor.

"You? Impartial?" Even as the words crossed his lips, Trevor knew he had crossed a line. Bruce was very defensive of his unique variety of news reporting.

"I don't have to take this!" Bruce flipped closed his notepad and started to leave.

"Wait!" Trevor grabbed Bruce by the forearm. "I didn't mean it. It's just that this Madison business has me a little upset. The man is scared to death and the police seem hell-bent on making the charges stick."

"So you insult me? How does that help matters?"

"Sorry for that. I was just implying that the *tone* of your story might sway public opinion. You know how highly respected you are on this island. If a hint that the police were off-base slipped into your story, it might go a long way in displacing some already misplaced guilt." Trevor held his breath. Would Bruce fall for such obvious flattery?

"It is true that I'm very highly regarded," Bruce replied. He would!

"I'm not saying I'm prepared to distort the facts," he went on, "but I suppose it would be a shame to slander the character of a man like Madison."

"Good man." Trevor clapped Bruce on the back with a heavier hand than necessary. "There is one other thing you could do, you know."

"I've just said I won't distort the facts."

"No, nothing like that. I mean the ad."

"What ad?" Heavens, Bruce was slow to catch on sometimes!

"The lonely hearts ad. If you reveal who placed it, then that might clear Madison's name."

"I already told you all, I have no idea who placed it."

Trevor was impatient, but treaded lightly. "Are you sure you couldn't do a bit of fishing around and figure it out? You still have the man's letter? You have the envelope he pushed under the door?"

Bruce thought for a minute, then uttered, "I'm not too sure."

"Maybe you wouldn't mind having a look," Trevor suggested. "It might save Madison's life. You, Bruce, might single-handedly save Madison's life."

"I'll see what I can do. It's late now. Let me go." And off he went.

"Don't forget, Bruce," Trevor shouted, following him as he left the bakery. "A matter of life and death." Bruce kept walking and, without looking back, waved his hand in the air.

Randolph pulled up in the bakery truck right then and saw Bruce leave. "Any luck, Dad?" he asked, as he slammed the door of the vehicle.

They entered the shop together just as Raoul reached the bakery in a taxi. (All the drivers knew Raoul and drove him for free, trips he repaid at the Belly with rounds of rum or beer.)

"Raoul!" Trevor said, surprised. "What are you doing here at this hour?" Though it wasn't ever too late to find company or comfort at the bakery, it was unusual for Raoul to seek either at this time of night. Twice in three days meant something was up. "Trouble with the missus?"

"No, everything's good," Raoul said. Without explaining his private interest in the bicycle case, he added, "The police have been to see me. I was just wondering about this murder talk. What's the word?"

"Good question," Trevor said. He proceeded to recount to Randolph and Raoul the conversation he had had with Bruce. He told them he harbored little hope of learning the truth about the ad, but he hoped he had made Bruce feel important enough to use his news story to Madison's advantage. If not, however told, the story would serve its purpose. The islanders, at least those in town who knew Madison, would be outraged to see such an honest man accused. And, too, spreading word of Rena's disappearance could only help Madison's case. Somebody might have seen her, might know what happened or where she was.

Flimsy hopes, these, but maybe Bruce would surprise them.

There was little else to do, they all agreed, but await the morning edition, so Trevor and Randolph locked up the bakery and drove the bakery truck home, dropping Raoul at his cottage on the way. Tired and tense, Raoul crawled into bed and—lucky again!—succumbed to the still-awake and amorous Ms. Lila. When they had finished canoodling, he dozed in the crook of her arm, until at last even the moon succumbed to morning.

Fisherman Suspect
in Glutton Hill Murder
Search Warrant Expected

Sources tell this reporter that charges will shortly be brought against Mr. Madison Fuller for the cold-blooded murder of Ms. Rena Baker of Glutton Hill. Mr. Fuller, fisherman, of Port-St. Luke, denies the charges that he killed Ms. Baker, his longtime girlfriend, and then placed an ad in this very newspaper to solicit her replacement. The investigation, led by Officers Arnold Tullsey and Joshua Smart of local football renown, pointed to Mr. Fuller when it was learned that the missing Ms. Baker routinely took the fisherman his lunch. The loyal readers of this paper will recall that in the ad allegedly placed by Mr. Fuller, a young woman with a bicycle and cooking skills was sought. Though Ms. Baker was not known to own a bike, and was in fact known to be an avid and exclusive walker, police surmised that, as the only lady currently missing on Oh, she could be none other than the victim of the hit-and-run near Thyme, at the scene of which a mangled and abandoned bicycle was discovered. Police Chief Lucas Davenport has ordered that the investigating officers file a petition to obtain a search warrant for the home and property of Mr. Fuller, who has already undergone a preliminary interrogation. Police have also interviewed the two young men who happened upon the mangled bicycle, Mr. Jarvis Coutrelle of Beaureveille and Mr. Randolph Rouge of Port-St. Luke; Mr. Rouge's father, Trevor Rouge, who may face obstruction of justice charges for his role in the tampering with and the concealing of evidence; the inhabitants of Glutton Hill and its outlying areas; Ms. May Fuller, the suspect's sister; and a high-ranking government official, privy to details about the night in question. Though, across the island, friends and family of Mr. Fuller are rallying to assert his innocence, this reporter can take no official stance except to confirm the fact that Mr. Fuller has no prior indictments or police record of any kind. Efforts by this paper to ascertain the identity of the individual who anonymously placed the lonely hearts ad of which Mr. Fuller is accused have so far proven unproductive. We are however confident that, with the rainy season nearly upon us, they will soon bear fruit.

16

Little Dagmore Bowles proved himself as resourceful a lad on sea as he had on shore. In no time he had endeared himself to his father's crew for his skillfulness in ridding their ship of its rats. He achieved this remarkable feat by trapping the little pests in an equally remarkable web of homemade piping and tubes, and smoking them to near-death. Then he collected their dizzied bodies and flung them into the sea.

Captain Thomson Bowles couldn't have been prouder. He immediately recognized in his brand new son the heir that his sea-searching heart had desired, and his little Dagmore's rearing became the order of every day. The captain enlisted Enoch Bell, a scientist on board, to furnish the rudimentary elements of Dagmore's education: reading and writing. It seemed implausible to the boy that Enoch's markings in his leather notebook could have any correspondence to the words they spoke every day, but Dagmore played along, fearing it might be as easy to become *un*-adopted and *un*-christened as it had been to become so. Dagmore enjoyed being a pirate son on the captain's ship much more than he enjoyed being an orphan boy on an island.

Before long, his lessons with Enoch, which had begun as obligatory curiosities, became genuinely fascinating and pleasurable. Not only did Enoch's markings begin to make sense under Dagmore's pen, but Enoch himself was a wellspring of unimaginable tales. Enoch had been a seaman for a very long time, searching the corners of the globe for undocumented animals and plants. He was a prolific artist, too, and showed Dagmore all sorts of biological sketches with arrows and annotations and cross-sections colored and magnified. His stories were so engrossing that Dagmore happily practiced his alphabet and grammar, for it was his secret hope to assist Enoch in his note-taking at the ship's next stop.

While Enoch sharpened Dagmore's language skills, the deckhands honed his mathematics. They taught him all their favorite card games, which demanded that he count and add and subtract. They would have let him win, of course—he was the Captain's son, after all—but this particular charity was not long required of them, for the boy showed an innate talent for calculations, both of the men's hands and of their bluffs. Though he readily outsmarted them at cards, they trumped him in matters of life, about which he was only too eager to listen, peering into the men's bragging faces with such awe and admiration that each felt as important as a king of hearts or diamonds.

To supplement the deckhands' arithmetic and Enoch's anatomical poetry, Captain Thomson Bowles took Dagmore under wing in the fields of geography, astronomy, navigation, and the sea. With spyglass, sextant, and globe, Thomson taught Dagmore about the earth and the heavens, following each lesson with a cup of tea and a lecture on men. He explained their whims and humors, their weaknesses and strengths. Whether it were easier to dominate a man or a mountain (he told his son), he wasn't sure. And a woman? Well, that was a different conundrum entirely.

Dagmore didn't know women and conundrums from whisky and codfish, but no matter. Evening tea with his new father was the best part of the day. The Captain shared with him his finest stash of crumbly biscuits and allowed him to sweeten his tea with sugar or honey, according to his mood. He felt a right gentleman in the Captain's quarters, with his leather shoes and china cup. He could hardly believe his luck.

One night as Dagmore and Thomson sat down to tea, Dagmore asked him, "Father, when can I be a pirate like you?"

"What are you talking about, son? I told you I'm not a pirate," his father replied.

"What are you?"

"Some days I'm a merchant, some days an explorer. Mainly it's this wretched sea that keeps me out here. Heaven knows what she hides from me, but I'd scour her very depths if I could." He gazed out at the water through the porthole in his cabin, for what felt to Quick, or rather Dagmore, like a very long time.

"Sir?"

The Captain turned his eyes back to those of his son. "But of course, I can't do that," he smiled. "Instead, I'll just cross her end to end and find what I find."

"So you're a seaman?" Dagmore suggested.

"Yes, you could say that. And when I get back home every so often, people like to hear about all the marvels I've come across and the riches I've found." His eyes drifted away again.

"Will I be a seaman, too, father?"

"For a while. But you're a smart boy, son, and you have to study. We'll have to send you to school. You might want to learn about engineering or biology or history. A smart man like you can't spend his life arguing with the wind and the waves, can he?"

"No sir," Dagmore agreed, his little heart sinking into the pit of his stomach. He didn't know exactly what school his father had in mind, but he didn't see how attending one could mean anything short of separation from this man he had already grown to love. Dagmore could simply not allow it.

While his father's tired gaze drifted back to the sea, Dagmore got up and poured him some brandy. Captain Thomson downed the shot in one gulp, then patted the boy on the back and gently pulled him onto his knee. In silence they both watched the black water, and Dagmore reached a decision: to be the best seaman ever. From that moment on he would make himself so useful—no, utterly indispensable, he planned to be—that not only would the captain never agree to his going off to some lonely school, but he would forget the idea altogether!

The next day Dagmore put his plan into action. Always an obedient and helpful child, he became as if possessed by an unrelenting will. He swabbed the deck and assisted the cook with breakfast, then he washed and dressed and met Enoch for his daily lessons. Only on *this* day, he had little interest in calligraphy and spelling. He wouldn't give Enoch a moment's peace until the man agreed to explain to him every last one of his biological annotations, even the ones in Latin. Dagmore knew that, sooner or later, the ship would have to land somewhere, and when it did, he intended to be the pride of the landing party, observing more astutely than anyone else. He would even ask the Captain for his very own book in which to take notes and draw sketches.

Dagmore studied feverishly, every day of the week. He would gobble his lunch and instead of napping afterward would devote his afternoons to maps and astronomical charts. Soon he could name every star and constellation, and draw the outline of all the lands he never even knew existed. After his evening tea with the captain, he would retire to his bunk, where he memorized poems about the sea, from a slim blue volume that Enoch had given to him.

Dagmore's transformation didn't go unnoticed on the ship. How could it? Every man on board had his own explanation for it, though these told more about the men themselves than they did about Dagmore. Enoch's hairy chest grew puffier, as he attributed the boy's enthusiasm to the masterful inspiration of his teacher. The deckhands, with whom Dagmore rarely ever played cards anymore, decided that the Captain was behind all this activity, torturing the poor lad to study day and night. Only the Captain, who prided himself on his discerning taste, knew the truth: he had seen through Quick's ragamuffin exterior and had adopted himself a real prodigy!

In fact, the Captain admired his son almost as much as his son admired *him*. Thomson couldn't wait to get home and show off his boy, take him to a tailor for some suits *à la mode*, and to a restaurant, and the theater! He would take him to a physician, too. Have him checked out, though he appeared to be of plenty-robust stock.

So it was that the Bowles gentlemen, Dagmore and Thomson, toiled at cross-purposes. The one worked and studied and wrote and memorized and flaunted the fruits of his labor in front of his sea-faring father. He predicted the weather by watching the moon and navigated the ship by the wind and the stars. He even gained dominion over the other men's tempers, for they felt both pity and pride in his presence, and were reduced to good behavior whenever he was around. The other planned and prepared and laid the ground for a proper city upbringing. He noted the best schools and devised a budget to pay for them. He made a list of all the prominent men he knew. Every night he wrote a letter to a different one, expressing his desire to introduce his son to society and his hope that each man would champion the boy's admittance to the tightest circles. The letters would be delivered first thing when they reached home.

That's right. Dagmore had no idea of it, but he was headed home. Or to what would be his home for a while. He would need his skills of observation, alright, but not to impress his father on any expedition. He would need them to survive in a strange, new world, where there were no such things as manchineel trees or waterfalls. Where the seaman he had taught himself to be, would have to roll up his wanderlust and tuck it away, like a sail in need of mending.

Oh, but when it unfurled! What winds would await! What fortune, beneath the glittering, glassy surface of the wretched sea!

17

Had you been a firefly on Oh, navigating the moon-bathed night that would culminate the next morning in Bruce's inflammatory front-page report—the one about the murderous Madison—you would have lit up quite an array of characters, in various shades of optimism. Raoul, gratified, asleep in the arms of Ms. Lila and biding the hours till morn. Madison, hopeful and alone in his room, discerning in the shadows on the ceiling Rena's returning silhouette. Bruce, chipper at his typewriter, an icy tumbler of pineapple juice dripping onto his desk. And Officers Tullsey and Smart at a rum shop, downing congratulatory shots. Their search warrant had come through and would be executed at dawn. Only May would you have found turning in her bed, tossed by a sea of bad dreams, if none so immediate as the one splashed across the headlines that morning when she awoke.

May found the *Morning Crier* curled up at her doorstep. (Bruce offered home delivery for a fee.) With foreboding and a cup of tea, she sat in her kitchen and unfolded it. She was quite prepared for some embarrassing, even worrisome, mention of her brother on Page 5 or Page 6. The accusation that screamed at her from the front page—**Murder**—well, for this she was *not* prepared, and her tea cup crashed to the floor.

May gripped the newspaper and read on. Her shock turned to fright, paused at despair, and stopped finally at rage.

"'Efforts by this paper to ascertain the identity of the individual who anonymously placed the lonely hearts ad of which Mr. Fuller is accused have so far proven unproductive'? How dare he?" May shrieked. "That weasel Bruce would have the whole island believe he doesn't know who wrote the ad? What does he take us for?" May stomped her foot, nearly impaling her pinky toe on a shard of wet porcelain.

As her temper cooled and she cleaned up the broken bits, May realized that Bruce had unwittingly slipped her the key. The ad was the answer! If she could figure out who placed it, then half of the wholly circumstantial evidence against Madison would crumble like May's china cup. But how could she go about that?

May paced her little kitchen, back and forth and back and forth, but found she was getting nowhere.

Bruce knows who wrote it, he simply *must*, she reasoned. Why won't he say? Surely he would not be so stupid, so self-serving, as to jeopardize a man's freedom to protect some love-sick fool? Surely not just to sell papers?

Pace though she might, May could come to no better answer. A murder suspect as unsuspecting as Madison made for hefty profits.

"I've got to get to Bruce," she said and sat down again.

May looked around the kitchen, as if further instructions might present themselves on a breadbox or a shiny pot. When they didn't, she got up and paced some more. Back and forth and back again, until a thought crossed her mind: how had Madison fared with

Trevor? she wondered. With the shock of the morning news, she had almost forgotten having sent him to seek advice. (His return from the bakery the night before had found her already fast in a fitful sleep.) Anxious though she was, she couldn't bring herself to wake him, not with the morning paper that awaited.

"He'll be up soon enough, I suppose," she said to the empty room, and poured herself a fresh cup of tea.

May stepped out onto the verandah and into the morning air, pure and almost heartening. The sun hadn't long begun its climb, and together with the flowers, she turned her face to watch it. Her eyes were locked on the burning orb for so long that they began to hurt, until finally with a jerk she forced herself to look away. Angry from the spots that taunted her vision, she grew uneasy again and stormed back inside.

Seated at her kitchen table, May sipped and reflected. She prayed, too, that Madison would have good news to relay about his tête-à-tête with Trevor. If anyone could help them solve a problem like this, Trevor would be it. Trevor was wise and kind and respected. He knew everything about everyone, was always willing to help a friend in need, always eager to solve a riddle, and he was friends with everyone, wasn't he? With the police, all the islanders, and...of course! With Bruce!

May relaxed, if tentatively, for the first time since the day before, and heaved a sigh of relief. She saw in Trevor's friendship with Bruce her brother's exoneration. Chances are they wouldn't have made the charges stick, she told herself, seeing how Madison is innocent. But on Oh you just never know, do you? A baker in the hand would be worth more than two bumbling policemen snooping in the bush. She sighed again, more confident now that hers and Madison's was a battle that could be won, and her mind drifted to Trevor. It drifted to his shop and his bakery crowd, to Bruce, Randolph, even to the Officers Arnold and Joshua who she knew spent time there.

Then it drifted to Trevor's best pal, Dr. Branson Bowles.

Perhaps I should tell you more about May and my Branson while Madison sleeps. We'll have to go back some twenty years, but that's to be expected. New stories often have old beginnings, fresh plots rooted deeply in the past. Especially where lonely hearts are concerned.

———

At the age of fifteen, May fell in love with Branson, on a Sunday morning when he rescued her lazy black-and-white pup from a petty thief named Melvin Jones. Melvin had swiped the furry bundle from under the feathery tamarind tree in May's yard, and Madison chased him through town, past the post office, the middle school, and the Staircase to Beauty salon, tackling him finally (flailing pup still in hand) at the church where May and her family worshipped, just as the congregation was pouring out. When May realized what Branson had done for her, she was smitten, and she flirted in the only way she knew how: with fish broth, corn chowder, and cashew nut ice cream.

Branson, who was sixteen and boasted a burgeoning appetite, couldn't but capitulate to May's steamy sauces and spicy sweets, and before long he was quite in love himself. In fact, practically from the day that Branson saved May's stolen puppy, the three were never apart. Branson walked May and her puppy to school; in the evening May and her puppy brought Branson his supper. Branson so adored May's cooking—the pleasure her dishes gave him was so deep and true—that May went to great lengths to expand her culinary repertoire. She borrowed books from the local library and listened to cooking shows on her battery-powered radio, studied spices and herbs and consulted her elders, and experimented with marinades and dough.

While May cooked, Branson studied. He wanted nothing more than to make a fine future for himself and for May and to make her his bride. He would finish school first, then go to the island's teaching college. He would get a job and a loan and build her a house, and they would live happily and heartily ever after off his teacher's stipend and May's saltfish souse.

Branson told May about his plans on a day so sunny it made the sea look silver and gold. May had prepared for them an abundant lunch of fish, breadfruit, cabbage salad, and cake, and packed it in a hamper woven of palm leaves. From a quiet bay, they rowed off in a small fishing boat, a boat that had once been my own. It was a sturdy little craft, nicked and dinged from years of use and wear, but seaworthy (within reason) and clean, and painted a bright shade of yellow. It was Branson's pride and joy as a young man, for it gave him a sense of freedom and authority that no other aspect of his young existence afforded him. In it he could command the direction that his life should take, and at what speed; this was a great satisfaction, a salve for the terrible patience that growing up required.

They reached a secluded cove and went ashore, Branson dragging the heavy boat onto the sand, May balancing the heavy lunch in her dainty arms. Not far away they spread a blanket and May laid out the meal. The anticipation of May's cooking was as exciting to Branson as the sight of her setting up their picnic. She had beautiful hands that danced around pots and utensils and gourds and cutlets with a fluidity as smooth and graceful as the gentle tide that lapped against the rocks at the cove's outer edges. At home, too, Branson enjoyed watching May prepare a meal, as much as he enjoyed eating it. Her recipes and movements were nothing short of magic.

Which was fitting, for a magical day ensued. They ate and talked and dreamed and made plans, laughing and touching in between. When the sun began to set, they stood arm in arm and watched it gently bend toward the horizon. Then they gathered their things quickly and May jumped into the boat, while Branson pushed it off into the water. Aboard, they sat opposite each other, and Branson softly rowed them home. Had you seen it, you would have said that their black silhouette against the sun's golden flare looked just like a frame from a movie. The proverbial happy and sunsetted ending, that no storm would dare to mar.

―――――――

In her kitchen, May finally heard Madison stir. She had just enough time to wonder if Branson still had that old fishing boat of his before the memory of it, and her unanticipated smile, dissipated in favor of more pressing matters.

"Madison, are you up?" she hollered. "Come out here. I need to talk to you about Trevor. Did he have anything helpful to say last night?"

Madison yelled back from the bathroom, but between the door's thick wood and the sink's splashing water, May couldn't make out his words.

"Come out of there, will you?" she shouted. "We need to go see Trevor together. He has to make Bruce come clean about that ad. Bruce must know who placed it. Who it is on this island who has a fishing boat and wants a woman to cook for him with her dainty little hands."

May froze, hearing her own words.

A minute later Madison emerged from the bathroom, still rubbing his face with a towel. "What were you saying?" he asked her. But when he reached the kitchen and lowered the towel from his eyes, May was gone. By her chair, for the second time that day, a puddle of tea dirtied broken china bits and seeped into the cracks of the tired floor.

———

Branson Bowles lived on a fine piece of land. From a dangerous height it overlooked the sea and a small private beach, the latter accessible by a steep rocky path. Branson had inherited the house and property from *me*, I'm proud to say—his teacher's salary would never have permitted him residency in such a prime locale. This particular morning found Branson lying on the beach in question, worn from a long and early swim, his eyes closed and the rising sun drying the salt water on his body. As he lay there contemplating the day's chores (buy bath soap and breadfruit, sweep the kitchen, bathe the dogs, prepare his lessons for the following week), the last person on the island (in the world, for that matter) whom he expected to see coming down the treacherous pathway to his beach was May Fuller, for he had spent the last fifteen years avoiding her, and she him.

So impossible was her presence there that, when he saw her, he blinked and rubbed his eyes. She must be some trick of the sunlight, a mirage, he thought. The more he blinked, the closer she came, and the near-naked Branson was overcome with a slew of emotions at once: embarrassment, fear, excitement, curiosity, and hope, to name a few. He jumped up and tried to collect himself, wrapped his towel around his waist, and knocked the sand from his hair. He looked around the beach, as if he should somehow tidy it up, too, before she reached it, but by then she was already just a few feet away.

"Branson, I have to talk to you about something extremely important."

Branson found May's matter-of-factness unsettling, at this their first meeting in years. "May? What are you doing here?"

"I'm here about the ad in the *Crier*," she snapped. "A good cook, dainty hands. Is that what you want?" She shook her hands in front of his face.

"A what?" he replied, backing away and swatting at her flitting hands. "What are you talking about?"

"A good cook," she insisted, moving her face nearer and nearer to his. "With dainty hands. Is that what you want? Is it?" May was yelling now, her lips achingly close to Branson's.

"I don't know what you want me to say" was all he could manage to get out.

"Branson," she tried more calmly, "you still have that fishing boat that used to be your dad's?"

"Sure. It's right there," and he pointed to it a short distance away, bobbing on its mooring. "Do you need me to take you somewhere?"

"Don't be stupid. I don't want to go anywhere with you," she nearly spat at him. "I just want you to tell everyone that you placed that ad in the newspaper, that ad for a good cook with dainty hands, and that it was *me* you were looking for, to row around with you in your silly boat."

"Why would I do that?" Branson asked her.

"Because it's the truth, and if you don't fess up to it, the police are going to use the ad as evidence against my brother. They think he killed his girlfriend Rena, and then advertised for her replacement!"

"I didn't kill anyone! I can't admit to that ad," he yelped. "I mean, I do have a fishing boat, and I'd be happy if you wanted to row around with me in it sometime, and you know what a fantastic cook I always thought you were. But I can't do it!"

"No one thinks *you* killed anyone. It doesn't matter if you admit to the ad."

"It matters to *me*," he argued. "I can't have everyone thinking I'm the kind of man who hunts for women in the island paper. I'm an instructor at the Boys' School, for heaven's sake!"

"I know what you are. You're as soft as guava jelly if you don't come forward and help my brother! They could put him in jail!"

"But May, I didn't do it."

"So it wasn't me you were looking for with that ad?"

"No! Yes! I mean, 'yes' to you, 'no' to the ad."

"You're not making any sense. Are you going to tell everyone you wrote the ad or aren't you?" she demanded.

"May, how can I?" Branson pleaded, his voice an octave higher in its desperation. "Come inside and I'll make you some tea. We can talk this over calmly. I'll show you the house. The kitchen floor needs sweeping, but otherwise it's in order."

May stared at him, flabbergasted. "Just tell me one thing, Branson."

"What's that?"

"What does a bicycle have to do with anything?" she asked. "In the ad you said you wanted a lady with a bicycle. Why?"

"May, I really don't know. Please, forget about the ad and come inside," he begged. "You seem a little upset."

May clasped her head in her hands and let out an exasperated scream. Then she ran over to Branson's fishing boat, gave it a good strong starboard kick and ran up the rocks with her skirt pulled up over her knees.

Branson was stunned. He could do little more than watch her as she struggled up the steps, the sun on her shoulders, the foliage on either side of the path framing her tense and hurried body, her slim fingers gripping the hem of her white cotton dress.

As he looked at her, he realized he hadn't seen anything quite so beautiful for a very, very, very long time.

———

May's interview with Branson had left *her* a little stunned, too. When she reached the top of the path, she could feel her face hot, her cheeks flushed. Her palms were sweaty. She must have run up the rocks too quickly, she tried to convince herself, for it was foolish to think that Branson might still have such an effect on her. Not after so much time and so many tears. What kind of man was he, May asked herself, to put his pride above her brother's freedom? To have turned his back on their budding love? Alongside these impossible questions in May's mind, another germinated, most impossible of them all. Was Branson still in love with her? Did he really want her back, after all these long and lonely years?

May didn't have time to dwell on Branson. Urgent matters awaited. The sun was up proper now, to light up what it would, and the fireflies made their retreat. Nighttime had delivered our cast to their matutinal chores, Trevor and Randolph to their loaves and their cakes, Raoul to his riddle, Branson to his dusty kitchen floor, his heart troubled by the morning's peculiar events.

Only Arnold and Joshua lay snoring still in their respective beds, the search warrant for Madison's property cooling on Arnold's bedside table. Drunk from the congratulatory rum of the night before, they pulled their sheets up over their heads and they slept and they dreamed, like two tired fireflies made redundant by the bright new day.

18

Ah, the sting of a first love failed! Never so acute as on Oh, where the bees themselves raise their brows and look down on your aching, itchy welt. Not that first loves alone will disappoint, mind you. Every day, somewhere on the island, a fisherman falls short, or a housewife wanders. Somewhere else, the beetles gossip about the islanders' betrayals, while the iguanas mock the mistresses and cuckolds. Not even the undeclared lover is spared, for the wind will ridicule him his cowardice.

So take heed if ever you find yourself embroiled here, and never expect that the canopy of trees will watch your sunburned back. On Oh loyalty and love are sticky business. Just take Branson and May, for instance, or little Dagmore and the sea that tossed him to and fro. Devotion is as capricious as the hurricane's winds, which—out of the blue—will veer abruptly from a seemingly certain path. But take heart, too, for the island's fickle nature gives rise to a convenient absolute: hope. Harbor it right next to your fishing boat!

Who's to say that one day your crush won't come round, or that with a bit of persuasion your neighbor's spouse won't notice your charms? Perhaps a mudslide will wash away your heart's obstacles or a rain shower reveal a tender secret. If a cyclone can be swayed, then where is the islander whose allegiance can't be coaxed? The palm whose formidable trunk might not be bent?

Sooner or later, even the most stubborn of dry spells will end in a sudden and inevitable splash.

19

Captain Thomson took Dagmore home shortly after his ninth birthday, celebrated aboard ship with as much fanfare and dignity as a gang of rude sailors could muster. The day in question wasn't the anniversary of little Dagmore's birth, not exactly, but the anniversary of the day that he had become Dagmore Bowles. Whether he was nine (or eight or ten), no one was completely sure, though this in no way diminished the felicity of the occasion. The crew had swabbed and polished the deck until it sparkled, and in the shade of the sails laid as fancy a table as the galley's provisions and the cook's imagination would allow. There was fish, for sure. Breaded fish, boiled fish, fish minced with onion and swimming in oil. There were potatoes and plantains, cornmeal and dumplings. For dessert, the cook had attempted a pineapple cake that, despite its filling of oldish jam and its somewhat charred underside, would have cut quite a figure center-table, had the sun not melted the sugary frosting that oozed down the sides of it like so many opalescent tears.

Every man on board took part in the celebration, which was as bittersweet as the wine they shared. Little Dagmore had had a good run; his plan had worked after all, at least for a little while.

He had so proven himself in his studies, and carved out such a niche for himself in the Captain's crew, that he had managed to stave off attendance at a proper school at "home" (wherever that was) for nearly two years. He had made himself an expert on every island the ship visited and revisited, knew each one's flora and fauna, its shoals and corals. Too much so, in fact. In his zeal for his academics, he had unwittingly exhausted, or nearly, the expertise of Enoch and his own father, who could no longer justify limiting his son to a life at sea.

Dagmore's birthday party thus doubled as a farewell, and not a soul there didn't feel as if he were sending off a son of his very own. Most of the men had even scrounged some sort of gift to bestow and to be remembered by. From homemade paper or cloth wrappings, little Dagmore pulled seashells, calabash shells turned into decorative bowls, a homemade deck of playing cards, kerchiefs blanched white by the sun, and a hand-carved wooden flute. Enoch gave him a book of poems, and his father, a brand-new leather notebook with his initials impressed into the cover. Lucky for them all, Dagmore had turned into quite a little gentleman by then, having mastered his father's stern but genteel manners, and so the only public tears that day belonged to the pineapple cake.

When darkness fell, Dagmore could no longer restrain his sorrow, and neither could anyone else. Tears flowed freely, and the men's collective hiccups and sobs bounced contagious throughout the ship's hull. They covered its slippery deck from end to end and climbed over the coarse and sturdy rigging to the very tips of the drawn and rugged sails. From there they tumbled out to sea and were eclipsed, finally, by the enormity of the waves.

Dagmore would celebrate fifteen birthdays in his new home, but none that would match the last one on his father's ship. Nearly half of them would be feted rather unceremoniously (little cakes in foil cups, a new box of pencils) at the "proper" school his father had found for him in England. It was a stuffy place, he thought, but he flourished there—if only because it broke his heart to think of disappointing the Captain, who came to visit him as often as he could (and wrote to him every day in between).

Captain Thomson had spared no expense. Dagmore's new home was certainly one to envy. Marble and ivy halls with masters who coddled the youth and genius (and wealth) in their charge, horses or cricket on Saturdays, and tea every afternoon. While the other boys seemed content with long runs on the manicured lawns and weren't bothered by the oft-cloudy skies, Dagmore quietly puzzled at his new life. Calculus and Plato and museums were all well and good, especially if they made his father proud, but the white shirts and porcelain cups so precious to Dagmore at sea, were in his new home merely a reminder of all he missed. The waves and the wind that smelled of saltwater. The stars, which here seemed not to burn as brightly. And there wasn't a palm or a mango for miles and miles, at least as far as he could tell. There were apples and pears to eat, and berries of every color. Dagmore did enjoy those. When he crawled into bed at the end of every day, however, he missed the tree frogs, the way their chirping had lulled him to sleep when he was Quick and alone.

Dagmore's nostalgia grew, until it was the only thing he could talk about when his father came to visit. Captain Thomson understood. If anyone knew the draw of the sea, it was he. There would be plenty of time for islands and ships, he assured his son, if he only finished his studies first. His future was bright, but its brightness had to be backed by degrees and certificates. Dagmore loved his father so much, worshipped him, really, that in the end he couldn't argue. He resigned to busy himself with his books, and quietly counted the days until he would serve under the Captain once again.

In the meantime, when the first four of Dagmore's birthdays at school had gone by without any sea change in his disposition, Captain Thomson got an idea. It seemed clear to him that what his son was missing was music. The tweet of the frogs, the whistle of the wind, the lap and smack of water on wood. So he arranged for Dagmore to make some music of his own. After Dagmore's thirteenth birthday, the Captain took him a piano. Not just any piano, but one with a top that curved and gaped, covered in a red cherry finish. It was housed in a lecture hall at the school and at first Dagmore had no idea what to make of it. Shiny and big and imposing, it reminded him vaguely of his father's ship, but when he touched the keys and their dull, random notes rang out, he jerked, startled.

"Well?" his father said.

Dagmore hadn't the faintest idea what to say, but his father's eyes were moist with anticipation and excitement, and so Dagmore smiled at him, and one smile led to another, which led to a series of exchanged giggles, and finally a guffaw from Captain Thomson.

"That's not all," his father told him. There was Miss Veronica, too.

"Miss Veronica?" Dagmore said.

The two words conjured an image of youth and bounce in Dagmore's barely teenaged head, but alas Miss Veronica was a "miss" by marital status alone. She turned out to be close to seventy, sprightly if spindly, her bounce now a mere shadow of what it must have once been. Miss Veronica, he was told, would give him a piano lesson every afternoon when his schoolday was done. Dagmore, on principle, would never have dreamed of refusing a gift from his father. This one, though, this mammoth, noisy instrument with its comparatively tiny and twittering teacher appealed for the sheer strangeness of its proportions, principles aside. So Dagmore, with a "pleased to meet you, Miss" and a peck on his father's cheek, sealed the deal.

The three birthdays after that found Dagmore much happier indeed, to his father's delight. The boy demonstrated a unique and natural talent, and he and Miss Veronica forged quite a friendship over scales and minuets. She couldn't have imagined that when Dagmore played, the *reason* he played, was to take himself as far away from her as he could go. The piano, like his father's ship, carried him across the sea, and back to the islands that he was missing more than ever. Music became his solace. The notes that mottled the parchment, like whirring fruitflies on coconut flesh, oozed from his fingers and transported him. Every trill was an island bird, every swell a thunderstorm that diminuendoed into the drip of lingering drops of rain. Not only did the music tell him what to do, where to pause, where to breathe, when to tread lightly and when to pounce, but the starkness of the keys, the black against the white, reminded him of the simplicity of his youth. On an island you always knew who you were, regardless of what name they gave you.

As Dagmore graduated to fugues and sonatinas, his playing acquired an almost magical allure. Soon the clouds cottoned on, and the birds, who thumped at the windows of the lecture hall when Dagmore was late to his lesson. His was the song that, until now, had only been whispered by the wind, a remnant of

Dagmore's island world that haunted him since the day he had left it. Thus, Dagmore threw himself into his playing, not for his father, or Miss Veronica, not because he possessed a natural talent for it. He threw himself into it, like a dolphin tossing in the sea, because it was his only means of escape, his only way home *for real*.

By the time a few more birthdays had come and gone, Dagmore was a true virtuoso, having mastered the twists and turns of some of the most famed and daunting sonatas ever composed. He had never slighted his academics—quite the contrary—still everyone agreed (the Headmaster, the Captain, Miss Veronica, and Dagmore himself) that his bright future was best secured at the Conservatory, though university might rather have seemed the next logical step. For the first time in his life, through his music-making, Dagmore had managed to genuinely please both his father and himself at once. He was *so* happy at his piano, so joyfully lost in the sounds of the birds and rain and wind, that he hardly noticed the absence of the real thing anymore. He didn't miss the seas, or the sun, as much as he once did, for they trickled out of his fingertips every time he pressed a key.

Captain Thomson was as pleased as rum punch and, one hot and sunny day, took the grown-up Dagmore from his proper school and set him up in a stylish apartment a stone's throw from the Conservatory—where, as it happened, Dagmore didn't spend as many birthdays as he had planned. A year had hardly passed when his teachers decided he'd surpassed them all. There wasn't a concerto he couldn't play, no emotion he couldn't evoke, from *allegro* to *legato con amore*. His *grandioso* was grand, his *grave* dignified, his *leggiero* light as air. His talents were such, it was deemed sinful that he should keep them to himself, and so before long the island rain that dripped from his fingers, fell in concert halls dripping in velvet. Pretty soon, every rich father wanted Dagmore to mentor his musical daughter, every rich mother sought his presence at her swank soirees—where to the delight and amazement of all, Dagmore could entertain them with equal flair in matters of Bach and biology, Schubert and sugarcane. Thus the next few birthdays passed to the tinkling of champagne flutes and the swoosh of silk.

Even so, island boys born to read the stars and chat with the breeze can only hide behind fake piano rain and rustling petticoats for so long. Dagmore was no exception. There were rats in need of catching and corncobs to roast. Sunlight destined for his brow that was tired of tip-toeing through a cloudy English veil. Dagmore became Dagmore on Oh, after all, and Oh had decided that it wanted him back.

As fate would have it—*island* fate—around that same time Captain Thomson found himself caught up in a terrible squall. He had never seen anything like it. Angry gales tossed his massive ship windward and leeward, while a vengeful wave bobbed it up and down like an empty nutmeg shell. The strategies that had served the Captain and his men so well during a near-lifetime at sea were suddenly and decidedly not going to be enough. The wind was blowing in two directions at once and the water seemed to leap straight up into the sky. What, Captain Thomson wondered, had he and his men ever done to deserve all of this?

In the end there was little more to do than huddle together and say their prayers, so that's what they did. To the accompaniment of pleas and mea culpas and apologies and promises barely discernible in the noisy storm, each clutched in strained and whitened fingers some icon to his faith. The cook held his Bible, the deckhands their rum, Enoch his favorite book of poetry. The Captain held and pressed to his lips a bundle of letters from his son. The early missives, accounts of cricket and badminton and the Natural History Museum, betrayed the false bravado with which they were composed and had broken the Captain's heart every time he read them. The ones after that made less and less an effort to hide Dagmore's melancholy, even as they bragged of his success. Then came the ones about the music lessons. About Ms. Veronica's nit-picking, or the Variations on a Theme that reminded Dagmore of the time he and his father watched a bird peck into a coconut, beak-rhythm on shell. Next came fame and fortune and private lessons in private apartments, and these had evoked from the Captain a devilish smirk that his not-quite-old-aged face had almost forgotten.

Sitting close in the circle of his men, the Captain replayed every letter in his head, and somewhere between Dagmore's first football match and his first performance at the Royal Hall, wind and wave conspired. A leeward tilt, then a starboard tongue of wave, jumped-aboard and demanding passage. Water slid across the deck and burrowed deep into the heart of the vessel, where it lay down, stretched itself, and got comfortable. Then it silently swallowed the Captain's ship, in a black and easy yawn not even the moon could bear to watch.

———

Dagmore spent the last of his birthdays in his home-that-turned-out-not-to-be-a-home packing trunks and signing papers. He was almost twenty-five and his father was dead. His piano no longer trilled birdsong or rained rain. It plunked and sputtered and twanged. His stylish apartment sold, its contents had been disman-tled into crate-size portions of memories hammered shut and sent away. Dagmore would meet them again at the port from which he would embark on the rest of his life. He was headed home, for real this time. Not to the sea, not exactly. Though he would journey by ship, he would never sail the globe from end to end, looking for whatever it was his father couldn't find. No, Dagmore was headed home to Oh, to the island where Captain Thomson Bowles had opened his heart to a scared little orphan called Quick, and given him a finer start in life than he could ever have imagined.

At least, that's what Dagmore wanted to believe, that his return to Oh was a tribute to a great and generous soul. Partly it was. Partly, he was running from his sorrow, like his father had run from his.

If the place Dagmore chose to run away to was Oh, there was a very definite reason for that. When you're born under the stars and weaned on pineapple juice, when there's sand in your bones and sea salt in your blood, an island is your fate. No matter how many sonatas you master and how many fancy shoes you buy. Time away is always just an interlude, even *years* abroad just a moment's head-turn from the blistering tropical sun. You can tell yourself you're moving on—or up—but sooner or later you'll find yourself moving back, as Dagmore did.

To the island with a name almost as beautiful as his own.

20

When the *Morning Crier* crying **Murder** hit the stands, Raoul was first in line to buy one. Despite his tryst with Ms. Lila the night before, he had woken up agitated, and eager to discover how much of a mess of things Bruce had really made. (Raoul knew a mess was guaranteed, but as to the degree of it, Bruce sometimes surprised him.) As he walked home to have his breakfast, he read the front-page article about Madison Fuller, collecting flies in his head along the way.

Although Bruce hadn't stressed Madison's reputation or good name, like Trevor had asked him to, Raoul knew that Trevor's belief in the boy's innocence was right. This was one fly, and it suggested two more: if Madison wasn't the murderer, but the police thought he *was*...oh, dear. Raoul didn't dare finish his thought. And, if Madison *wasn't* the murderer, then who was? Each of these flies triggered others in turn.

How would this Madison Fuller protect himself from the unchecked investigators on Oh?

Was Rena really dead, if some vandal in-the-know was ordering Raoul to find her? Surely even a graffiti-painting thug would have little use for a corpse. Presumably, Rena Baker was alive but merely lost.

Was this thug then her killer? That hardly seemed likely; had he done her in, he would know where he had done so.

Or was he boasting of his crime by taunting Raoul? Egging him on, daring him to find the evidence?

So on and so on, the flies that accompanied Raoul home multiplied in the wake of the ones that came before.

By the time he reached the cottage, his tummy was grumbling for breakfast and his head was a-hum with bugs. The paper, which he would re-read a dozen times that day, was folded in thirds. He grasped it tightly in one hand and slapped it, over and over, against the palm of the other as he studied the cottage wall that had once borne Rena's name. The scraped and yellowish wall now housed only the sloppy pink cloud that Raoul had painted in the dark to cover the letters. Annoyed, he realized he would have to scrape the wall again to put on a more even first coat of paint. Ms. Lila was picky about things like that.

Raoul started to calculate how many hours of his next "day off" the second wall would require, when he remembered that the third was as yet unfinished, too. He sighed and went to have a look at it, to remind himself how far he had gotten before leaving it to go and search for clues.

"What the...?" he said when he saw it, and dropped his paper on the ground.

Now *this* scraped and yellow-ish wall was marked with pink, too! Only instead of a cloud there were letters. Another request from the murderous message-writer? A clue to Rena's whereabouts? Raoul stood back to take in the words. D-A-G M-O-R-E. DAG MORE. What did that mean? He read it again. "Dag more" was no kind of command. "*Dig* more," maybe, but this definitely said DAG. As Raoul repeated the strange syllables over and over, and surveyed the wall again, he realized the words were not two, but one. DAGMORE was what the wall said.

Huh.

Not *Captain* Dagmore? The one who had crossed Raoul's mind only two days before, the one so worried about magic? What could he possibly have to do with any of this? Dagmore was long dead, jumped from the rocky perch where once he lived. All of Oh knew the story (or so they thought!). Did this mean that Rena was dead, too? Had she done herself in just like Dagmore? Perhaps her murderer had pushed her off a precipice? Was that what the message meant?

Suddenly Raoul's appetite was gone. His head was a hive of questions and there wasn't an answer in sight. Lovelorn fishermen and hits-and-runs and Rena Baker messages might all be connected, but surely this dead Dagmore was a separate kettle of fish?

"Just a minute!" Raoul said out loud. How had this message appeared on his wall when his paint tins and brushes were put away and locked up? He picked up the newspaper, ran to the front of the house and burst inside.

"Now what?" Mrs. Lila asked him, looking up from her breakfast. But Raoul was too busy to answer. He rushed to where he had stored his paints and brushes and they appeared to be untouched. One of the brushes seemed a bit wet with paint still, but was that the one he had used late at night, and in the dark not properly cleaned? Or had the vandal been inside his home?! Raoul dropped immediately to the ground and crawled backward from the closet that housed the paint paraphernalia to the cottage's front door. He could see no sign of drippings or dirt or footprints anywhere on the floor. Next, he crawled to each of the windows, but they were all pristine as well. Had the picky, polishing Ms. Lila inadvertently wiped away the traces of whoever had broken in?

"When was the last time you cleaned the floors and the windows?" Raoul asked her as she shared a fishcake with Fragile, who sat on her lap.

"Why?" she demanded defensively. "Are they dirty?"

"No, damn it! They're as clean as can be!"

"Why are you so upset? Aren't they supposed to be clean?"

"We've been robbed, and you've wiped away the clues!"

"What in the world are you talking about?" Ms. Lila asked him. "I don't see anything missing."

"I don't see anything either! That's the problem!"

Before Raoul could keep Ms. Lila talking in circles the whole of the morning, making them both late for work, she deposited Fragile on the floor, stood up, and gently pushed Raoul onto his favorite chair. She put two fishcakes in front of him, and a stiff cup of coffee, which she demanded that he down in one gulp. Then she returned to her place at the table and as a calmer Raoul sliced tentatively at his breakfast, she asked him to begin all over again with whatever it was he was trying to get off his mind. "Take your time, dear," she said.

Raoul told her about Trevor's talk with Bruce, about Bruce's article, about how Madison couldn't possibly be a murderer. He told her he was mulling the lot of it over in front of the first vandalized wall, when he peeked around the corner and found the name DAGMORE splashed across the next.

"Dagmore?" she interrupted. "Dagmore Bowles? The dead one?"

He told her he wasn't sure, but that there had never been another Dagmore on Oh as far as he could recall. He told her that he couldn't imagine how all of it fit together, the anonymous messages, and the hit-and-run, Rena and the suicidal sea captain. Then he told her the worst of it: that whoever had painted Dagmore's name had broken into their house to get at the brushes and Playful Rose.

She assured him she hadn't cleaned for at least three days and that if there were no clues to be found, it was because the culprit hadn't left any behind.

"Not unless," she chuckled, "it was the work of a ghost. Maybe old Dagmore is your message-writer. Do you think we could get him to paint the whole house?"

Raoul was in no mood for jokes. Certainly not jokes about spirits or spooks, which were in his book just another branch of magic. His very own wife should know better and he told her so. No fishcake, however golden or crispy, was worth listening to this!

Raoul started to get up from his chair, to gather his things for work, but a repentant Ms. Lila stopped him.

"Now, now," she said. "Don't get so hot and bothered. I have an idea that might help."

"What's that?"

"You want to know if your two messages, FIND R. BAKER and DAGMORE, are connected, right?"

"Right," he answered cautiously.

"Well, you can't talk to Rena, not unless you find her first, and since you haven't the faintest idea where to look—"

"Is there a point to all this?" Raoul interjected, offended.

"You can't talk to Rena, but you can talk to Dagmore Bowles— or at least to the next best thing. His Mrs. Jaymes."

"His *who?*"

"Mrs. Jaymes. She was his cook and his housekeeper. She married his handyman, Hammer Coates, after she married off Dagmore to some girl she hand-picked for him herself. She looked after Dagmore. She knew his life inside and out. My guess is she was his only friend in the world. If it weren't for her, Dagmore Bowles would have lost his sanity in that big empty house of his.

"He jumped off a cliff and into the sea. That doesn't say 'sane' to me."

"Maybe," Ms. Lila agreed, "but I know for a fact that if anyone can tell you about that crazy old Captain, it's Dorothea Jaymes."

Hmm.

Ms. Lila might be right, but Raoul was bothered by the prospect of interviewing the Captain's former maid. It smacked of ghost-hunting, and though his methods were unorthodox, he hadn't yet ever resorted to *that!*

What truly troubled him, though, was a different ghost entirely: Rena Baker's. He didn't really believe she was dead...or didn't *want* to believe it. But finding a dead man's name on your doorstep—or nearly—was bound to rattle even the staunchest proponent of the plain-as-noses-on-faces philosophical school.

21

The *Morning Crier* was notoriously hit or miss. Either it scintillated to the point of selling out, or was so dull that not even the chickens could abide it at the bottom of their coops. The edition that named Madison Fuller a suspect in the murder of Rena Baker was of the former sort, striking a bull's-eye of the kind that only Bruce could manage. No islander talked of anything *but*. Raoul couldn't stop re-reading it. At the bakery they couldn't stop discussing it. May Fuller couldn't get it off her mind.

As she walked farther and farther from Branson's beach and from their stunning early morning interview, her thoughts turned more and more to Madison and the accusations against him. She was so agitated and so angry by the time she reached her house, that she walked right past it and headed straight to the grimy-windowed office of the *Morning Crier*. There was no time, she decided, to explain things to Madison or to cajole Trevor into getting the truth from Bruce. May would handle the matter herself.

"Bruce!" May shouted, as she burst through the door. "Where are you? I've got some business to discuss with you!" Bruce didn't answer, because he wasn't there. He had opened up the office and lined up his pencils, then gone off to the bakery for breakfast. (Not that her shouting would have bothered him if he *had* been there. He had grown accustomed over the years to women barging in and yelling at him, what with his line of work.)

"Bruce!" May tried again. "I'll find you," she yelled at the empty room and rushed back out the door. No use wasting all this anger, she thought, and she proceeded to the bakery, where she planned to give Trevor a good talking-to about his friend Branson, who—she was still convinced—had placed the ad and now would not admit to it. When she got there and found Bruce as well, she was only too happy to kill two birds with one stone.

"Aha! There you are!" May planted herself an inch from Bruce's face.

Poor Bruce! May was not the only one of a mind to reprimand him on that shiny, early morn, for Trevor and a handful of bakery regulars were already up to their elbows in biscuits and how-could-yous, while Bruce, for his part, countered with how-could-I-whats.

"I thought you were going to help matters, not make them worse," Trevor scolded him.

"What have I made worse? I put right in the article that the man had no prior indictments!" Bruce replied.

"And you accused *me* of obstruction of justice!" Trevor added.

"Ooohh," Bruce growled. "You all think I invent the news, do you? I simply report the facts as they stand."

"Facts?" May squealed. "You want to talk about facts, do you? Well how about, as a matter of *fact*, you tell us who it was who placed that stupid ad that has those stupid officers accusing my brother of murder."

"How many times do I have to say it? I don't know who wrote the ad!"

"With all due respect, Bruce, you have to admit that's hard to believe," Trevor said, in defense of May's position.

"You!" May whirled around and pointed her index finger right at Trevor's nose. "You're one to talk! It's that stupid friend of *yours* who placed the ad, and now he's too ashamed to come forward and save a man's life!"

"What are you saying?" Trevor asked her, confused.

"Branson Bowles is what I'm saying. Just ask *him* what he knows about dainty hands and good cooking!"

Trevor couldn't imagine Branson doing something so outlandish as to advertise for love. Nor could he believe for a minute that, had Branson done so, he wouldn't speak up and save the day. He tried to say as much to May: "I hardly think…"

"I'll say, you hardly think," she interrupted him. Then she stomped out the door, twisting her torso back inside to add, "If you don't get Branson to come clean, I'll smash that big hat of yours flat as a roti skin!"

Such fury, and without May's even knowing yet that the police were at that very moment elbow-deep in hers and Madison's personal effects, executing the search warrant they had procured the night before. Unawares she continued her walk home, alternately cursing under her breath and beseeching the skies, eyes heavenward.

How could Bruce be so irresponsible? she asked herself. How could Trevor stand by and watch? And Branson! Well, he was the most shameful of all! How could he do this to her? And why, she wondered, did it bother her so much? She was worried about her brother, yes, but there was more to it than that.

May always spoke her mind, to others and to herself, and what her mind was saying now, May didn't want to hear. All it talked about was Branson Bowles. About their long-ago plans for marriage and for a house with a verandah. About how Branson had studied harder than ever before, as if his zeal could somehow make the school years pass more quickly, while May had baked and stewed and fried. She recalled how her father, wary of love too-young, had taken every step imaginable to ensure that Branson and May were kept apart. How weeks went by in which May didn't see Branson or hear a single word from him.

Perhaps she had been mistaken about him all along, her teenaged heart had told her. Whenever she caught a glimpse of him in town or at the market, and hoped to read in his eyes some declaration of love or some flicker of shared suffering, he averted her gaze.

Young Branson wasn't avoiding her, or with his avoidance declaring his indifference. The very sight of her moved him to tears, and he was forced to look away to maintain his public composure. He missed her more than he knew it was possible to miss a person, and yet he feared that she wasn't missing him nearly as much as that. Surely if she were, she would find a way to slip him a note or send him a message. (Neither Branson or May had a telephone back then, the Oh-Tel Communications Company having temporarily run out of numbers.)

Thus each had engaged in his (and her) private suffering, avoiding gazes and entertaining doubt, neither suspecting of the other's pain. When the school year finished and another had come and gone, Branson decided that May no longer even remembered who he was. She remembered—of course she did—but while Branson's heartache had matured into a steady, romantic malaise, May's had blossomed into vexation. How dare he let her go without so much as a second thought! All those recipes, her most expert and delectable, devised for him alone! May got herself so worked up that when she sought out Branson's eyes at the market after that, it was to stare into them, mean and indignant.

It was all much more than poor Branson could take, and when it had come time to enter the island teaching college, he couldn't bear Oh or the threat of encountering May a moment longer. He decided to pursue his training elsewhere, far away from the island and its constant reminders of May's porridge and her conch fritters.

He had no idea of it then (and still doesn't), but Branson ended up not far from where little Dagmore himself had studied years before, though Branson had no inclination for pianofortes (and Miss Veronica was now long dead). Branson's interlude away from Oh was even lonelier than his father's, if only half as long. *His* belly, too, hungered for the sea, his heart throbbed with the pulse of the tide. He could swear he heard the chirp of the tree frogs when the wind blew just so, although sometimes the chirp sounded more like May's hiccups, the kind she got whenever she cried. Was she sad that he had gone? Branson wondered. Had he got it wrong when he ran away from Oh?

No matter. You're always in time to change your mind where an island's concerned. Because sooner or later—like I said—you'll find yourself moving back.

22

The small ship that carried Dagmore home to Oh quietly laid anchor not far off the coast on a Friday night. When the islanders awoke on Saturday morning, they drank their tea, ate bread with jelly, and dressed to go to town. Saturday was the biggest market day of the week, and in Port-St. Luke the vendors' stalls bustled with buyers and sellers and fishermen peddling their wares for Sunday dinner. On this particular Saturday, as the islanders headed to market, descending their respective hillsides in cars or buses or on foot, they were all stopped dead by the sight of Dagmore's ship in the harbor below. It wasn't actually *his* ship—he only had it on hire—but it was the best and brightest he could find to bring him back to the island, and the most spiffy the islanders had ever seen. It shone so golden in the morning sun that vehicles stopped in the middle of the road to let their passengers jump out and look down on it.

By the time the islanders reached town, the market square was abuzz with rumor. It was the Prime Minister's ship, purchased with siphoned funds. No, no! It belonged to a movie star, the one who played a battlefield warrior in the new picture at the Loyal Cinema. Surely it belonged to the Queen herself, who must have come to pay a visit. Dagmore's appearance, when he finally disembarked, did little to dispel the rumors. In his father's honor, he had donned a captain's cap of blinding white, and an expensive blue jacket with brass buttons so shiny, they gave the sun's brilliance a run for its money. He might very well indeed have been the Attaché of a minister or a monarch.

At the very least, he must be a Captain, they decided, based on his attire, and so began his life on Oh as Captain Dagmore Bowles. Though the only craft he would ever command after that was a small fishing boat, Dagmore liked the title, for it reminded him of his father, Captain Thomson Bowles, and he would wear it proudly for over thirty years to come.

Captain Dagmore's first order of business was to find himself a place to live. After stops at the Police Station, the Fire Station, the Customs Office, the Stationer's, the Library and the Island Post, where he signed, stamped and sealed a series of forms declaring that his boat was in the harbor, he set off to explore the island on foot. Though twenty years had passed since his boy days of itchy feet and rats, he could still climb about an island as well as anyone. He went up and down Dante's Mountain, circled Glutton Hill, and took a swim in Crater Lake. The latter went far in cementing Captain Dagmore's celebrity across the island, for everyone on Oh knew that Crater Lake was bottomless and that if you dared dip even a toe in it, you were doomed to be sucked away to your death. That Dagmore had survived the ordeal, they said, might mean he was some sort of devil.

It wasn't long before Captain Dagmore found the piece of land he wanted to purchase. He spotted it from the top of Mt. Tulip (so called for the way its summit dipped and peaked), and the sight of it nearly knocked him over. It was his beach! The one where he had defied the sun and leapt from an almond tree to save his father's life. It was exactly as he remembered it. The sandy coastline where the crew had rowed ashore and where Captain Thomson had made him his son, the woods just a ways inland, and a steep and stony perch above that jutted out and over the sea. There, Dagmore decided, he would build himself a house, a villa to make his father proud, and to forever keep watch over the beach where they had met. After visiting the respective Offices of a Surveyor, Solicitor, and Architect, Dagmore went to the Savings Bank, where he deposited, drafted and designated a series of notes, and *voilà*! Both the beach and the perch were his.

Dagmore lived on his ship for three months, while materials were got in and blueprints drawn up for his new home. When ground was finally broken and the first pillars cast, he paid the men extra to work longer and harder and in a matter of weeks enough of the structure was complete that Captain Bowles could renounce his ship and move himself in. Only the ground floor was covered and there was still no electrical current, but there was plumbing and flooring and room for all of Dagmore's crates, which in the meantime had arrived. He had even shipped his piano (though it no longer made him happy), because it was a gift from his father and he couldn't bear not to have it near.

It took almost six months after that for Dagmore's crew of masons and builders and painters to finish his lavish estate. While the men laid more piping and wires and tiles, Captain Dagmore unpacked his past. He arranged his rugs and furniture and his clothing and books, and the mementos of his musical career. He hired a cook and housekeeper (Dorothea Jaymes), and settled into an entirely pleasant and leisurely routine. He woke early every morning, when the temperatures were coolest (though, mind you, still very hot), breakfasted, climbed down the rocky steps that nature had cut into the side of his cliff, and went for as long a swim as he could endure. After that, he ran up and down his private beach, did his calisthenics, and napped in the sand while the sun dried his wet and sweaty body. Back up the rocky steps for a cool shower and a hot lunch, he then dressed and walked to town, where he bought the daily paper and lost an hour or two to dominoes or old talk in his favorite bar. When the sun began to set, he went back home, and in the evenings he sat on his verandah, where the moon kept him company as he read.

In between the various activities of Captain Dagmore's typical day, he could be caught staring, lost in reminiscence and previous lives. From his beach he looked to the woods where once he hid, and remembered the first time he met his father. From his house on high, he looked down at the water or up at the sun and marveled that he had come as far as he had. When he floated in the sea, he gazed up at his beautiful home, its windows mirroring the sun's glow, and he hoped that his father was proud.

In truth, the house that Captain Dagmore Bowles had built inspired far more than pride. It was the envy of all the islanders. Even the island itself took note of it. Poised as it was on its imposing and jutting plateau, the sun was moved to parch it, while the wind billowed through its windows and porticos with alternate whistle and hiss. Its positioning hampered the birds and dazzled the butterflies into a stupor; the house towered over the sand below, blanketing the beach in shadow much of the day. To all of this, though, Dagmore was oblivious. He felt rather as if the sun shone for the sole purpose of watching over him, and that the bewildered birds and butterflies wavered at his windows for his delight. The wind was kind enough to sing him to sleep at night, and the shade of his stony hillside, to keep him cool. He couldn't imagine a more perfect existence, and every evening from the first-floor balcony, he thanked his lucky stars.

Is it any wonder, that on a rocky and muddled footing like this one, a mountain of trouble was soon to ensue?

23

As May neared home, thoughts jumping in her head (Branson Bowles, the *Morning Crier*, Trevor's hat) like drops of oil in one of her skillets, she spotted the Police pick-up truck parked in front of her house. Her heart sank as her temper flared, her walk turned into a run, and in a flash she was bounding up the front steps.

"Madison!" she cried out. "What's going on?"

May didn't have to wait for Madison's reply, because as soon as she walked in the door, she could see for herself. Officers Tullsey and Smart had the entire place in disarray. They were opening drawers and emptying cupboards and thumbing through books on bookshelves. Madison sat incredulous on the sofa.

"They say they have a search warranted," he mumbled.

"Let me see it!" May snapped. Officer Smart handed her a piece of paper that showed signs of having spent too much time in the pocket of his hot and heavy uniform. She unfolded it, read what it had to say, then handed it back to him as if it were something dirty and repugnant, her thumb and index finger barely holding its uppermost edge.

"If this isn't the most ridiculous thing I've ever seen in my life!" she started. "Disrupting the lives of honest, hard-working people, while liars and rascals run about the island making all kinds of trouble!" Her rant went on for a good five minutes and spared no one: not the Prime Minister, the Chief of Police, or the local pastor, who should have foreseen what was coming and said a prayer. May criticized the legal system and the tax laws and the local bus schedule (or lack thereof), and finished off with the price of cheese. Officers Arnold and Joshua looked at each other, and at Madison, none of them quite sure what to do.

Finally May insisted, "You have your warrant. Get on with it! But don't think for a minute I'll have you leaving my house in a mess!"

With that, the officers returned to their search, May trailing close behind and ensuring that everything they touched was put back where it belonged. The sitting room, with its cupboards of extra cushions and its desk drawers full of old newspapers (which May used to wrap up Madison's daily catch) proved of little interest.

The officers moved on to Madison's bedroom, where they filled a whole sack with evidence. They took the yellow shirt he always wore to take Rena dancing, thus establishing a relationship with the victim. They took a pair of mud-covered shoes, thus placing him at the scene of the crime (never mind that most of the island was muddy for four months out of the year). They took his fishing pole, thus proving unequivocally that he was a fisherman.

The next room was May's. All the officers did there was peek in through the door, for May's expression assured them that entering would be at their peril.

They concluded in the kitchen, which was tantamount to her bedroom, as far as May was concerned, and her sharp and angry eyes followed the officers' movements even more closely.

They unfolded all her dishtowels and tapped on her wooden spoons, uncorked her spice jars, examined the bananas that hung from a hook, and sniffed May's salt and pepper. It was all she could do to contain her temper, and that she managed to was testament to just how much she loved her brother. Her inclinations were to clobber Officer Tullsey with her grandmother's teapot, after pouring its boiling contents all over Officer Smart. For Madison's sake, May bit her tongue.

"Are you done?" she asked them, when they had gone through the fridge, too, poking their noses into every jar and bottle.

"Please, miss, kindly keep quiet. This is official police business."

Officer Smart will never know how close he came to a good dousing with hot tea right then. Lucky for him, his partner distracted May from her thinning patience just in time, with a terrible, fateful question.

"What's that?" Officer Tullsey asked.

May let out the slightest of sighs and closed her eyes for a second. Officer Tullsey pointed to a squarish lump that rested atop her china cabinet.

"It's nothing," May said, composing herself. "Just an old basket."

"Why's it covered up?" Officer Tullsey persisted.

"I threw a beach towel over it to keep out the dust."

"To keep out the dust or to keep the basket hid?"

"Why in the world would I hide an old basket?" May argued, her usual, indignant self. "And if I *were* going to hide an old basket, do I look so stupid as that? To toss a piece of cloth over it to make it go away? Like a child who thinks he's invisible if he closes his eyes?"

"I don't know anything about that, lady, but we're going to have to take a look at the basket," Officer Tullsey said. "Joshua, go up and get it."

Officer Smart pulled a chair from May's table and slid it near the cabinet. A stern glance from May suggested he first remove his shoes before stepping on it, which he did, then he climbed on it and off it again, basket gently in hand. He set it on the table and Officer Tullsey pulled off the beach towel to reveal a basket that wasn't old at all, or if it was, it was so well cared-for that its age was a tribute, not a flaw. Inside it, they found a hard plastic dinner plate with a faded pattern of leaf or fruit, or maybe both; a knife, fork, and spoon; and a stack of bowls with plastic covers, on which someone had written in the center of each, in black ink, a thick and rudimentary "R".

"What's all this now?" Officer Tullsey asked May.

"It's a plate and some food containers," she answered. "You can't see that?"

"Why's there writing on the lids? Are they yours?"

From the sofa in the sitting room, Madison almost let out a groan, but May threw him a harsh look and he suppressed it.

"No, they aren't my lids," May said matter-of-factly, offering no further explanation.

"Are they his?" Officer Smart asked, indicating Madison with a tilt of his head.

"Of course they aren't! Does he look like a man who has to cook for himself?" May replied.

"If they aren't yours and they aren't your brother's, then whose lids are they? Did you steal them?" Officer Smart looked May straight in the eyes.

"Is that why you were hiding them?" Officer Tullsey chimed in.

"No, I didn't steal them," May said curtly. "They belong to Madison's friend."

"What friend?"

"His girlfriend."

"What girlfriend?"

"He only has one girlfriend. What kind of man do you think he is?" she hissed at them.

"Are you trying to say that these lids and utensils that you were hiding in a basket under a beach towel on top of a cabinet belong to the victim?"

"I'm saying they belong to Rena. I don't know about any victim."

"How do you explain Rena Baker's things in your house, if she isn't dead?"

May was speechless. If she hadn't known any better, she would have thought for sure she was dreaming and would have shook herself awake. Alas, hers was a nightmare that was very real and becoming more nightmarish by the minute. She took a deep breath and with uncharacteristic calm addressed the officers.

"Rena and Madison are in love. Rena cooks him lunch every day and sometimes she takes it to him in those bowls with those lids in that basket. Sometimes in between a lunch and another, the basket and the bowls and the lids all end up here. It's as simple as that."

"Is it?" Officer Tullsey asked. "Are you sure it's not as simple as your brother got rid of Rena and hid her bowls and basket where he thought no one would find them?"

"In plain sight?" May squealed. "Are you both mad?"

"They weren't in plain sight. They were under a beach towel," Officer Smart corrected her. "I'm afraid we'll have to take these, too."

In the end, besides the yellow shirt, the muddy shoes, the fishing pole, the beach towel, and the basket (with all that was inside), Officers Tullsey and Smart made off with a beer tumbler, dishwashing gloves, an apron, an umbrella, and a box of macaroni, but not before May made them polish all her drinking glasses and every last of her utensils, to rid them of the smudges the officers had left behind.

They headed to the truck to deposit their plunder and were about to dig up May's vegetable garden on the way (to see what evidence they might find buried there), when May put her foot down.

"I have tried to be cooperative with the pair of you, and with your foolishness, but enough is enough," she threatened. "Touch so much as a leaf on a tomato plant and neither one of you will know what hit you!"

"Fine!" Officer Smart yelled back at May, emboldened by the screen door that separated them. "We already have more than enough."

"Enough for what?" May hollered.

"A warrant."

"You already have a warrant. What more do you want?"

"Not a search warrant," Officer Smart yelled from the window of the truck as Officer Tullsey put it in gear and pulled onto the road. "A warrant for arrest."

May rushed outside, but all she could do was watch them drive off, the sun refracted in the lenses of Officer Smart's sunglasses, which appeared to shoot broken-rainbow daggers in every direction.

24

When things start off badly on Oh, generally they tend to get worse. A longer-than-usual dry season will typically end in fire; a too-wet rainy one won't stop until every river has flooded its banks; and a mudslide isn't a mudslide until it has carried off a dozen homes. A tingling tooth will always need pulling, a grey hair will turn into ten, and that spot of humidity on your ceiling will eventually come crashing down on your head.

The islanders don't worry about trouble. They take challenge in stride, rally in the face of seeming defeat, and are as routinely resilient as the island itself. So acquainted with trouble are some of them that they tend to seek it out, to slip it on like a favorite pair of football boots. These daring and misguided souls would tell you that problems follow them wherever they tread. They would argue that any fight is heaven-sent and preach the folly of forgiveness. Oh has no interest in characters like these, brawlers and scrappers who wage imaginary war. The island much prefers the subtler charms of the innocent and true, of the gentle and unsuspecting. What fun in an enemy poised for the fight?

A surprise attack where none is expected, now that's a fish of a different color! The tug and jostle, the thrill of defeat. What's more, an unwary adversary, once bested, will on Oh come back for more. Take a snapper, for example (a red one, or yellowtail), hooked and reeling, who will flop and dance until he finally falls down dead. Or a lizard who will turn himself a dozen shades of green to save his skin.

Trial is the spice of island life, and every island creature knows it. From bakers and newspapermen, to the birds in the treetops and the fish in the seas.

25

Against his better judgment, Raoul took his wife's advice. After an obligatory stop at the headquarters of Customs and Excise, where he told his staff that a pressing case required his attention, he left for the Office of Vital Records to find Mrs. Jaymes's last known address. She was apparently Mrs. Coates now, longtime widow of Darion Jaymes and re-married to a so-called Hammer, presumably the handyman of which Ms. Lila had spoken. They lived on Ladywood Road not too far away, but because Raoul was anxious and pressed for time, he took a taxi instead of going on foot. When the driver deposited him at the Coateses' front gate, it was just after nine o'clock.

"Hello," he called out, as he tapped on the frame of the open front door. "Mrs. Jaymes? I mean, Mrs. Coates? Are you there?"

The years (well over ninety of them) had slowed Mrs. Jaymes down (although not to the extent you might expect), but her mind remained as sharp as ever, and her tongue as pointed. When she reached the doorway, she surveyed Raoul suspiciously. "Who are you?" she asked him.

"I was wondering if I could ask you some questions. I'm with the government."

"Questions about what?" she snapped.

"Mrs. Jay—," Raoul stopped himself. "Mrs. Coates—"

"Mrs. Jaymes is fine," she interrupted him. "Hammer gave me his name too late for it to stick," she explained.

"Thank you," he nodded. "Mrs. Jaymes, I'd like to talk to you about a previous employer of yours. Dagmore Bowles."

At the mention of the name, Mrs. Jaymes was clearly taken aback. "Who did you say you were?" she asked.

"My name is Raoul Orlean. I'm head of Customs and Excise and I'm doing some research for a case."

"Dagmore's been dead thirty years."

"Yes, I'm aware of that. He...er, that is, his estate, is not in any trouble. I just need some background information."

Mrs. Jaymes was about to send the tax man before her straight to the devil, when his name triggered a faraway memory.

"Did you say your name was Raoul Orlean?"

"Yes."

"Then if memory serves, you met my employer once many years ago, Mr. Orlean."

"That's right!" Raoul confirmed. "We had a conversation once, he and I. You know about it? May I come in?"

It turned out that Mrs. Jaymes and Dagmore Bowles were indeed as close as Ms. Lila had said. Mrs. Jaymes was the one constant in Dagmore's rocky years on Oh and the only companion in whom he could confide. Well she remembered hearing about his chat with Raoul Orlean at the Belly years before, and for that reason, she stepped aside and invited Raoul to come in.

"Thanks to you he finally gave up on that silly Abigail Davies he was so smitten with," she said.

"Did he?" Raoul said. "That's good." Raoul had never been a fan of Abigail Davies. Abigail, still the island's most sought-after midwife despite her years, had been the best friend of Raoul's first wife, Emma Patrice. Emma Patrice went missing a few years after she and Raoul wed. She skied down a long, slippery slope during a holiday with him in Switzerland and never made it to the bottom. He didn't think her disappearance intentional, not exactly, but her body was never recovered—despite a team of sniffing Saint Bernards—and, well, you never know one-hundred-percent-surely, do you? He couldn't help but wonder if Abigail knew more about his wife's whereabouts than she had ever said.

"Would you like some tea?" Mrs. Jaymes offered. She and Hammer had already finished breakfast, but she was happy to put on a pot.

"No, thank you. If I could just ask you some questions."

They sat down, Mrs. Jaymes growing more and more animated as her memories of Dagmore flooded to mind. "What is it you'd like to know?" she asked Raoul.

He didn't dare reveal that Dagmore's name might somehow be mixed up in the Rena Baker case splashed across the headlines, so he simply replied that confidentiality forbade his telling her the circumstances surrounding his official investigation. He infused his tone with all the authority he could muster, hoping it would sway Mrs. Jaymes to cooperate. "I'd like to know everything you can recall, from the time Captain Dagmore came to Oh and moved into his villa," Raoul ventured.

"Oh my," Mrs. Jaymes said, clapping her palms to her smiling cheeks. "I haven't thought about all that in years!"

"But you remember?"

"Remember?! Why, I could tell you the story of Captain Dagmore Bowles, and that miserable old house of his, just like he would tell it to you himself!"

Mrs. Jaymes proceeded to do just that, as Hammer puttered outside in the garden and Raoul, in a notebook he had brought from his office, wrote down every word she said.

———

Captain Dagmore had no sooner settled into his relaxing life on Oh than he started second-guessing his early morning swims and his sandy siestas. His walks to town, too, had grown tedious; his rum punch tasted weak; and evenings home with little more than the moon began to pale in comparison to the life he had left behind. He had come back to Oh to honor his father and his fatherland—what Mrs. Jaymes meant by that was another story entirely, she explained—and a daily walk to town for dominoes was just not enough.

As Dagmore strolled along the harbor one typical afternoon, fielding "Hello, Captains" and trying to put his finger on the problem, his eyes looked down into the murky port waters. Suddenly he was reminded of the island's reefs and corals. Then one-by-one its waterfalls and forests came to mind, followed by its plantations of pineapple and cocoa. Could it be as simple as that? he wondered. Had Dagmore, snug in his hilltop villa, taken Oh and her beauty for granted?

He stopped and directed his gaze out to sea, to the fishing boats that dotted the wavy surface and the cargo ships he could barely make out in the distance. Before long, Dagmore felt himself swept up in a wave of nostalgia for the years he spent criss-crossing islands with his father's crew. ("His father, Captain Thomson, had a ship, you know," Mrs. Jaymes told Raoul.) All at once he missed making notes about trees and sketching bugs and indigenous vegetables. He missed the thrill of discovering a secret beach or a nest of tiny birds. He gripped his belly and doubled over, right there in the center of town, painfully homesick, though he was as "home" as he had ever been.

Dagmore decided then and there that it was time to roll up his sleeves and to remember what island life was all about. What kind of islander had he become, lounging all day in the sun and the sea, when there were hills to be climbed and monkeys to be studied and bigger fish to fry? He headed straight for Higgins Hardware, Home, and Garden. There he purchased a long piece of rope, sturdy gloves, a set of graduated shovels, a bucket, and a canvas sack. At Samuel's Sundry, he bought books filled with empty pages, a box of pencils, and a caramel candy that he ate straightaway. He just had time to pop into a shoe shop that was about to close its doors for the evening, and there he got himself a pair of hardy boots with laces. With his packages in hand and his head full of plans, Dagmore was far too impatient for his usual long walk home that day and instead jumped on a bus for Tempperdu, which was more or less where he was headed.

The Captain spent months after that putting his new tools to good use. He covered the island end to end and filled half a dozen notebooks with drawings and data and poetry inspired by Oh's scenery. His canvas sack during that time housed any number of petals and pineapples, iguanas, crabs, beetles, and leaves of banana. He had observed the waterfalls they called the Seven Brothers, had canoed up and down Oh's canals, collected water samples from Crater Lake, and scrutinized the surf at Black Pearl Beach, which had stolen many a swimmer over the years.

Dagmore's research wasn't limited to pollen and lizards. He indulged in every island delicacy as well, consulting the local ladies for recipes and advice on how to cook everything from cou cou to callaloo soup. He planted his own corn and pigeon peas. He even learned to spice rum, and which bush to boil for tisanes to cure any ailment.

The island's history drew Dagmore's attention, too. Its forts and caves and cannons and peaks that had all played part in the island's colorful and violent past. He studied the remnants (linguistic, architectural, sartorial) of the island's invaders over the centuries, and read all that he could find about Oh's governance.

Occasionally he consulted some islander who might be able to share his or her particular expertise (which vines to feed a goat, what phase of the moon was conducive for planting yams), but for the most part Dagmore's wanderings were solo, his company primarily the island itself. Though his haughty hilltop abode had bothered the butterflies and encroached upon the stars, the island embraced the new-and-improved Captain Dagmore, who devoted his every waking moment to what Oh had to offer. The wind was always at his back, the sun shed light on whatever puzzled him, and it only rained when Dagmore's hardy boots and laces were in need of a good rinse.

Still, the grass is always greener on the other side of the fence, and this new arrangement was satisfying Dagmore little more than the last one had. When he had hopped about islands as a boy with his father's men, there was someone to share the findings with. Why, the men on Captain Thomson's ship had been known to debate the merits of a particular kind of fish for two or three nights running. Dagmore's notebooks now stirred no such dialogue. When he found a perfect shell or saw a perfect sunset, the best he could do was reproduce a poor sketch of it. Soon Dagmore grew nostalgic for the English gatherings—"Yes, England!" Mrs. Jaymes boasted. "He studied there and lived there until his father died."—where he had pontificated on bee nectar and Beethoven, the silked and powdered audience hanging on his every last word.

So now what? he asked himself, one fine day on Dante's Mountain when the clouds had hung themselves over his picnic lunch, cooling his hot head and soothing his itchy feet. Abandoning his research hardly seemed the answer, but neither could he scrounge a crew with which to debate it in the evenings over cigars and spiced rum punch.

Or could he?

Dagmore had an idea. He finished his fried fish and home-made bread as quickly as his teeth would allow, put his boots back on and tied them tight, packed his things in his bag, slung it over his shoulder, then stood up and brushed himself off. With a furtive glance left and right for the too-chatty goatherd Pedro, who would certainly have cost him some time, Dagmore dashed back down the mountain and into town.

Later that night, Mrs. Jaymes couldn't get him to eat any dinner.

"Captain, aren't you going to have any supper?" she called up to him in his study, where he had locked himself away since returning from town earlier that day.

"Just leave it, please, Mrs. Jaymes," Dagmore yelled down to her. "You can go, if you like."

"Well, you leave me no choice," Mrs. Jaymes yelled back in reply, not hiding her anger.

She wasn't angry that Captain Dagmore had let his supper get cold, or that her own culinary efforts had gone to waste. Heavens, no! As long as Mrs. Jaymes got her pay every week, which she did, it was no concern of hers if Captain Dagmore ate her food or not. If he failed to include her in the household affairs, well, that was another matter entirely.

Mrs. Jaymes knew that something was afoot at the villa, and she was loath to set foot outside of it until she knew exactly what. The captain had come home at a very unusual hour in the middle of the afternoon (he typically conducted his research until dusk), with small but mysterious packages from town, some of them tied with delicate ribbons that gave Mrs. Jaymes an awful sense of foreboding. She dilly-dallied in the kitchen and tidied up where no tidying was needed, but no sign of the Captain (or what he was up to) came, so finally she collected her things and took herself reluctantly home.

Reluctantly, because Mrs. Jaymes had a knack for sniffing trouble. And her instincts had served her well that day at Dagmore's. Those fancy packages of his were indeed going to be a problem, though this would not have immediately appeared the case to the innocent onlooker. They contained little more than writing materials: the finest quality paper to be found on Oh, envelopes to match, the ink of blackest black, and a stick of golden wax for sealing up the whole kit and caboodle with a capital B (a stamp of which Dagmore had inherited from his father, Thomson Bowles).

Dagmore spent all of that evening drafting and composing, folding and sealing. When Mrs. Jaymes arrived the next morning with fresh eggs for his breakfast, she found him next to a tall stack of thick envelopes, hard at work writing more letters still. He was dressed in such finery as she had never seen him. Her hunch of the day before was full-fledged fear now, and she couldn't hold her tongue a minute longer.

"What in the name of all things holy are you up to? And why are you dressed so?" she demanded to know.

"Calm down, Mrs. Jaymes. It's just a few invitations," Dagmore assured her. "Don't worry about a thing."

Invitations? She didn't like the sound of this at all! Mrs. Jaymes furrowed her brow and studied the Captain. As near as she could tell, he had no inkling whatsoever that he was stirring a hornet's nest. Funny, that, she thought to herself, her own intuition so feverishly astir that she was sure she heard the angry insects buzzing about her head.

"What sort of invitations?" she asked, skeptical and stern.

"Invitations for some old acquaintances of mine, from…" (Did Dagmore really start to say 'from home'?) "…from my piano days."

"Piano days? What's 'piano days'?"

"I used to play. Concerts. I'm very good, you know. Better than very good. I was quite sought-after, to tell you the truth."

"So you're inviting your old friends to a concert. Is that it?"

"Not exactly. I'm just inviting them to visit. I was a guest in some very fine homes and I thought it might be nice to repay some old kindnesses."

"And when these—what did you call them?— 'acquaintances' turn up? Then what?" Mrs. Jaymes was unconvinced of the harmlessness in hosting old piano people.

"We will show them some island hospitality! We'll give them a bed, and they'll swim, and sun themselves, and in the evening we'll have parties."

"Parties?! Good gracious!" It was worse than she had imagined!

"What's the matter with you? Who doesn't like a party? We'll get you in some extra help, if you need it. I'll pay you extra, too."

Mrs. Jaymes puffed her chest and put her hand to her temple and let out a long, significant sigh. Her worries had nothing to do with finger sandwiches or pineapple cake or with whatever extra cooking the presence of the guests would require. It wasn't even the guests or a party per se that had her hot and bothered. It was a funny feeling about *these* guests and *these* parties, and in all her years (Mrs. Jaymes was not yet forty then) her funny feelings had never failed her once.

"You've given me an idea, though," Captain Dagmore continued.

"An idea?" Mrs. Jaymes wrung her hands.

"What you said before about a concert. Maybe I *will* play for our guests. You're absolutely right, you know. They'll expect it."

"But you never play," she said.

She was right again. Not once since Dagmore arrived on Oh had he dared touch a key on the piano Captain Thomson had given him after his thirteenth birthday. The mere idea of it made him sad, as if to play a note were to lose his father all over again. Hundreds—thousands—of deaths on every page of every musical score. Dagmore couldn't bear it, and yet, as he watched Mrs. Jaymes and her wringing hands and considered the company he hoped to draw to Oh, the thought of his fingers on the soft, smooth ivory struck him as a comfort, not a punishment. The memory of a life gone by—and the music that had marked it—began to buzz in Dagmore's ears. His hands became fists, then opened, the fingers spread and taut. Dagmore looked at his palms, as if trying to place them, to remember how it was that he and they were acquainted. He looked up at Mrs. Jaymes, whose eyes awaited his in near horror, and he hurried to the room where the piano had stood silent for nearly a year.

"Captain, no! Are you sure?" she implored him, rushing behind and grabbing at the hem of his fine coat.

"Mrs. Jaymes! Please!" he scolded her and twisted free of her grip. "Get a hold of yourself!"

Captain Dagmore gently pulled out the bench and sat down. Slowly he lifted the lid that protected the keys. As he did, a gnat lazily swooned upward from C-sharp and Dagmore flicked at it with the back of his hand.

"Captain, I really don't think...," Mrs. Jaymes started, but before she could finish, the room was awash in a bath of notes— two, three, four at a time, flat and sharp and jumping and pinging and splashing against the walls and onto the floor.

"We're doomed!" she cried, raising her eyes and her hands heavenward.

The Captain, meanwhile, had grown more animated than she had ever seen him, and this only added to her discomfort. His head was bobbing up and down, his toes rising and falling on the pedals and his hands a fluttery blur that slid around the keyboard. Without skipping a beat he shouted to her, "We'll need to find a tuner," but she didn't know what to say to that.

When Dagmore finally had enough, or when the song was done, Mrs. Jaymes wasn't sure which, he got up and rubbed his hand lovingly across the flat, curved piano top.

"Not bad, eh, Mrs. Jaymes? A bit of practice every day and I'll be as good as I ever was." Dagmore looked the instrument over from stem to stern, as if he were noticing it there in his house for the very first time. "Now, shall we see about some breakfast? I need to get to the Post."

Mrs. Jaymes knew when she was defeated, nay, when she couldn't even compete. There would be no conquering this great noisy beast in the sitting room. The best she could do, for now, was to dust it every day and say her prayers.

She scrambled the Captain's eggs that morning, whisking them into a frenzy to match her own, and burnt his toast to a crisp, not from any ill will in his regard but from sheer discombobulation. After breakfast he left with his fine, fat envelopes, still wearing what Mrs. Jaymes now recognized could only be "piano clothes." He told her he would send his letters, then would bring back a man to get the piano tuned up. To Mrs. Jaymes's knowledge, no such man on Oh existed, and under any other circumstances, the prospect of his coming might have made her wary, even bothered. On this particular day, however, she didn't care if the Captain brought a stranger home. Mrs. Jaymes was too preoccupied with those dratted invitations that, as she sipped her solitary tea, had already begun their journey to heaven-knew-where and -whom. Compared to the mysterious hands for which they were destined, a piano tuner (albeit unknown) was indeed a paltry affair.

26

Lunchtime was nearing, and Raoul was growing impatient. Though the story of Captain Dagmore and his research touched Raoul's truth-seeking heart, and though he was intrigued by the Captain's piano-playing and curious to know what came of his invitations, Raoul's notebook was over half full, and he was not one clue closer to finding out how the Captain was connected to Rena Baker—or if he really was. He couldn't help but wonder if his time might not be better spent scouring the island with his magnifying glass.

"Mrs. Jaymes," he interrupted her, "this is all very interesting, and I can certainly see what a pleasure it is for you to remember your dearly departed friend, but perhaps I've learned all that I need to. I'm very grateful for your time."

"Learned all you need to?" she rebutted. "You haven't heard the half of it! You couldn't possibly understand."

"Understand what?"

"About Dagmore and his life on Oh. He *had* to live here, you see. Even though he never figured out how to get along with the island—he did try, believe you me—it still wouldn't let him go."

"I don't understand," Raoul admitted.

"You certainly don't!" Mrs. Jaymes chided him. "Dagmore tried everything, but he never quite...*fit* here, if you know what I'm saying."

As a matter of fact, Raoul did know. How many times had he asked himself why everyone around him was thinking *one* thing, while he was thinking something else? Why every islander but *he* swore by moonbeams and raindrops, while he declared loyalty to his library books and the principles of Stan Kalpi maths? (Stan Kalpi was the mathematician-musician hero of Raoul's favorite book. Mr. Stan let his observations guide him, and kept the variables of his equations neatly in line.)

Raoul turned his attention back to Mrs. Jaymes. "I don't see what pianos and party invitations have to do with fitting in."

"Why, nothing at all! That's what I'm trying to tell you. Those invitations were only the beginning of the trouble in that house. It had a mind of its own, that villa, sending the Captain messages that he refused to see or hear."

Houses sending messages? Imagine that! Raoul knew a thing or two about houses and messages. Maybe he could learn more from Captain Dagmore than he realized. He thumbed through the remainder of his notebook and glanced at the clock on Mrs. Jaymes's wall.

"Well," he conceded, "I suppose I could stay a few minutes more. I *would* like to know how those invitations turned out, I admit. You say the Captain went to town for a piano tuner?"

Raoul opened his notebook to a clean page and smoothed it on his lap, then prompted Mrs. Jaymes to go on.

"He came back with Hammer," Mrs. Jaymes said, pointing through the window at her husband. "He wasn't my husband back then."

Outside, Hammer had finished his gardening. He had deduced that his lunch would be delayed, and patiently he waited, swaying in a hammock, stretched between two royal palms.

———————

As Mrs. Jaymes suspected, Hammer Coates, the piano tuner Captain Dagmore found, turned out not to be a problem. He turned out not to be a piano tuner, either. He was simply the best the Captain could find in town, where all the islanders swore that no one on Oh had ever touched the insides of such an instrument. Famed for his general handiness—he could fix almost anything with some cardboard and a piece of string, they said—Hammer was hired, and Dagmore took him home.

At the Captain's house, Mrs. Jaymes greeted them cautiously, as she did almost everything now, sure as she was that disaster would strike at any time. From the safety of her kitchen, she listened to their muffled puzzlings over how to get the piano in tune, and when strange buzzes and plinks wafted into her sanctuary, she promptly set off for the sitting room with ice-cold lemonade. There she found Hammer bent over the piano's innards and the Captain bent over Hammer, humming loudly into his ear.

"Mrs. Jaymes!" Dagmore said excitedly, when he saw her come in. "Where there's a will, there's a way, Mrs. Jaymes." He smiled triumphantly.

"How so, now?"

"I hum the pitch, and Mr. Hammer here tightens up the pins. Or loosens them, as the case may be. We'll have her fine-tuned in a jiff!"

They took a short break and downed the cold drinks, then got back to work. The Captain sounded like an angry, monotone duck, and Hammer looked like a man possessed, fully intent on comprehending every word the duck had to say. "A fine pair!" Mrs. Jaymes said to herself, as she took the tray of empty glasses away.

It took the two men the better part of a day, but as the sun began to set, Hammer Coates packed up his tools and shook the Captain's hand. With his pocket full of Oh's rainbow bills, Hammer set off, and Dagmore sat down to his newly tuned piano. He practiced well into the evening, not stopping even for his dinner, a habit Mrs. Jaymes was beginning to get used to, though its implications continued to perturb. For an entire week Dagmore did little more than play the piano, in fact. The music that in England had reminded him of Oh, on Oh was sending him back, magically, into the company of his father. He could smell his father's whiskey and cigar, could hear him shuffling his feet in a nearby chair, listening as Dagmore played for hours. It seemed impossible to him that mere notes could conjure up such physical sensations, but that's exactly what they did. Alas, when Dagmore finished his piece, and turned to ask his father what he thought, to explain to him why he had altered the *andante* ever so slightly, his father was gone.

Dagmore played four, five, sometimes six hours a day. Anything to keep his father's spirit close by. The practicing paid off, for his skills and his memory were as sharp as they had ever been, his interpretations never more masterful. Even the wary Mrs. Jaymes found herself humming along to an especially lively passage one afternoon as she stewed her plums. Could her instincts have misled her? Was it possible that things weren't destined to be as bad as all that? She was rather enjoying the music that now filled her days, and couldn't quite work out how this piano might bring about the disaster she had been fearing. Dagmore was calmer, too, than he had been in a good long while. He would have spent the rest of his life at the keyboard, warmed by his father's nearby love, had those plum invitations he had sent to drizzly England not suddenly born some juicy island fruit.

It was a typically windy day on Oh, the day trouble first came knocking. Mrs. Jaymes had just come in from hanging the Captain's freshly laundered tops and bottoms to dry on the line, when she heard pounding at the door.

"Afternoon! Is someone there?" a voice shouted.

Mrs. Jaymes, who had grown complacent and forgotten her fearfulness, what with all that classical music clouding her head, threw the door open without thinking twice.

"Hello, can I help?" she asked cheerfully. As the words left her lips and her eyes fell on the official shirt of the man who stood before her, her jaw fell, too, the *allegro* in her head suddenly stamped-out. "Island Post" the pocket of the man's shirt said, and below the words, a small, embroidered pineapple of green and brown, it's bulbous body sporting a pair of wings.

Mrs. Jaymes had no time to react before the man had pushed into her hands a thick stack of cards and letters, mumbled something she didn't understand, tipped his hat and turned back down the road.

"Wait!" she called to him pitifully, but he didn't hear her, and she didn't know what she would have said to him if he had. With shaky hands she shuffled through the pile. The envelopes were beautiful, in spite of what must have been a long and arduous journey. The handwriting was curled and confident, romantic even. The paper, solid and strong. The stamps, in every color. Mrs. Jaymes retched and steadied herself against the frame of the door. "I knew it!" she hissed. Her knack for sniffing trouble was always on the nose.

For a moment she contemplated tossing the lot of it right into the sea, waxy seals and all, then reason prevailed. A known threat is far more easily dealt with than an unknown one, and something told her that the authors of those letters she held would not be kept at bay. (Right she was, as it turned out, for many were already at sea, half the way to Oh.)

"Captain!" she cried, bursting into the sitting room right in the middle of a delicate *decrescendo*. "Look at these!" She handed him the bundle as if it were proof positive of a crime just committed or a lie just told. "Now what are we to do?"

The Captain got up from the keyboard and gently folded the wooden cover over it. He took the envelopes from Mrs. Jaymes and sat on the divan to look them over. Without even opening them, he was moved to half-a-dozen shades of a smile, as he recognized their senders from the return addresses or the script.

"Oh, Mrs. Jaymes," he said, "let's hope it's good news!" He pulled them open one by one and read every line on every page of every letter. He chuckled, he marveled, sometimes he talked back to them, unable to contain himself. Mrs. Jaymes watched him, stunned into anticipatory silence and chanting Hail Marys in her head. When he had finished, he gently returned the last one to its envelope, which he reverently placed on top of the stack with the others.

"Well?!" she nearly yelled.

"They're coming! They've all said yes!"

"All who? When?"

"Not all at once, don't worry. Some of the letters are two months old. Others were sent just over a week ago." (It wasn't uncommon on Oh for mail to arrive in spurts.)

She looked at him with a blank expression that prompted greater specificity on his part.

"It looks like the first guests will arrive in about ten days. Just three of them. Professor Emmitt Abbelscott, with his wife and daughter. Then a large group a month after that: all the Shelbys, with the Fitches. Won't that be lovely!"

Mrs. Jaymes didn't know about Applescotts or Finches, but she did know about "lovely," and it hardly seemed the most suitable word for the awful news that she was hearing.

"'Lovely,' did you say, Captain?" she asked. "Are you sure about that?"

"Well, of course, I am. I'll tell them all about the island. I'll finally have people to discuss my research with, Mrs. Jaymes—people who can appreciate the island like no islander ever could."

Mrs. Jaymes took little consolation from this explanation of the Captain's, this metaphorical rubbing of salt in the wound, and for lack of a more fitting reply, she grumpily returned to the kitchen. The Captain didn't notice her departure. His guests' arrival dominated his every thought and sense. He could smell the feast they would share, could feel their admiring eyes upon him and his home, and hear their sighs of wonderment at the island's vistas. In his head he saw the scenes exactly, and he went to his study to jot down some ideas. He would show his guests a fine time indeed! he told himself, giggling like an excited child. Seated at his desk, he pulled out a sheet of paper, dipped his pen in ink and began to make some notes, never doubting for a moment that everything would go perfectly—melodically—according to his plan.

27

Arrest Made in Glutton Hill Murder
Plans for Trial Under Way

A warrant for arrest was executed late last night by Officers Arnold Tullsey and Joshua Smart at the Port-St. Luke home of fisherman Madison Fuller. Mr. Fuller is charged with the murder of his girlfriend, Ms. Rena Baker of Glutton Hill, who recently went missing, the likely victim of a hit-and-run perpetrated on the Thyme shortcut. The warrant was issued on the basis of evidence collected after a thorough search of the suspect's home earlier in the day, namely incriminating articles of clothing, a telltale fishing pole, kitchen items, a beach towel, and the very same picnic basket in which the victim is known to have delivered lunch to the accused every day. As many readers will recall, Mr. Fuller allegedly placed an anonymous ad in this newspaper soliciting a young woman to cook for him, which not only confirmed police suspicions of his involvement in the Rena Baker case, but also led investigators to speculate that Mr. Fuller was orchestrating what may well have proved the second in a string of murders. The Chief of Police, Lucas Davenport, has already set in motion the plans for Mr. Fuller's trial, which promises to be a legal spectacle, drawing a record number of observers from Port-St. Luke, Glutton Hill, and respective outlying areas. It has not yet been determined if the prosecution will be represented by the legal authorities of Oh, or if experts will be called in from the neighboring islands of Killig or Esterina. The date of the trial will be finalized once details such as this, and the matter of sufficient seating in the courtroom, have been ironed out. All efforts will be made to ensure that the trial does not interfere with the island's annual Rainbow Fair. For the record, Mr. Fuller adamantly maintains his innocence; his sister, Ms. May Fuller, maintains it even more adamantly than he. As this edition went to press, Mr. Fuller was not yet represented by legal counsel.

The day the news of Madison's arrest broke, Trevor's Bakery was packed morning to night. Every islander who could find the time stopped in to make a purchase, knowing full well that the bakery was—hands down—the best place to put his (or her) finger on the pulse of the island. There, every theory was tested, every opinion flaunted, and no one wanted to miss a word. Extra bread sales were a by-product of island tragedy, and Trevor always tallied his take at the end of such days with a bittersweetness in his heart.

The general consensus of the clientele was that Madison was innocent. His quiet life had conducted itself well under the radar for as long as anyone could remember and this murder business was surely just a blip, one that would fall away as suddenly as it had arisen. Cries rang out of police brutality and persecution of the common man, until some smart and cheeky feminine soul shouted, "What about the common woman?" This marked an abrupt shift in the discoursing crowd now forced to recall that a woman was dead. At least she seemed to be. The brutality wasn't at the hands of the police, then, but of man in general, who no longer knew how to respect a woman, and would sooner kill her and feed her to the fishes than treat her as he ought! "Now wait just a bloody minute," said an offended masculine voice. "How do you know Rena is dead? There's not even a body, and you're calling every man a murderer?" And the discourse shifted again.

Like a seesaw on a playground, the debate bounded from one side of the story to the other and back, the customers in the crowded bakery space mimicking the to-and-fro with bobs of their alternately convinced and convinced-again heads.

Amidst the public debate that ensued, a number of those present struggled with more private concerns about the case of Madison Fuller and what was coming to be known as the Bicycle Trial. Foremost in this group was Branson Bowles. Seeing May again the day before, when she had stomped onto his beach, had stirred in him feelings he had been denying for years. Poor May! He couldn't imagine how much she must be suffering. Her brother arrested! Branson was suffering, too, for he knew that May held him responsible for Madison's dilemma, and he wondered if he ought not come forth and claim the lonely hearts ad, whether he had written it or not. Would the police believe him if he did? Would it be enough to clear Madison's name and to win back May's respect and her affection? Was Branson's dignity worth her tender dasheen and her dainty touch?

While Branson, nervous and worried, shook his head from side to side, Trevor moved his up and down in an effort to see one wave of customers over the next. He was anxious to close his doors for the day and to reflect on the problem at hand, for which he felt somewhat responsible, since Madison had turned to him for help. Trevor never liked to disappoint, and disappoint he arguably had, if Madison was sitting somewhere behind bars. Trevor couldn't even point a finger at Bruce, whose report had merely brought to light the mess that the police were cooking up—a mess that at the end of the day couldn't really amount to much, could it? Madison was innocent. Of that, Trevor was absolutely sure, and so truth would prevail in the end.

Trevor tried to believe in these arguments he elaborated in his head, but nothing on Oh was so straightforward. All the more when Oh's authorities came into the picture, dancing their procedural dances to the islanders' drums. If the case went to trial, as it appeared it would, Trevor was not at all confident that the evidence misconstrued by the police wouldn't be misconstrued by the public, too. The island's justice wasn't always just.

As Trevor's thoughts thus meandered, his hands waved and grabbed and wrapped and saluted, serving up drinks and loaves and making conversation and correct change. His son Randolph assisted, carrying out hot trays of fresh goodies as the shelves were emptied and emptied again. Like his father, outwardly he managed to keep time with the talk and the orders, while inwardly his heart went out to his friend, poor Madison.

As poor Madison pondered his problems in the lonely jail, back at the bakery for the evening rush, Raoul Orlean pondered a few things, too. It seemed to him that this bicycle affair had gone a bit too far, even for Oh, and he wished that everyone would stop talking about it. They were making more and more of a mountain out of a molehill. Didn't they see that? There was likely no crime, so far no victim, and, near as Raoul could tell, not an evil bone in Madison's body. The case was barely a case at all, and Raoul doubted if even *Oh's* police force could make the charges stick.

The islanders, naturally, weren't helping. With their gossip and their speculation they were letting the matter swirl irresponsibly and irretrievably out-of-hand, and Raoul wanted nothing to do with it. He had no idea why someone had written Rena's name on the side of his house, but the more he heard it mentioned, the less interest he had in finding out.

Truth be told, he was more interested in why someone had painted Dagmore's name on his cottage, and although he had taken his leave of Mrs. Jaymes the day before without learning all that he could, he had promised her to return to hear the rest. The story of this Captain Dagmore was rivaling that of Raoul's favorite book, the one about mathematician Stan Kalpi. Like Dagmore, Stan Kalpi had abandoned his future to go home and look for his past. Raoul had never done that, not exactly, but he recognized the importance of one's roots above all else—roots were as hard and irrefutable as facts—and so he fancied himself, too, a Stan Kalpi of sorts (for that, and for his devotion to detail and his love of absolutes).

Rena Baker? He wouldn't waste his time! Raoul's flies were now aflutter with the story of Dagmore and his house. What messages did Dagmore's house send to him? Why didn't he see or hear? Were they words on walls, like in the case of Raoul? Perky pink on faded pastel? And what was the trouble that Dagmore's invitations invited? Raoul couldn't wait to visit Mrs. Jaymes again, to address these flies and more. Mostly, though, there was a great big horsefly he hoped to hush: how had a questing and bookish sea captain, with whom Raoul was beginning to feel a kinship, gone out of his tree, and ended up dead in the water?

———————

It was nearly midnight when the bakery quieted down. Most of the flood of customers had come and gone by ten, but the next two hours witnessed a steady flow of the men-about-town who, with nowhere else to party, dropped in at the bakery whenever Trevor stayed open late. Raoul had gone home when the tide of islanders ebbed, and Randolph left soon after. He was headed to the courthouse where Madison was jailed, hoping to finagle a visit despite the late hour. Branson, who remained at the bakery with Trevor, was a bundle of nerves. He could hardly stand still as the young men talked about trials and evidence and a fisherman maybe gone mad, but he resisted, so that he could speak with Trevor alone after the partiers departed.

Finally, the last one sensed that the conversation and his welcome were wearing thin, and he grudgingly said his "good nights." Such was Branson's relief as he watched the man walk out—palpable, practically—that it drove Trevor to ask him, "What's going on with you?"

"Aren't you worried about Madison?" Branson replied.

"You know I am! But you look like you just killed Rena yourself. What's the matter?"

Branson sighed. He hadn't yet gotten round to telling Trevor about May's visit and her accusations, but once he did, Trevor suddenly recalled, and made sense of, May's scene at the bakery the day before. He started to laugh.

"What's so funny?" Branson said, offended.

"What's so funny is that silly woman thinks you're *so* in love with her, you would put an ad in the *Morning Crier* to get her back."

Branson looked at Trevor sheepishly and didn't say a word.

"Don't tell me you did it! *You* placed the ad?" Trevor was incredulous.

"No, of course I didn't! You know me better than that. But she thinks I did."

"Who cares what she thinks?"

"I do." Branson explained that seeing May again had reminded him how much she once meant to him, that he had fooled himself into believing a stint off the island had erased his feelings. It simply wasn't true.

Trevor didn't like where Branson was headed. He remembered how much his friend had suffered at May's hands, and he still blamed her for Branson's eight-year absence from Oh. "Do you really want to jump back into that mess?" he asked him. "May didn't seem too keen on you yesterday, when she was standing here spitting fire."

"She hates me alright," Branson confirmed.

Trevor wasn't following and said so.

Branson sighed impatiently, failing to see how his dearest friend could fail to see the solution, obvious as it was.

"If I go to the police and say that I'm the one who placed the anonymous ad, then that would clear Madison's name, and May won't hate me anymore."

"Says who?" Trevor objected. "You don't know if she still has feelings for you—it didn't look to me like she did—and how can you be so sure, if she does, that this is all it will take to win her back?"

Branson was silent.

"Have you thought about *this*," Trevor went on. "Suppose you speak up and tell your lover's lie, embarrass yourself and maybe lose your job, and they still keep Madison in jail. They have a whole sack of evidence against him, you know, or so they think. Next thing, you'll be in jail right there with him and charged as his accomplice. Heed my words."

Well! Branson hadn't thought of that! It never occurred to him that a phony confession might backfire and that he could lose his job, or worse, land himself behind bars. That certainly wouldn't do. He looked at Trevor helplessly and Trevor looked back, like a parent who scolds a child while inside his heart is breaking.

"You know better than this, Bran," he said, and he rubbed the top of Branson's shoulder between his thumb and fingers. "When did a lie ever put things to right?"

28

Since most of Oh is tucked into thick and fertile greenery, the islanders call "country" everything more than a half-dozen kilometers
from Port-St. Luke, Oh's bustling capital. The farther beyond the out-
skirts of "town" you go, the deeper into the country you are considered to be, regardless of the fact that much of the so-called country
is speckled with towns of its own. Take, for example, a town on Oh's
northern tip (Port-St. Luke resides in the south): officially denoted
Chanterelle, you are as likely to hear it called Rainbow City, especially
in the run-up to (and in the wake of) Oh's annual Rainbow Fair.

The Fair was born of Chanterelle's fortunate latitude and lon-
gitude, which had positioned it on a hillside point from which
an inordinate number of rainbows could be spotted, though in
Chanterelle-proper little rain ever fell. The rainbows that were
seen there much of the year derived from downpours elsewhere,
and from the mist that Oh's wind skimmed off the sea and lifted
into Chanterelle's sunny view. The rainbows' numbers were greatest just as the island's dry season drew to a close, when random,
gentle rains began to foreshadow the storms to come, which is
more or less when the Fair took place every year.

Though purportedly in honor of the delicate and ephemeral rainbows visible from Rainbow Hill, the Fair itself was a rather raucous event. It started early in the morning, when the ladies of Chanterelle sold fried bakes, saltfish souse, and freshly prepared pineapple juice. When breakfast was done, the footballing started, with spectators swapping their juice for local beer or mixing it with local rum. Rough under the best of circumstances, island football spiked with booze was especially bad. Tempers flared and supporters shouted and words grew more colorful with every yellow card.

When the matches ended and the music began, there was more food and drink, more fish broth and mauby, and the already excited crowd got wilder still. The partying continued throughout the day and into the night, the height of the revelry (or the depths) witnessed as the moon climbed up the dark sky that had long since swallowed the town's famous rainbows. The islanders danced and jumped and caroused until morning, when they crept home exhausted and gratified, ooh-ing and ahh-ing at the renascent rainbows they had all but ignored the day before.

The event was as awaited as Carnival or Christmas. Most years, the islanders' anticipation was ignited by an early shower, or even a drizzle that augured the rains to come. Some years, it was spurred by an outright downpour, and Fair-goers geared themselves up for an equally frenzied fete. Every once in a while, though, when the moon was blue, the island announced the Chanterelle bash with a bang, with a storm that downed a bike on a muddy backroad and carried off the body of a fisherman's girl.

When something like *that* happened, every Rainbow reveler was dead sure the Fair would be a real humdinger.

29

For the second time in three days (it was Sunday, but Customs and Excise never closed, what with the ships and planes arriving every night and day), Raoul's morning consisted of the briefest of stops at his workplace and a lengthy visit to Mrs. Jaymes's house on Ladywood Road. The story of the colorful Captain Dagmore was, on its own, enough to lure Raoul from the grey of his office walls. The fact that every member of his staff on duty was now nattering on about Madison Fuller and the girl he had allegedly killed, only added to Raoul's agitation, and to his hurry to put headquarters behind him.

"Get back to work," he ordered them all as he left. "We're not in the business of scuttlebutt here!" (Or so Raoul thought. His employees knew better, for scuttlebutt occupied far more of their workday than either customs or excise ever did, especially on a weekend.)

When Raoul reached the residence of Mrs. Jaymes, he found her on the verandah with Hammer, sizing up the garden and discussing the arrangement of the flowers in their beds. Hammer, who was in spirit as resourceful and handy as ever, was far less so in body. So to busy his nimble spirit, he engaged in gentle, incessant gardening, planting and re-planting the flowers and shrubs.

"Good morning," they said to Raoul in unison, interrupting their debate.

"Back so soon!" Mrs. Jaymes exclaimed, unable to disguise her glee. "Are you here to investigate the Captain some more?"

"Yes," Raoul confirmed, "if I may."

"Come in, come in," Mrs. Jaymes urged him, getting up from her chair and leading him inside the house. "Hammer was just about to start in the garden. Weren't you, dear?"

Hammer tipped his hat in reply and Raoul flashed him a polite smile.

Once inside, Raoul and Mrs. Jaymes repeated the ritual of the time before. Tea (no, thank you), fluffed cushions, the smoothing of impatient notebook pages. Mrs. Jaymes asked Raoul where she had left off in her story and he told her, at the part where Dagmore's guests had said yes and were just ten days from Oh.

"The part," he added, "where everything was going exactly according to plan."

––––––––––

The sun was hot and curious on the day that Dagmore hummed his way to town to collect his first visitors, and it was as anxious as Mrs. Jaymes to see what the fuss was all about. Under the sun's glaring eye, the whole island had spruced itself up for the Abbelscotts' arrival. The trees were pert and green, the flowers full and rich, the blues of sea and sky impeccably coordinated. The temperature was high, but the winds just high enough to make the sticky heat tolerable. The trio of guests—Emmitt Abbelscott, his wife Anna, and their daughter Martine—had traveled to Oh by ship and were walking the plank that would lead them to Dagmore just as their host neared the harbor. Wishing to make a big splash, the Captain had forgone his piano clothes in favor of his finest seaman's attire, the very same white cap and brass-buttoned jacket he had worn when he himself disembarked on Oh, well over a year before.

"Welcome!" Dagmore greeted them, reaching the dock and extending his hand to give the professor's a shake. To Anna he bowed his head and smiled, then looking down at the girl who clung sleepily to her mother's side, he said, "You must be Martine. My, how grown-up you are!"

While the Abbelscotts' eyes adjusted to the island sun, Dagmore arranged for their belongings and for a vehicle to take them all home. As they drove up the steep and winding roads that carried them higher and higher above Port-St. Luke, the Abbelscotts admired the shrinking and picturesque capital and the crystalline water that stretched as far as they could see. So entranced were they by the scenery, that they spoke of little else, asking Dagmore a million questions, which he was both happy and proud to answer. When they finally reached the villa, Mrs. Jaymes silently served them pineapple juice over ice, on the verandah, from which they gazed in awe at the beach below.

"It's marvelous," Anna announced, and Dagmore sighed complacently. So far, everything was going as expected. Neither he nor the island had failed to impress.

They finished their drinks and a tour of the house, and while Anna and little Martine went to rest before dinner, Dagmore and Emmitt took a walk down the rocky path to the beach. Once utterly assured that the beach was Dagmore's and Dagmore's alone, Emmitt stripped down and waded in, leaving his shirt, socks, trousers, and under-things in a pile in the sand. Mrs. Jaymes, who was cooking dinner at the time, poised to spot any signs of trouble, caught sight of him from the kitchen window and, startled, dropped a plate. It smashed apart on the tile flooring, tiny pieces of it scattering every which way.

The first casualty of the Captain's cockamamie plan to host a houseful of strangers! she thought, and it gave her pleasure to sweep up the miniscule ceramic flecks, each one yet another sign that her fears were well-founded and her suspicions well-placed.

In the mornings, Dagmore took the Abbelscotts on island tours, dazzling them with the local flora and fauna, and with his knowledge of both. In the afternoons, after the lunch prepared by Mrs. Jaymes had been enthusiastically consumed, they lounged on Dagmore's beach and swam in his private bit of sea. In the evenings came more island delicacies, followed by cocktails and cigars in the sitting room. There, the guests were equally enthralled by Dagmore's piano-playing and by his lectures on Oh's every aspect, from its cocoa plantations and its honeycombs, to its plantains and its bush tea. When, with heavy heart, the Abbelscotts finally packed their cases and went home, promising to return again soon, Mrs. Jaymes surveyed the damage and was irked to find that it amounted only to the broken plate, and the extra bedsheets she had had to launder. Miffed that her instincts were still just that, she sat and shook her head.

Storms that took too long to brew were bitter cups to swallow.

———

Raoul crinkled his brow and looked at Mrs. Jaymes, visibly disappointed. "Then everything *did* go according to plan," he complained. "You said those invitations were trouble. That the house was sending messages. What about all that?" he cried, as if accusing her.

Mrs. Jaymes, forgetting her glee from remembering Dagmore, responded in kind. "Aren't you reading what you're writing down in that book of yours? You must be as single-minded as the Captain himself! A thunderstorm doesn't come out of nowhere," she declared.

"Doesn't it?" Though flattered, now, to be compared to the Captain Dagmore he had once met, Raoul was confused.

"Well, of course not!" she replied. "It collects itself. Gathers itself up. The sky calls out to the wind, and the wind musters the clouds, who plump themselves up until they blot out the sun. Then the lightning turns up and the thunder behind it. *That's* when the rain comes," she announced triumphantly. "You can't have a downpour until you line up a few clouds!"

Hmm. Raoul recalled the story of mathematician-musician Stan Kalpi. Mr. Stan had lined up his variables, but never any clouds. He *had* played music on his homemade not-quite-guitar-but-more-than-mandolin, which, Raoul reasoned, was not so very different from Dagmore and his piano. He decided to give the story another chance.

"Very well, Mrs. Jaymes. Carry on," he said, checking his watch and turning to yet another page in his nearly full notebook. "Line up your clouds."

Mrs. Jaymes barely had time to get things in order, to polish the silver and wax the floors, make up the beds and put up pineapple preserves, when next Captain Dagmore set off to town humming. She had only just liberated herself of the Abbelscotts, and already the Shelbys and Fitches were bearing down on her. She feared the villa would never be quiet again—and for a long time it wouldn't. Dagmore had grown so accustomed to the camaraderie of his English friends that he couldn't abide an empty house anymore, not even when, alone, he played the piano to summon his father from the beyond. The company of a spirit, while soothing, was not the kind of company with whom he could argue or smoke or take tea. His father's ghost never answered when Dagmore posed a question, never applauded when Dagmore played, not even after the most rigorous of *rinforzandos*. If filling the villa with living, breathing visitors meant Dagmore had to tolerate Mrs. Jaymes's complaints and admonitions, he found it a small price to pay.

As he had forewarned her when the letters first arrived, a large group indeed were the combined Shelbys and Fitches. The former were four sisters, aged twenty to twenty-five, accompanied by their twenty-six-year-old brother, who served as chaperone. The Fitches, in an unlikely pairing with the garrulous youths, were a somewhat crusty financier, his fussy wife, and his even fussier mother-in-law. Dagmore had cast a wide net with his invitations, and in hindsight the Fitches were not the most sparkling of his associates. Still, Phillip Fitch was an intelligent man and highly regarded in his field.

Because the Shelbys and Fitches shared so few interests (the ones wanted to see every corner of the island, while the others preferred to observe it from Dagmore's verandah), their presence posed a challenge for both the Captain and the cook. Dagmore was quite content to spend his days with the Shelby siblings, accompanying them on nature walks or to town on market day (where each bought a coconut-leaf hat with a coconut-leaf bird on a stick poking out of the top), but even a man as adept as *he* couldn't be in two places at once. Dagmore regretted leaving the Fitches to fend for themselves at the villa, though the arrangement didn't disturb the Fitches in the least. They took great comfort in Mrs. Jaymes, whom they turned to for hot meals, cold drinks, and more chats than she cared to count. Dagmore, upon returning in the evenings with the happy siblings, was forced to endure Mrs. Jaymes's rants before she would set so much as a salt-shaker on the table where the guests were to dine.

One day when the Fitches had Mrs. Jaymes's dander up good and thick, she almost quit the villa for good. They had pestered her morning and afternoon with silly questions—"Is it always so hot?" and "How fast does a pineapple grow?"—and when Mrs. Jaymes caught sight of the returning Shelbys, the protruding birds on their hats jerking and flitting above their heads like flustered green gulls in miniature, it was all the silliness she could take.

"Captain, I can't stay here a minute longer!" she blurted out. "It's too much. Too much!"

"Calm down, Mrs. Jaymes, what's happened? Is everyone alright?" For a minute he feared one or more of the Fitches had fallen into the sea.

"Oh, they're fine! *I'm* the one going mad listening to their nonsense! Do you know what they asked me today? 'How many times a year does it rain?' Like we have nothing better to do around here than sit and count the raindrops. And what about those Shelbys? Traipsing about the island every day like a bunch of children skipping school. Don't they have lives of their own? Don't they need to get home and do whatever it is they do?"

"They'll be leaving next week, Mrs. Jaymes, if it makes you feel any better. They're just visiting, taking a little holiday. Surely you've done that yourself."

Mrs. Jaymes watched him, appalled. She most certainly had done no such thing! "Where in the world would I be going off to, to do nothing but waste my time and someone else's?" she challenged him.

"They aren't wasting my time, Mrs. Jaymes. I want them here."

"Don't I know it! That's the problem."

"Mrs. Jaymes," he reasoned with her, "for two months now you've been preaching about some sort of trouble. But what has happened really? Has a single thing gone wrong? Everyone's having fun. What's the matter with that?"

She couldn't think of anything to say, her broken plate an admittedly brittle argument, and simply repeated the warning she had delivered so many times before.

"I'm telling you these people are trouble!"

Dagmore comforted her and convinced her she was wrong (or so she let him think), and Mrs. Jaymes agreed to stay—but only because in her heart she knew her predictions would prove correct, and she wanted to be there to see it when they did.

Still and all, apart from a cranky cook, the friends and colleagues that showed up on Dagmore's doorstep did him a world of good. Dagmore once again felt at home on his island, which he thoroughly enjoyed showing off, and he felt at home in his house, where he entertained his intimate audiences with his music and his island lore, both of which met with their applause. The house that Captain Dagmore Bowles had built soon became quite renowned in his former circles, and before long not a single English acquaintance had failed to turn up, unannounced even (poor Mrs. Jaymes!), for word had spread that Dagmore would turn away none.

The tales of his generosity and his wealth took on a life of their own. Those who had been fortunate enough to benefit from his hospitality told stories of a luxurious mansion perched high above its own sandy shore. They talked about the breathtaking views and the stars and moon that seemed to shine for the sake of the villa alone, and they talked about Oh. About Crater Lake, from which only Dagmore had ever emerged alive, and about the island's rainforest full of wild monkeys. They recalled dishes with potatoes in shapes and colors they had never seen and drinks made from fruits they had never tasted.

Whether for his magnanimity or for the exotic locale in which he had made his home, Dagmore, too, became the subject of speculation, the embodiment of mystique. Hailed as a sea captain, a scientist, a virtuoso, and a wealthy eccentric, some began to wonder if Dagmore and his house were real. Suddenly he found himself in great demand, as important figures from the corners of Europe came to verify his very existence. Within a few short years, his house boasted the most prestigious of houseguests, from princes and painters to writers and entrepreneurs. His sitting room rang with the arias of opera divas and his divans cushioned the bottoms of top-level leaders.

As the caliber of Dagmore's acquaintances grew, his interactions with them gradually shifted. The crowd that now came to call wasn't interested in lizards or almond trees (and wouldn't be caught dead in hats with protruding coconut-leaf birds). It was more likely to debate the merits of the latest novel or coup d'état than to discuss the differences between island limes and lemons. This didn't bother Dagmore. He could hold his own with the best of them. What mattered most was that he wasn't alone, that he had peers with whom he could joke and discuss. If at the end of the evening they begged him to tickle an ivory or two, well, that just sweetened the fish pot.

In short, the Captain was becoming a snob and Mrs. Jaymes didn't like it one bit. He lived on the island without *living* on the island. All he ever wore were piano clothes; he had even hired a local tailor to sew him some new ones "with more fashionable lines" (the tailor's first attempt had produced an unfortunate jacket of striped green and blue). He never walked to town to play dominoes anymore, rarely took a swim, and took his guests on only the most perfunctory of island tours. The guests themselves were even worse. They treated Mrs. Jaymes like a common servant, rarely uttering a word that wasn't a request (or an order) and their "pleases" and "thank yous" were as perfunctory as their sight-seeing. Mrs. Jaymes was almost nostalgic for the inquiring Fitches.

Over five years had passed since then and, despite the fact that tragedy had yet to disrupt the Captain's plans or to waylay a single visit, Mrs. Jaymes never ignored the intuitive twitches that told her it was coming any day. The passage of time hadn't dulled her instincts; it had sharpened them. Her initial fears, she realized, had been misplaced. The visitors were not to be the cause of the problem—not exactly. Although with their talk of taxation and Timbuktu they had inched the Captain's thoughts from sunny picnics and lucky stars, the desertion was his alone, and jealous Oh would exact a mile of revenge. Mrs. Jaymes's only worries now, where the houseguests were concerned, was what misfortune would befall them when it did.

30

After leaving the house of Mrs. Jaymes (where, along with Hammer, he was treated to one of her scrumptious Sunday lunches), Raoul returned to work. He accomplished little, for his mind raced with thoughts of Captain Dagmore and the misfortune the island was about to unleash on him and his visitors. Though Raoul was normally intolerant of tales about island mischief, the story of Dagmore Bowles exerted an almost hypnotic effect on him. Whether this was attributable to Mrs. Jaymes's telling of it, or to the fact that the dead man's name had turned up on his house, he couldn't say. So enthralled was he with Dagmore, in fact, that the buzz about Madison Fuller and his upcoming murder trial flew right through Raoul's head without stopping. Let the islanders deal with islander nonsense! Raoul was too old to be bothered. He had his job and his wife and his house still to paint, and his private Dagmore mystery to solve. He decided Ms. Lila had gotten it wrong: it was *a* baker that the graffiti had told him to find, not Rena, and it had done so as a prank and nothing more.

He really should have known better. On Oh it's not as easy as that! Such simple solutions were rare, especially for Raoul, who, without knowing, was lining up a few clouds of his own. His wife, for one. She was none too pleased with the state of her cottage. She could almost live with its untouched front, faded and yellow, yes, but no worse than it had looked for months. The other sides, though, were an incongruous combination of colors and letters. The first, on the left, was covered in a first coat of pink; the second, in back, boasted a rosy blob that covered the mysterious BAKER; and the third, on the right, said DAGMORE in pink on yellow. When Raoul got home from the office, Ms. Lila gave him a piece of her mind.

Before he could cross the threshold and say "good evening, dear," she had pushed him back outside for a tour of the house. She started with the wall that said DAGMORE and worked her way round, complaining as she went. Raoul's day-off Tuesday was coming and she expected him to make some much-delayed headway.

"The day after tomorrow? Do you hear?" she insisted.

"I had planned on spending my day off with Mrs. Jaymes," Raoul objected. "She still hasn't told me anything to explain why Dagmore's name was so important that someone should paint it on our wall."

"I couldn't care one ripe fig about Dagmore, and neither should you!" she shouted. You don't care about Rena Baker anymore. *Her* name showed up on the side of the house, too. You're not bothered by a missing girl, but you're bothered by a ghost? Since when do *you*, Raoul Orlean, even entertain the notion of a ghost? 'Ghosts are no different than magic.' I've heard you say it a thousand times!"

Raoul tried to interject some sort of explanation, but Ms. Lila was on a roll. He wanted to tell her that this Rena had probably just run off, that there was no evidence whatsoever that a crime had been committed. His research on Dagmore, well, that wasn't ghostly.

That was philosophical curiosity, along the lines of Mr. Stan, and she, as a librarian and a woman of books, ought to understand as much! Had she stopped yelling at him for even a moment he would have told her so, but the best he could do right then was try to keep up with her as she stomped along the perimeter of the cottage. Past Dagmore, past the pink blob, carping all the way.

As Ms. Lila rounded the corner of the only wall that had an even coat of paint, she looked at it and stopped dead in her tracks. Raoul, who had been following close behind, ran right into her and knocked her down. The two of them lay on the grass looking up at the once pink wall that now appeared splotchy and faded, dotted with small and angry white-ish ghosts.

"What did you do here?" Raoul asked her.

"Me?! Not a thing! I looked at this wall a few minutes ago and it was solid Playful Rose, just like you left it."

"What the devil?" Raoul said, trying to decipher the splotches. He stood up and distanced himself, and, oh, dear. Not again. The angry splotches that marred the pink wall clearly told him to FIND R. BAKER. Raoul sat back down on the grass and emitted a long, sorry sigh. He should have known better, indeed. He had turned his back on a mystery—Stan Kalpi would have been vexed—and now the mystery had come back with a vengeance. Raoul could sense the rage in the dull, eerie letters where the pink paint had been removed.

"Are you sure you didn't hear anything?" he asked his wife. "Is it possible someone sneaked inside for some paint thinner?"

"Well of course it isn't! I'm not daft! I should know if someone came into my own house, shouldn't I? It's not as huge as all that—though you'd never know it to judge by how slowly you're getting it painted."

Suddenly, Raoul jumped up. Perhaps the person who had removed his pink paint was still hiding in the bush. Raoul crept stealthily (as stealthily as he still could, at his age) around the house again and into the woods that bordered his yard.

"Well?" Ms. Lila asked when he turned up a few minutes later.

Raoul shrugged. Nothing. No footprint, no clue, no sign that any human had passed within feet of the cottage. The wind picked up just then and he got a spooky chill. Ms. Lila felt it, too, and her eyes met his. Raoul might not entertain the notion of a ghost, but Ms. Lila was not so discerning.

"One thing's for sure," she said, her arms folded to keep herself warm. "We won't have a moment's peace around here—or a properly painted home—until you find out what happened to that girl." She looked up at the air around her, to determine if some specter or spirit were looming, but there was none that she could see. "I'm going inside."

Raoul stayed out on the grass, alone in the dusk, taking stock of the week he had had. A girl was missing, a man was in jail, and Raoul's house had been marked up three times. Twice with the name of the missing girl, and once with that of a dead man. A dead man with a story that Mrs. Jaymes was taking a terribly long time to tell. Raoul stilled his mind and let the flies in his head flutter freely. There was one whose hum out-hummed the others,' and that one told him that the mysteries of Rena Baker and Dagmore Bowles were intertwined. Raoul didn't believe in ghosts, but he believed his eyes and his ears. The humming hunch in his head was not to be ignored, nor was the fact that both Rena's name and Dagmore's had appeared plain as day on his walls. Very well then, he told himself. He would take up his Rena Baker business again, but he would not forgo Captain Bowles. He would see

Mrs. Jaymes the very next day. Then, on his day off, the day after, he would do some old-fashioned snooping for plain-as-noses-on-faces clues.

Pleased with his plan of action, Raoul joined Ms. Lila inside, had his dinner, and went to bed. He dreamed about storm clouds and notebooks that filled themselves up with writhing, wriggling letters that started out pink and turned blood red. When he woke up, his head hurt. He skipped his breakfast and rushed to head-quarters, where he made his now routine excuses and headed to Ladywood Road. He accepted Mrs. Jaymes's tea today, for his empty stomach was grumpy and grumbling.

Opening a fresh notebook that he had brought with him from work, he readied himself to listen to her tale.

"Now, then, Mrs. Jaymes," he pleaded. "Let's get straight to the 'downpour' part, shall we? *Please*."

The trouble at Captain Dagmore's house began with a handful of birds.

The guests at the time were a violist from Spain, named Juan, who spoke little English; his translator, Daphne, a famed linguist with whom he had fallen madly in love; a pair of geologists, named Peters and Stewart, back from gathering rocks in Africa; and an Irish doctor versed in liver disease, whose nickname was Ruck. The afternoon they arrived, the weather was sunny, as it always was on Oh when it wasn't raining, and Mrs. Jaymes's pots were astir with swordfish, dumplings, callaloo, carrots, and coconut milk.

While the dinner cooked, she served local beer on the veran-dah, where Dagmore and his company waited to admire the sun that was about to set. The conversation progressed somewhat bumpily, despite the illustrious minds and talents present, owing to Juan's lack of vocabulary (Daphne was too tired from the trip to translate) and the doctor's accent, which posed a bigger problem with each beer that he downed. The geologists were distracted by Dagmore's mountain perch and his rocky path, and leaned dangerously to get a better look at both, speculating between themselves as to the composition and age of each.

It didn't worry Dagmore much that the guests weren't immediately hitting it off. He had entertained enough to know that a houseful of strangers was like one of Mrs. Jaymes's stews. It would take some time for each component to soften and relax and mix with the others; but once they did, what a rich and nuanced treat everyone was in for! In the meantime, they would enjoy the sunset, then sit down to eat, and if after that they were so inclined, Dagmore would play his piano an hour or two before sending them off to bed.

The island cooperated nicely, unveiling for the newly arrived a spectacular sunset in bloody red, brassy orange-yellow, and, as the sun dropped out of sight, a flash of vibrant bluish green that amazed and startled even the tired translator.

"What was that?" she asked, and all five looked to Dagmore in alarm.

Dagmore was thrilled. He told them not to worry, that green flashes were rare but not unheard of at sundown, not on islands in general, and especially not on Oh, where—as they could see for themselves—rainbows staggered across the sky even in the near-dark, and without a drop of rain required. He beamed, prouder of his island than he could remember in a long time, and felt certain that the flash boded well for the group's sojourn. Dagmore was excited to see what the week would bring, and he made a toast in honor of the five travelers who had come so far to see him.

In her kitchen, Mrs. Jaymes was excited, too. Through the window she had witnessed the flash and, like Dagmore, didn't doubt its significance on this very evening, with its visiting violinist and geometrists. Unlike Dagmore, who raised a glass in celebration, the abstemious Mrs. Jaymes downed one for courage. Her twitching instincts told her that the nay-saying Captain would soon be put in his place.

When her pots were done stewing, she announced that dinner was served, and Captain Dagmore and company took their places at the table. The meal was enjoyed but uneventful, as was Dagmore's concert (Beethoven, Sonata n. 14) and the dessert (carrot cake with nutmeg ice cream) served in the sitting room. Finally, after midnight, the guests were shown to their rooms, amidst a chorus of "good nights" and "*buenas nocheses.*" Their bellies were full, their eyelids heavy, and the night lay promisingly ahead.

Mrs. Jaymes saw to their last wishes (towels, extra pillows, glasses of water), then set off to bed herself. She had taken up residency at the Captain's house some year or two before, unable to keep up with the comings and goings of his visitors if she came and went herself every day. Besides which, she couldn't be sure that whatever malicious wind was headed for the villa wouldn't blow through it in the middle of the night.

She said her prayers and rolled her hair in curlers, wrapped her head in a scarf, and fell asleep almost instantly. A few doors down in either direction, her houseguests were not so lucky. Though each had fallen wearily into bed, once there, they were suddenly wide awake. Whether the ill effect of the tropical clime or of the sugary nutmeg ice cream, they tossed and turned, unable to shut an eye. They felt every bump in their unfamiliar mattresses, heard the strange, unsettled rustling of the island's nocturnal animals, grew anxious and hot, and sweated in their sheets. The strangers to Oh would have welcomed even an ill wind on that night, so long as it kissed and cooled their clammy skin.

While Dagmore and Mrs. Jaymes snored unencumbered by heat or nutmeg, the tucks and grooves of their respective mattresses suitably snug, Juan and Daphne bickered *en español*, Peters and Stewart knocked and pinged on the common wall between their rooms to calculate its thickness, and Ruck tapped Irish folk songs with his fingers on his chest. It took over two hours before they were bickered-, knocked-, tapped- and tuckered-out, and went to sleep.

Then—oh!—just two hours more before they were—again!—wide awake.

The sun had decided that its climb required music on that particular morn and so it had enlisted more than a few of Oh's finest chirpers. Well before dawn they took to their task with gusto, their little chests plump and proud, their beaks pointed heavenward. Because Dagmore's house was the highest around, they situated themselves on its windowsills and sang their feathered hearts out. Any other time of day, the birds would have been quite a treat, for their music was masterful. It had melody, harmony, duets and quartets, choruses, verses, and rounds in every key. At scarcely five o'clock in the morning, however, as they lined up on the sills of the open windows and tweeted *en masse* their first notes in the pre-dawn dark, "treat" was not the word that burst from the sleepy, uncensored lips of the Captain's guests, who fell out of their beds, alarmed.

"¡Dios mío!" cried Juan, and Daphne promptly translated, embellishing with extra decibels.

"Bloody hell!" exclaimed first Peters then Stewart.

"What in the world...?" Ruck began, twisting all about himself to see why he was no longer in his bed.

At the commotion in the rooms, the birds became confused. Was their audience the rising sun or these writhing bodies that seemed to join in their dewy song? They sat on their sills and twisted their heads inside the house and out. Not knowing where to aim their tunes, they compensated with ever-increasing volume. The five visitors moaned and complained and covered their heads with their pillows, struggling to reclaim the sleep they had fought so hard for a mere two hours earlier. They were still spent from their journey and loopy from what little sleep they had managed. They needed to rest!

The birds didn't care that they were troubling some of the greatest minds of the Captain's day; on the contrary, they took the moans and the complaints that came from the house as some odd form of human participation and, spurred on, sang even louder. Soon, their numbers had doubled and doubled again, as had their volume, while the sun rose higher and hotter in the sky. The triple assault on the restless guests—light, heat, noise—was too vicious to ignore. They got up, drowsy and sweaty and anxious, and began to fight back.

They coaxed and shooed the birds, joining forces first in one room then the next, clearing each sill only for as long as the five of them shook their pillows at it. As soon as they moved on to the next sill, the birds came back, excited by the human play they inspired. The houseguests ran from window to window, room to room, waving their pillows and cases above their heads, swinging them in front of their chests. They cursed and commiserated in louder and louder voices, so as to hear each other above the birded din.

When Captain Dagmore finally awoke and pounded on Mrs. Jaymes's bedroom door (she had heard the skirmishing, but had pulled the sheets up to her nose and stayed in her bed), quite a callithump was under way, the birdsong mingled with the cuss and howl of the sleep-deprived quintet that ran higgledy-piggledy and brandishing linens about the villa's upper floor.

"Mrs. Jaymes, please!" the Captain cried out.

In her room, Mrs. Jaymes crossed herself, slipped out of bed and into her slippers, then padded over to the door. She opened it only enough to poke her wrapped and curlered head into the corridor.

"Mrs. Jaymes, thank heavens!" the Captain said when he saw her. "You have to do something!"

"What do you want *me* to do? You're the scientist. You sort it out!" She locked herself in her room and began to sing Ave Maria, which only contributed to the noise.

"Capitán, ¿qué está pasando?" Juan shouted, when he saw Dagmore appear in the hall. Juan held his pillow in one hand and his violin in the other, as if he might have to escape at any time and couldn't bear to leave his instrument behind.

"Captain, what's happening?" Daphne parroted in English and in near hysteria. In *her* free hand, she held her favorite feathered handbag, into which she had stuffed what clothes and *bijouterie* it would accommodate.

"Bowles, what the hell's got into these infernal birds?" (It was Peters or Stewart. In the fuss, Dagmore had forgotten which was which.)

Ruck said something, too, but Dagmore couldn't make it out. One of them had just flung a pillow too forcefully, busting it, and fluffy feathery stuffing flew at their eyes and into their mouths. They swatted at the air and at their tongues, now adding to the ruckus of the island's birds and the cook's Ave Marias the sounds of five sleepy people spitting mad and coughing feathers.

It took until high noon, when the sun had climbed as far as it planned to go, for the birds to abandon their singing and disappear as mysteriously as they had come. By that time, Juan, Daphne, Peters, Stewart, and Ruck were good and roused, somewhat sloppily dressed, and slumped over the dining table, awaiting Mrs. Jaymes's somewhat sloppily prepared lunch. When the Captain had finally coaxed her from her room, all the birds having flown away, to her was left the task of setting things aright—sweeping up feathers, remaking beds, and scrubbing window sills of the muck the excited birds had left behind—while the Captain calmed down his guests. They were weak from hunger and the heat and lack of sleep, and gobbled down in ravenous silence the fried fish (a bit too crisp) and chips (a bit too limp) that Mrs. Jaymes harriedly slammed before them long after one o'clock. Normally, Mrs. Jaymes put a pinch of love in the dishes she cooked, even those meant for the Captain's troublesome table, but the morning's mayhem and the birds' droppings had put her right off her pots.

With their hunger satisfied, the guests were feeling a bit more cheerful, and though they were too tired to smarten themselves up and take an island tour, an afternoon on Dagmore's beach appealed to one and all. They collected cold drinks and clean towels, books and reading glasses, goggles and fins, and with the Captain in the lead, off they paraded to his private stretch of Oh's coast. There they laid out their beach towels and the accessories that each had brought, and they surveyed the scenery of which they were part.

"Capitán, es maravilloso," Juan said, almost in a whisper, so moved was he by the blue of the water, sandwiched between that of the sky and the soft white of the sand.

There was no need for Daphne to translate. The emotions that the island's beauty had evoked in the violinist were felt by all of them, Dagmore included. For the first time in hours, he began to relax, and to forget about Mrs. Jaymes, who had been wagging her finger at him in warning ever since lunch. They all relaxed, in fact. They swam, and chatted, and began to get along more easily, just as Dagmore had planned and expected. Finally they stretched out in the sand and, exhausted, went right to sleep. It was half past three or thereabouts, and the tropical sun was still high in the sky.

Dagmore was used to daily naps in the sand, and, besides that, he was an islander from birth. His dark brown skin paid little mind to the sun that danced on it day in and day out. The visitors he had entertained over the years were not so lucky. They were mostly white, and usually pale, and had to take precautions. Still, Oh's sun had posed few problems, as Dagmore's acquaintances, especially of late, were more likely to spend their afternoons sipping iced tea in floppy hats than sweating on the shore.

The unlucky five that lay resting on the Captain's beach were the rule's exception. So tired were they from the dawn's tribulations that they slept long and deep in the sun's rays. Only when the sun began to dip toward the horizon, and the air slightly cooled, did they awake with a gentle shiver. Their first impression was collectively a good one: they opened their eyes and began to come to their senses, felt refreshed and rejuvenated from their nap. As smiles of pleasure tried to cross their faces, though, they realized in a flash that something was horribly wrong. Their faces were stiff, and smiling was a painful chore. They sat up to stretch, to figure out what was going on, but moving their arms and legs was painful, too. With cautious, puzzled hands they examined their afflicted limbs. Panicked, then, and fully awake, they discovered that their skin was hot, hot, hot.

To the reliable and unfortunate Mrs. Jaymes again fell the task of sorting things out. Over a nice cup of tea, she had finally collected herself and put the miserable day at the villa behind her. Now her pots had begun to boil and hiss with the dinner she was preparing, and the evening presented itself calmly enough. But as her adept hands opened and cleaned the fish destined for the Captain's skillet, she heard nearing the villa a hubbub not indigenous to Oh.

Mrs. Jaymes sighed, and crossed herself. With a sense of dread, she went out to meet the clamor halfway, hoping to keep any messes from coming inside.

"Mrs. Jaymes, thank goodness!" the Captain cried. "They've all burned up!"

Behind him, Mrs. Jaymes saw the whining and moaning quintet struggling to walk, the books and towels and bags they had so neatly packed for the beach now clutched haphazardly or dragging on the ground behind them. They were all talking at once, all griping, and the closer they got to the house, the more easily verified was the Captain's claim. Their five white houseguests were now undeniably red.

"Don't just stand there," she told the Captain. "Go and find some aloe."

Aloe. Of course! He had pages of notes about aloe plants.

Mrs. Jaymes took the guests inside, had them bathe in cold water and put them to bed. She brought them cool cloths and bowls with water and ice. When the Captain arrived with the fat and spiky aloe leaves, she cracked them open and applied the gooey insides to the visitors' taut, burned skin. After that, she turned her attention to Dagmore, who, in his rush to bring the aloe home, had scratched himself with the leaves' sharp points. Like gruesome breadcrumbs, tiny droplets of blood marked his nervous peregrinations through the villa. Mrs. Jaymes patched him up and wiped up his trail, then got back to the fish in the kitchen.

It was late when dinner was finally served, and Mrs. Jaymes, for the evening's distractions, had overcooked the fish again. After slow and labored treks from their various bedrooms, the guests arrived at the table in various states of undress and disarray, both modesty and vanity at odds with their efforts to tolerate the painful sunburns. Through the open doors that led to the verandah, a cool breeze wafted in only periodically, while the mosquitoes poured in in droves. To keep them away, the Captain kept most of the lights turned off.

Thus on the second night of their stay, Juan, Daphne, Peters, Stewart, and Ruck, in the faint light of strategically positioned and mostly ineffective mosquito coils, tried to eat now cold, over-cooked fish, their arms and fingers almost too burned to bend. The meal was interrupted by yelps of pain and by mosquito-triggered slaps of skin on skin (which in turn triggered yet more painful yelps). When they were finished eating, the guests remained at the table, knackered, but wary of the heat in their bedrooms, where Mrs. Jaymes had locked shut the windows to ward off a repeat of the morning's bad luck. Eyes closed, their heads resting on sweaty palms, they yawned in the semi-darkness and fanned themselves with floppy cotton napkins.

"¡Ay de mí!" breathed Juan, but Daphne didn't bother to translate.

Things were not going gaily at the Captain's house.

Just how bad things would get at the Captain's house, Raoul wouldn't find out that day. He had had his fill of Mrs. Jaymes. Surely she was belaboring the point because it gave her such pleasure to reminisce. By the time he bid her farewell and took his leave, Raoul's head was hurting again. His instincts still told him that Dagmore Bowles figured somehow in the Rena Baker affair; but his practical side said enough was enough. Stan Kalpi wouldn't waste time on worthless variables and neither would he. Especially not when his equations were in such urgent need of solving. Though Mr. Stan, in seeking his path, was known to heed the songs and scents on the breeze, to Raoul's knowledge, he had never heeded, or needed, a ghost's story to finish his own.

31

Raoul returned to his office just before lunch, determined to delve into the matter of Rena Baker as soon as he had had a bite to eat. As if to scold him for his procrastination, however, for his morning of Mrs. Jaymes's tall tales when murderers and missing girls awaited, the island hurled him headlong into the bicycle business before he could so much as unwrap his tuna.

Madison Fuller's murder trial was the first ever on Oh, and Police Chief Lucas Davenport had his hands full planning the ordeal. Interest in the case had flooded the island, and its citizens spoke of little else. Because so many islanders planned to attend the trial, it had been determined that the best place to conduct it was outside. Laborers had been hired to build benches and to construct a dais. Chief Davenport found himself under pressure to pull off what was becoming a national event without a hitch, and he simply couldn't do it alone. How was he meant to fight crime if he had to get in speakers and microphones and prosecutors from other islands? There were press passes to organize (for Bruce) and security and crowd control. Public toilets, water to drink, tarpaulins if it should rain. He was the people's protector, not a damned party planner!

"Miss Simms," he shouted to his secretary in the next room. "Get the Prime Minister on the phone!"

Miss Simms did as she was told, setting off a string of official, confidential, parliamentary calls that masterfully passed the buck from Chief Davenport to the PM, to the Minister of Culture and Tourism, the Minister of Justice, and back to the Chief of Police, who in a desperate flash of buck-passing brilliance landed it definitively with the Office of Customs and Excise. If microphones, speakers, toilets and tarps were to be got in, then Customs clearance was required. Wouldn't it make good sense, he convinced the Prime Minister, to centralize the planning? If every government branch had a hand in the affair, how would the left one know what the right one was doing? By the time the Head of the Office of Customs and Excise (poor Raoul!) found the buck on his desk, it was a signed, sealed, and delivered Prime Ministerial decree.

"Damn it to hell!" Raoul swore. How was he meant to look for Rena Baker if he first had to round up tarps and toilets for an *al fresco* fiasco? The assignment had Raoul cursing with unusual oomph. The combined force, however, of the PM's decree and Raoul's professional integrity precluded his declining the job. In fact, he wasted no time getting started. He picked up the phone and made an appointment with the Chief of Police to discuss what articles were needed, and how many of each. An hour later he was seated in front of Lucas Davenport's desk, pad and pencil anxiously in hand.

"So, what are we looking at here?" Raoul asked the Chief. "Chairs? Tents? What kind of crowd are we expecting?"

"We already have workmen building benches and a dais, so you don't have to worry about chairs. Tarpaulins or tents, that's up to you. We need to keep the spectators hydrated and dry. We also need a public address system, portable toilets, and a prosecutor."

"A prosecutor. Sure." Raoul scribbled something on his pad. "You need me to sort out a visa for him?"

"No. I need you to sort out a prosecutor. I hear Monday Jones from Killig is good. He's never lost a case."

"What are you saying? I'm with Customs. Prosecution is *your* business."

"My hands are tied, Raoul. PM's orders. He doesn't want too many cooks spoiling the broth, so you're in charge of the whole stove, the kitchen, and the kitchen sink."

Raoul raised his voice. "What do I know about prosecutors?" It was bad enough he had been saddled with the logistics of this dog and pony show. Now they expected him to round up the dogs and ponies, too?

"Sorry, man. Who are we to question the authority of the powers that be?" the Police Chief replied, tilting his head upward. Raoul followed the Chief's gaze, half expecting to see the Prime Minister's photo stuck to the ceiling with Sellotape.

Though Raoul didn't have all the information he needed, he got up and stormed out of the office. He supposed that Lucas Davenport wasn't to blame for the way the duties had been meted out, but he found it galling that Customs and Excise should be called on to do the work of the Police. He hoped at least to manage it without speaking to the Chief in person again, and to that end, Raoul headed to the office of the *Morning Crier*. He figured Bruce, who knew all about the Bicycle Trial, could get him up to speed.

———

"The way I see it, your problem is the crowd. They'll turn the trial into a real bashment," Bruce predicted.

"Bashment, eh?" Raoul repeated.

"Barbecued-chicken stands, fresh sorrel, rum on the sly, and DJs ready to blast their racket the minute the gavel goes down for the day," Bruce elaborated. "How'd you get involved in all this anyway?"

"Hell if I know," Raoul told him. "They want to centralize the planning, and it looks like I'm the eye of the storm."

"Customs and Excise? How do they figure?"

"The prosecutor's coming from abroad, so is the public address system and the toilets and tarps. Since Customs has to be involved, they decided I should do it all."

"You up on the facts of the case?"

"Only what I read in the paper. In my official capacity, I'm more concerned with the crowd than with the criminals on the dais. I won't tolerate tomfoolery at a formal government hearing."

Bruce shrugged his shoulders. "You may not have a choice, Raoul," he said with foreboding, and repeated it for effect. "You may not have a choice."

Bruce suggested that Raoul accompany him to the bakery, where from Trevor and whatever customers were around, Raoul might get a feel for how excited the islanders were about the trial. Raoul agreed, not least of all because, in his personal capacity, he was still as determined as ever to delve into the matter of Rena Baker. As Raoul and Bruce walked, they discussed the weather, not for small talk, but because weather was a real concern of Raoul's in light of the outdoor trial he had to coordinate.

Typically on Oh, the harder the first rain fell, the longer the wait until the rainy season started. Since the storm that led to the discovery of the bike had been such a doozy, Raoul figured he had a good month to get the trial wrapped up before it began to rain every single day. (And a month to get his house painted, a niggling gnat reminded him.)

"Well, close to a month, anyway," Bruce told him. "The Fair's coming. You need to finish up by then."

"True. True," Raoul agreed. "How long does this sort of trial usually take?"

"Hard to say. We've never had one here before."

"Mm," Raoul answered, too preoccupied with the clouds to banter further with Bruce. He kept his eyes on the sky as he walked, searching for some sign of what the island had in store for them, and when.

———

The bakery, it turned out, was not as busy as Bruce had hoped. Trevor and Randolph had gone to the courthouse jail to talk to Madison about a lawyer. Patience, Trevor's wife, was manning the shop, something the Bicycle Trial was forcing her to do more and more often of late. The presence of Patience, who only shared gossip in private, dissuaded customers from lingering, so when Raoul and Bruce arrived, they found her there alone.

"Can I help?" Patience asked, as the two men reached the counter. She assumed they had come for bread.

"No Trevor, eh?" Bruce said, in what was both a question and an observation.

"He went out. What do you need?"

"Raoul here is setting things up for the Bicycle Trial and I thought Trevor might give him an idea of what people are thinking, is all."

Patience, who up to then had treated the men dismissively, suddenly became animated. Her husband had taken the trial to heart, and she didn't like his getting mixed up in (even alleged) murder.

"So you're the one! Sending an innocent man to jail!" she accused Raoul. "And without a stitch of evidence, too!"

"I...uh...I...," Raoul offered, a little stunned by Patience's attack.

"Calm yourself," Bruce intervened. "He's not Police. He's just Central Planning."

"Planning of an innocent man's demise, maybe! You have Trevor at his wits' end. Randolph, too. How any of you can have a hand in it, I don't know."

"What makes you so sure the man is innocent?" asked Bruce, indignant.

"Madison's not a criminal! There's not even a body. How can they say there's been a murder?"

"There is a girl missing," Bruce countered. "How do you explain that?"

"A missing girl is a missing girl. A missing girl is not necessarily the same as a dead one! You want to put a man away for not necessarily committing a crime?"

"Bruce and I really have nothing to do with that side of things, ma'am," Raoul said. "Not officially."

"You see this?" she shouted at him, ignoring his words entirely. "Do you?" She held a perfect, honey-scented, golden doughnut right up to Raoul's face. "You see this doughnut with the hole in the middle?"

Raoul and Bruce nodded, not understanding where Patience's line of reasoning was headed, but suddenly very hungry for doughnuts.

"The doughnut has a hole because that's how doughnuts are. Some of them have holes. We make them that way, missing the centers. On purpose. Sometimes missing things are just supposed to be missing. It doesn't mean they were murdered!"

"You can't know that about Rena Baker," Bruce said.

"The police can't know the contrary!" Patience rebutted. "Now, do you need some bread or don't you?"

Bruce and Raoul looked at each other and replied in unison, "Two doughnuts, please."

They paid for them and left the shop, eating as they walked back to Bruce's office. Though Raoul was enjoying the sweet, warm snack, their encounter with Patience had left a bad taste in his mouth. He didn't doubt that she was absolutely right. He decided to test the waters with Bruce.

"You think she's right?" Raoul asked him. "About the girl, I mean."

"She could be," Bruce mused, not too worried, for he had confidence in island institutions like the press and the justice system. "That's what the trial is for. Whatever needs to come out will come out there."

"I sure hope so," Raoul said, rather wishing they might have avoided a trial altogether. He examined the half-eaten doughnut in his hand. The doughy semi-circle, the missing center now lost to the nothingness beyond the doughnut's golden edge. In his head a tsetse fly darted and a smile broke out on his face.

"What is it?" Bruce asked.

"Hmm? Oh, nothing," Raoul said. "Nothing."

But it wasn't nothing. It was something. A variable in the equation. The solution's next logical step. Raoul had seen it. He had seen it very clearly.

32

Less than an hour later, Raoul was at the airport, sleuthing. Dare he hope he had found a way to stop the trial before it started? If he could prove that Rena Baker wasn't dead, the charges against Madison would have to be dropped. His doughnut with its missing middle—it's purposefully missing middle, as Patience pointed out—had reminded Raoul of the obvious. Like bakers who knew of every hole they—on purpose—poked out, Customs kept track of every islander who poked his (or her) head past Oh's borders. Rena might not be dead but simply ducked-out, departed, run-away. If that were the case, it would be on record, in the registers of Customs and Excise.

During Raoul's early Customs career, at the airport, he had monitored the comings and goings of locals and foreigners alike. It might just be possible that Rena Baker had sneaked off the island on a pre-dawn flight, her departure recorded by some drowsy or hung-over entry-level officer, who didn't remember what he had done and so had not spoken up when Rena went officially missing.

How had Raoul not thought of it before? Wives (and girl-friends) had been known to make themselves disappear, and husbands (and boyfriends) were in no way to blame if they did! This much Raoul knew firsthand. If Rena Baker was one of these "lost" island loves, it would warm the cockles of Raoul's heart to catch her out.

Raoul needed no credentials or warrant to gain access to the airport logs he wished to examine. He was practically a legend at Arrivals and Departures and the young man on duty was happy to hand over everything he wanted. Raoul began with the log for the day that Rena went missing. Nothing. Next he checked the logs for seven days before and after. Still nothing. Had Rena kept herself hidden and sneaked off well after Madison's arrest? Raoul pored over the entries for every single day since the mangled bike was discovered. No Rena Baker had departed from Oh by plane. If she left by boat, then Raoul might never find her; the record-keeping of the maritime officials was notoriously fluid.

Raoul's mind raced. He felt certain the answer was right at his fingertips and yet the pages he flipped and turned offered up no clues. What was he missing? Was he going too fast? A man's freedom was at stake. He couldn't dawdle. It was almost four o'clock! Raoul closed his eyes and took a deep breath. Stan Kalpi would never approve of such haste. Raoul needed to keep calm and to line up the variables he had so far.

He took the departure registers, which were in a jumbled mess on a table, closed them, and stood them upright, putting them in order by date. He noticed their spines all had bright green dots stuck on them, which signified round-trip travel.

"I need the orange dots!" Raoul cried out, smacking his forehead with his palm. "I need the one-way registers right away."

The young man brought him the registers marked with adhesive orange dots and took away the others. Again Raoul began with the day the bike was found. Nothing. He checked seven days before and after. Still nothing. He checked every single day since Rena went missing. Nothing nothing nothing. Raoul felt the answer close at hand. He started again on the one-way data for the day that Rena disappeared, checking it carefully line by line. Most of the names belonged to foreigners, who had no reason to come back to Oh. Amongst the few declared citizens with no return ticket, Raoul recognized all the surnames but one (he knew all the family names on Oh, as most islanders did). The unfamiliar surname was Arbe.

It was nearly five o'clock by then, but the Office of Vital Records wasn't far away. Raoul rushed out of the airport and jumped in a taxi. He got there just as a young lady was locking the door. She told Raoul he would have to return in the morning.

"Sorry, miss. This is official business," Raoul said, pulling rank and flashing a badge that said he was Head of Customs and Excise. She wasn't at all convinced it meant she had to work over-time for his benefit, but she chose not to argue.

Raoul felt a tinge of guilt for inconveniencing the girl. He didn't really know what he was looking for. The name he hadn't recognized had nothing to do with the case as far as he could tell, but it bothered him that he had never come across it in all his years of checking passports and collecting tax. "I need you to look up a person, please," Raoul told her. She passed him a form, which he filled out in block letters. Personal/Fiscal Data requested for Oh citizen of family name: A-R-B-E. First name: K-A-R-E-N. (Signed, R. Orlean.)

The young lady disappeared into a back room and returned after just a minute. "You sure you have the name right?" she asked Raoul.

"Yes, I'm sure. Karen Arbe. A-R-B-E."

"I don't have a record for a Karen Arbe," the young lady told him.

"What does that mean?" Raoul asked.

She shrugged her shoulders and handed him back his form. "It means Karen Arbe doesn't exist. There's no one on Oh by that name."

Raoul thanked her for her assistance and left. He didn't know what to make of his discovery. Oh had only *one* unaccounted-for female when Raoul went into the Office of Vital Records, and now it had *two*? His investigation seemed to be making matters worse! If Karen Arbe didn't exist, then who signed the register and flew out on a one-way ticket? Frustrated, Raoul crumpled the useless paper in his hand. He walked forward a couple paces and spotting a rubbish bin in the distance, stopped and took aim, about to throw away the balled-up form. As he did so, the setting sun fell into his line of vision and momentarily blinded him (as, you've seen, the sun on Oh sometimes does). It pushed him, as if back in time. He withdrew from its shine, turned his face away, and like a corkscrew unwinding, he un-made the last of his moves. He lowered the arm that was poised to toss out the paper, walked backwards a couple of paces, and un-crumpled the crumpled form he held in his hand. As he flattened it out and studied it in the sun's angry rays, the solution to the riddle appeared.

"I see it," he said, as if answering to the sun itself. "I see it very clearly."

Waving the wrinkled form wildly over his head, Raoul flagged a taxi. He had to get to Bruce before Bruce put the morning edition to bed.

33

Mystery Woman Runs Away From Oh
Is Rena Baker Really Dead?

According to an official airport departure roster that has recently come to our attention, the day of the discovery of a mangled bicycle on the Thyme shortcut, a young citizen of Oh calling herself Karen Arbe left the island, on an early morning flight, for a one-way journey to an unknown destination. Based on the required information supplied by the young lady at the time of her departure, her itinerary was to take her to Killig, where she was to board a series of connecting flights. Her ultimate destination, although recorded with her departure data, is illegible. Whether this is owing to her own efforts to conceal her whereabouts or to the poor record-keeping of the officer on duty at the time is impossible to ascertain; while passenger departures are reported in the registry, the names of on-duty Customs officers reporting said departures are not. What makes the one-way flight of the young Ms. Arbe particularly significant is that no Karen Arbe is listed in the birth registries of Oh. This begs the question, if it was not Karen Arbe who left the island that morning (since Ms. Arbe does not exist), then who was it? There is in fact a young female citizen of Oh who is presently missing, Ms. Rena Baker of Glutton Hill, better known as the alleged victim in the Bicycle Trial soon to take place in Port-St. Luke, where Madison Fuller is facing charges for Ms. Baker's murder. Because the body of the allegedly dead Ms. Baker has never been recovered, this reporter is forced to ask himself if Ms. Baker and Ms. Arbe might not be one and the same. Evidence would indicate that they are: Ms. Arbe departed the same day that Ms. Baker supposedly died; Ms. Baker's body has never been found, suggesting she may be vacationing in the illegible land whose name she scrawled in the airport roster under the pseudonym of Karen Arbe; the name of RENA BAKER is easily scrambled to produce the convenient alias KAREN ARBE, a coincidence that we are not prepared to attribute to the magic of Oh or to island caprice. As the trial of Mr. Fuller gears up—if indeed a trial is warranted—we can only hope that the prosecuting authorities will have the foresight to read not only between the lines, but between the letters.

Bruce was delighted to cause a stir with his news report, because, he believed, that was what effective journalism aimed to do. Police Chief Lucas Davenport, upon reading the article about Karen Arbe at work the following morning, immediately summoned Officers Tullsey and Smart to his office. He sent them straight to Bruce's house.

The officers banged on Bruce's door, threatening him with charges of obstructing justice and demanding he tell them how he came upon the information contained in his inflammatory report.

Bruce refused to reveal his sources, but he suggested the officers investigate his theory and verify it for themselves at the airport. "Don't think we won't do it!" they threatened, and suggested in turn that Bruce not leave the island until further notice. (Police procedure called for confiscation of his passport, but Arnold and Joshua both forgot about that.)

They stormed off, while Bruce (*déshabillé* and drinking his morning Milo) stood grinning in the doorway, watching them go. For fun, in his head he scrambled his name into possible aliases, just in case, and nearly laughed out loud when he came up with DEREK CABLUNE.

Bruce's mood was not the only one lightened by his headline. Trevor and Randolph were happy and hopeful, as was Branson, and May. They couldn't prosecute her brother for a crime that hadn't been committed, could they? Patience was thrilled that her husband might soon be able to wash his hands of the Fullers forever. Even Ms. Lila had visions of a dismissal and of four finally finished cottage walls. Raoul, cloaked in blissful journalistic anonymity, went to work on what should have been his day off, to wait for the call from Chief Davenport, or the Prime Minister maybe, informing him that the trial had been called off.

Not taking the article quite so blissfully, apart from the police, was the accused. Madison, who learned of the development through one of his more literate jailers, wrangled with doubt and despair. He didn't want to believe that Rena would leave him at all, let alone in such underhanded fashion, and yet it was the only explanation that made any sense so far. Did Rena's disappearance mean she didn't love him? Or did it mean she didn't love him *enough*? Of the two scenarios, he tried to calculate which was less painful, but his fisherman's mathematics came up short.

———————

By noontime, the call Raoul awaited had come through. The Chief of Police wished to see him at the station straightaway. Raoul groaned as he hung up the receiver. Why couldn't they tell him over the phone that the trial was undone? Why drag him to another face-to-face with the useless Lucas Davenport? Cursing under his breath, he collected his things and set out, thinking only of the celebratory beer he planned to down at the Belly, once the Chief told him the case was dismissed.

At the police station, Raoul sensed a somber mood as he was shown into Chief Davenport's office. He attributed the sobriety to collective disappointment on the part of the police, who would not only have to cop to poor policing, but would have to renounce the bogus Bicycle Trial they had expected Raoul to arrange.

The Chief sat at his desk, quietly studying some papers, seemingly unfazed by Raoul's arrival. Raoul sat down, cleared his throat, and broke the silence.

"Looks like Bruce's article has added some salt, pepper, and vinegar to the plans," he said. "Have the police corroborated the newspaper's story?"

Chief Davenport looked up from his papers, as if annoyed that he and Raoul were forced to have the conversation they were having, what with so many more important official things either one of them could have been doing.

"Yes," he replied. "A woman named Karen Arbe did leave the island."

"Then you're dropping the charges against Madison Fuller?" Raoul preceded him, anxious to get the Police Chief to the point.

"Why on earth would we do that?" Chief Davenport asked him in turn.

Raoul was stunned into momentary speechlessness, his flies quiet with disbelief. When he had collected himself, he argued that the charges should be dropped because there was no dead body, so technically no murder, and in all likelihood Rena Baker and Karen Arbe were one and the same.

"Let us suppose for a minute that Rena Baker did leave the island using a false name," the Chief said. "Do the laws of this land not require that a passport be shown prior to leaving the island? Are we to suggest to our citizens that the authorities of Oh were sleeping on the job? That they let a woman go without proper documentation? Are we to imply that our own government workers don't know how to read? That they mistook one name on a passport for another?"

Raoul was flabbergasted. "But you might have an innocent man in jail!"

"Which is precisely why we must proceed with the trial, don't you see?"

Raoul did not and said so.

The Chief continued: "Even if a woman going by the name of Karen Arbe left the island, what does that prove? Any woman on Oh could wake up and decide to call herself Karen Arbe. Maybe she wasn't an islander at all, but a foreigner who checked a wrong box or signed the wrong register. Bruce Kandele's fancy theory is just that, a fancy, a whim. It's completely inadmissible as evidence. He peddles invisible girls with mixed-up names just to sell a few papers. Meanwhile, there are hard, tangible truths to take into account. Truths like that mashed-up bicycle that was run over by a very real vehicle."

"The Prime Minister?" Raoul tried. "He supports the Police decision to pursue this matter?"

"Oh, yes. He's the reason I had to inconvenience you. He wanted me to express our position to you in person."

"But he can't possibly think—"

"Raoul," the Chief interrupted, his hands opened and pleading, his tone condescending, his eyes again lifted ceilingward. "The authority of the powers that be."

Raoul stood and snorted disdainfully.

Chief Davenport, in reply, waved him out of the office, like a gnat from a bowlful of mangoes.

34

Raoul was furious when he got back to his desk at headquarters. The smug Police Chief had gone too far. Encouraging false charges was bad enough, but dismissing Raoul? How dare he?! They wanted a trial? Fine! They would have their trial. Raoul was a government official and a professional and would coordinate it to the best of his abilities. If they thought they could stop his finding Rena Baker, however, they all had another think coming.

"Stupid girl!" Raoul swore. He was more sure than ever that Rena Baker was Karen Arbe. A fly in his head confirmed it beyond all reasonable doubt. She thought she could get away via Killig, did she? Well, Raoul had connections in Killig. He had been involved in more than a few cases over the years in which Killig had figured, and he hoped he might call in a few favors. He dispatched a flurry of unofficial letters on official pale green letterhead, explaining about Rena. If there was record of her passing through the airport at Killig, perhaps there was record of where she had passed on to. Next, he sent a telegram to Mr. Monday Jones, Killig's top prosecutor, inviting him to Oh on behalf of the Prime Minister and the Chief of Police. Once that was taken care of, Raoul went to the Belly for a much-deserved drink.

"What a horrible day off!" he complained aloud as he walked there. "Even worse than last week's with all its painting and its BAKER problems." His cozy corner at the library seemed as far away as the neighboring isle to which Rena had likely fled.

While Raoul drowned his sorrows and thought about the bicycle crime's alleged victim, Trevor and Randolph tried to sort out legal counsel for the accused. They had been conceded a visit with Madison in his cell and tried to focus on the problem at hand instead of on the squalid surroundings, which were dark and mostly cement, with a tiny window and a crooked cot. Everything appeared as clean as one could hope to find in a courthouse jail, though the smell that permeated the corridor of barred rooms belied the apparent lack of filth.

Not wishing to stay there longer than necessary, and not wishing it for Madison either, Trevor got down to business right away.

"Madison, we need to find you a lawyer," he said. "A good one. Do you have any money?"

"I have a little something in the Savings Bank," Madison replied. "May has access to the account. I don't know what kind of lawyer it will buy."

"Don't worry," Randolph assured him. "We'll loan you the rest. Are you okay in here?"

"I suppose," Madison shrugged. "They let May bring me food from home."

Randolph was nearly shaking, despite his efforts to put on a brave front for his friend. How could Madison be so calm under such conditions? What Randolph didn't realize was that Madison's mind wasted little energy fretting about the upcoming trial, because it just didn't seem possible to him that he might be convicted of a crime he hadn't committed.

What did worry Madison was Rena. She wouldn't just up and leave him. Something terrible must have happened. He spent his days praying for her, picturing her safe and sound, and grappling with theories as to her whereabouts that he might offer to the police. Not to get himself freed, but to get his Rena found (which, at the end of the day, was the same exact thing).

Randolph and Trevor kept Madison company for the thirty minutes allowed, then they left him, having promised to hire a lawyer on his behalf. Trevor had suggested they try to get Glynray Justice, who boasted not only a first-rate reputation on Oh, but a name that (the three of them agreed) meant he couldn't fail.

Trevor sent Randolph to help Patience in the bakery and went himself to the Law Office of Mr. Justice to discuss Madison Fuller's case. Like all the islanders, Glynray had followed Madison's story in the news, but only Glynray had seen right through the shoddy arguments and the immaterial evidence on which the police had based their arrest. He felt confident he could exonerate Madison, and regardless of what he felt, he wouldn't have passed up a chance to be part of the island's first murder trial ever. He even offered his services *pro bono*, thus boosting the public images of attorney and client alike; for surely a lawyer of his repute would only defend a killer—and for free!—if wrongly accused.

When Trevor had finished at the lawyer's office, he went back to the bakery, his spirits lighter with Glynray's services secured. He sent Patience home, after telling her and Randolph about his interview with Glynray Justice and allaying his wife's fears at their continued involvement in Madison's messy dilemma. Patience was indeed calmed by what her husband told her, but still she felt compelled to admonish him. He had done his part and should now leave well enough alone, did he hear? Trevor scratched his head through his very big hat and made her a meaningless pledge. He would have nothing more to do with murder. He promised.

Women!

Trevor was not alone that day in marveling at the oddities of womankind. Branson too wondered about the more delicate sex, as he lay on the beach relaxing after an afternoon swim. Now that May was in his life again (albeit to chide and badmouth him for sending her brother to jail), Branson couldn't help but think of ways to win her back. He suspected that behind the passion with which May blamed him for Madison's arrest, she might be harboring a passion of a different sort.

Just his luck, he thought, that a murder was what had reignited their love! He could hardly fan the flames with flowers and chocolates while May's brother languished in jail. He considered once again confessing to the ad that had incriminated Madison, but knew in his heart he was incapable of such dishonesty, even for a worthy cause. The possibility of jail time, which Trevor had so astutely pointed out, was an effective deterrent as well.

Branson looked up and admired his house on its hill. In the sunlight, its windows appeared to be made of pure gold. What a life he could give to May now! He closed his eyes and pictured her puttering in his kitchen, heard her humming as she sewed in the sitting room. He imagined every one of the villa's empty bedrooms filled with their toddlers and babies. How far he had come from the days when all he could offer May was a fishing boat and a seaside picnic!

Branson propped himself on his elbow and, shielding his eyes from the sun, he stared at the very boat in which he and May had spent such happy hours. He knew it had once been his father's pride and joy (another reason Branson always treasured it so), and he wondered if Dagmore had ever been as happy as he in the sturdy craft. Branson didn't often let himself think of his father, Captain Dagmore; the memory was too painful. Dagmore had died when Branson was ten years old and his mother, who couldn't bear to stay in the house her dead husband had built, took Branson and made a home in the heart of town. Not until she died herself nearly ten years later, and Branson went through her things, did he discover that the house was his—"To my beloved son Branson Bowles I bequeath the acreage in my possession and the constructions thereupon," the Captain's tucked-away will resolutely attested.

By then, the house was an eyesore, completely rundown, and Branson's heart ached too badly to stay on the island, especially in a ramshackle dwelling. Only when he returned from his studies in England did he decide to fix the place up and move himself in, making of the house (like his father had before him) a tribute to the man who gave him his name.

Though Branson and Dagmore had each lovingly and in his turn transformed the house into a lovely jewel, neither had—so far—managed to fill it up. Fancy furniture and fancy guests, or shelf after shelf of glossy textbooks, these were not the stuff that made a house a home. Those things—the love, the warmth, the security—were as elusive to father and son as were the mysteries of the vast, enchanting sea.

35

"Raoul, you better have a look at this," Ms. Lila announced when Raoul finally got home. The sun was just setting and enough daylight resisted for her to show him what she had to show him. She took him outside, pulling him by the hand to the wall of the house, the once one-coated pink one, where FIND R. BAKER had shown up in ghostly grey-white letters. The second sighting of Rena's name had so stunned and overwhelmed Raoul that he had forgotten to cover it up. Ms. Lila, who now adopted the habit of checking the walls when she got home from work, had discovered that below the "D" in FIND, the letters A-G-M-O-R-E were etched vertically in the same wispy and phantom hand. A cryptic crossword seemed to be suggesting that Dagmore and finding Rena were inextricably connected.

Raoul was spellbound. He got close to the wall, touching the new letters, smelling them to establish what chemical might have created them. Paint thinner? Turpentine? When the daylight faded, he got his headlamp and strapped it to his head. He continued his examination of the wall, studying the ethereal outlines through his magnifying glass. He crawled across the yard and through the bush

241

but (again) could find no footprint or clue. His head was foggy with beer from the Belly and with way too many flies: the patronizing Police Chief, Karen Arbe, Monday Jones, and now Dagmore (again) to top it off? Raoul was too tired to fathom how it all tied together, or if it really did. The mysterious message seemed to suggest so, but what did it want Raoul to do?

To start, he dragged out his paint tins and painted over the strange messages (the criss-crossed FIND R. BAKER and DAGMORE; and the DAGMORE in pink on yellow, which he had so far left untouched). Plain-as-noses-on-faces clues were one thing, but he didn't need his business splashed plain-as-day on his house. While he worked in the near darkness, Ms. Lila, who had gone in for a minute to see about supper, joined him and kept him company.

"You know what this means," she said, watching him and hating the words she was about to say.

"What?" Raoul asked.

"You'll have to go back and see Mrs. Jaymes."

"Really?" he said, sounding more delighted than he meant to.

"She's the only one who knows anything about Dagmore. But don't bother with that story of hers. Just ask her outright if she knows anything about Rena." Then with a sad resignation in her voice, Ms. Lila added, "And please pick up more paint tomorrow. At this rate, we're bound to run out."

———

Raoul was giddy when he woke up the next morning. He had turned his back on Dagmore more reluctantly than he'd admitted. The fact that he had an excuse to see Mrs. Jaymes again was putting a skip in his step. As usual, he put in an appearance at work before he rushed off to Ladywood Road, stopping en route at Higgins Hardware, Home, and Garden to order two tins of Playful Rose. Mrs. Jaymes was pleased to see him arrive, and she put on a pot of tea. He assured her, however, that he had come not to hear Dagmore's story, not exactly, but to ask her some very important questions about a very important matter.

"Sounds serious," she said.

"It is, Mrs. Jaymes. Have you ever heard of a girl named Rena Baker?"

"The missing girl from the newspaper? What do you want to ask me about *her*?"

"I know it may sound odd, but we have reason to believe that there is a connection between Dagmore Bowles and this young girl's disappearance."

"What in the world do you mean? Dagmore is dead. Since before the girl was even born, I'd venture. How can he be responsible for her disappearance? Didn't she go missing just last week?"

"Yes," Raoul conceded. "Yes." He felt like a fool for suggesting that a ghost had had a hand in a murder, let alone a murder he knew in his heart had never taken place.

"Did Dagmore have any connection to the Baker family while he was alive?" Raoul persisted.

"He didn't mingle much with the locals. I don't know any Bakers, and I can say for certain that the Captain didn't either. Do you think the girl is dead?"

"Honestly, Mrs. Jaymes, I do not." Raoul should have kept his theory to himself, but he had to unburden his head and he felt a kind of closeness to Mrs. Jaymes. "I think she may have run away."

"Yes, I read about that lady with the strange name who ran off. You think that was her?"

Raoul nodded.

"Anything is possible on Oh," Mrs. Jaymes continued. "She wouldn't be the first one to fight with the island and lose."

A fruitfly flitted inside Raoul's head. "What do you mean by that?"

"I mean maybe she was one of those islanders—like the Captain—who belonged here but didn't really belong here. So, like the Captain, she left."

"You mean she killed herself?"

"I didn't say that. There's lots of ways of leaving."

Now a handful of fruitflies assembled in Raoul's brain. Could that be the connection to the Captain and Rena? His body had never been found. Was he really dead? Had he run off like Rena? Like Raoul's first wife Emma Patrice so many years before? Was the answer still somewhere in the Captain's tale?

"Mrs. Jaymes," Raoul said, "do you think you could tell me a little bit more about Dagmore's life?"

Mrs. Jaymes was only too happy to oblige. Where had she left off? Oh, yes, that's right, with the visit of Juan, Daphne, Peters, Stewart, and Ruck. It ended as badly as it had begun, she told him. The guests were stuck inside for most of their stay, playing cards while they waited for their skin to blister and pop. Finally, the five of them left the villa, but word of the disastrous visit got back to Spain and Ireland and England (which might not have been so terrible, except that the next batch of Dagmore's visitors to Oh coincidentally capsized en route).

Words like 'curse' and 'magic' had begun to be uttered and Dagmore noticed that more and more time passed between one visit and the next.

"That's where Hammer came in," Mrs. Jaymes said, and she waved to him in the garden. She explained that, with Hammer's help, the Captain devised and implemented a series of measures to protect his visitors from the birds and the bees (the bees being unquestionably the worse of the two). They attached tiny spikes to the window sills, so that the birds had nowhere to perch, and Hammer uprooted Dagmore's larkspur and lavender, in favor of bleeding heart and pineapple sage, whose flowers would draw hummingbirds instead of stingers. Dagmore even kitted out the shoreline with umbrellas and life-vests, just in case.

"The next visitors, they were okay?" Raoul asked, hoping to hurry her along.

"Oh, heavens no! They had the worst time yet." She leaned in closer to him and added knowingly, "Bad barracuda. Nearly died."

"From the fish?"

"From the *island*," Mrs. Jaymes said. "The island sent that poisoned fish straight to the Captain's table. After that lot, no one ever visited him again."

"That's when he killed himself?"

"No, not then! That's when he got his fishing boat. The very day they left."

"Fishing boat?" Raoul asked, thinking of fisherman Madison Fuller, and of the fisherman with the lonely heart. Was fishing the connection?

"You see, the Captain tried everything—from his piano to horticulture to hummingbirds, as he put it—and nothing worked. He scoured the island from bottom to top, opened up Oh to the famous and rich. His happiness was on Oh, Dagmore was surer than sure of that. But he couldn't figure out where on Oh it was *exactly*. He looked behind clouds, under bushes, and on top of the highest hills. It wasn't in his garden or his sitting room, or under the umbrellas on his beach. Not in the rainforest or Fort Tuesday or Tempperdu."

"Did he ever find it?" Raoul asked anxiously, interested not as a government official investigating a case, but as an islander to whom happiness had more than once proven elusive.

"He thought so. He said he caught sight of it as he walked home past the lumberyard of Higgins Hardware, Home, and Garden. It was covered in dust and wrong-side up, but it was there behind a stack of plywood, no mistaking it."

"What was?"

"The fishing boat! That was supposed to be his happiness."

"Ah." Raoul was growing restless. There seemed to be some similarities shaping up between Dagmore's story and Rena's, and even Madison's, but none that made much difference. There was a mountain of pre-trial work to do, Raoul's subordinates were beginning to whisper about his absences, and he was wondering if maybe Bruce wasn't right. Maybe the truth would surface once the trial got under way.

"I'd love to hear more, Mrs. Jaymes, but I'm afraid I really must be going," Raoul said, closing his notebook and capping his pen. "Can you think of anything else that might be worthy of mention?"

Only, she said, that from the minute the Captain brought home the fishing boat, she noticed a fullness to his cheeks and a quickness to his step that she hadn't spotted for a very long time. 'It's a boat, Mrs. Jaymes. Isn't she a beauty?' he had happily panted. It wasn't a beauty, Mrs. Jaymes assured Raoul, but the Captain planned to fix it up. He wanted it, he had told her, because his happiest days were the days he spent at sea. He thought maybe what was missing all along was a boat of his own.

"Was it?" Raoul asked her.

"Oh, heavens, no!" she laughed, as if Raoul had posed the most preposterous of questions. "It wasn't a boat that was missing. It was a girl."

36

With Officer Raoul Orlean at the helm, the ship of Oh's justice was moving full-steam ahead. Not too enthusiastic at first about his role in the Madison Fuller affair, Raoul was keen to get the trial started. He had come to the conclusion that the police might be their own worst enemies, and the sooner they were up on the witness stand, the sooner the sensible Glynray Justice could crumble their case. Raoul had come up with nothing to crumble it in the interim.

To expedite his duties, which left Raoul no time for anything else—not for painting, for sleuthing, for Mrs. Jaymes—Raoul turned the prime-ministerial Decree that had put him in charge of the Bicycle Trial into a virtual laissez-passer. Like a badge, he flashed it to access the government's coffers and bypass its convoluted protocols, and in the space of a week was able not only to procure the prosecutor Monday Jones from Killig, but to fly in the tarpaulins, toilets, speakers and mics. With Oh's own Ministry of Health he had arranged for a medical station and water to drink, and he had personally taken the construction team in hand. Thanks to his insistence, the dais was done, and so was much of the seating.

Raoul sent word to Police Chief Davenport to get his witnesses ready, that a trial date was officially set, for the Monday one week to follow. In the meantime, the remaining details would be wrapped up; the last of the seating seen to; the jury selected; and lawyers Justice and Jones would consult with their clients, Madison Fuller and the Island of Oh, respectively. When Chief Davenport balked and asked Raoul "What's the hurry?" Raoul blamed the rain that was due soon thereafter, and promptly displayed his laissez-passer to remind the Chief who was now really in charge.

———————

A frenzy fell across Oh that week leading up to the trial, as the various players prepared themselves for their parts. Chief Davenport arranged for Officers Tullsey and Smart to round up jurors (not a problem, because jurors on Oh are paid, and no islander declines easy money), while the Chief himself reviewed with the Prosecutor the evidence gathered to prove Madison Fuller's guilt. They drew a timeline and a map of Oh and discussed every piece of evidence and every clue (from the bike to the beach towel to the shortcut to Thyme), and how each fit into the murderous puzzle.

"Don't worry too much about the evidence, Davenport," Mr. Monday Jones assured him. "I've yet to lose a case. Just make sure there's a corkboard close to the jury, where I can pin up all my points."

"Yes, sir!" the Chief agreed. Clearly, the Island's case was in capable hands.

Chief Davenport immediately phoned Raoul to order the corkboard, then escorted Monday Jones to the Hotel Sincero, where

Raoul had set him up in a suite on the government's dime. (This, to the delight of the hotel's owner and Raoul's pal, Cougar Zanne.)

While the Prosecution baked in the sun at Cougar's, the Defense cooked up its strategy at the bakery. Together with Trevor, Glynray Justice, too, made a timeline and studied a map, and refuted the pieces of evidence one by one. The Island's case was full of holes, he said, and Madison, as good as a free man.

"You sure?" Trevor asked.

"I couldn't say with one-hundred percent certainty, but the evidence they have is completely circumstantial. Is there anything else you can tell me to help clear Madison's name?"

Trevor had no arguments on hand, but he had solved a problem or two in his day (his bakery business was built on it), and he felt sure there was a solution he had overlooked. He and Glynray re-examined the facts, inside-out and back to front, wracking their brains for the better part of an afternoon.

"Aha!" Trevor cried out suddenly, slamming his hand on the bakery counter. "Madison couldn't possibly have hit Rena and run. He doesn't own a car."

"No?"

"No! Does that help?" Trevor asked Glynray anxiously.

"It surely doesn't hurt," the attorney said, making a note on his yellow pad.

With that, Glynray left for the courthouse jail, to present the Defense's case to Madison, including their ace in the hole, the fact that Madison owned no vehicle. As he walked across town, Glynray noticed a hustle and bustle unusual for Port-St. Luke on a run-of-the-mill late afternoon. He never suspected that the to-and-fro of islanders was as earnestly involved in the Bicycle Trial as he.

Indeed both jurors and spectators ran busily about. There were new clothes to purchase and hair to plait, time off work to ask for, shoes to shine. The trial was turning into a real to-do, and no one dared show up uncoiffed or ill-prepared.

For his part, Raoul had got a trim and a shave, had arranged for security to safeguard the site, and for seats for the VIPs. On the dais, the jury members would sit to the right, facing not the crowd, but the Prosecution and Defense tables set up next to each other on the left. In the middle, a judge's bench had been erected for His Honor Maxted Samuels, the magistrate assigned to the case (Oh only had two and the other had recused himself, on account of his being a fisherman in his spare time).

Those with a special interest in the case, May, Branson, Randolph, Trevor and his wife, were of two minds as the trial date neared. They were eager for the evidence to be presented and for Madison's acquittal, but apprehensive that things might not go as they thought.

Bruce was excited about the Bicycle Trial, from which his front pages would indubitably benefit, and about the Special Access press pass that Raoul had arranged for him.

Madison was none of the above. Not eager, not apprehensive, not excited. At least not about the trial. He considered it a mere formality, since he had done absolutely nothing wrong. All *his* mind could focus on was Rena.

Rena, who, officially missing for days now, bobbed and floated far away with the fishes, her soul no longer troubled by the island's senseless trials.

37

L ife on Oh doesn't lend itself to readiness. Carry your umbrella, not a drop of rain will fall; don't, and you're in for a drenching. Plant your sorrel in time for Christmas, and your flowers will be finished before the first halls are decked; but delay, and you'll be lucky to have a sprig by Old Year's Night. Coop up your chickens, pen in your goats; still they'll find a way to get away from you.

The locals know all this and more, and yet they conduct themselves as if they have a say in what goes on around the place—and why not? Predictably fickle as the island is, one day it might just leave them to their own devices. They build themselves houses, and fishing boats, fashion happiness with hammer and nail, and hope each morning for sunny skies and kindly tides. When the tides pick up and the storms roll in (as they inescapably do), the islanders cover their rooftops with plastic and wait for the clouds to pass.

Like a pair of fencers forever *en garde*, island and islander thrust and parry, attack and dodge, until the one lashes out in a poke to the heart, that the other is helpless to foil.

38

When Monday morning rolled around, Raoul proudly surveyed the scene of his Bicycle Trial. Every last variable was in place, right down to the scant clouds and the abundant sun. Only Justice was missing, Raoul thought to himself, referring not to Glynray, but to the hallowed institution. He prayed it would turn up by the trial's end.

Glynray Justice was of course present, as was Monday Jones, both sporting their finest ties and most fashionable suits, despite the island temperatures. Madison wore a tie as well, but sat in shirtsleeves at the Defense table, looking achingly at May in the audience. As a family member of the accused, Raoul had assigned her a place among the VIPs, represented on that first trial day by some of Oh's lesser ministers (Sanitation and Traffic), and by Chief Davenport and Officers Tullsey and Smart. Branson, Randolph, Trevor and Patience sat somewhere in the middle of the crowd, while Raoul circulated its borders, assuring himself that no islander fell out of line. Bruce had predicted correctly: outside the official court perimeter established by Raoul, vendors of fruit and drink and floppy hats opened up for business. Bruce himself, press pass prominently displayed, meandered through the makeshift court, now eavesdropping on spectators, now listening in to legal counsel and clients.

The trial was set for eight a.m. (which on Oh might mean nine or even ten), but with Raoul on the clock, things got started by eight-thirty-five, as Judge Samuels arrived. The police band broke into the national anthem, which everyone sang wholeheartedly, and when it was finished the trial began.

"You may be seated," the judge said to everyone there, before addressing the trial's key figures,

the jurors: "Members of the jury, have you been sworn in?" he asked. (They had.)

the Prosecution: "Mr. Jones, are you prepared to speak on behalf of, and act in the interest of, the eminent Island of Oh?" (He was.)

and the Defense: "Mr. Fuller, do you understand the charges brought against you and do you submit to the representation of Mr. Justice here present?" (I do, Mr. Fuller said.)

The judge then ordered the trial to proceed, with the opening statement of Prosecutor Jones. Mr. Jones was a seasoned attorney and knew how to win over the toughest of crowds. His arsenal was stocked with charm and a flair for the dramatic, and his rugged good looks didn't hurt. He slowly stood up and straightened his tie, calling attention to his good taste and to his concern for detail. With deliberate, suspenseful steps he approached the microphone that stood in the middle of the dais, positioned himself with his back to the Defense, and splayed a semi-circle of charisma, like a hand-painted fan, that went from the judge on his left, to the jury before him, to the audience on his right.

"Your Honor, members of the jury, sisters and brothers, good morning," he began, distributing his personality along the whole of the fan's arc. "Welcome. Welcome to what I promise you will be a tribute to the investigative skills of the authorities of your great island nation. Behind me, sisters and brothers, sits an unlucky man, a man who lost his way. To find it again—to clear his path—he ran over a woman, a fellow human being, who he felt was barring his road. That's right, my friends," he replied to the anxious stirring of the horrified crowd, "he ran down Miss Rena Baker, killed her, and dumped her body in the sea, which, as you are all aware, is in great supply here, and unforgiving."

"Objection!" May cried out, standing up from her VIP seat. "Madison has never thrown a woman in the sea in his life!" May's friends and supporters hooted and cheered.

"Order! Order in the court!" Judge Samuels shouted, pounding his gavel. "There will be no objections during opening arguments! Mr. Jones, please continue."

Branson and Trevor looked at each other, worried. Branson wished he could sit closer to May, to hold her hand and comfort her, but a teacher at the Boys' School was not as Very Important a Person as a Minister in charge of sewage.

"As I was saying, ladies and gentlemen, the sea is unforgiving. So unforgiving, that we have no body to show you. The Defense will argue, 'no body, no crime,' but there *is* a body, my fellow citizens"—so had he beguiled them with his performance thus far that they forgot he was a citizen of Killig—"there is a body in the sea. Because we can't see it, does that mean it isn't there? Do we see every swimming fish and every coral reef when we look at the sea from our windows? Of course we don't! Does that mean we believe them not to be there? Of-course-we-don't," he finished, punching the last four words in an ominous, sing-song baritone.

255

"The last thing I wish to say, before we begin, ladies and gentlemen of the jury, is this: I've always been a lucky man. My momma, rest her soul, named me Monday because I was born on a Monday, and that's my lucky day. I ask therefore that you show no bias toward the young man accused of this heinous crime, simply because fate has seen fit to start his trial on *my* lucky day, not his. The law requires us, all of us, to treat him as an innocent man until the trial is over, even if in our hearts we know him to be guilty."

Solemnly he walked back to his place at the table, while the spectators applauded his eloquent speech and the display of integrity with which he had closed it.

Monday Jones was a tough act to follow. Glynray Justice, though one of Oh's top attorneys, lacked Monday's stage presence and hoped the plain truth would trump showmanship.

"Members of the jury," he said, wasting no words on the audience or even the judge, "I would like to start by responding to something said a moment ago by my esteemed colleague. Mr. Jones, here, has suggested there are plenty of fish swimming in the sea, and that we ought not to assume otherwise because we don't see every one of them." He paused for dramatic effect, inspired by the stage and by the rapt attention of the spectators.

"Well, he's absolutely right." The crowd collectively gasped, and Glynray paused again before going on. "Mr. Jones would have you accept that the fish you cannot see are vibrant and alive, and so too would I ask you to accept that Rena Baker is vibrant and alive. We have no proof to the contrary, and the fact that we can or cannot see her is not the matter at hand. What matters here is the future of a wrongly accused man, a man accused of murder when there is no corpse to be found. Remember, ladies and gentlemen of the jury, that your verdict must be based on the truth—the truth as supported by irrefutable and *visible* (here he raised his index finger) evidence. You may not—indeed you *must* not—base your ruling on what you cannot see. Do not determine my client's guilt or innocence on the basis of invisible fish."

Though the trial had barely begun, the judge called a short recess after the opening arguments, both sides having succeeded in riling up the crowd. Raoul was chagrined by the interruption, for once the gavel went down, the islanders would mill about, visit the toilets or the beer stalls, and start heated debates from which it would be hard for him to herd them back inside the official perimeter.

During the break, Monday had his corkboard wheeled close to where the jury sat, and Glynray conferred with Madison and with Trevor, who had sneaked up onto the dais.

"Great start," Trevor said, though whether speaking to Madison or Glynray, he wasn't sure. "Invisible fish. That was good!" He clapped Madison on the back.

"We've got a long way to go," Glynray cautioned. "They'll call the police as witnesses first and go through the evidence piece by piece. I'm sure that shyster will drag it out for days."

"Then you get to cross-examine?" Trevor asked.

"That's right."

Through a megaphone, Raoul's voice could be heard requesting that everybody return to their seats, so Trevor gave Glynray and Madison a nod, then jumped down off the dais. On the way to his place in the crowd, he stopped by May to say hello and wish her well, and to assure her that Glynray wouldn't let them down. On the one hand, May felt relieved that the trial was finally under way, but on the other, she was scared to death. Every word that the loquacious Prosecutor spoke sent chills up and down her spine.

As Trevor reached his place next to Patience, Monday Jones arose from his chair and called his first witness, Officer Arnold Tullsey. Officer Tullsey stated his name for the record and Monday swore him in.

"May I present Exhibit A," Monday announced, flamboyantly waving high in the air a copy of the *Morning Crier*, sealed in a clear plastic bag. "Can you describe this item for the court, please, Officer."

"Yes, sir, that would be a newspaper, sir," Arnold answered. He spoke his words close into the microphone, rendering them almost unintelligible.

"Thank you. No need to get so close to the mic, son. Now, tell the court please why this particular newspaper is so important." (Bruce beamed, somewhere amidst the onlookers.)

"It's the edition with the ad, sir."

"The ad?"

"Yes, sir, the ad for a lady," Arnold explained.

"Would that be the lady sought to fill the vacancy left behind by the murdered Rena Baker?"

"Yes, sir. The ad came out the same day the mangled bike was discovered. It seemed obvious that whoever placed the ad needed a woman, to fill in for the one he got rid of by knocking her off the bike."

"I see," Monday said, pinning to his corkboard a large, glossy photograph of the newspaper. "What makes you so sure that Mr. Fuller placed this ad?"

"The ad was placed by a fisherman, and that's what Mr. Fuller is. We confiscated a fishing pole when we searched his house."

"Would this, Exhibit B, be the fishing pole?" Monday asked, showing Arnold another glossy photo, then tacking it to the corkboard as well.

Before Arnold could reply, Glynray jumped up and interrupted.

"Objection, Your Honor! It's common knowledge that my client is a fisherman, an activity in which he takes great pride. The witness is suggesting that Mr. Fuller tried to hide his occupation, when in fact he has nothing to hide, occupational or otherwise."

"The objection is sustained. The jury will disregard the fishing pole," the judge ruled. "Mr. Jones, kindly remove the photo."

"Of course, Your Honor," Monday conceded. "There's plenty more where that came from." Turning back to Arnold, he continued. "Was there anything else about the ad to indicate that Mr. Fuller was the one who placed it?"

"Yes, sir. He wasn't just asking for a lady. He wanted a lady who cooked and who had a bike. Rena used to cook him lunch every day, but Rena was a walker. We suspect he wanted a lady who had a bike, so she could get his food to him a little faster."

"Yes, that makes good sense," Monday agreed.

"Speculation, Your Honor!" Glynray called out.

"Overruled," the judge declared. "I agree completely that the testimony makes good sense."

"Thank you, Your Honor," Monday said, bowing to him slightly. "Officer Tullsey, let's try another Exhibit B, shall we?" Again he wagged a clear plastic bag high in the air for the audience to see. In it was the beach towel the police had found at Madison's house, the one covering the picnic basket that belonged to Rena Baker.

"Can you tell the court what this item is, please?" He handed the towel to Arnold and pinned a picture of it on the board.

"That's a beach towel, sir. We found it at Mr. Fuller's house."

"Where exactly at Mr. Fuller's house did you find it?"

"It was on top of a basket belonging to Rena Baker," Arnold said.

"Is *this* the basket that belonged to Miss Baker?" Monday tacked a photo marked "Exhibit C" onto the board.

"Yes. Her things were inside it, with big R's all over them."

"Thank you, Officer. Right you are." Monday attached to his corkboard pictures of the articles found in Rena's basket—a dinner plate, knife, fork, spoon, three plastic bowls tucked one inside the other, and three plastic lids (Exhibits D, E, F, G, H, and I).

Like so, the questioning continued for three days, until Monday Jones's corkboard was completely covered, with pictures of exhibits J through P as well. Halfway through Arnold's testimony, Monday had excused him and called to the stand Joshua Smart instead, so both of the officers could take a turn. When the Prosecution finally rested its case, the most damning pieces of evidence were Madison's ad (the Prosecution excluded the notion that someone else might have placed it), Rena's basket (particularly the initialed lids inside it), and a pair of Madison's muddy shoes, muddied presumably when he picked her remains up off the shortcut that leads from Thyme to Port-St. Luke.

———

It took the remainder of that first trial week for Glynray Justice to cross-examine Officers Tullsey and Smart. Exhibit by Exhibit,

Glynray ran down the list of incriminating items, refuting every one as best he could, first and foremost the classified ad.

"Tell me, Officer Tullsey, how is it that the Police determined my client to be the author of this ad, placed anonymously, if I'm not mistaken, in our only island daily?"

Arnold opened his mouth to respond, but Glynray kept talking.

"I mention that it is our *only* island daily," he explained, "so as to remind the court that the entire population of Oh reads this newspaper and this newspaper alone." (Publicity! Bruce hadn't thought of that!) "If the entire population reads the *Morning Crier*, then the pool from which to fish out the writer of that unusual ad is vast, Officer Tullsey, is it not?"

"I suppose."

"The ad might have been placed by any one of the hundreds of spectators seated here before us. Not to mention those seated at home, listening to our proceedings on the radio." (Raoul, hoping to stem the number of onlookers, had arranged for radio transmission of the trial.) "How did you narrow it down to my client?"

"Your client was the only one who was missing a girl."

"I see, and did you bother to interview the editor of the paper?" Glynray asked.

"Yes, sir. He told us the ad was anonymous, like you said. Someone slipped an envelope with cash and an unsigned note under the door of the *Crier* offices."

"Do you have a girlfriend, Officer Tullsey?"

"No, sir," Arnold said.

"Do the court the favor of reading the ad aloud, please, would you?" Glynray handed Arnold the plastic bag that housed Exhibit A.

"Honest man, early 40s, athletic, with fishing boat seeks honest woman, early 30s, with bicycle, cooking skills, and dainty hands. For immediate marriage," he read.

"How old are you, Officer?"

"I turned forty last month."

"Do you like a nice home-cooked meal?"

"Who doesn't?"

"So, you just turned forty, you find yourself with no girl, and admit to liking good home-cooking. Did you perhaps buy yourself a birthday present, Officer? Get yourself a boat and put an ad in the local paper to get your forty-year-old life in order?"

"Absolutely not!" Arnold said. "I don't need the newspaper to find myself a girl."

"And yet you don't have one," Glynray said.

"Objection, your honor!" Monday Jones hollered, standing up. "Now who's stabbing at invisible fish?"

"Sustained. Move it along, counselor," Judge Samuels ruled.

"Fine." Glynray feigned frustration, but was satisfied that he had made his point, as the animated whispers from the crowd clearly indicated. He made a show of rifling through a stack of papers, then started in again on Officer Tullsey.

"Allow me to read to you a piece of your own testimony from earlier this week. Speaking about the newspaper ad in question, you said, and I quote, 'Rena was a walker. We suspect he wanted a lady who had a bike, so she could get his food to him a little faster.' If Rena was a walker, and the alleged victim of the crime with which my client is charged was a biker, then how do you figure Rena and the victim to be one and the same?"

"No one but Rena is missing, so she must be the one who's gone. Who's dead, I mean," Arnold added for clarity.

"How do you know that no one else is missing?"

"We canvassed all the surrounding areas, and everyone is accounted for. No other missing persons have been reported anywhere on the island."

"Okay. Assuming you are correct, and Rena was the biker on that fateful night, where did she get the bike?"

"We don't know."

"And why would an inexperienced cyclist choose the wettest night of the year so far, and the roughest road she could find, to go cycling?"

"We don't know that either."

"The truth is, Officer, that you don't know for a fact that Rena *did* do any of those things, do you? No proof she got a bike. No proof she rode it on the Thyme shortcut. No proof she got knocked off her bike and killed," Glynray said, counting off the proofs (or lack thereof) on his fingers as he spoke.

"No, sir."

Glynray went on to lure similar admissions from Arnold and Joshua regarding the rest of the evidence. If Madison truly wished to hide Rena's basket, would he not have found a better means than a beach towel tossed on top of it? (He would, they said.) Weren't the Officers' shoes muddy, too, on that day of the hit-and-run, when they jumped off Jarvis Coutrelle's bus and landed him in a ditch? (They were.) Didn't Joshua himself own a yellow shirt that he liked to wear when he went dancing? (Yes, sir.) Wasn't it possible the dishwashing gloves retrieved from Madison's kitchen were for washing dishes and not for keeping fingerprints off corpses that didn't exist? (It was.)

The Defense position appeared to grow stronger as the week went on. Late in the afternoon on Friday, shortly before court was to recess for the weekend, Glynray neared the end of his cross-examination. Because the Prosecution had insisted the lids with Rena's R's on them were especially incriminating, Glynray chose to end with those, hoping to send the crowd home for the two-day hiatus on a pro-Defense note.

Officer Joshua Smart was on the witness stand, when Glynray brought up Rena's basket and its contents.

"Can you remind the court of the items found in the picnic basket, hidden under the beach towel, in the kitchen of my client?" he asked.

"Yes, sir, there was a plate with a faded design, a knife, a fork, a spoon, and three plastic bowls. There were three lids for the bowls, too."

"Are these the lids?" Glynray held up the bag with Exhibit I, three plastic lids, each marked with a big black "R".

"Yes."

"Prosecutor Jones was disturbed by the fact that these lids were marked with Rena's initial. Would you say that's accurate?"

Joshua said it was, adding, "It proved they belonged to the victim."

"We have already established that the confiscated picnic basket belonged to Rena, have we not? That it was the basket in which Rena took lunch to her beloved Madison every day?" Glynray went on.

"That's right."

"If the basket belonged to Rena, then why does the Island find it damaging that Madison should store lids clearly belonging to Rena inside it?"

Joshua hesitated. "I couldn't exactly say."

"Are you personally acquainted with the Defendant, Officer Smart?"

"Not really."

"Then you don't know firsthand what an honest, loyal man he is. And he *is* an honest man, and a loyal one, which is why he would never dream of storing any other woman's lids in the basket belonging to his girl. Would you agree, Officer Smart, that only a dishonest man would dream of such a thing?"

"I guess so."

"Which makes my client an honest man?"

"I guess."

"Thank you, Officer, for that character assessment," Glynray said smugly. "May I remind the court that my client, an 'honest man' according to the testimony of the Prosecution's own witness here today, has maintained his innocence since this alleged crime and these heinous charges first came to light. No further questions, Your Honor."

The court was recessed.

39

As Bruce had predicted, the spectators lingered long after the Bicycle Trial broke for the weekend. They made of the open-air court a real Friday-night party-ground, eating, drinking, and dancing well into the wee hours. In a solitary corner at the out-skirts of the merriment, May sat in contemplation, encouraged by the trial so far, but not daring to take her brother's freedom for granted. Branson, who hadn't kept his eyes off her the whole week, saw her sitting alone and decided to approach her.

"May? You good? Would you like a drink or something?"

May looked at him, still upset at his silence about the ad and yet not entirely displeased to see him there. "I'm fine," she said, too tired to argue or plead with him.

"Looks like Justice is doing a good job, eh?"

"For now," she said, her thoughts not fully there with Branson on the edge of the court-cum-carnival. In an act of unusual daring, Branson sat down beside her and took her hand in his.

"Don't worry too much. Trevor says Madison's lawyer has a trick or two up his sleeve. He's sure holding his own for now against that fancy Monday Jones."

"What I don't understand is what happened to Rena," May confided desperately to Branson. "Where in the world could she be?"

Branson didn't know what to say.

"That fool brother of mine," May went on, gradually feeling more like herself with Branson at her side, "isn't even concerned about the predicament he's in. All he can think about is that crazy girl, rest her soul."

"You think she's dead?" Branson asked.

"I wish to heaven I knew," May replied.

Neither of them said another word after that. Branson simply held May's hand for as long as she would let him.

———————

Back at Raoul's cottage, where to his dismay not a single message had turned up since the trial began, Raoul was outside staring at the silent walls. Because of his recent busy schedule, he had all but abandoned Dagmore, and apart from arranging the trial, he hadn't accomplished a thing in the way of finding Rena (his sources in Killig had so far proved unhelpful); and yet, the ghostly messenger failed to insist about the one or the other. Confused as he was feeling, Raoul had rather hoped a new word would appear, to guide him, but the weekend came and went without so much as a letter.

A new week began, as it always does, dragging into court another lucky Monday. Amidst an ominous flurry of whispers and conferrals on the dais (during which Judge Samuels wrapped his pudgy fist around the mic to silence it), the Prosecution called Officer Tullsey back to the stand, having requested a redirect. The crowd sensed something sinister was coming, and Glynray Justice braced himself for bad news, though what it might be, he couldn't imagine.

"Members of the jury, Your Honor, ladies and gentlemen, good morning," Monday Jones began with characteristic gravitas. "I have a confession to make." He turned to the audience, that they might fully absorb what he had said, and for a minute they half expected him to admit to the murder himself. When they were suitably on the edge of their seats, Monday continued. "It has come to my attention that in examining my first witness, I failed to address a very crucial piece of evidence, and for this I beg your forgiveness." The crowd was simultaneously disappointed and intrigued, the Madison Fuller camp rather terrified.

"I submit to you, members of the jury, Exhibit Q." He held up for them another large, glossy photo, this one of a boat. "Exhibit Q is nothing less than the fishing boat belonging to the very fisherman responsible for the newspaper ad and for Rena Baker's murder, Madison Fuller." With that, Monday pointed dramatically across the dais, fully extending his arm and his index finger in Madison's direction.

The spectators sat quiet and perplexed, failing to see the significance of the boat of a known fisherman.

"Officer Tullsey," Monday said, "do you confirm for the court that this is a picture of the boat belonging to Mr. Fuller, and that it is currently in the custody of the Island Police?"

"I do," Arnold said.

"Can you tell us what was found in the boat when you confiscated it?"

"Yes, sir. We found a bucket of worms and a lantern, some towels, and, I believe, an empty thermos."

"Is that all you found? Are you sure?" Monday insisted. Smiling he added, "Take all the time you need to respond."

Arnold looked at him, puzzled, then testified, "Oh, right! We found blood! There was blood on Mr. Fuller's boat."

At the word "blood," Madison's ears perked up and the crowd commented noisily.

"Order in the court!" the judge cried, smacking his gavel repeatedly.

"Objection, Your Honor!" Glynray yelled out. "The Defense was not informed of this piece of evidence."

Before the judge could sustain the objection, or overrule it, Monday was back at the microphone, reiterating again his apologies for overlooking Exhibit Q and theatrically begging the forgiveness of the Defense.

"I'll allow it," Judge Samuels said. "An honest mistake is an honest mistake. Defense can cross-examine again when Mr. Jones is finished."

At that, Mr. Jones jumped right back into his questioning.

"Officer Tullsey, please tell us how much blood you found on the boat. A few droplets? Smears from one end to the other? How would you describe it?"

"Hard to say, sir. More than droplets, but less than smears," he answered.

"I see. How long have you been a police officer, if I may ask?"

"Close to fifteen years."

"My compliments on a fine career," Monday said. "Is it your professional opinion, based on fifteen years of police work, that the blood evidence found on Mr. Fuller's boat is not inconsistent with the blood you would expect to find if one, say, dumped a dead body into the sea?"

"You could say that," Arnold said, feeling especially important.

"Thank you, Officer. The Defense may question the witness."

Glynray got up, agitated, with only one question in mind.

"Officer Tullsey," he sharply said, "are you completely sure that the blood on Mr. Fuller's boat belongs to Rena Baker and not to a fish?"

Arnold reflected a minute. "Not completely sure, no."

"Your Honor," Glynray said firmly, turning to the judge, "I request that the court have the blood evidence analyzed before this case goes any further."

Judge Samuels agreed to Glynray's request that the blood be checked, but was reluctant to postpone the trial in the meantime. That is, until Monday Jones rested his case a short time later. The Prosecution had no witnesses apart from the two policemen, whose testimony was finally finished, and so the judge agreed to a day's delay while the blood was looked into. He adjourned the court until the next morning, when the Defense would be asked to call its first witness.

The spectators dispersed, tittering and speculating, Branson and Trevor among them. Branson, noticeably disturbed by the short morning's events, spotted May on the VIP bench and ran to console her. Her patience where he was concerned, however, was inversely proportional to the strength of the Prosecutor's case, so she snapped at him and sent him away. Trevor, meanwhile, equally disturbed, rushed to consult with Glynray on the dais, as the police took Madison back to jail. Glynray wasn't worried about the forensics, he said, but he feared that the jury had been irrevocably swayed by the blood-spattered boat, whose picture spoke a thousand words from its position smack-dab in the middle of Monday's corkboard.

"I'll do my best tomorrow," he promised Trevor (as he had promised Madison, too, a moment before), "but I'd be a hell of a lot more convincing without a bloody fishing boat hanging over my head!"

———

As the organizational head of the Trial, to Raoul fell the handling of the blood that afternoon, and he discovered that Oh simply wasn't equipped for forensic testing. The blood had to be sent to Killig for analysis there, which posed an additional problem, for it was spattered on a fairly large boat. Raoul couldn't slip it in a bag marked Exhibit Q and send it out on the earliest flight.

After conferring with his colleagues in Killig, it was determined that Raoul should collect samples of the blood to be analyzed, and merely send *those* off (by air or by sea) to the lab. He was instructed to shave off thin slivers of wood from the bloody spots on the boat. Raoul had no idea how to do such a thing, and by the time he learned that this was the most expeditious of options, it was well past sundown. Since the day's last flight to Killig was long gone, Raoul decided to get the samples—at all costs—on the five a.m. flight the next day. To do so, he enlisted the help of his friend Fred Nettles, a builder well-versed in wood.

It was nearly nine o'clock when Fred and Raoul arrived at the police repository where oversized evidence was housed. Because in the judicial history of Oh, "oversized evidence" had been encountered less than a dozen times, the repository amounted to a shed behind the police station, where the police band stored its extra marching drums. The shed had no windows and no electric lights. Luckily Raoul, who kept his investigative gadgets near at hand, had in his bag his headlamp and strap, which he fastened onto his head. While he bent and aimed the lamp's beam at the traces of blood, Fred used a plane to slice them off the boat. As he expertly slivered the wood into curly shavings, Raoul stood at the ready with a plastic bag in which to catch them.

By nine-fifteen, Fred was headed home and Raoul was on his way to the airport, to wrap up his samples for the morning flight.

40

Before the trial started on the Tuesday morning when the Defense was to call its first witness, Raoul went up on the dais to speak with the judge. He told him the state of forensic affairs and informed him it would be at least another twenty-four hours before they had news about the blood from the boat. The judge passed the word on to Monday and to Glynray, who was saddened at the prospect of opening his case in the shadow of such damning evidence. He had intended, lab results in hand, to clear up the fish-blood mix-up first thing, then call a string of character witnesses to attest to Madison's honesty and to his love for Rena Baker. With the expected day-long delay, Glynray would have to change tack. He would call Madison to the stand and they would face the Prosecution's accusations straight on.

"Do you swear to tell the truth, so help you God, Mr. Fuller?" Glynray asked him.

"I do," he swore, and the questioning began.

"Let's get right to the heart of the matter," Glynray said. "Were you aware of the blood on your fishing boat?"

"Of course," Madison said.

"How do you explain it?"

"It's fish blood. I normally wash the boat off at the end of the day, but I could tell by the sea and the sky we were in for some rain. So I just tied the boat and left it. I figured the rain would wash it off for me."

"But it didn't?"

"It was so hot, I guess the blood dried pretty good before the storm came. Or maybe the way the rain was angled, it didn't hit every inch of the boat."

"So you *didn't* kill your girlfriend Rena Baker, and dirty your boat dumping her body into the sea. Correct?"

"Absolutely," Madison confirmed. "I love Rena. She's all I think about, and I pray every minute that she'll turn up safe and sound."

"Objection, Your Honor!" Monday jumped to his feet. "Let's not drag the good Lord into this ugly mess." The more pious of the spectators applauded and hollered "Amen."

"Sustained. The jury will disregard the defendant's last statement," Judge Samuels ruled, to the hisses and boos of Madison's friends and acquaintances.

Having justified the bloody boat to the best of his abilities, Glynray moved on to the rest of the evidence presented the week before. Again he went through the various exhibits and with Madison's help explained away every last one. It took him almost the whole of that Tuesday, which he hoped to close on a positive note.

Accordingly, he asked that the judge please read out the charges against his client.

Before Judge Samuels could reply, Monday Jones volunteered to do the honors. "Mr. Madison Fuller of Port-St. Luke is charged with the vehicular homicide of Rena Baker of Glutton Hill, and with the disposal of the remains of the victim," Monday read slowly.

"Thank you, counselor," Glynray said with a smirk. "Members of the jury, please take note that the primary charge in this case is vehicular homicide, which in legal terms refers to the killing of one person by another person through the use of a vehicle. In laymen's terms, it means running someone over. I am sure that my esteemed colleague Mr. Jones will agree: a key element to the charge of vehicular homicide is a vehicle." Glynray paced the stage and looked into the crowd as if to give the impression his well-planned words were dawning on him right then and there.

"Mr. Fuller, do you own a car or other vehicle?" he turned and asked Madison suddenly.

"No, sir."

"Have you ever owned a car or other vehicle?"

"No, sir."

"Which means that it would be impossible for you to run someone over, not that you would ever be so inclined. Is that correct?"

"Yes, sir. That's absolutely correct."

"Thank you, Mr. Fuller." Looking at Monday Jones, Glynray added haughtily, "Your witness," knowing full well that their time had run out.

As the outdoor courtroom emptied, Branson elbowed his way through the crowd to get to May. According to his calculations, the testimony had gone well enough that she wouldn't rebuff him. May allowed him to escort her all the way home, in fact, where she offered him a cup of tea. It struck Branson, as he and May quietly sipped lemongrass on the verandah, that when May wasn't screaming at him, or accusing him of something, he felt quite like a teenager in her presence. It seemed impossible to him that their young love had ever been interrupted by misguided glances and years abroad, and even more impossible that a newspaper ad and a bizarre hit-and-run had sent their separate paths colliding once more. Branson watched May admiringly and mulled over such impossibilities, never imagining that, an island away, two other paths were about to collide (that of Betty Grewber and her own bit of lemongrass tea), or that the victim of the collision would once again be May's brother Madison.

———————

Betty Grewber lived on Killig, where she was a technician in a scientific lab. Having unluckily drawn the night shift that week, she sat in a hot, dingy staff room having her supper of tuna pie and boiled lemongrass, when her supervisor came rushing in.

"Betty! Thank heavens you're here. I have a rush on some blood from Oh."

"Oh?" Betty said.

Her supervisor, who had spoken to Raoul the day before by phone, briefly explained about the Bicycle Trial and the boat with the blood, and told Betty to get right to it. They had already wasted most of the day, because airport officials failed to inform the lab that the blood had landed that morning. Betty's supervisor set the package on the staff-room table and left.

"Oh, my," Betty complained, looking at the sloppy, hastily taped envelope sent from Oh. She ripped it open and inside found

Raoul's official request for the analysis (which was neat and precise) and the bag that held the bloody shavings from Madison's boat. She examined them through the plastic, trying to decide the most efficient way to test the spatters of blood. From the pocket of her lab coat she pulled a clean pair of rubber gloves and stretched them over her hands. She opened the bag, reached in and grabbed the shavings, then laid them out on the table to get a closer look. When she had made up her mind about how to proceed, she abruptly stood up, toppling her cup of tea and spilling its contents all over the bloody bits of boat laid out before her.

Betty looked around frantically to see if her supervisor were anywhere near. (She wasn't.) "Oh, my!" Betty said again, nearly in tears. She surveyed the table helplessly, then with her crumpled paper napkin and the sleeves of her lab coat, Betty wiped up the evidence of what she had done. When she was finished, she rolled up her sticky cuffs, stuffed the shavings from Oh in her pocket, and walked casually into the lab to execute Raoul's official request.

———

Monday Jones had Glynray Justice pegged. If Glynray thought he could end the day on a high note, casting a five o'clock shadow on Monday's case, he was sorely mistaken. Like a swatted-at wasp, Monday showed up on Wednesday buzzing mad. The various players had barely taken their places on stage when Monday put Madison on the stand for cross-exam.

"Mr. Fuller, it is your testimony that you do not own a car," Monday declared.

"That's correct."

"Allow me to read to you the charges against you one more time: 'Mr. Madison Fuller of Port-St. Luke is charged with the vehicular homicide of Rena Baker of Glutton Hill, and with the disposal of the remains of the victim.' Do those charges anywhere specify to which vehicle they refer?"

"How should *I* know? They're *your* charges."

"You're absolutely right. I'm far better qualified to answer the question, and I can tell you that the charges do *not* specify to which vehicle they refer. Do you know what that means?"

"No."

"It means that you don't need your own vehicle to commit vehicular homicide."

Madison didn't know what he was meant to reply to that, and so he said nothing.

"Do you have a driving license, Mr. Fuller?" Monday asked him.

"Yes."

"Is it true, as your sister told Officers Tullsey and Smart when they first showed up at your home, that you spent an entire day driving around the island looking for Rena?"

Madison looked at Glynray for help, but Glynray sat stoically, not daring to let his face reveal his feelings.

"Yes," Madison said softly.

"Could you speak up, sir," Monday insisted.

"Yes," Madison said angrily. "My girl was missing and I borrowed a car to go and look for her. Yes." Glynray sighed, and at the front of the murmuring audience, May hid her face in her handkerchief and cried.

"In other words, Mr. Fuller, what you are saying is that you do have access to a motor vehicle. Is that an accurate statement?"

"Yes," Madison said hopelessly.

"Good," Monday said. "We've sorted out the matter of your vehicle, now let's discuss your fishing boat. You have testified that you left your blood-spattered boat on the beach, where you expected the rain would clean it."

"That's correct."

"Do you really expect us to believe that a seasoned fisherman, like you, would leave his boat to the mercy of the pummeling rains? That he wouldn't wash it himself and then cover it with a protective tarpaulin?"

"I didn't have a tarp that day, so I figured I'd let the rain do my washing for me. Since the boat was bound to get wet," Madison explained.

"I see. Do you also expect us to believe that an experienced fisherman, like you, would leave a bucket of worms, half-full and wide open, exposed to the elements? If the rain water had filled up your bucket, wouldn't your boat be swimming in bait?"

"I guess I just forgot about the worms."

"Allow me to suggest a more plausible scenario, if you will, Mr. Fuller. I believe you *did* wash your boat that day the rains came, as was your habit, and I believe that you put away your worms and that you covered the whole lot of it with a tarpaulin. I also believe that later that day, after you killed Ms. Baker, when darkness had fallen, you uncovered your fishing boat, wrapped her body in the tarpaulin, and rowed out to sea. I believe that you threw her overboard, tarp and all, and that as you did so, your boat got smeared with blood, and your bait bucket, tucked away somewhere, became dislodged and uncovered. You rowed to shore, under cover of night, and tied up your boat again, not realizing that Rena's blood was all over it and that your worms were unsecured."

"Objection, Your Honor!" Glynray shouted. "The Defense is engaging in speculation. Pure, vile speculation!"

The crowd was in an uproar, half of them cheering on Monday Jones, the other half galled, and complaining on Glynray's behalf.

Judge Samuels hammered away with his gavel. "Order! Order!" he cried, but it took Raoul and his megaphone to get the islanders to hush.

"Members of the jury," the judge said, "I will allow the remarks of Mr. Jones, but only insofar as they represent his personal theory regarding the night in question and not insofar as they necessarily refer to the events as they actually transpired."

The jury members looked at each other perplexed, and Raoul, behind his megaphone, resisted the urge to speak up. He wasn't satisfied one bit with the way the trial was being handled, and as the officer in charge of the proceedings, he took the mishandling to heart.

Without giving Madison an opportunity to say another word, Monday called out, "Nothing further," and Glynray was back at bat.

Glynray redirected a series of questions at Madison to counter the Prosecutor's so-called personal theory. He brought to light the fact that two days went by before the boat was ever confiscated, and that a guilty man would have gone back to the beach to make sure nothing was amiss. Madison had not, because he was too busy looking for Rena. Too busy scouring Oh to be bothered scouring his boat. (That Madison had scoured the island in a motor vehicle was an unfortunate coincidence for Glynray's case.)

Having drawn from Madison all the useful information he could, Glynray's defense was reduced to the character witnesses he had lined up. He planned to exhaust the court with dozens of them, before resting his case. That day alone, he managed to get three or four on the stand, among them Randolph Rouge and Branson Bowles. The former had attended secondary school with the accused, and was one of his closest friends; the latter, in his capacity as teacher at the Boys' School, could attest to the fact that Madison selflessly volunteered his time there every year, for a fishing demonstration on Career Day.

After Glynray finished with Branson, the judge adjourned the trial for the evening. Stepping down from the dais, Branson found May waiting for him, beaming. Despite the bad turn the trial had taken, in terms of worms and boats and vehicles, it appeared that she was happy with what Branson had said on the witness stand. Soon Randolph, Trevor, and Patience joined them, and together they reassured one another, Randolph and Branson repeatedly complimented for their articulate testimony.

Taking advantage of May's good mood, Branson put his arm around her waist and escorted her away from the court. Trevor shot him an admonitory glance, which Branson pretended not to see. He had May in his arms and that was all that mattered. He would testify for Madison a hundred times if he could.

As the Rouges left to go back to the bakery, chattering along the way about the day's ups and downs, Bruce and Raoul bumped into each other in the crowd that still milled about. Although Bruce wasn't to blame for the failings of the court, Raoul couldn't help but be upset with him for ever suggesting that a trial would yield the truth—a theory to which Raoul had let himself helplessly cling.

"It's not going very well, is it?" Raoul said sharply.

"It certainly isn't," Bruce agreed. He didn't say it out loud, but he had come to the same conclusions as Raoul: Madison was innocent and the trial was hurting more than it was helping.

The pair of them stood there silently, each wondering what he might do to change the tide of the trial. They watched the outdoor court empty and enjoyed the evening air. It was a perfect island night, the kind that only Oh could fashion. A not-too-warm breeze carried the scent of frangipani and of oniony swordfish stewing for someone's supper. Crickets and frogs chirped and whistled in time with a reggae love song that sifted from a distant radio. The island felt contented and still. Soon the stars would come out, if only to marvel at the peace the moon commanded.

So incongruous was the stillness with the tenor of the day nearing its end, that both Bruce and Raoul were moved, simultaneously, to action. All the trial talk of fishing boats had got Raoul to thinking about Dagmore Bowles again. He harbored little hope that a visit to Mrs. Jaymes would help, but at least it was something to do, something to try. If he hurried, he could chat with her for an hour or two before she went to bed. Bruce, on the other hand, had a more immediate something to try and—smiling his strange bakery smile—bid the already departing Raoul a good night.

41

It was well into evening when Raoul reached Mrs. Jaymes's house. He apologized for troubling her so late and, without any pretense as to his presence, simply asked her if she might spare an hour or so to tell him more of Dagmore's story. He told her he'd like to hear about the fishing boat, particularly. Mrs. Jaymes replied that there really wasn't a lot to say in that regard, that the boat hadn't amounted to all that much in the end, but she was certainly delighted to continue her tale.

She invited him in and started in on her story, which Raoul continued to take down in his notebook, just in case something salient emerged.

"You said something about the Captain and a girl last time, too," Raoul reminded her. "Do you remember?"

"Oh, yes," she said with a disgusted puff. "I couldn't forget *that* one any more than the Captain could."

———————

As the months went by, Mrs. Jaymes warmed more and more to the Captain's fishing boat. It was still an old wreck, if you asked her, but it was taking shape, as was the Captain himself. He devoted hours every day to sanding, smoothing, and sealing, and by the time the boat was ready for its first coat of paint, the Captain was cheerful, muscular, and tanned the color of pure dark chocolate. He looked so good, it got Mrs. Jaymes to thinking. The Captain had already tried everything to busy his body and mind, from communing with family ghosts to hosting timorous violinists. What he needed next wasn't a boat of his own but a woman. A fine island girl!

It was a doubly good idea, because Mrs. Jaymes would recruit Hammer Coates's help in finding the Captain a wife. For years she had wished to broach any subject with the handyman that wasn't related to nuts or screws or weeds in need of pulling, and had always chickened out. Thanks to the Captain's fishing boat, Hammer was at the villa every day from sun-up to sundown, and with the excuse of the Captain's wellbeing, Mrs. Jaymes would finally have a reason to pull him aside for a private chat.

In the beginning, Hammer didn't much fancy the idea of butting into the Captain's affairs, but the thought of butting into Mrs. Jaymes's intrigued him, and so he agreed to go along. They began taking strolls through town to evaluate the pool of pretty girls, and in a few months Mrs. Jaymes had compiled a list of over two dozen candidates to work her way through. She hadn't yet figured out how she would introduce the females into the Captain's house, but once she did, surely from a pool so deep he would find at least one that was pleasing.

While Mrs. Jaymes elaborated her bride plan, the Captain, clueless, busied himself with his boat. It had become his newest obsession, and for it he abandoned even his precious piano temporarily. Once he and Hammer had finished the basic renovations, the Captain began to embellish his boat with glossy varnish and brass touches, and gadgets for every purpose. It was the most kitted-out boat of its size on Oh (it held no more than two persons at once). Dagmore painted it, and repainted it as soon as its sheen was faded by the salt or the sun. He spent more time in the boat on sand than he ever did at sea.

This doesn't mean the boat wasn't a seaworthy craft. It was. He and Hammer had taken it out to ascertain as much, having first had it blessed by a Baptist pastor, and they both came back dry as bones. After that, the Captain took it out alone now and then, but being at sea made him sad, while the *possibility* of setting sail excited him. So in the end, sea-captain Dagmore enjoyed his boat more on land than on water.

Try though she might during the early months of the Captain's boating, Mrs. Jaymes couldn't coax him to invite some fine island girl for a day at sea. She had offered not only to make up their picnic lunch, but to provide the woman as well.

"Row her up the coast a piece and lunch on the shore," she suggested, but Dagmore only looked at her like she was mad.

Having failed to hit the mark by direct strike, Mrs. Jaymes opted for a subtle, sneak attack. Suddenly she was demanding more help at the villa (something the Captain had always promised her, she reminded him) and parading in front of him every day candidates for the positions of dishwasher, laundress, flower-gardener, and assistant cook. Still, the Captain didn't bite. A good year and a half went by, maybe more, and Mrs. Jaymes had recruited every fine girl she and Hammer could find at the market, in church, and in line at the Island Post. Captain Dagmore, though, preferred to buff his boat alone. Mrs. Jaymes had all but decided to throw in the beach towel, when fate gave a push to her plan.

Although the Captain was not the sort of man you could tell what to do—he had to make his mistakes for himself—you could plant a seed in his soul that, over time, would bloom. Mrs. Jaymes had done just that for years, when she complained about his troublesome visitors. He knew deep in his heart she was right all along, but not until the bad barracuda and his guests' near demise had he acknowledged the raging blossoms in his bosom. The germ Mrs. Jaymes had lodged in his heart *this* time around had taken root far more quickly, unbeknownst to her or to the Captain himself.

As he walked to Higgins in town one day, where he planned to purchase some brass cleaner and extra-soft cloths, he pondered Mrs. Jaymes's incessant matchmaking and how problematic he was sure a woman would be. Far more so than a boat, he reasoned, which required only a bit of scrubbing and polish. He could prop it in the sand and forget about it; if he never got it wet, it wouldn't complain.

Dagmore decided to stop at the Savings Bank before he did his shopping. He liked to check on his accounts from time to time, to make certain the island bankers had his interest at heart. There was a long, slow line, as usual, which Dagmore would normally have forgone in favor of a rap with his knuckles on the Bank Manager's office door. On this particular day, it so happened the Captain found himself waiting behind a pretty young thing (at least from the back), with an hourglass shape clad in tight white cotton. Her dress was dotted with dainty purple flowers and cinched at the waist with a shiny black belt that matched the shiny blackness of her high-ish heels.

Dagmore found himself staring at her, amazed. It wasn't desire that determined his interest but awe. Mrs. Jaymes must be completely mad, he told himself, to think a creature as complicated as this could solve a man's problems. "Imagine!" he scoffed.

"Pardon me?" the creature, hearing him, turned back and said. She was as tall as Dagmore, but because of her shoes and the way her cotton dress propelled her chest upward, he found himself face to face with her ample cleavage.

"Did you say something, sir?" she tried again, calling Dagmore's attention to her face. Its features were regal, strong cheekbones and full, humid lips. Her eyes were black pools, deeper than any sea he had ever peered into.

"No. No, I didn't," he managed to whisper and she smiled at him, then turned around again.

Dagmore's heart was racing. He couldn't remember what he was doing at the Bank, and he had no idea which account was his. It seemed to him that all that mattered in the world right then were the purple blossoms raging over the poorly contained bosoms of the girl that stood close enough to touch.

To think, a creature as complicated as this could solve a man's problems.

Imagine!

———

Before Mrs. Jaymes could reveal the identity of this creature that was sure to cause more problems than she would solve, Raoul decided to call it a night. It was enough that he saw Dagmore's son, Branson, mooning over May Fuller all day in court. Raoul wasn't up to hearing about the Captain in love, not with murders and missing women to sort out. He said goodbye to Mrs. Jaymes and went home on foot. He wondered, as he walked, if he ought to ask Branson Bowles about his father. He tried to remember how young the boy would have been when his father killed himself. Ten maybe? Raoul supposed the suicidal Captain was a sensitive subject for Branson, and he decided to leave it alone. Besides, hope how he might for some clue in the Captain's story, there didn't seem to be a single one.

Raoul reached home and crawled into bed. Ms. Lila had left him some supper, but he wasn't hungry. As she snored gently next to him, Raoul replayed the day's events in his mind, the particulars of the trial, Captain Dagmore and the girl at the bank, and... Bruce! It struck Raoul suddenly that as he left the court that evening, Bruce had spoken to him with a strange smile on his lips. A strange smile that Raoul had seen before.

"I wonder what in the world he's up to now," Raoul sighed. Inside his head, though, a quiet and desperate little fly prayed that Bruce had indeed got up to something.

And, whatever it was, it had better be awfully good.

42

Honest man, early 40s, athletic, with fishing boat STILL
seeks honest woman, early 30s, with bicycle, cooking skills,
and dainty hands. For immediate marriage.

Bruce was up and at the bakery early on the Thursday of the
second week of trial. He knew he was in for a busy day of
court reporting, and he wanted some of Trevor's whole wheat
buns to boost his stamina. Truth be told, he also suspected a hero's
welcome at the bakery, and who would pass up one of those?

"Bruce!" Trevor exclaimed, holding the *Morning Crier* in his
hand. "Do you realize what this means?"

"If you mean," Bruce replied, "that the real killer is still out
there somewhere and still putting ads in my paper, then yes, I do."

"I wonder if Glynray has seen it?" an overjoyed Trevor asked
no one in particular.

"Seen what?" Patience asked, coming into the bakery from the
storeroom in back, where she had been counting bags of flour.

291

"This!" Trevor held out the morning edition.

Patience wiped her hands on her apron and took it from him. "What's this supposed to mean?" she asked, confused, looking alternately at her husband and at Bruce.

"It means whoever placed the first ad is still out there," Trevor said gleefully. He grabbed Patience by the waist and danced her around. "Wait until May hears this!"

Trevor was so excited he didn't know who to call first, Glynray Justice or May Fuller. He phoned the lawyer's office, only to discover that Glynray, no slacker, was already at court with a copy of the paper, waiting for an audience with the judge. Next, Trevor called May, but she, too, had seen the ad and reached the same happy conclusion as everyone else. She rushed to court to see if Madison would be freed on the spot, but it wasn't quite as simple as that. Still, Judge Samuels did declare a day of recess, mostly to diffuse the reaction that the news of the ad had triggered. He figured the lawyers could sort the matter out for themselves, while *he* could spend a much needed day at the beach.

Not only did the lawyers not sort it out for themselves, but each dug in his heels, adamant about making a public show of the new piece of evidence. Glynray didn't want some quiet dismissal of Exhibit A (the first lonely hearts ad) in light of the ad just placed, and neither did Monday, who felt the new ad needed rebutting head-on and on stage. The day off was thus for nothing. Worse, while Judge Samuels blew off steam, the local gossip only picked some up.

Raoul had experience with newspaper ads, having placed one or two in the past. He knew there was always more to them than met the eye. Though he hadn't seen the *Crier* that morning, he heard about the second lonely hearts ad the minute he got to court. Mr. Justice and Mr. Jones might be content to discover the ad's merits in front of an audience, Raoul thought to himself, but *he* was not. He thought it best to investigate them beforehand and in private, and for that he sought out Bruce.

Raoul couldn't have imagined the two blows the day would hold for him. Before he could even get to Bruce, the first one came at him all the way from Killig. Raoul had stopped at his office, and there he had gotten a terrible call. The official results of the blood analysis were in and they weren't good. As it happened, they weren't bad, either. They were inconclusive, which was worse.

"Are you sure?" Raoul asked Betty Grewber's supervisor.

"I'm one-hundred percent sure of inconclusiveness, sir," she answered. "I have the technician's report right in front of me. Perhaps you sent us an insufficient sample. If you'd like to send another, we'll be happy to run the tests again."

Raoul hung up, cursing Fred Nettles. Bloody builder must have shaved the samples too thinly, Raoul thought. Poor Fred! His shavings were perfectly proportioned. The blame lay with Betty and her lemongrass. She needed her job, you see, and couldn't admit to her spilled cup of tea, which as it turned out hadn't contaminated the sample all that badly. Betty was almost positive the blood wasn't human but fish. Still, she dared not say so to a scientific certainty, lest her lemongrass lead her to wrongly rule out a murder.

With a shake of his head, Raoul imagined the field day the Prosecution would have with the results, and he hoped his chat with Bruce would bring better news.

It didn't. Bruce told Raoul—off the record—that the two lonely hearts ads were placed by two different lonely hearts. Or so he thought. One of the ads was hand-written, the other typed. One on graph paper ripped from a schoolbook, one on writing paper pulled from a box. One was tucked in an envelope with cash, the other was clipped to one of Oh's rainbow bills.

"In other words," Bruce summed it up, not seeming terribly concerned, "Madison is technically not in the clear, and they told me this morning that I have to testify tomorrow."

"For the Prosecution or the Defense?" Raoul asked.

"Both," he said cheerfully. "But don't worry. I know just what I have to do."

"You have to tell the truth," Raoul said reluctantly. "What else can you do?"

Bruce didn't answer. He flashed Raoul a knowing grin and harrumphed.

———

When the trial reconvened the next day, lawyers for both sides champed at the bit to put Bruce on the stand and address the new lonely hearts ad. First, however, Raoul whispered something to the judge, who motioned for Monday and Glynray to approach the bench, where the judge whispered to both of them in turn. Then the lawyers whispered to each other, whispered to the judge again, and finally took their seats—all of which sent whispers rippling through the crowd. What was going on? everyone wanted to know.

Judge Samuels pounded his gavel and announced that the results of the blood found on Madison's fishing boat were inconclusive.

This meant the blood and boat meant nothing, he instructed the jury, and he ordered the lawyers not to mention them again until closing arguments. Judge Samuels was cranky and impatient that morning, for his previous day off had, by contrast, reminded him of the trial's tedium. He was tired of exams and cross-exams, of directs and redirects, when it was plain enough where the trial was headed.

In light of the ruling regarding the results, Glynray requested that Judge Samuels have the boat's photo removed from the center of Monday's corkboard, but the judge, angered that Glynray had mentioned the boat against express orders not to, punished him by denying the request and allowed the photo to stay.

Because the Defense had the floor, Glynray was the one who called Bruce to the stand. After necessary but banal questions concerning his full name (Bruce Kandele), domicile (Bishop Street, Port-St. Luke), and occupation (the *Morning Crier*'s editor-in-chief, copyeditor, reporter, and special correspondent), Glynray brought up the subject of the classified ad.

"Please tell the court how the ad that appeared in your newspaper yesterday differs from the ad you published nearly a month ago, or Exhibit A," he said, holding up the first ad in its plastic bag.

"They're identical. Yesterday's ad contains one extra word, 'still,'" Bruce answered.

"Is it your opinion that both ads were placed by the same person?"

"I couldn't say, but it would be quite a coincidence for two different people to place identical ads."

"Both of the ads were placed anonymously, that's right?" Glynray asked.

"Yes, sir. Found them both slipped under the exact same door."

"You are no doubt aware that the Prosecution is convinced my client placed the first one," Glynray said.

"Exhibit A? I'm aware."

"You said it was unlikely that two different people placed the two ads in question."

"I said it would be quite a coincidence, yes."

"Assuming that the party responsible for Exhibit A and the party responsible for yesterday's ad are one and the same, do you have an opinion as to whether or not my client is that party?"

"I don't see how he could be, unless they let him out of jail to slip a note under my door."

"Thank you, Mr. Kandele," Glynray said. "I wish to state for the record, Your Honor and members of the jury, that Mr. Fuller was not at any time released from custody to deliver correspondence to Mr. Kandele or to anyone else. I have no further questions."

Monday Jones pensively rubbed his palms together as he approached Bruce on the witness stand.

"Mr. Kandele," he began. "I would never cast doubt on the veracity of your testimony, but, if it pleases the court, I would like to ask that you produce the original ads that were slipped under your office door."

"I'm afraid I can't do that, Mr. Jones."

"Why is that?"

"I don't have the first one. I threw it out after it was typeset."

"And the second?"

"Yes, sir, I did keep that one."

"Yet you can't submit it to the court?"

"No, sir, Mr. Jones. I'm a journalist, and therefore my sources are privileged. If I started revealing every piece of information I got, what kind of reporter would I be?"

"You're a man of principle," Monday nodded. "I like that. Surely, though, as a reporter, you can appreciate the potential fact-finding significance that this second ad would afford us."

"I can. But that doesn't change the fact that a journalist never reveals his sources."

"Then tell me this, sir," Monday said, changing direction. "How can I be sure the second ad exists at all? Maybe you invented it. Maybe you slipped it under the office door yourself to influence the jury in Mr. Fuller's favor."

"That's absurd!" Bruce cried out, insulted. "Why would I slip an anonymous ad under my own office door? I am in possession of a full set of keys to the newspaper office."

Monday could feel the sympathies of the jury slipping away and adopted a harder line.

"Alright, Mr. Kandele. I'll go along with you. Let's assume that Mr. Fuller did not place the ads in your paper, not either one of them. Is there anything in your journalistic experience, any case study, any news story you've written, that says a man not guilty of newspaper ads is automatically not guilty of murder?"

Bruce stared at Monday and swore under his breath. It seemed the Prosecutor had one-upped him.

"Not to my recollection," Bruce answered vaguely.

"Let's make sure I have that right, Mr. Kandele. It is entirely possible that a man who has *not* placed an ad in your newspaper, has in fact committed murder. Is that your testimony?"

Bruce threw Glynray a threatening glance, and with raised eyebrows urged him to object.

"Objection, Your Honor!" Glynray shouted, stumbling as he jumped up from his chair. "He's badgering my witness."

"I'll allow it," the judge said.

"Thank you, Your Honor," Monday said. "Mr. Kandele, is it your testimony that a man who has *not* placed an ad in your newspaper could in fact be a murderer?"

"Yes," Bruce said. "It looks that way."

Raoul was upset. The Bicycle Trial was turning into a kangaroo court—with *his* name all over it. He was "Central Planning" and the one they would blame if the case went awry in the end. Things were looking terrible for Madison. Bruce had been tricked on the witness stand, and Glynray had spent the rest of the day boring jurors and spectators both, with a list of character witnesses nobody cared about. As near as Raoul could tell, few truths had been exposed by either side, and still a girl was missing. He had the weekend to figure something out—if he could—before closing arguments began on Monday.

Luckily, whatever ghost or vandal or meddler was mucking up Raoul's walls was inclined to agree, and he (or she) was about to point to him in the direction of the missing girl.

43

Raoul rushed home from court on Friday evening, resolute in his intentions. Before the weekend was done, he would come up with a clue, if it meant he had to go all the way to Killig himself to scour the airport registers there. As it turned out, that wouldn't be necessary, for the answers he sought—or the hint of them—were no farther than his own backyard (there, and perhaps Ladywood Road).

Raoul stormed into his cottage when he got there, gave his wife a peck on the cheek, and pulled out the notebooks from his sessions with Mrs. Jaymes. Next he gathered up his newspaper clippings of every article about the Bicycle Trial and its run-up. Finally, he dragged out his personal trial dossier, which contained everything from copies of the request for blood analysis to invoices for toilet rentals and tarps. He sat himself down in the middle of the sitting room and spread all his papers around him, a doughnut of variables and he, the hole. "I'm not moving from this spot," he shouted to his wife, "until I've solved the riddle!"

Ms. Lila looked at him with a mix of pity and amusement, for she had an announcement of her own to make, one that would supersede Raoul's by a mile. No sense torturing him, she thought, and simply blurted it out: "You've got a new message on the wall outside."

"I do?" Raoul jumped up, betraying his enthusiasm, which surely went against every tenet of the plain-as-noses-on-faces school of thinking.

"See for yourself."

Raoul ran outside. His first pink wall, where Dagmore and Rena had once appeared interconnected, now boasted a new intersected cross. Dagmore's name had re-surfaced in vertical ghostly white-ish squiggles, but this time, the D in DAGMORE led to a horizontal DAVIES.

Davies?

Raoul went back inside to reason with Ms. Lila. "What does Davies have to do with anything?" he asked her. (He already knew the answer, but was hoping he was wrong.)

"Only one 'Davies' of any relevance around here," she said, tilting her head suggestively. She meant Abigail Davies, island midwife, and, if not Raoul's enemy, certainly not his friend.

"It figures that wretched woman would have her hand in this!" he complained. "I can't bear the thought of going to see her."

In addition to the bad blood between Raoul and Abigail on account of her being his (missing) first wife's confidante (and, he suspected, her accomplice), there was a little matter of his granddaughter, Almondine, which had never sat well with Raoul. Abigail had been his daughter's midwife and, though Raoul couldn't prove it, had had a hand in little Almondine's mysterious (and maybe magical) arrival.

"I won't do it," he said. "I won't go begging that woman for information. If she has any, I'm the last person she'd tell it to anyway. She's proven that time and again."

It pained Ms. Lila to see her husband tormented by old hurts, and she suggested that, since the name Davies had shown up interlocked with Dagmore's, maybe Raoul could ask Mrs. Jaymes about the connection between the two.

"A fine idea!" Raoul exclaimed, grabbing her by the shoulders and planting a congratulatory kiss on her lips. "I'll go see Mrs. Jaymes in the morning. But just to be safe, I better study my variables a while longer." She nodded at him affectionately, as if in agreement, and went to the bedroom to read. Raoul plopped himself back down into his doughnut.

"Wait just a minute!" he called out as he settled on the floor.

"What is it?" Ms. Lila came running.

"Dagmore and Abigail! Of course they're connected! How could I forget? The one and only time I met the man, years ago, he was asking about Abigail. He was in love with her and was sure island magic was somehow keeping them apart. Well, you know what I think of that kind of talk, and I told him so! The first time I went to see Mrs. Jaymes she said *I* was the reason Dagmore finally gave up on Abigail."

Before returning to bed, Ms. Lila said something like "That's wonderful, dear" or "I'm glad you're getting somewhere" or maybe even simply "good night." Whatever it was, Raoul didn't hear it. His head was buzzing and his neck hurt from surveying his circle of clues. What did it all mean? Things seemed to be coming full circle and yet the ends weren't quite matching up. He pored over his doughnut until late in the night, but still he couldn't put his finger on the part of it that was missing.

44

In the morning, Raoul woke up early, and chipper. Back to Mrs. Jaymes's house he rushed, not even bothering to stop at his office first. How lucky, he thought, that two whole days lay ahead before the trial reconvened! If he could get her to line up the rest of her clouds, he was sure he could work out the Rena riddle in time.

"Mrs. Jaymes," he yelled through her open front door. "Mrs. Jaymes, I need to talk to you. Are you there?"

"What's all this excitement on a Saturday morning?" she inquired as she reached the doorway and invited him in.

"Mrs. Jaymes, I have to ask you about Abigail Davies. About her and the Captain."

"You want to hear now, do you? I tried to tell you last time and you ran off."

"You mean the girl at the bank? That was Abigail?" Raoul was stunned into momentary silence. Abigail's name had turned up on his wall just two days after she turned up in Mrs. Jaymes's story.

"It was Abigail, alright. 'I found her, Mrs. Jaymes! I found her!' the Captain came in yelling. He didn't even know her name. I was so happy for him. Until he told me who the 'her' was."

"How did he tell you if he didn't know her name?" Raoul asked, making furious notes in his notebook as he took a seat on the sofa.

Dagmore told her how tall the girl was, she explained, and described the girl's deep eyes, her moist lips and her regal cheekbones. He said her shape was pleasant, slim in the middle and wider below and above. When he got to her bosoms, poorly contained in their cotton, Mrs. Jaymes had cottoned on.

She told Raoul: "'Not Abigail Davies?!' I shouted, and I described Abigail to him again, with a woman's eye for detail, and we agreed it had to be her. 'You don't want that one,' I told him. 'She has a handful of children, and she can't yet be more than twenty years old.' All he wanted to know was if she was married. I told him she wasn't, though a decent girl with a handful of children ought to be, but he didn't care. You know what he said?"

"What?" Raoul asked.

"'Thank goodness!' So I said, 'Don't think for one minute that I'm going to start changing diapers and cooking up bottles at *my* age, Captain!' He had his hand in another hornet's nest and didn't even know it."

———

Before settling into midwifery at the age of nineteen or thereabouts, Abigail Davies had assumed a number of positions, each of which compromised her in turn. She had worked for a plumber, a painter, and a bookkeeper (who insisted on showing her their pipes and strokes and assets), and by the time Dagmore set his sights on her, she knew all too well that a sea captain would be no less of a distraction. Abigail had four little mouths to feed and her only concern was her gainful work, assisting the young island ladies who, like her, had had their fill of men.

Dagmore had little experience with courtship (he had filled up his share of female houseguests, but they always came and went) and so approached the matter of Abigail like any other of his island research projects. Notebook in hand and packed lunch tucked in his shoulder bag, he began to follow her around town, recording her every move, every purchase, and every preference, so as to formulate his plan of attack. He couldn't blurt out his attentions like some rash, lovesick fool, not with a woman as practical and experienced and intelligent as Abigail must be. He would declare his feelings and his intentions more efficiently, scientifically. What sensible woman would refuse an advance unspoiled by poetry, one perfectly timed?

It took a week for Dagmore to collect the data he needed. He learned that Abigail woke up every day by six a.m., dressed and fed her babies, and left them in her mother's care (Abigail still lived with her parents and siblings). She walked to town, treated herself to a leisurely breakfast of coffee and buns in a shop by the docks, then spent her mornings visiting clients at their homes. In the afternoons she ran her errands and, at the end of the day, went home by bus.

These were just her movements; a seasoned researcher like Dagmore was capable of discovering far more than *that*. He noted that she preferred her buns with raisins, that she always stopped to admire jacaranda trees, and that when she had extra cash, she bought herself skin cream made from honey. On a hot day she fancied ice cream, always vanilla, and she never carried an umbrella when it rained. Instead, she removed her shoes and went on her way in stocking feet (thanks to a gossipy shopgirl, Dagmore also discovered Abigail wore the kind of stockings that stopped mid-thigh).

He observed that Abigail's favorite color was red. She liked her mangoes soft, her plums stewed, and her favorite fish was snapper. She wore dresses and skirts, not denims or trousers; she could carry a tune; and she was always on time. Her fees were fair, her services fairly sought-after, her demeanor reservedly firm.

Had Abigail lived alone, Dagmore would have called on her at her house, and professed his love there, but because she lived with her babies and brothers and sisters, that wouldn't do. Dagmore's declaration required some peace and privacy. He hated to admit it, but he would have to ask Mrs. Jaymes for help. He sat her down and explained that he planned, very plainly, to tell Abigail Davies she had stolen his heart and he wished her hand in exchange. He wanted Abigail to marry him and live with him at the villa, with her four little ones, for whom he would happily provide.

"You can't tell her that!" Mrs. Jaymes hollered when she heard the plan.

"Why not? It's the truth."

"For one thing, if you tell her you want to take care of her and her babies, she might just say 'yes' for the free room and board," Mrs. Jaymes explained.

"That's unfair of you to say, Mrs. Jaymes. You don't even know her!"

"Nor do you! You can't tap a woman you don't even know on the shoulder and tell her, 'Let's get married and live on a mountaintop.' She's likely to call the police!"

"I see no point in games or pretexts," he objected. "My mind and my heart are made up. She's the only one I want."

"Maybe so, but it's a safe bet she doesn't want *you*. She has no idea who you are."

In spite of her feelings for Abigail, Mrs. Jaymes found herself dispensing romantic advice, telling the Captain what it was that every woman needed and longed for. It was not the time to be avoiding poetry, she chided him, the more the better! The same for flowers and chocolates and pretty things. If he wanted to conquer a woman, he had to write her a song and row her in his boat and not send her a marriage contract by way of the Island Post.

"Fine," the Captain replied, and retired to his study to compose an invitation.

"Dear Ms. Davies," he wrote, then decided that was too formal and wrote "Dear Abigail" instead, but that looked too forward. He ended up with "To Abigail Davies from Captain Dagmore Bowles." He wrote that although she didn't know him formally, they had met once at the Savings Bank and she had struck him then as a very fine girl. He hoped that she would find it agreeable to take tea with him in his home, and if so, he would be happy to meet her in town and escort her up his hill. He suggested the following afternoon, and said that he would wait for her at the port at three o'clock. Then he sealed the letter with a dollop of wax (in red, her favorite color), and he impressed his "B" upon it.

Now, how would he get it to her? The surest way, he figured, was to catch her on her way home in the afternoon. He put on piano clothes and polished his shoes, perched his hat on his head and, shouting "Off I go" to Mrs. Jaymes, went to the bus stop to sit and wait. When Abigail finally turned up, Dagmore, faced with her heaving cleavage, was a fish out of water. He flopped through his introduction and his discourse in a manner that boasted little of either efficiency or science, and sloppily thrust his invitation at her as she boarded the bus.

Back at the villa, Mrs. Jaymes wanted to know how the Captain had fared, and he honestly couldn't say. He told her he got nervous and tongue-tied but had delivered his invitation and time would tell. He would go and wait for Abigail the following day. In the meantime, and in hopes that she would indeed come to tea, he had Mrs. Jaymes prepare all her favorite things: raisin buns and stewed plums, and jam made with soft, ripe mangoes.

Abigail did show up at the port at three o'clock to meet Dagmore, but only to tell him that it was not agreeable to her to take tea with him or with any man, and to advise him to set his sights on some other fine girl, of which the island was overrun. Then she stormed off somewhat snootily, her hips bouncing to and fro in a way that made the Captain love her even more. He was determined to win her heart.

"Plan B, Mrs. Jaymes!" he announced coming into the kitchen after his failed rendezvous.

"What would that be?" she asked him.

"I'm not sure but we'll figure it out."

His use of the plural irked her at first, but when the Captain recounted how Abigail had rejected him and haughtily swung her hips, Mrs. Jaymes was miffed on the Captain's account.

"How dare a girl like that turn her fanny to the likes of you!" Mrs. Jaymes exclaimed. "Why, she should thank her lucky stars that you ever laid eyes on her! You want Plan B?" she said to Dagmore. "You go back to that bus stop tomorrow and take her these buns. They're full of raisins, just like she likes, and as light and airy as they come. Take her a poem, too. Go look through all those books of yours and copy something about the moonlight or the stars. Go on!"

Dagmore did as he was told, and returned to the bus stop the following afternoon armed with pastry and poetry. When Abigail showed up, he presented her with Mrs. Jaymes's buns and recited a poem comparing her eyes to the sun and her teeth to the twinkling stars. The bus pulled up just then and before Abigail could wag her hips at him and hop on, he invited her again, "Would you like to have tea tomorrow?"

"No, I would not," she told him, "and I believe I said so yesterday."

The Captain went home defeated, again, and reported what had happened. "The tongue on that child!" Mrs. Jaymes said, shaking her head.

Together they devised Plan C, cream made from honey, for Abigail's skin (bought from the pharmacy in town), coupled with another poem. "A longer one, this time!" Mrs. Jaymes insisted.

Plan C proved no more effective than Plan B. When Dagmore invited her to tea the next day. She said, "I told you yesterday and the day before, I don't want to have any tea."

When the Captain returned home defeated for a third time, Mrs. Jaymes had a revelation. "I know what Abigail Davies is up to," she said smugly and pointing her finger. "She's playing hard to get, the greedy thing. We'll have to raise the stakes."

They came up with Plan D, a dress for Abigail that Mrs. Jaymes sewed herself. It took her over a week to finish it, but it was a stunning piece of island haberdashery. Its burgundy bodice was fitted, with flowing cap sleeves, its skirt full and flowered in petaled specimens of yellow and red, sliced here and there by leaves of dark and light green.

"It's lovely, Mrs. Jaymes," Dagmore praised her, and left for the bus stop, dragging the dress behind him. Although Abigail had accepted it and carried it onto the bus, she once more declined the Captain's invitation, and, for her part, invited him to stop inviting her.

"Hmm," Mrs. Jaymes said. "Perhaps the girl isn't as greedy as I thought. Maybe you would do better to lavish her with your true feelings, instead of with lavish gifts. What if you wrote her a poem of your own?" Thus was hatched Plan E, or the Elegy to Abigail Davies on the Occasion of First Sighting Her at the Savings Bank.

Now, *this* was a hit at the bus stop! The passengers, who had rather begun to look forward to Dagmore's antics, were enthralled by his lyrics and iambs. He depicted Abigail as a latter-day island Beatrice who alone could illumine the seaway that the adrift and mid-life Captain was meant to follow. Without her, his redemption was doomed to lie hidden amidst the waves.

"You're very persistent," Abigail admitted, but despite the standing ovation that the other riders felt moved to produce, Abigail still declined tea with Dagmore. She knew too well the trouble that men caused. It started with a cup of tea, then there was sugar and "Honey," and before you knew it your belly was bursting. Abigail had had enough of that for now.

If his lofty words hadn't quite done the trick, perhaps Abigail would be swayed by something more down-to-earth. Plan F was a basket of fruit. Mango, papaya, guava, banana, soursop, and a small-but-still-significantly sized watermelon. When Dagmore showed up with such abundance, Abigail was too stunned to speak. To Dagmore's renewed invitation to tea, all she could manage in the form of refusal was a firm shake of the head.

"Not a single word of complaint?" Mrs. Jaymes asked, delighted. "A good sign. A very good sign."

Plans G and H were executed in tandem, fresh grouper and a fresh hen, respectively, which Mrs. Jaymes herself went to the fish and poultry markets to purchase. So as not to arrive with sweaty fish and chicken, Dagmore had left it a bit late and almost missed Abigail. When she saw him coming, she quickly jumped on the bus that had stopped in front her. She urged the driver to leave, but he, along with the other regular passengers, had taken an interest in the business of Captain Dagmore (there being little else of interest on his daily route), and he insisted they all hear Dagmore out.

"Abigail," he huffed, tired from running to get to her in time. "How are you today?" There had grown a strange familiarity between them in spite of themselves, owing to the constancy of Dagmore's efforts to court her. She nodded at him through the open door of the bus but didn't say anything. He gave her the grouper and the hen and again invited her to join him for tea at the villa. She accepted the gifts, said "no, thank you," then took her seat and stared straight ahead, making it clear that her transaction with Dagmore was done.

As the bus pulled onto the road, the riders' tongues loosened and they bothered Abigail about the kindly Captain Bowles. The men were annoyed that Abigail was making a fool of an island man, and jealous of all the free food she was getting; the women were appalled by her snobbish pride, and jealous that such a distinguished and wealthy man as Dagmore sought Abigail's hand, not theirs. By the time Abigail got off the bus, her fellow riders were in such a lather that the "good night" she uttered was met with hostile indifference and all but ignored.

This got her to worrying. Abigail's midwifery business was doing well enough, but it wasn't booming, despite the islanders' enthusiastic love-making. The midwife market was saturated with ladies older and better known (though not more talented) than she. Her income depended on the locals' acceptance of her as a humble and compassionate being. If word of this Dagmore business spread, it was likely to jeopardize her work. She decided then and there, though it pleased her little, that the next time the Captain showed up at the bus stop, she would publicly accept his invitation to tea, and then deal with him in private at the villa.

How dare he compromise her bread and butter with his fowl and big, stinking fish?

———

"So Abigail finally went to the villa for tea?" Raoul asked Mrs. Jaymes.

"Even better. He got her on a picnic. Eventually. That's when she told him she only accepted to protect her reputation."

Mrs. Jaymes explained that the day of the failed fish and fowl, Dagmore had come home especially downhearted and had taken out his fishing boat. He rarely put it in the water, as much as he loved it, and when he did, he always let it bob close to home. That day, though, the smooth, quiet sea had beckoned.

"Dagmore felt the sky overhead and the sea underneath and it calmed him," Mrs. Jaymes said. "He breathed in the sea air and thought of his sea-faring father. He rowed up the coastline and even went ashore."

She leaned closer to Raoul and added, by way of aside, "He hadn't been exploring in years, you know. He still hadn't learned to live on Oh, although he could imagine himself nowhere else."

"How does Abigail fit into all this?" Raoul wondered aloud.

"She fits in because when the Captain went ashore, he found an enormous jacaranda tree, thick with purple blossoms. He remembered seeing Abigail admire jacarandas when she passed them, and he remembered the purple flowers on her dress the first time they met. Maybe tea in a fancy villa was too stifling for a girl as free and strong and modest as Abigail, he figured. Maybe she would prefer a simple picnic out of doors. Soon after that, he went to the bus stop and said to her very directly, straight from his heart, 'Would you like to go on a picnic? There's a beach not far from me with a beautiful jacaranda tree. I can take you there in my boat.' And she made a big show of saying 'Thank you for your invitation. Let's go on Sunday'—."

"—because she wanted everyone around to know she hadn't refused him," Raoul chimed in.

"Yes," Mrs. Jaymes confirmed. "The Captain thought his heartfelt words had done it. Or his jacaranda Plan J. But that one failed as miserably as his Ice-cream Plan before it."

45

It was Saturday afternoon at the Orleans, and, like every Saturday, Ms. Lila was preparing one of Raoul's favorite meals, minced beef in mango and beer, with a side of fried plantains. On Saturdays they always ate an early dinner, after which they took a stroll to the Loyal Cinema for the early showing. Ms. Lila was in the kitchen, busy peeling and slicing, when Raoul returned home from his most recent tête-à-tête with Mrs. Jaymes.

"Any luck?" she asked him, quickly adding, "did you ever pick up the paint?"

"No," he sighed, then added, "I ordered it but have to pick it up next week."

"Mrs. Jaymes didn't tell you anything about Abigail?"

"She told me, alright," he said. "Try making heads or tails out of any of it."

"Oh, dear. Is she losing her mind? She *is* well past ninety," Ms. Lila said.

"Her mind is sharp as a tack! The problem is Dagmore's story. It only skirts the issues. Fishing boats, Abigail. None of it connects and none of it has anything to do with Rena Baker. Mrs. Jaymes is certain that the Captain didn't even *know* a Baker on Oh."

"Well, what did she tell you?" Ms. Lila asked. "You've been there the better part of a day."

While Ms. Lila saw to her starches and minced her meat, Raoul pulled out his notebook and relayed to her all that Mrs. Jaymes had relayed to him. He told her about the Savings Bank and Abigail's bursting bosoms, about Mrs. Jaymes's doubts and Dagmore's insistence. He told her about the Captain's plans to win Abigail's heart, from his very first declined invitation to failed plans B through J.

"So the jacaranda plan didn't work either," Mrs. Lila remarked as she stewed. "What happened? You said Abigail agreed to a picnic, if for all the wrong reasons."

"Let's see," Raoul said, fishing in his bag for his notes. "Mrs. Jaymes had so much to say I could barely get it all down." He opened up what was now the third notebook filled with the facts of Dagmore's life and began to read aloud.

————

Mrs. Jaymes had been trying to get the Captain on a picnic with a pretty girl for longer than she cared to remember. When he came home on a Friday evening, however, announcing his Sunday plans with Abigail, she had second thoughts. Now that Abigail's visit was nigh, her doubts about the girl's suitability came back—as did her twitching instincts, which told her that things were not destined to end happily. Because she didn't know what to do to fix them, in an unusual departure from her custom, Mrs. Jaymes kept her doubts to herself and prepared a potato pie for the picnic.

Dagmore asked her to stew some plums, too, to bread and fry some snapper, and to ice some bush tea. For his part, he spent all of Saturday cleaning the beach and polishing his boat. Everything had to be perfect if he was to propose to Abigail that they wed.

Despite the Captain's careful plans—or because of them, Mrs. Jaymes would have argued—there was to be no proposal that Sunday. Close to twelve o'clock on Saturday night, the skies erupted in a loud and pounding rain that drenched the island non-stop until dawn. The sky seemed to clear as the sun came up, but by lunchtime the clouds had overtaken it again.

"She's not going to come on a picnic with all this rain," Mrs. Jaymes gently warned the Captain.

And she didn't.

Though Abigail assured the Captain, at the bus stop the next day, that she still had every intention of joining him for an outing (where she planned to tell him in no uncertain terms to leave her alone), every time they tried to meet after that, their plans were thwarted. If they scheduled a picnic, it rained; an afternoon tea, then one of her children came down with a cough; a picture show, and the current went. Abigail got some new clients, too, with precarious pregnancies that demanded her attention twenty-four hours a day. Months went by during which Dagmore wasn't able to reach her to reschedule their latest rescheduling. When Abigail finally had time on her hands, Dagmore was so discouraged and depressed that he couldn't muster the will to call on her, and by the time he snapped out of his funk, she was busy again, with her clients, her babies, her clients' babies, or with Easter, Christmas, All Saints Day or Guy Fawkes Night. Before Dagmore knew it, a year had gone by, then two. Abigail must have thought she had rid herself of him for good.

Mrs. Jaymes, meanwhile, began to think that she would never marry Dagmore off. All he wanted was Abigail, and since he couldn't have her, he sulked. Every time he went to admire the nearby jacaranda that had almost brought them together, the sun sparkled glorious in the sky; but the minute he tried to arrange for Abigail to go see it with him, the clouds rolled in faster than he could say 'Abigail Davies.' It seemed to Mrs. Jaymes that the island itself kept Abigail and the Captain apart, though when she suggested as much, he told her she was mad and to keep her instincts to herself, thank you kindly.

———

Raoul stopped to flip through his notebook, as if re-checking his facts.

"Go on," Ms. Lila said. She was skinning her mangoes and Dagmore's story was good company while she worked.

"Well," Raoul said, flipping some more, "it went on like that, back and forth, for three years, if you can believe it. Three whole years the island managed to keep Dagmore and Abigail apart. That's Mrs. Jaymes's theory. The Captain refused to believe it, rightly so, and so what did that crazy old woman tell him to do? Come and talk to *me*!"

"Why you?" Ms. Lila asked.

"Well, not me *exactly*, but that's what happened. She told the Captain to seek the advice of his island chums, only he didn't have any. He came up with the idea to talk to someone who knew Abigail, and he happened to know that Abigail's best friend was Emma Patrice, who I, at the time, was courting."

"That's when you met him and he talked about magic?" Ms. Lila asked. "I thought you said he didn't agree with Mrs. Jaymes."

"I don't know what he believed, to tell you the truth," Raoul answered. "He asked me if I could give him a clue about Abigail's heart." At this, Ms. Lila chuckled, knowing the rapport that there had always been between Abigail and Raoul.

"Exactly," Raoul said, agreeing with his wife that the Captain's question was completely absurd. "I told him I could *not* give him a clue to Abigail's heart, and then he said his cook had this crazy idea that some kind of island magic was keeping Abigail and him apart. He said for years they tried to make a date and every time they did, it poured with rain or someone died and there was a funeral to attend."

Ms. Lila was laughing so hard now, she had to temporarily abandon her chutney. "Imagine, asking *you* of all people about Abigail and magic in the very same sentence! What did you tell him?"

"I told him I knew from Emma Patrice that Abigail didn't want a man, that she had had enough of them already and the kids to show for it. I told him he was barking up the wrong tree. 'There's plenty of fish in the sea.' That's what I said."

"What about island magic? Did you say anything about that?"

"Not a word. The best part is that Mrs. Jaymes says he took my advice. Listen to this."

———

Dagmore decided that Raoul was right about Abigail. He decided, too, that he had barked up her tree long enough. It was time at last to give up. And he *would* give up, he promised Mrs. Jaymes, after one last howl. He would leave Abigail alone forever, only not without the picnic she had promised him (where he would make a final attempt to convince her of his devotion). He ordered Mrs. Jaymes to prepare the food and the hamper, and he practically kidnapped Abigail one Sunday as she came from church. Abigail was so shocked, she had no time to decline, or even to react.

The sun was shining, but Dagmore was ready for anything. He had armed himself with an enormous umbrella, under which they would picnic regardless of what fury the jealous island clouds might decide to unleash. Under a mango tree on a beach near where he had nabbed her, Dagmore laid down a soft, clean blanket and laid out their picnic lunch. There was snapper breaded and fried, macaroni pie, boiled dasheen, and cool cabbage salad. There was ice-cold water, fresh guava juice, and homemade pineapple wine. For dessert, stewed plums and fried dough dusted with nutmeg and cinnamon.

Sadly, Abigail, once seated and calm on the blanket with the food spread out before her, became aware of the fact that she had been ambushed, hijacked, and plopped at a picnic against her will. She scolded Dagmore for his effrontery, and to her own cries and hollers mixed those of the island skies, which broke into thunder and burst into rain before Dagmore had time to erect his umbrella. When Abigail finally stormed off, after rudely assuring Dagmore that she didn't love him and never would (mind you, he hadn't yet got round to declaring himself), the food was a soggy mess of limp dough, battered cabbage, and runny purple mush. Not even the satisfaction of a final howl had the island conceded the Captain.

"Oh dear," Ms. Lila said. "The poor man! So Abigail never went to his villa or saw the jacaranda tree."

"Mrs. Jaymes said Abigail did go to the house one time after that, but Dagmore was married by then. I would have stayed to find out the details, but my head was hurting." Raoul took a deep breath and gathered his strength. "I'll spend the day tomorrow making calls to Killig, see if anyone has turned up any signs of Rena Baker. It's going to be Monday morning before you know it." Ms. Lila walked over to her husband and gave his shoulders a sympathetic rub.

Raoul closed his eyes, enjoying her touch, and muttered, "I might stop at Mrs. Jaymes's for a quick hour or so before I go to headquarters. You never know. Maybe I'll get lucky."

46

As Raoul would discover the next day from Mrs. Jaymes, the next chapter of Dagmore's life had no leather notebooks or visitors or badly behaved birds. Dagmore retreated to his house, where he divided his time between the sea and his sonatas, rarely going out but for quick trips to the Savings Bank or the Island Post. He devoted less time to his fishing boat on shore, though he put it in the water almost every day. He rowed from his property around the southern tip of the island until he could see the harbor of Port-St. Luke. He rowed straight out to sea until he almost lost his bearings. He rowed up the coast to the beach where he had found the jacaranda, but never went ashore again to see it up close.

With Abigail definitively out of the picture, the island calmed down, and after a few years, Dagmore did, too. He stopped moping, stopped fretting about what he should be doing and just did it. He read his books and smoked cigars on the verandah of his beautiful house, while the stars flickered above him. He played sonatas and felt the presence of his father nearby, and he spent hours in his boat, Oh's sea close enough to touch, daydreaming of Captain Thomson and his pirates.

Life at the villa was peaceful for once. It wasn't unhappy or unpleasant. It also wasn't joyful or very alive. When the Captain turned forty-five, Mrs. Jaymes, without discussing it, started matchmaking again. Ten years had passed since she and Hammer had first strolled through town evaluating candidates, and a whole new generation of young girls had grown up in the meantime. Dagmore had no interest in marrying. Dagmore had no interest in *not* marrying. Nothing much interested him at all, apart from his boat and his piano, so when Mrs. Jaymes brought home Verissa Peterkin, Dagmore didn't put up a fight.

She was almost thirty years old and a distant relative of Mrs. Jaymes. Verissa, who had not had her fill of men, wanted nothing more than to marry a man to take care of her and to have a houseful of babies. She knew how to cook and to clean and to sew, and, Dagmore couldn't help but notice, she was agreeably big on the top and the bottom and nicely thin in the middle, just as he liked. They were wed by a preacher in a private ceremony on the Captain's beach, attended by Verissa's parents, Mrs. Jaymes, and Hammer Coates. The sea was calm that day, and the sky quiet and clear. The island blessed the union of Dagmore and Verissa with a cool, soothing breeze that kissed their cheeks when they said their "I do's." It was fine with Oh that Dagmore take a wife, as long as he didn't love her, and Verissa fit the bill.

There was a semblance of marital bliss in the Bowles villa. Dagmore and Verissa got along well enough, and Mrs. Jaymes had stayed on to help care for the babies that were bound to turn up any day. Hammer still came to unclog the pipes or to tune the piano, which the Captain still played when he wasn't rowing his boat, and sometimes, after Hammer finished his work, he let Mrs. Jaymes make him a snack that he shared with her in the kitchen. Things were almost cheerful in the Captain's house.

Although Dagmore didn't mind his wife's company, he felt sure that the company of his own son or daughter would be preferable to hers, and to that end (and to Verissa's), he applied himself wholeheartedly. Their tolerance of one another was all that Dagmore and Verissa shared; she, too, thought a baby would be more fun than a forty-something sea captain who preferred the company of his boat and his dead father to hers. Thus, she, too, applied herself to the production of a little Bowles, creeping from her room into the Captain's on a nightly basis (and sometimes in the mornings). When months of trying produced no heir or heiress, Verissa and Mrs. Jaymes conspired to improve the odds. They consulted local experts and collected the bush leaves and herbs renowned to boost fertility, virility, and motility, which both Verissa (knowingly) and Dagmore (unknowingly) consumed. Nothing worked.

Dagmore, though disappointed, was used to renouncing his desires, and the fact that he had ended up with a wife unable to conceive seemed par for the course. Verissa, on the other hand, was not accustomed to disappointment. In fact, she was rather used to getting her way, and if Dagmore wasn't up to getting her pregnant, she would resolve the problem herself. "By whatever means necessary," she told Mrs. Jaymes.

Whatever Verissa did, it paid off. Eventually, she was with child. Dagmore marveled as her body grew and swelled. Her agreeably big top and bottom got bigger, while her nicely thin middle filled out. It was an awesome sight to witness, and it reminded him of his scientific research projects of many years before. But though the pregnancy itself amazed him, Dagmore felt no attachment to the baby in his wife's belly. He couldn't imagine holding it or looking into its eyes. When it finally came, nine months later, Dagmore didn't know what to expect.

The delivery of the baby took place in one of the villa's guest rooms. It had been outfitted for the happy occasion, and the presence there of Dagmore was strictly forbidden (which was just as well, because Verissa had absolutely insisted that her midwife be Abigail Davies, known for her skill and discretion). After Verissa and the baby were both cleaned up, and the bed and bedroom tidied, Abigail sneaked away, and the Captain was called to see his wife and son. He took the infant in his hands and held it close. As he felt its warmth against his chest and saw its eyes peer into his, he knew he could never love anything more than this child in his arms. Was this what Captain Thomson had felt when he first peered into Quick's orphan eyes? Dagmore wondered.

Mrs. Jaymes watched the Captain and beamed proudly, feeling rather responsible for what her instincts told her was a happy ending at last. "Well?" she urged him. "Don't just stand there. Give the boy a name!"

Dagmore smiled at her. "Branson," he said. "We'll call him Branson Bowles." What did it matter, Dagmore later confided to her, that the baby was Verissa's not his?

"What are you talking about?" Mrs. Jaymes barked, and Dagmore explained: nearly a year had passed since his wife had last crept into his bed.

Verissa's betrayal and Dagmore's acceptance of it were not the only secrets that Raoul would discover at Mrs. Jaymes's house that Sunday. Before he went to see her, Raoul had gathered up his circle of clues, his notebooks, his clippings, his dossier, and he carried them with him, that he might have another look at his variables in the harsher light of headquarters. So shaken was he—literally—when he learned about the Captain's son Branson that he knocked his bag off of Mrs. Jaymes's sofa and onto the floor. As the contents tumbled out, the folder that contained Raoul's personal dossier emptied, its invoices and photocopies and whatnot scattering themselves all over the sitting-room rug. Amongst the whatnot that Raoul rushed to pick up was a photograph that caught Mrs. Jaymes's eye.

"What's that?" she asked him, pointing to it. On her face was a strange look, one that Raoul had never seen her wear before.

"This?" he said, picking it up and handing it to her. "It's a photo. Of Rena Baker. The missing girl."

"Are you sure?" she asked him.

"Yes, I'm sure," Raoul answered, his flies sensing that something significant was about to happen. "Why?"

"It's like seeing a ghost," she said quietly, and she leaned back in her chair, studying Rena's photo. Suddenly she felt very weak.

Raoul rapped on the window and motioned for Hammer to come inside.

"What's wrong?" Hammer said, when he came in and saw his wife's face. In reply she handed him the picture. Hammer didn't say anything, but from the look on his face, it was clear that he was just as surprised as she.

"What's going on?" Raoul demanded to know. "Surely you've seen Rena Baker's picture before." Then Raoul realized—stupid Bruce!—that the *Crier* had never once published Rena's photo.

The entire island had taken Rena's demise for granted and had focused on murder-suspect Madison instead of on the missing girl.

"What is it?" he demanded again, about to faint from sheer curiosity. "Have you seen her? Do you know where she is?"

"No," Hammer said, handing the photo back to Raoul. "Nothing like that. It's just that she's the spitting image of Dagmore Bowles at that age." Raoul took the picture back and looked at it, but didn't know what to say. Hammer walked over to Mrs. Jaymes's china cabinet, opened a drawer, and pulled out a photograph. He gave it to Raoul.

"That's Dagmore," Hammer said. "A few years after he came to Oh."

The photograph was old and bent, but there was no denying it. Rena bore an uncanny resemblance to Dagmore. Was she a reincarnation of the dead man? A ghost come to life? These were not typically the kind of hypotheses Raoul posited, and only after the initial shock subsided, did he realize the more plausible explanation for Rena's appearance.

Dagmore Bowles was Rena Baker's father.

Raoul did some quick mathematics. Rena was younger than Branson by about ten years. Raoul's research into her background had revealed her to be an orphan, raised in an orphanage run by Seventh-day Adventists.

"How is this possible?" Mrs. Jaymes asked. "Dagmore has a daughter?"

"You had no idea?" Raoul asked her, not sure he believed her ignorance. Mrs. Jaymes knew the Captain's every private thought. How had he not told her about fathering a child?

Unless.

Mrs. Jaymes and Raoul together reached a single conclusion: "He didn't know."

They stared at each other a moment, unsure what to think, then Raoul snapped into action. He hastily grabbed his things from the floor and stuffed them into his sack. His head was buzzing and humming. He would have run right out without a word, had Mrs. Jaymes not shouted after him to ask where he was off to.

"I'm sorry, Mrs. Jaymes," he yelled over his shoulder as he stormed out the door. "I'll be back." Then, deciding she deserved more explanation than that, Raoul elaborated:

"There's a midwife I must see immediately."

47

"Abigail!" Raoul spat the name as he stomped from Ladywood Road to the wooded lane where he knew Abigail resided. He hadn't yet pieced together exactly how she fit into the riddle, but he was sure that she did. He was willing to bet Dagmore's daughter was no secret to *her*! "Damn her mischievous midwifing!" Raoul cursed.

As for Rena's disappearance, he should have guessed it, shouldn't he? That Abigail had had a hand in a girl running off. Hmph!

Raoul was enraged and excited at once. Enraged because Abigail had yet again been brewing her special brand of magic (and splashing it all over Raoul); and excited, because this time he thought he had her caught. His rage and his excitement were such, that he forgot how much he hated the idea of confronting Abigail face-to-face. He marched right up to her door and pounded on it with his fists.

"Abigail! Are you in there? Abigail!" he shouted.

Abigail opened the door with a mocking grin that for a split second rattled Raoul's resolve. "It took you long enough," she said.

Raoul opened his mouth to make a very loud point, then lost his train of thought as his brain processed Abigail's words. "What do you mean by that?" he asked suspiciously.

"You're here about Rena Baker, aren't you?"

"So you *do* know where she is?" he accused her.

"Of course I don't!"

"Then why am I here?" Raoul asked. (He meant: Why had Abigail been expecting him? But it came out wrong.)

"How should *I* know why you're here," she said, laughing at him.

Raoul's fury faltered, but luckily his flies rallied, and he found it again: "I want you to tell me about Rena Baker. I know you know she's the daughter of Dagmore Bowles."

"How do you know that?" Abigail asked, trying to gauge how much Raoul really did know—and how certain he was of his knowledge.

"A ghost told me," he blurted out, before he could catch himself. Abigail raised her eyebrows.

"I mean," he corrected, "that I received information connecting you with Rena Baker and Dagmore Bowles. I know she's his daughter and I know *you* must be the one who delivered her without ever telling him. Now, where is she?"

Abigail's face suddenly went dead serious and she grabbed Raoul by the front of the shirt. "Now you listen here," she told him. "I have no idea where Rena Baker is, but I suggest you stop yelling at me, dig out your giant magnifying glass, and go find her, do you hear? Not that it's any business of yours, but, yes, Dagmore Bowles is her father. And, yes, *I* delivered her. Now, why don't *you*, before that innocent Fuller boy spends his life rotting in jail?

Don't you see that time is running out? The trial is almost over and you haven't done a thing!"

Abigail released her hold on Raoul. She gave him a stern—no, fierce—look straight in the eyes and slammed her door in his face.

Raoul was in shock. He gradually regained his composure and his balance, and flattened out his shirt where Abigail had crushed it. Even his flies were stunned. They didn't make a sound. How dare she treat him that way? If she thought she could manhandle a government official and get away with it, well...well, he didn't know how to finish that sentence, but even so!

Underneath Raoul's bruised ego, however, some niggling gnats took flight. Had he misunderstood? Had Abigail truly been expecting him? Why was she so quick to admit that Rena was a Bowles? Secrets were her stock in trade. She built her business on them. And why was she so adamant that he find Rena? Why her concern for Madison Fuller? Truth and justice were not exactly what motivated a secret-keeping midwife. On the contrary: every female confession she protected implied a lie to some island male. Where was the justice in that? Was Abigail connected somehow to Madison, too? If she thought he was innocent, why wouldn't she simply speak up? Heaven knows her voice carried far and wide on Oh.

With so many questions and still no sign of Rena, there was little else for Raoul to do but go to his office and put in more calls to Killig. When he wrote to his colleagues there to ask for their help, he had included Rena's picture—the same one that had jarred Mrs. Jaymes. Hadn't any of them recognized her? Had she disguised herself somehow? Perhaps Raoul, in his first round of letters, had not made the gravity of the situation clear. Grave it was indeed, now, and he planned to make sure they all knew it. If he could convince them to put Rena's picture on the front page of the Killig Gazette, maybe someone would remember seeing her there, before the jury on Oh reached a verdict. Raoul punched his fist into his palm, angry with himself for not having sent clearer instructions in the first place. He forgot that his initial inquiry had been informal at best and that the jurisdiction of Customs and Excise extended to pallets of pineapple and VAT. Missing girls were not his mandate. If the Chief of Police found out what he was up to, there would be hell for him to pay.

Raoul, though, couldn't worry about Lucas Davenport or about the authorities that resided on the Police Chief's ceiling. Closing arguments were less than twenty-four hours away. Raoul dialed and debated like a man possessed, begging anyone on Killig who would listen to pass Rena's picture around. He spent the rest of the day in his office and only stopped his phoning when it grew too late to expect an answer at the other end. He went home and fell into bed, utterly tuckered out.

Despite his exhaustion, Raoul didn't get much rest. His fitful sleep was troubled by two vying, last-ditch hopes: that someone, sooner or later, would come through from Killig; or that his niggling gnats, if left alone, would hatch into clues Raoul would be quick enough to catch.

48

"Order! Order!" Judge Samuels shouted before the trial had officially reconvened. Bicycle Trial Week Three was beginning, and the crowd was in a frenzy. It took more than a few smacks of the judge's gavel to get the spectators in line. When at last they were, Monday walked pensively to the microphone and opened his closing arguments.

"Your Honor, members of the jury, brothers and sisters of Oh, our journey together draws to a close. I told you when we first embarked on this trial together that it would be a testament to the investigative skills of the authorities of this great island nation and by God it has been so. Or almost so. Sisters and brothers, we have a troublemaker in our midst, a troublemaker no better than the Devil himself, and that is the editor of your island paper, Mr. Kandele."

Ooh, this Monday really was too much! Bruce thought to himself, squeezing his hands into fists.

"What I mean, ladies and gentlemen, is that this man has sought fit to undermine the institutions of justice and truth by hiding beneath the cloak of the *Morning Crier.* When we asked Mr. Kandele the truth not two days ago, when we asked him to show us a classified ad that he would have us believe exonerates Mr. Fuller, he said he could not, because he is a journalist. *I* say he could not, because he is a liar, a liar who placed a phony ad hoping to steer the hearts of the jury. But righteousness has thwarted this lying devil, ladies and gentlemen—as righteousness always will—because with his silence, Mr. Kandele has spoken volumes. Do you know what he has said, my friends?"

The crowd collectively shook its head.

"I'm here to tell you," he reassured them. "His silence has said that, in *truth*, he is not in possession of any evidence whatsoever to clear the criminal who sits before us." (Monday pointed dramatically at Madison.)

"Truths are what matter, fellow citizens," he continued. "Truths, like a missing young lady, ripped from among us in her prime. Truths, like Mr. Fuller's fishing boat, which was covered in blood not deemed to have come from a fish, as he claimed. These are the truths we must bear in mind, not those spouted—unsubstantiated—from the mouths of trouble-making newspapermen."

Having thus discredited Bruce and the second lonely hearts ad, Monday removed his eyeglasses and rubbed the bridge of his nose, a gesture the audience ate up. This Monday Jones was a serious man!

For the rest of the day, he regaled the crowd with his continuing monologue, revisiting his exhibits, and incriminating Madison a dozen times (the accused was in possession of an umbrella, the crime committed on a rainy night; he was a depraved alcoholic, as witnessed by the beer tumbler found at his home; et cetera, et cetera). Monday reminded the jury that the corkboard was covered in evidence based on which they must find Madison Fuller guilty (though really it was covered in photos and nothing more).

"Finally," he reminded them, "when we began our journey into this ugliness, when we delved into the darkness that is Mr. Fuller's evil heart, I beseeched you to treat him as an innocent man for the trial's duration, for the law requires you to do so."

Monday stood in front of the jury. Slowly, he made eye contact with every juror, one by one. "Members of the jury," he said at last, "I say to you now, the trial is done."

Monday Jones's closing arguments were so thorough and so moving that when Glynray Justice took the floor the following day, investing his words with the same emotion and authority that the Prosecutor had, he came across as derivative and fake. When, like Monday, he revisited the exhibits, refuting the charges a dozen times (hundreds of people on Oh own umbrellas; who doesn't drink a beer on a Saturday night, but still make it to church on Sunday?; et cetera, et cetera), they thought him tedious and an out-and-out copycat. Though Glynray's speech, on paper, hit all the right points and raised all the right questions, it just didn't do justice to Madison's case.

He talked about the blood, which was neither fish nor female and could not be used against Madison. He pointed out that the killer still likely walked the streets, since he had placed a second classified ad. Every time he said "ladies and gentlemen of the jury," it sounded as if he were desperate and begging them for something he didn't deserve. By the time he was finished, the Madison camp started to think that Monday Jones was right—the trial was done, and how!

The jury was excused for the night and asked to report to the courthouse the following morning to begin deliberations. The judge warned that as long as the jury was out, the outdoor court was to stand empty and was not to be commandeered for dances, rallies, meetings, or festivities of any sort.

May was beside herself with grief. Branson had held her hand for the entirety of Glynray's closing, but was afraid to speak to her when Glynray was done. It had gone so poorly, he thought for sure she would be furious at him. She wasn't, and even sought his shoulder to cry on, literally. She was no longer upset that Branson hadn't come forth and admitted to having placed the first ad, because she was certain (though they never discussed it) that it was he who had placed the second, in an attempt to save Madison's life. Besides which, she now realized the Bicycle Trial was bigger than that. It had gotten away from them all, and the ad alone was no longer enough to exonerate her brother.

Branson took her home and did his best to comfort her, but like Glynray's closing, he felt that his words, if accurate and on point, lacked the conviction they needed. He didn't say it out loud, at least not to May, but the best they could hope for now was a juror or two with an ounce of common sense, who hadn't been bamboozled by Monday's "brothers *this*" and "sisters *that*." Branson made sure that May ate some dinner, then obtaining her promise to try and sleep, he left her and went to the bakery. There, he found Trevor and Randolph behind the counter in a somber state.

"Good night," Branson said quietly, not wishing to inject the silence with too much sound.

"Hey," Trevor replied. Randolph lifted his chin in a solemn greeting.

"It doesn't look good for Madison, does it?" Branson asked.

"No, it doesn't," Trevor sighed.

"I thought for sure when the second ad came out that Madison was as good as freed," Branson said, pounding the counter with his fist. "Man!" He turned his back to Trevor and looked out the bakery window into the dusk. In the glass of the door, Trevor saw Branson's reflection. His face, which Trevor could read like a book from Ms. Lila's library, looked odd. Trevor opened his mouth, wanting to ask Branson if he had had anything to do with the second lonely hearts ad, but stopped himself. Trevor wasn't convinced that his friend would tell him the truth. Nor was he convinced that he could stand another truth that day if he did.

Across town from the bakery, at the Buddha's Belly Bar and Lounge in the Sincero Hotel, Bruce and Raoul commiserated over fruity, multi-colored cocktails Cougar Zanne was testing for his Rainbow Fair menu. (Cougar was unbothered by matters of justice or truth, and no island event—Rainbow Fair, Marimba Competition, Harvest Football Tournament—was spared a signature Cougar cocktail.)

"Did you hear that bastard? Calling me the Devil?" Bruce complained to Raoul, sipping a green sample from a tiny paper cup.

"Forget that, Bruce! An innocent kid is probably going to jail for the rest of his life," Raoul said.

"You never know," Bruce shrugged. "Maybe someone on the jury will see sense."

"I know one thing." Raoul let out a sigh. "And that's that Rena Baker and Karen Arbe are one and the same. Rena Baker went to Killig. I don't know how, or if she stayed, but she went."

"I think so, too," Bruce said. "But the police told you Karen Arbe was inadmissible."

"Come on, you two, cheer up!" Cougar said, arriving with more cocktails to sample. "The Rainbow Fair is almost upon us," he added with a wink.

"Cougar, knock it off, will you?" Raoul said. "We're trying to talk business here."

"Okay. But first try these red ones," he said, leaving the cups on the table.

Raoul continued talking. "Rena could have easily slipped through Customs with her own passport, even if she signed Karen Arbe's name. It's not like in my day, when a man took his stamp and his inkpad seriously."

Bruce didn't answer, because he didn't know what to say. Though neither Bruce nor Raoul knew it, the two men were sharing the same thought, that somehow they had failed. Bruce was a reporter and should have blown the lid off the case long before Madison faced a life sentence. And Raoul, well, the Bicycle Trial was his baby, though he hardly recognized it now. How had it turned out so differently from what he had pictured?

Raoul tapped his temples with two fingers, as if to loosen from his brain the solution to his problems. Where could that stupid girl be? he wondered. Where would she have gone off to?

"Wow, this one's not too bad," Bruce said, swishing a mouthful of Cougar's red concoction.

Could he initiate an international search for Karen Arbe without involving the police? Raoul asked himself.

"Sangria and...vodka, is it?" Bruce said, studying his cup.

Was there any chance Rena might change her mind and come back on her own? Did she have any idea of the danger that Madison faced?

Raoul had a horrible thought: What if Rena *had* heard about Madison and just didn't care?

"You gotta try this one, Raoul." Bruce nudged him with his elbow. "It starts off sweet and fresh, then it really cuts loose and coldcocks you."

49

What the island of Oh wants, the island of Oh gets. There's no way around it. If it wants you to suffer, you will. No amount of precautions or safety-nets will protect your hand or your heart, if either is meant to break. Likewise, when island fortune favors you, you'd be hard-pressed to duplicate the warmth of Oh's sun on your back, or the sweetness of its fruit on your lips, no matter how far and wide you travel. If you do travel, if you go away, you will never really be gone, never free of Oh's magic. Your mind will forever return to Oh's wind and its rains, to its shady mangroves and its yielding sands. You'll still feel the heat of its passions, should you bury yourself deep in Alpine snow.

You'll remember Oh's cool reggae groove and its icy juices, even as you sweat in some other palm-tree'd locale, perhaps as close as Killig (which, at first glance, might appear to mimic Oh's wonders).

If you can relegate your returns to Oh to the back of your mind, to your daydreams and your fantasies, then pat yourself on the back. More often than not, Oh won't let you off so easily. It will blow its breezes through your head and confound you, fool you into thinking that you want to go back, that you need to. It will trick you into believing that you have unfinished business there, a mystery to solve perhaps; or will guilt you into accepting that a life needs saved and only you can save it. It will knock on your door or send a letter, and you will hop on a boat or a plane.

If Oh wants a murder trial, it gets one of those, too; and if it wants newspaper coverage, it fashions it. Just ask Bruce Kandele, who knows better than any. By Wednesday of Trial Week Four, as the jury continued its deliberations and the official verdict loomed, Bruce was waging an all-out press campaign to discredit Oh's legal authorities and lay the ground for Glynray's appeal. The Rainbow Fair, which was to start on Friday night, had been all but forgotten, except in Chanterelle, where organizers worked day and night to get everything ready. They feared, this year, that the Bicycle Trial might overshadow the town's annual to-do.

What luck that, as Bruce typeset the Thursday edition on Wednesday afternoon, through the grimy-windowed office of the *Morning Crier* his eye was drawn to a newsworthy sparkle.

"Damn," he sighed, grabbing his camera and rushing outside. He needed a rainbow like a fish needs a bicycle. "This one really *will* have to go on the front page, now won't it?"

Rare Sun Halo Rings In The Fair
Rainbow City gears up for annual festival

At approximately 4:57 p.m. yesterday afternoon a rare weather occurrence was cited in the skies over Port-St. Luke. A circular rainbow, also known as a halo, was visible around the entirety of the sun's circumference. The phenomenon, which differs in shape from the traditional arc or semi-circular rainbows more common to Oh, was last witnessed on the island some eleven years ago in the northern parish of St. Charles, on the cusp between the dry and rainy seasons. The halo's appearance is especially fitting in light of the annual Rainbow Fair in Chanterelle, which opens tomorrow night and runs through Sunday. According to island belief, sun halos herald major meteorological events, though none was documented subsequent to the St. Charles halo. There is no official record of halos on Oh prior to that; unofficially, local history confirms them as portents of drought or flooding. Organizers of this year's Fair see the unusual rainbow as an auspicious sign for the event, which has been overshadowed by the Bicycle Trial murder case, recently turned over to the jury. The officials of Chanterelle have sent a formal plea to jury members, who have been in deliberation for over six working days, requesting that a verdict be reached by tomorrow; they have also petitioned Judge Maxted Samuels to reconvene the trial immediately for the delivery of the verdict, should it be reached before the end of the week. They hope to avoid that islanders, wishing to partake of Rainbow Fair offerings over the weekend, might feel shame in doing so while a man's fate remains undecided. Although the run-up to the Rainbow Fair has been lackluster compared to that of previous years, as public attention focused almost exclusively on the trial, the Rainbow City authorities remain confident that actual attendance figures will outdo expectations by far. It would be negligent and irresponsible of this reporter not to suggest that the unusual halo phenomenon might also be a portent of a major judicial event, with the Bicycle Trial verdict expected at any time. What will the halo signify for the defendant, Madison Fuller, and for us, the citizens of Oh, as we look to our leaders in hope, and with faith in their ability to oversee the fair and reasoned judgment of one of our own? Will they embrace this challenge like the halo embraced the island sun? Or will they blind us with science, and dazzle us with an empty ruling wrapped in layers of colored and bent legality?

50

"Raoul, hurry! You'll be late!" Lila called to him as he washed and dressed for what was setting itself up to be a very busy Friday. Early that morning Raoul had been alerted that the jury was back and that Judge Samuels had reconvened the court for ten a.m. There was likely to be a real ruckus when the verdict was read, and Raoul would have to be ready for anything. He prayed that Madison would be acquitted, in which case Rena's whereabouts would no longer matter, and Raoul could get back to the business of painting his house.

It was nearly nine o'clock as his wife yelled out to him from the kitchen. Normally an hour would be plenty of time to down a cup of tea and head to trial. On this particular Friday, however, Raoul's judicial duties had been superseded by a Customs emergency that meant he had to rush. Not five minutes after getting the call from the courthouse in town, Raoul had got another from the airport. It seemed there was a problem there that only he could resolve. He hoped to do so quickly, and get back to the outdoor court before the session began. If Raoul wasn't present for the ruling, there was no telling what mayhem the crowd might get up to.

"Can't someone else handle the airport?" his wife protested. "You can't miss the most important day of the Bicycle Trial so far!"

"That's the problem," Raoul explained to her, annoyed with his Customs colleagues. "Everyone's excited and off to the trial. There's a skeleton crew at the airport—and everywhere else." He kissed her on the cheek, grabbed his megaphone, and promised to meet her at court as soon as he could.

Raoul's absence went unnoticed as the Trial prepared to resume. Though a ruckus might be in the making, as the spectators and key players took their places on the benches and the dais respectively, the mood was one of somber anticipation. Few dared even speak, and those who did, did so in a manner more befitting morning mass than mayhem. Despite the relative silence, there was excitement in the air. It was a beautiful day on Oh. The sky was a vibrant blue, and the hills strangely lush and green, considering there had been no rain since the night of the hit-and-run over a month before. On either side of the dais, flamboyant trees and jacarandas framed the judge and jury in red, orange, and violet.

The islanders were anxious. The suspense of awaiting a verdict had come to an end, and the Rainbow Fair was about to start. The timing was perfect. The fact, though, that a man might be sent to prison for life, guilty or not, was a prospect worthy of a respectful hush, so they filed in and filled the benches calmly and quietly. Behind his own bench the judge fidgeted, and Glynray was nervous at his table. Madison appeared indifferent, though he had lost weight from worry that Rena might have willingly run off. He cared little what happened to him now, since a life with her seemed to be out of the question. (His attitude galled Glynray, who needed his client's full participation if he was to appeal a guilty verdict and win.)

Branson, Trevor, and Patience were all as nervous as if they were about to be sentenced themselves. They had managed to sit in the front row, together with May. The ladies clutched their handbags with white knuckles, while Branson and Trevor looked at each other, at Madison, and back again, shaking their heads and unable to say a word. Randolph was too agitated to sit still, so he hovered at the outskirts of the court, his hands clenched into fists that he hid in his pockets. Only Raoul missed out, thick in the midst of his airport problem. Although he was angry not to be present at court, he was glad they had called him. The problem was delicate, and no one could have handled it more logically or expeditiously than he. Still, he had to hurry, if he was to arrive at the outdoor court before the verdict was delivered. Ms. Lila, who had already taken her place in the crowd, looked over her shoulder nervously, wishing her husband there in time.

The temperature was very high. From the dais, as Glynray looked out at the crowd, he saw it speckled with fluttering kerchiefs and fans and newspapers, as the onlookers tried to keep cool. Ten o'clock had come and gone, albeit not by much, and there was no sign of prosecutor Monday Jones. The judge had ordered that they wait for his arrival before proceeding.

At ten-thirty, Monday at last showed up. He offered no explanation for his delay, but made a show of hurrying to his place on the dais, leaving the islanders to assume that some very important and urgent business, which only the likes of Monday could appreciate, must have made him inevitably tardy.

Finally! the judge said under his breath. He hit his gavel twice and turned on the microphone. "Order! Court is now in session!"

Quiet came over the already hushed crowd. The judge continued: "We are here today for the reading of the verdict in the case of Oh versus Madison Fuller, on the charges of the vehicular homicide of Rena Baker of Glutton Hill and the disposal of the victim's remains. Ladies and gentlemen of the jury, have you reached a unanimous verdict?"

"We have, Your Honor," said a petite, resolute woman who had served as the jury's foreperson.

The judge then asked her to state her name and domicile for the record, but before she could, literally in a flash, the sky cracked with lightning, and rain poured where before there wasn't a single cloud in sight. The spectators, at least those without a direct relationship to Madison, jumped up screaming and ran for cover. Those related to him looked at the judge pleadingly, unbothered by the shower that drenched them. The judge, who feared he might be electrocuted by his microphone, ran from the dais waving his arms and shouted, "Recess! Rain recess!" The jurors scattered like mice.

Ms. Lila looked around, worried, for Raoul. This was precisely the sort of development that he had planned for, but only he knew what plans to deploy. He was nowhere to be spotted. Meanwhile, the crowd ran helter skelter, seeking cover under the narrow canopies of the chicken vendors and fresh-juice stalls. Bruce, who had been lurking at the back of the crowd, had the good sense to climb onto the dais, disconnect the sound system, and cover the giant speakers with their plastic casings that lay nearby. "Next thing you know they'd be arresting Raoul for damaged property!" he said to himself.

Raoul was frantic. His airport problem was solved and he was en route to the trial in a taxi. He couldn't get there fast enough. He had been nervously tapping his feet, as though he might propel the vehicle farther with the sheer force of his will, when the rain came so hard and so suddenly that the driver was forced to slow down. Raoul was nearly mad with frustration. He imagined the confusion at the outdoor court, with no one there to direct the setting up of the tents and the tarps he had laid in for just such an occasion. He stuck his head out the window and cursed the rain. "Now?" he yelled up to the sky. "A man's life is at stake!"

Slowly and surely the driver made his way to the court, stopping his vehicle as close to its perimeter as he could. "Wait for me right here!" Raoul ordered, as he jumped out into the pouring rain.

With his megaphone in one hand and an umbrella snatched from the taxi in the other, Raoul rounded up the team of officers providing security and started giving orders to erect poles and tarps. Bruce saw him and came running.

"Raoul! Where the hell were you? I disconnected the sound system for you, and I covered the speakers. Everything okay?" Bruce asked.

Raoul wanted very much to tell Bruce about the morning he had had at the airport, but it wasn't the time for that, and besides, it was way too noisy to talk. The rain was loud and growing louder as its fall was stopped by the tarpaulins being stretched high over the outdoor venue.

"See if you can round up the judge and the jury, will you? And get Madison and the lawyers back on stage, so we can get this over and done with!" Raoul shouted.

It took over an hour, but Raoul managed to get most of the court and the entire dais covered, and the sound equipment dried and safely situated. The rain never ceased, but it slowed considerably, and gradually the court filled up again, though muddied and damper for the wear. Raoul had hoped to share a private word of encouragement with May and Branson, and the rest of the bakery crowd, before the session, but without waiting for Raoul's thumbs up, Judge Samuels had resumed the proceedings. As if there had been no interruption, he again asked the petite, resolute Madame Foreperson to state her name and domicile for the record.

"Your Honor! Wait!" Raoul shouted into his megaphone from the back of the court.

"Mr. Orlean, what is the meaning of this?" Judge Samuels snapped into the microphone.

"Your Honor, the Office of Customs and Excise has some new information relevant to this case," Raoul said, again into the megaphone.

"This is highly irregular, Orlean! Approach the bench!"

Under the tented court, it was hotter and steamier than ever and the crowd, which now wanted only to get home and to get cleaned up, fanned itself impatiently and grumbled at Raoul, who, they figured, was only prolonging the inevitable.

"With all due respect, Your Honor," his voice boomed, "might I first present Exhibit R." As Raoul said "Exhibit R," he opened the door of the taxi, parked just a few steps away. A young woman emerged, dressed in bright yellow, and slowly walked toward the dais. The onlookers were confused, until Madison caught sight of her and stood up.

"Rena!" he exclaimed.

She ran to Madison and embraced him. Not with unbridled passion, but with genuine-enough affection. While Rena and Madison spoke to each other in soft voices, Raoul reached the dais and approached the bench. There he explained to the judge, and to Glynray and Monday, who had approached it as well, that Rena Baker had returned to the island that morning by plane and had been detained at the airport as a material witness. Raoul reported that she had learned of Madison's predicament and had come back to Oh to save him from a life in prison. The judge looked from Raoul to Rena to Madison and back again, not knowing what to do. Clearly, there was no murder to try, but he couldn't just up and adjourn the Bicycle Trial without official rhyme or reason. The court was in a frenzy, if a somewhat feeble one, due to the heat and humidity. Monday Jones was miffed; he had never before lost a case, and he was beginning to think not even his rhetoric could fix this one. Glynray was too stunned to speak and mutely awaited the judge's ruling with fingers crossed. Finally, Judge Samuels motioned with his hand for Monday, Glynray, and Raoul to move away from the bench, and he called the court to order.

"Order! Order!" he cried out, slamming his gavel. The court went deathly quiet. "In light of the unexpected arrival of the alleged victim," the judge began, "we must modify our scheduled proceedings and postpone the reading of the verdict. I will instead ask both the Prosecution and the Defense to question the material witness introduced by the Office of Customs and Excise, Miss Rena Baker of Glutton Hill." He ordered Rena to take the witness stand, and turned to Monday Jones. "Mr. Jones, your witness," he said.

Monday might be going down, but not without a fight. If this silly girl was to be the only blotch on his perfect record, he planned to give her a public talking-to that she wouldn't soon forget.

"State your name and domicile for the record, please, Miss."

"Rena Baker, Glutton Hill," she replied hesitantly.

"Are you aware, Miss Baker, of the trouble you have caused?"

Rena looked at Raoul, who smiled at her reassuringly. She opened her mouth to try and deliver a response, but before she could, Monday interrupted.

"I'll take your silence as a 'no,'" he said. "Allow me to enlighten you. Miss Baker, you have behaved very selfishly. You have brought a tremendous financial burden to the government of Oh, which spared no expense in its efforts to locate you and, failing that, to prosecute the man who murdered you."

"Objection, Your Honor!" Glynray called out. "Miss Baker has clearly not been murdered, nor did the authorities of Oh devote a dime to finding her. The Prosecution has labored under the assumption of her demise from the moment the case was officially opened."

"Sustained," the judge reluctantly grumbled. "The court recognizes that Ms. Baker is very much alive."

"Very well," Monday resumed. "Perhaps then you would like to enlighten *me*, Miss Baker. Please inform the court of the circumstances surrounding your disappearance."

"I didn't disappear," she said. "Not exactly. I flew out on a flight to Killig is all."

"And from there?"

"From there, nothing. That's where I've been all the time."

"What have you been doing there?" Monday asked her.

"Walking around. Exploring the island. Floating in the sea."

"You expect this court to believe that you ran away from *one* island, where a fisherman had pledged his love to you, to 'walk around' *another* island all alone?"

"I got itchy feet," she explained. "It's not as though all islands are alike, you know."

"What about Mr. Fuller?" Monday asked. "Don't you love him?"

"Yes. I do. That's why I'm here. I happened to see a copy of Oh's *Morning Crier*, and when I read that Madison was in trouble, I came right back."

354

The *Morning Crier*?! Bruce was tickled. He had gone international without even knowing!

"If you love him as you claim, then why did you leave him in the first place?" Monday snapped. "You would value a pair of itchy feet over a fisherman's loyal heart?"

"I just wasn't happy here. On Oh. I know it's my home, but it's never *felt* like home." She paused before continuing, as if unsure whether she should speak her heart. "Mr. Jones," she finally said, "have you ever heard of island magic?"

The spectators stirred and conferred in hushed tones. Had Oh had something to do with Rena's running away?

"What nonsense is this?" Monday Jones rebutted. "Your Honor, I ask that you instruct the witness to stick to the facts of the case."

Before the judge could rule, Glynray was on his feet. "Objection, Your Honor! Magic on Oh is not nonsense!"

"Sustained," Judge Samuels grumbled again. "The witness may proceed with this line of questioning."

"Thank you, Your Honor," Rena replied. She turned back to Monday and picked up where she had left off. "I'll take that as a 'no,'" she mocked him. "Allow me to enlighten you." The crowd sniggered, and Raoul nearly fainted. What was she saying? How had her testimony got mixed up with island magic?

"Oh is a very special place, Mr. Jones. A little *too* special for *me*, I'm afraid."

Monday looked at her like she was mad, but Rena kept talking.

"The sun plays tricks on everyone here. The moon, too. The leaves laugh at you, the birds butt into your affairs. Everyone's used to it. But with me, it's different. The island doesn't want me here, and Madison's love wasn't enough to make up for Oh's torments." She looked at Madison, begging his forgiveness with her eyes.

"Why on earth would Oh not want you on Oh?" a skeptical Monday Jones inquired.

Rena bowed her head and spoke so softly, she almost couldn't be heard. "I think it has something to do with my father."

"Your father? It was my understanding you were raised in an island orphanage."

"Yes, that's true. I was raised in an orphanage—where I never wanted for anything—but I discovered, recently, that my father was Dagmore Bowles." The crowd gasped in amazement and commented loudly. Branson Bowles's jaw dropped open and he turned to Trevor, whose jaw had dropped open in turn. Monday Jones thought perhaps the whole island was mad, and he didn't know what else to say.

"Order! Order in the court!" the judge shouted, banging his gavel.

"Your Honor," Glynray interjected. "In light of the fact that Mr. Jones is not familiar with the history of our citizenry, the Defense requests permission to take up the questioning."

"Permission granted," the judge ruled.

"Thank you, Your Honor." Glynray approached the witness stand as a puzzled Monday took his seat. "Miss Baker, you were saying? The island was tormenting you because you were Dagmore Bowles's daughter?"

"I think that might be the reason. It's legend on Oh that Captain Dagmore...my father...had lots of problems here. They say he never quite fit in, that the island drove him mad. That's why he jumped to his death from the rocky perch where he built his house."

"And you believe the island feels for you the same animosity it felt for Dagmore Bowles," Glynray deduced.

"Exactly."

"May I ask, Miss Baker, what the basis is for your conviction that Dagmore Bowles is—*was*—your biological father?"

"I received a letter a few months ago. Unsigned. Whoever wrote it said that he (or she, I don't know) had information proving I was Dagmore's daughter. He (or she) said that I must come forward and take back my birthright, the Captain's house on the hill."

Branson and Trevor looked at each other again, horrified by what they were hearing.

"Take it back?" Glynray asked. He had spent enough time in the bakery to know that Branson was Dagmore's son. "To my knowledge, the house is inhabited by Dagmore Bowles's only known offspring, Branson Bowles."

Rena covered her face with her hands. When she had collected herself, she let them fall and said, "The letter said something about that, too. The sender also had information proving Branson was *not* Dagmore Bowles's son."

The crowd was out of control. Branson was on his feet, as was Trevor, protesting loudly. "How dare she make up such lies?" Branson cried out.

"Wait! Wait!" Rena shouted over the din, waving her hands wildly. "I don't want anything! I can't stay here! I won't!"

The judge required the assistance of Raoul and his megaphone to get the court to quiet down. Branson and Trevor had all but jumped onto the dais to consult with Glynray about Branson's rights. Could he sue this imposter? Branson had the will! He could prove the Captain's house had been bequeathed to him. And what about his mother, Verissa, long dead? What had she done to deserve such slandering? When Branson finally calmed down and returned to his seat, he began to wonder if the island might not have a bit of animosity for him, too! With Madison exonerated, Branson could have finally declared his love to May, and now this pretender had come along to steal their house of wedded bliss from underneath them?!

"Miss Baker," the judge addressed her. "You are making some serious accusations, without any proof whatsoever. May I remind you that you are under oath."

"Your Honor, I don't want the house. I don't want to live on Oh. The Captain's son, Branson, he can keep it. Up until the time the Captain died, he *raised* Branson. *I* never even knew the man. If anyone has claim to the Captain's property, it's Branson, not me."

"Objection, Your Honor!" Monday jumped up and shouted. "Then why trouble us with all this needless information?"

"Miss Baker?" the judge said, inviting her to respond.

"Because once the letter came, that's when the island really turned on me. I knew all my life it didn't want me here, but it was as if putting in writing my relationship to Dagmore, suggesting I might lay claim to his home, had somehow aggravated the island in a way my existence never had before. I couldn't tell Madison or anyone about it. They would have thought I was crazy, or insisted that I stay, and, too, I didn't want to cause any problems for Dagmore's son...for Branson."

"How could you be so certain that the letter-writer was telling the truth?" Glynray questioned. "It's careless to put stock in anonymous communication."

"Yes, that may be," she said. "But inside the letter there was a picture of Dagmore Bowles from when he was about the age I am now. I look exactly like him. There's no denying I'm his daughter."

"Do you have any idea who sent you these letters, or what kind of proof the sender is in possession of?"

"No. The letter said when I was ready to pursue my claim to Dagmore's estate, I should put an ad in the paper."

"What kind of ad?" Glynray asked.

"Any kind. For a gardener or a housekeeper. As long as it said 'Call Rena Baker,' the sender of the letter would know to contact me. But I wasn't interested in staying on Oh, and especially not in the Captain's villa, so I never placed the ad. It was enough for me to know, after all these years, who my father was, and to understand why I've been so miserable here my whole life."

"Did the letter, by chance, say who your mother was, or if the sender was in possession of this information as well?"

"No."

Glynray could think of nothing else to ask Rena. It seemed to him that whatever else was left to say, was better said in private. Between Rena and Madison, between Rena and Branson, between Rena and an anonymous writer of letters.

"No further questions, Your Honor," Glynray stated.

He returned to his seat, and all eyes went to Judge Samuels. The outdoor court was completely silent, except for the hiss of the island wind and the chirp of some birds, who had taken advantage of a pause in the rain to make their voices heard.

Judge Samuels cleared his throat and adjusted his microphone. He complimented the efforts of both Glynray Justice and Monday Jones, thanked the jurors for their time, and thanked Raoul Orlean of Customs and Excise for his material witness. May thought she would burst before the judge at last declared: "The case is dismissed without prejudice."

Madison Fuller was a free man.

51

"Raoul!" Bruce called jovially, making his way through the animated and still-lingering crowd. "You did it, man!" He clapped Raoul on the back.

"I didn't do anything," Raoul said. "She showed up this morning on the early flight and they called me. It was you and your paper that did it."

"Maybe," he conceded, "but you knew from the start she wasn't really dead. And the way you delivered her to court? 'Might I first present Exhibit R,'" he mimicked Raoul good-naturedly.

Raoul shrugged. Bruce offered to buy him a drink at the Belly to celebrate, but Raoul declined. He had to attend to the dismantling of the makeshift court, and he wanted to meet up with Ms. Lila. Besides which, Raoul was too distracted to drink. Though Rena's return had saved the day, for Raoul it was far from satisfactory. He still didn't know who had painted on his walls, or why, and the fact that he had made the connection between Rena, Dagmore, and Abigail had nothing whatsoever to do with Madison. Not exactly. The truth had come out, and that was a good thing, he supposed, but he couldn't shake the feeling that there was still a piece of the puzzle he wasn't seeing.

For one thing, he never got to hear the details of Dagmore's death from Mrs. Jaymes. Someday he might go and ask her, but if magic was the cause—and Rena had suggested it was—then Raoul was no longer all that interested. A once-questing captain who lets an island bewitch him and kills himself, is a far cry from mathematician-musician Stan Kalpi, piano or no! Raoul had been a fool to think otherwise.

"Stan Kalpi would never have fallen for Abigail Davies!" Raoul said, louder than he meant to.

"What are you carrying on about?" Ms. Lila asked. She had elbowed her way through the crowd and gave him a peck on the cheek. "Congratulations," she said. "I bet you make the front page."

"Ha!" Raoul said, with a little chuckle. It would be satisfying indeed to read in the newspaper that he had one-upped the Chief of Police. A smile managed to creep across his face. Ms. Lila wore a smile as well, for now nothing would keep her husband from his paints. She would see to that herself.

As the trial crowd thinned, and the rain returned with renewed vigor, there were indeed quite a number of smiles to note.

Monday Jones and Glynray Justice had rushed to intervene in Branson's family dispute and, for separate fees, had happily agreed to sort out the Bowleses' affairs. Rena would gladly sign over her claim to the Captain's villa, for which Branson agreed to send monthly rent checks to Killig, thus financing her itchy feet. Though Branson would never doubt Dagmore was his father, Rena's eyes told him Dagmore was *her* father, too, and fair was fair (so the Captain had taught him). All that truly mattered to Branson was May, and she had agreed to marry him and live in his house on the hill.

Even Trevor smiled when he heard they were engaged, delighted that his dearest friend, after mere decades, had finally landed the one fish he wanted. The rest of the Rouges, Randolph and Patience, were simply content that their biggest concern now was the baking of buns and bread.

Eavesdropping, unassuming, on Trevor et al (and on Rena and Branson especially) was none other than Abigail Davies, who, like the rest of the island, had turned up to find out the verdict. *She* smiled, too, for it was right that young women got a share of their dead fathers' money. Mothers sometimes couldn't make ends meet.

Only two people weren't smiling the day the Bicycle Trial ended.

One was Police Chief Lucas Davenport, who still had a Bicycle Mystery to solve. (Patience is all it would take, though of this he had no clue.)

The other was Madison Fuller. Madison had discovered that his loyal, lonely heart wasn't worth a bit of salve and a pair of shoes.

Such was the magic of Oh: a fisherman cleared of murder the saddest man in Port-St. Luke.

52

You see? Oh got me again. I died—or rather the Dagmore I once *was* died—without knowing that Rena was my daughter. Without knowing that Rena *was*. Is that why the island did me in? Was Oh jealous that after all those years with an indifferent Verissa, I finally had a fling with true love? Did it blow me off my rocky perch to keep me away from my little girl?

Because that's what it did, you know. It swept me up, and hurled me straight into the sea! I remember light (that island sun!), and lift, and the sound of the wind. And then Captain Dagmore was gone.

I certainly never jumped! Not with Branson in my life. I needed—and *still* need—Branson's company, like I needed the air in my lungs or the breakfast in my belly. It kept me alive! (While Oh would let it.) Even in death, I've only ever left Branson's side when he was in England. Oh doesn't like that I should stray for too long.

Rena, now she's another story. She got away. Oh dragged her back to save Madison, it's true, but she's going off again, with an inheritance in tow. Leave it to Abigail to have sorted *that* out. She was always a practical thinker. Those jobs of hers, plumbing and painting and bookkeeping, they taught her about money, about settling accounts. The midwifing and the so-many pregnancies that so scandalized my Mrs. Jaymes, *they* taught Abigail the lengths to which mothers must go for the sake of their own. Don't doubt it for a minute: were Branson unwilling to pay Rena rent, Abigail Davies would FIND A WAY to make things right.

As for Raoul, if he had lined up his variables more carefully, he would not have judged Captain Dagmore so harshly. A 'far cry from mathematician-musician Stan Kalpi,' my itchy foot! Did Stan Kalpi have a son he adored? A son who would marry his true and dainty-handed love, under a jacaranda tree on a rocky perch overlooking the sea? (Hammer planted the jacaranda to mark the spot where I fell to my death.)

Did Stan Kalpi have a daughter? A daughter who had challenged an island and won? A girl so strong-willed she had broken the spell of two lifetimes? And love! What about love? Did Stan Kalpi ever get a taste of that? Because Dagmore did, however briefly. (Time softens the hardest of coco shells, I assure you.)

Dagmore Bowles was no 'once-questing Captain' who killed himself, no poor man's Mr. Stan. He was merely the victim of island love. *Fatal* island love that the likes of a Raoul Orlean will never have to know. Ignoring what Dagmore-gnats still niggle, Raoul will simply carry on as he's always done.

He will wait for the rain to stop, will pack up his speakers and his borrowed tarpaulins, and will ship them home to Killig. He'll collect his tins of paint from Higgins Hardware, Home, and Garden, and he'll get two coats on his cottage, all the way round. He will even manage to finish the sills and shutters, I should think, before the rainy season rolls in for good.

While Ms. Lila lovingly prepares him kingfish in coconut cream, Raoul will trim his Playful Rose in Coconut Cloud—never knowing that the lone ghostly plume in the sky overhead, was once a star-crossed Captain whose piano took him home. Or a tiny questing pirate, destined for an island named Oh.

Rainbow Fair Rained Out
Rainbow City cancels annual festival

For the first time in Oh's history, the Rainbow Fair was destined not to be. The yearly outdoor event, a two-day homage to the rainbows visible from the town of Chanterelle, famed for its sunny skies when neighboring areas are getting drenched, had to be called off due to inclement weather. It is widely accepted that the circular rainbow, or halo, visible around the sun in Port-St. Luke only two days prior to the Fair is to blame. Halos have long been considered harbingers of significant weather occurrences, such as floods or droughts, though up to now no such occurrence had ever been officially or specifically connected to a halo on Oh. This newspaper, which recently attained international renown for its coverage of the so-called Bicycle Trial, in which local fisherman Madison Fuller was cleared of charges he had murdered his girlfriend, is pleased to report the first documented incidence of an indisputably halo-triggered meteorological disturbance. In so doing, it scientifically sanctions what islanders have known all along: a rainbow around the sun is just too much. Such beauty is bound to take its toll. Organizers of this year's Fair had hoped the halo would mean good luck for the Rainbow City and had banked on record-breaking attendance figures, which, sadly, they attained. In a bizarre twist of island conditions as only Oh can twist them, by Sunday evening, as the weekend of the ill-fated Fair drew to a close, the skies suddenly and strangely cleared up, postponing the rainy season indefinitely. The officials of Chanterelle, when asked if they would consider holding the event at a later date, declined to comment. Speaking on condition of anonymity, however, a senior member of the town council confirmed that no Fair would take place this year, citing as the reason the clouds themselves, which, he claims, are not the mere wispy slivers they seem.

Acknowledgments

This book began with a dented bike on a rainy country road. A bike that took Raoul and Captain Dagmore, and their story, to Europe, the Caribbean, and across the United States, before it finally decided it was home. For directions en route, I would like to thank authors Janice Hally and Peter May; readers (and faith-keepers) Priya Balasubramanian and Dee LeRoy; and the cheer-leaders—Michelle Italia, Marie Lamoureux, Kari Winter, and *all* the others, found and familiar—who crossed my path and made it sunny. You are too many to list here, and that makes me lucky, indeed.

I have been blessed by the talents of Andrew C Bly (cover design) and Patti Schermerhorn (cover art) not once now, but twice; and forever by the generosity of my mother, MaryAnn Siciarz, without whom I would have no stories to tell.

For all of you, and for the ride, my gratitude is heartfelt and boundless; my love, to the fishes and back.

About the Author

Stephanie Siciarz was born in the US and is a graduate of Georgetown University and The Johns Hopkins University. She is a writer and translator and has worked for high-ranking officials in international, government, and academic institutions in the US and Europe. She currently resides in Ohio, where she is on the faculty at Kent State University. Her debut novel, *Left at the Mango Tree*, was named to *Kirkus Reviews'* Best Books of 2013.

www.ingramcontent.com/pod-product-compliance
Lightning Source LLC
Chambersburg PA
CBHW051523250626
47156CB00001B/206